THE END OF SORROW

A Novel of the Siege of Leningrad in WWII

John Verlin Love

WingSpan Press

Copyright © 2007 John V. Love
All rights reserved.

No part of this book may be used or reproduced in any manner without written permission of the author, except for brief quotations used in reviews and critiques.

This book is a work of fiction. Other than well-known historical characters and events, all names, characters, settings and incidents are either the product of the author's imagination or used fictitiously. Any resemblance to actual events, settings or persons, living or dead, is entirely coincidental.

Printed in the United States of America

Published by WingSpan Press, Livermore, CA
www.wingspanpress.com

The WingSpan name, logo and colophon are the trademarks of WingSpan Publishing.

ISBN 978-1-59594-165-7

First edition 2007

Library of Congress Control Number 2007927281

The poem "Prayer" in Chapter Eight is from *The Complete Poems of Anna Akhmatova* by Anna Akhmatova, Zephyr Press (from the Russian by Judith Hemschemeyer; edited and introduced by Roberta Reeder).

Dedicated to my wife Inessa.
Я тебя люблю.

And to all those involved in that fateful 900 day siege: the citizens of Leningrad, the Soviet soldiers who fought to defend it, and to the German soldiers who fought to take it. Good or bad, right or wrong, they were all in it together. It has always been this way, and always will be. This shared existence is the ground we stand on, and the actions we take today create the world we'll live in tomorrow. May we have the courage to try to understand those that would harm us, and the honesty to admit our fears.

Contents

	Prologue	1
	Part I	
Chapter 1:	Two Days in June	6
Chapter 2:	A Dream Incomplete	40
Chapter 3:	The Greenfinch's Song	68
Chapter 4:	The Last Line	96
	Part II	
Chapter 5:	All That Matters	134
Chapter 6:	Rats in a Whirlpool	178
Chapter 7:	Forever Hungry Ghosts	204
	Part III	
Chapter 8:	The Lake, the Moon, and the Lies	254
Chapter 9:	The Coldest Winter	316
Chapter 10:	Those Who Would Not be Defeated	384
	Epilogue	389
	Resources	394

Preface

This historical fiction novel attempts in every way to remain true to the events and circumstances that history has recorded for the siege of Leningrad. The stories within – though fictional – could very well have happened. The novel contains several real-life characters who interact with the fictitious characters created by the author. Some real-life characters may be obvious. Others not so. For the real-life characters, the novel stays as close as possible to the historic events they were involved in, whether it be deserting to the enemy lines, or buying tickets to a soccer game before the war started.

Acknowledgments

I have come to realize that this novel is not entirely mine. Like everything else, it is a conglomeration of the interconnectedness of the world I live in. The thoughts and ideas contained in this book are not all mine. They've come from my teachers, from books I've read, from people who've offered feedback on early versions, from the music I've listened to, the art I've seen in museums and nature, from casual conversations, and from sources which I don't fully comprehend. It is my honor to have been the receptacle for the characters and story of this novel.

I am deeply grateful to Harrison Salisbury and his book "The 900 Days," to Kyra Petrovskaya Wayne for her novel "Shurik," and to Elena Skrjabina for her diary entries from the war ("Siege and Survival: The Odyssey of a Leningrader"). Without their wonderful details and stories from the siege, this novel would not have been possible.

I would like to thank myself for keeping faith in my abilities as a writer, for persevering through those times when there was no encouragement, and for having the courage to quit my job to complete this novel. I am immensely grateful to my wife for her enduring support, both emotionally and financially. A special thanks goes to Felix Chevtchinskii for sharing his vast knowledge of all things, and to Lydia Chevtchinskaia for her help in taking care of our son. I am grateful to Kermit Moyer of The American University, Michael Neff, Charles Salzberg, Lihong Ma, Jack Mangold, Elisabeth Dearborn and Jeanine Cogan. And a special thanks to Susan Hadler for her unwavering encouragement and support.

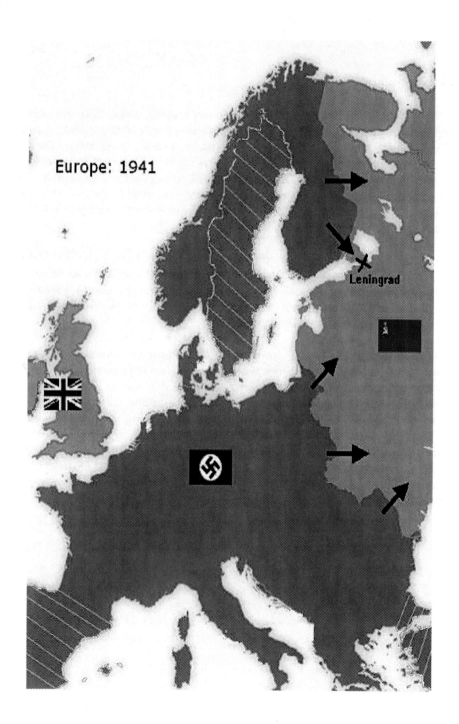

Prologue

The two German soldiers huddled together, trying to deny their shivering by discussing the bitter cold and the strange blue tint of the moon. They spoke in soft, sad voices that the stillness of the night carried far and wide over the freshly fallen snow. They wondered how much longer it would be before the sun once again emerged from the horizon. Of all the unusual things in this country, they agreed, that was the one that took the most getting used to – the shortest days and longest nights they'd ever known.

The moon was suddenly gone again – swallowed whole by another of the enormous dark clouds that floated through the black winter sky. One of the soldiers took out a flask, cursed the city of Leningrad, and then took a long sip. A small hole in the cloud allowed the moon to shine through, and for a few seconds, the entire area glowed pale blue. Tall, somber evergreens cast black shadows a hundred feet long, and a solitary tree stump in the middle of a white field stood out like a tiger on an iceberg.

When the stump appeared to move, the strangeness of the night threatened to become surreal.

"Dietrich, did you see that?"

"See what?"

"That dark spot out there," he said, motioning toward the open field in front of them. "I think it moved."

No sooner had they begun to examine the spot when the light was again lost, and everything settled uncomfortably back into the dark.

"There's nothing there. I knew you couldn't handle your liquor."

"To hell with you! I'm telling you I saw something move."

"All right, let's go to the nest. The moon should be back out in a minute. You'd better be right this time. I'm getting tired of your false alarms."

What had been vague, borderless figures only an hour before could now be seen clearly by the Russian soldier. Felix Varilensky had excellent nighttime vision and even without the help of the moon could make out the two Germans as they trudged through the snow over to the machine gun nest and then disappeared inside. Under his breath, he cursed whoever it was that had been spotted. For most of the men, there had been no training in how to crawl in thick snow across an open field in the middle of the night. For most of the men, there had been no training at all.

He studied the night sky and calculated how much time he had in between the clouds – in between the dark and the light. In the dark, he was invisible, immeasurable. In the light, he was just another man.

It wasn't long before the moon began showing its ashen face again. It crept along the edge of the monstrous black cloud – its frail light spilling over the rim and down to the frozen ground below. The light moved faintly from the top of the field where the Germans were, toward the middle of the field where he was. He dug a few more inches into the snow and stopped all movement as the light treaded up to, then around, and finally over him.

The machine gun nest was off to his right on a slight hill, no more than 90 feet away. As he lay motionless in the moonlight, he tried to wiggle his toes, but they were too numb from the cold for him to tell if he'd moved them or not. He needed the dark to return. That was where he lived now – where he walked, where he ate, where he prayed, and most of all, where he unleashed his anger.

And when the darkness did return, he slowly positioned his rifle at the machine gun nest. The ghostly light returned a few seconds later, just as he had calculated it would, and he found his target – a dim figure with binoculars looking out from behind the sandbags. Felix gripped his rifle tighter and slowly clenched his jaw until the gums around his loose upper tooth once again flooded his mouth with that thick, salty sensation he craved. He closed his eyes for a short second to concentrate on the sourness of his own blood. Then he opened his eyes and pulled the trigger. The bullet went straight through the German's hand to his cheek, and one after the other, the binoculars, and then the man, fell from sight.

The other German soldier quickly engaged the machine gun and bullets flew frantically in every direction. They struck all around Felix, but he remained still. Even when one of the bullets burned a hole straight through his left arm, he did not move.

After several minutes, the tat-tat-tat of the machine gun ceased and additional German soldiers could be heard arriving – barking out orders and demanding answers.

The snow underneath him turning red and the cold so intense that it was difficult to breathe, Felix waited. In his mind, he disappeared from the cold, and reappeared in that warm, familiar place where the sun refused to set, where the lazy afternoons went on forever, and where the shade of a tree was proof of God's unconditional love. In that peaceful place, he lay on the soft grass, Katya beside him – her seductive hips next to his, her outstretched forearm resting lightly on his bare chest. When he kissed the small of her wrist, the tender scent of lilacs and honey stayed on his lips. An insatiable zest for life and for Katya pumped through his veins, and the passionate love they'd made that morning seemed an eternity ago. He listened as she recited in his ear a poem she had written for him, the final words of it repeating themselves in his mind: *Love is the beginning, and Love is the end, and here in the middle is where we must mend.*

It was all so real – that bright yellow sun, that clear blue sky, that cool green grass. But that warm day was long past. That warm day was before it all began . . .

~

ОДИН – Part I

A man's character is his destiny. – **Heraclitus**

Глава Первая — Chapter One

Two Days in June

Eyes that pierce,
Beauty so rare.
Thoughts that intrigue me,
    love to share.
I with my body, a mind, and a soul,
I am but parts, you make me whole.
Will so strong,
    with good intention.
The road is long,
    our journey in question.

The End Of Sorrow

Day 1: June 21, 1941

Sunlight soaked every inch of Felix Varilensky's muscular back. His fair skin glistened with tiny beads of sweat as his shoulder blades tucked in and out of his torso in a mechanical rhythm. He was deep within himself, shutting out all sounds, all feelings, all thought. This focus – this inordinate ability to concentrate solely on what he wanted to – was his gift. In addition to helping him survive life as a Jew in the Soviet Union, it also made him a fearsome competitor.

He counted to himself as he lowered his body to the ground and pushed it back up again. 56, 57, 58. Even when his muscles were tired and wanted to quit, there was still nothing but the count. 61, 62, 63.

"Come on, Felix! You can do it!" one of his friends yelled.

"You've got him, Felix! He's slowing down!" said another.

"Let's go, Dima! Don't let Felix win again!" a girl yelled.

But it was too late. Dima collapsed in mid-pushup, and the cheers exploded.

"I knew I shouldn't have bet on you, Dima!" someone jested.

"How about pull-ups?" Dima said, very much out of breath. "I know I can beat him at that."

"No, it's hopeless. You'd think we'd know by now not to bet against a Jew – Felix always wins."

But even after the cheers faded away, Felix continued his silent counting. 69, 70, 71. He hadn't heard the cheers, nor the quiet that announced the end of the bet. There was only the one voice that he heard, and it was that voice that he remained true to. He had no idea whose voice it was, nor did he care much. It was simply there, in his head, and it never left him. It reassured him when things weren't going well, complimented him when no one else would, and pushed him when he could push no further himself.

The group, four young men and four young women, gathered around and began yelling once again.

"You can stop now, you show-off!"

"Hey, Felix! It's over. Let's eat now."

Even Dima, his conquered foe, joined in. "Felix, I'm done. You beat me."

But Felix, eyes tightly shut, arms bulging, a silent voice counting, kept doing pushup after pushup in a perfect, unbroken rhythm.

A young woman made her way through the group, and when she got to the front, she paused to watch the commotion: Felix doing his seemingly effortless pushups and his friends yelling at him – trying in vain to get his attention. She smiled for a brief second, and the inherent sorrow of her chestnut-brown eyes nearly disappeared.

"Katya, tell him to stop," a girl pleaded to her.

"No," said a young man, "let's see how many he can do!"

Everyone was laughing. Half of the group was yelling for Felix to stop, and the other half was yelling for him to keep going. Slowly, Katya bent her knees until she was sitting on her ankles and her head was next to his. "Felix ...," she said softly. "Felix, you've won. It's over."

His eyes opened immediately, and he stopped in mid-pushup. And as his eyes met hers, there was a period of time when he held the entire world inside his heart. In Katya's eyes – in those beautiful brown eyes that looked sad even when she was happy – he saw himself and knew he could do anything with her by his side. He wanted nothing more than to remain in that moment, but the commotion all around him wouldn't allow it. He noticed for the first time the crowd and the yelling and the laughter. Arms still extended, heart pounding vigorously, he realized suddenly how tired he was.

"Let's see how many more you can do!" Dima shouted as he sat on Felix's back.

"Yeah, let's see how many more you can do, Felix!" They all piled on top of him, and his arms finally gave way, sending the whole group tumbling to the ground amid a chorus of laughter.

Overhead, the 4:00 p.m. sun sailed through a bright aqua-blue sky, and in front of them, tiny waves from the Neva river lapped at the shore. Summer had finally arrived, and it brought Felix more joy than he had ever known in his life. And when the thought occurred to him that it might be more than he ever would know, he quickly banished that thought from his mind.

A soft breeze picked up the scent of freshly cut hay and blew it across the Neva river, past the large solitary oak tree where the picnickers sat, and on to the forest of birch trees that lay beyond. In the other direction, they could still see their home – the stalwart yet graceful Leningrad that never seemed very far away.

Katya sat with her back against the oak tree and watched a column of ants above her march into a small black hole underneath one of the branches. It was a hot day, though comfortable in the shade, and after the spring that had been more like winter, no one was complaining.

"I'm hungry. Let's eat."

"No, we have to toast first."

"Who brought the champagne?"

"Dima did. Dima, open the champagne!"

He opened the bottle of champagne and began filling glasses for everyone as they interrogated him about where he got it.

"My father gave it to me," he said. "But only after he found out it was for Felix's birthday. He loves him like he was his own son."

After he poured a glass of champagne for everyone, Dima led them in a toast. "Felix, may your next eighteen years be as happy as your first eighteen years."

A gentle smile spread from one ear to the other on Felix's face, and he indulged in a quick look beyond his friends – at the vast, wide-open space ahead of him where he could see for miles on end. *Only in Russia*, he thought. Only in Russia could there be so much beauty crammed into one glimpse – the long, narrow fields of wheat with their scattered blue flowers, the peacefulness of the birch trees swaying in the wind, the calm authority of the Neva river . . . . And what better time to be in Leningrad than during the White Nights – that time of year when the sun graced the sky both day and night. It was all his to savor. "Thank you," he said, "it's a good time to be alive. Now, let's eat!"

Spread out before them was a delicious medley of foods. All nine of them had brought something, and with very little planning, a festive meal was fashioned. A large smoked fish provided the centerpiece. It was surrounded by hard-boiled eggs, pickles, dark Russian bread, boiled potatoes with salt, thick eggplant spread, and a cucumber and tomato salad. For dessert, a large Napoleon cake awaited the picnickers.

"Felix, I see Katya brought some real Ukrainian *salo* for you. I thought Jews weren't supposed to eat pork."

Felix shrugged his shoulders. He didn't know much about his Jewish roots.

"She must really love you to let you eat that."

"What do you mean?" Felix laughed. "Salo is very good for you. You should try some."

"Salted pork fat is good for you? You Ukrainians are crazy."

"You saw how I won the pushup contest, didn't you? It's because I eat salo."

"Either that or all that vodka you drink!" someone yelled, and everyone laughed.

A large black fly landed briefly on the cake before Dima swatted it away. It then buzzed in front of Felix's face for a few seconds until he snatched it from the air.

"Did you catch it?" Katya asked, her face alight in amazement.

He nodded yes and began to squeeze his hand tighter, but Katya stopped him. "Let it go," she urged. And Felix knew that he could do no harm under that gaze. As he opened his hand, the fly buzzed away, and Katya silently mouthed *thank you* to him.

Felix situated his head comfortably in Katya's lap, and she gently stroked her fingers through his dark, curly hair. He thought back to that day thirteen months ago when they had first met. Her, carrying her sunflower-sized portrait of Lenin, and him carrying his big sign that read "Glory to the Workers of the World." It was the first May Day parade where he hadn't been overcome with feelings of patriotism. His love for his country had been trounced by a different sensation altogether. Fuzzy little caterpillars had crawled in his stomach. He'd felt some strange connection to every person he saw, and everything had a dreamlike quality to it. Most of all, he couldn't take his eyes off the beautiful girl at the end of his row with her shoulder-length brown hair and her fluid, effortless way of moving through time and space. Three times along the parade route, he'd run into the plump peasant girl in front of him because he couldn't stop himself from gazing at the woman over his left shoulder.

All during the parade, he memorized the words and gestures he'd use to approach her after the parade. But when the time came, he walked up to her and promptly forgot everything, ending up staring at her with neither a grin nor a word to offer. "Hi," she said somewhat nervously and turned to try to rejoin her friends. He grabbed her by the arm and forced himself to say something – anything – so as not to lose the moment.

"You were great in the parade," he said and immediately felt embarrassed by such a stupid statement.

"Ummm, thanks," she said and then added quite seriously, "You've got a nice sign."

It took him a second to realize she was gently poking fun at him, and when he laughed, she laughed too. She had a secretive, restrained laugh, and much like her delicate smile, it conveyed a sense of vulnerability that intrigued Felix. He'd found himself wondering how anyone could say a harsh word to her with those downcast, rueful eyes looking back at them, looking *through* them.

He still felt the same now, even though it seemed like an eternity since that day. Katya tickled his cheek with the sprig of lilacs she'd picked on their hike earlier that day.

"Look, here's one with five petals," Felix said, pulling the tiny branch from her hand. "That means you have to make a wish."

Katya closed her eyes tightly, but only for a second, then said, "Ok."

"You have to eat the flower now," Felix said.

"What? No, you don't."

"Of course you do. If you don't eat the flower, your wish won't come true."

"I think you're making it up," she said but then plucked the tiny purple flower and put it in her mouth anyway.

"What did you wish for?" Felix asked.

"I'm not telling. If you say what your wish was, it won't come true."

He laughed and kissed the underside of her wrist. She put her hand on his thigh and gently squeezed in return. Felix felt his desire rise and wished they could be alone. She could turn him on so easily.

Their friends were busy doing what most everyone did these days – chattering endlessly about the possibilities of war with Germany.

". . . my brother is in the army, and he's on that border. He's on one side, and the Germans are on the other. He tells me he sees more German troops arriving every day. And he says he hears tanks and trucks moving at all hours of the night up and down the riverbank."

"Pipe down, you provocateur!" someone jested, and everyone laughed nervously. They all knew someone who had been arrested for "panic-mongering." The position of the government of the Soviet Union was unmistakable and unwavering – just eight days ago, the official news agency, Tass, printed a statement in the newspapers throughout the country denying rumors of impending war.

"There's no way the Germans will attack. They learned their lesson fifteen years ago. They can't fight and win a war on two fronts. They'll finish off Britain before they look our way."

"I heard that Britain warned Stalin that the Germans would attack tomorrow."

"You can't trust the British," Dima chimed in. "They want to drag us into the war because they're finished unless they get some help. They want the Germans to attack us to relieve the pressure on them. But it's ridiculous for us to speculate on whether or not the Germans will attack. The Party has said there won't be a war. Stalin made the pact with Hitler to guarantee peace."

"So how do you explain all the German troops massed on the border?"

"I don't have to explain," Dima replied defiantly. "The Party knows more than we do. That's why they make the decisions. I just have to have faith in the Party, and I do. I'm beginning to wonder how much faith the rest of you have in the Party." The challenge was implicit in his voice.

"Dima, calm down," Felix quickly intervened. "We all have faith in the Party – most of us are in the Komsomol. But there's no reason why we can't talk about things – that's what students do. That's what they *teach* us to do. Besides, we're all friends here."

"Yes, friends who don't trust in the wisdom of the Party and who gossip like peasants in a village!" Dima yelled and then stormed away to smoke a cigarette.

"Don't worry," Felix reassured everyone, "you know how he is. He'll calm down in a few minutes."

"Hey Felix," someone said, "what are you going to do if the Germans attack?"

"He'll run to the front and fight them off with his grandfather's sword!" someone else yelled, and everyone laughed.

"No," a girl said, "Katya wouldn't let him. She'd make him be a chauffeur for General Zhukov." Everyone laughed again. "Hitler himself couldn't keep those two apart," she said, and they all looked at Katya and Felix.

Felix's gleaming iron-grey eyes once again met Katya's, and he agreed with the girl. Nothing in the world could ever separate them. Their unbounded love could surely overcome anything the world had to throw at them.

***

Alfred Liskof's calloused, sweaty index finger was wrapped tightly around the trigger, and it began to squeeze. Perspiration gathered around the barrel of the gun where it met the soft white skin of his temple. But something wasn't right, and the finger could neither squeeze nor release.

"Why do you keep doing that?" Franz yelled in an exasperated tone. "It *really* irks me, you know." Franz was a dozen yards back but catching up quickly now that Alfred had stopped. Because of his meager size, Franz was constantly lagging behind. His short legs had to move nearly twice as quickly as Alfred's if he wanted to keep up. "I hate it when you put that pistol to your head. What kind of a sick game is that?" he continued as he took off his helmet and placed it under his left arm.

Alfred lowered the handgun from the side of his head and noticed a small deer and her fawn grazing at the bottom of the wooded hill. It was 7:30 p.m. and soft beams of sunlight squeezed through the young leaves of the trees, splashing the ground around them. Alfred's left eye began to irritate him. This strange sensation focused his attention, and then he felt it – something gathering and racing down the side of his cheek.

Franz approached Alfred. "Are you crying?" he asked incredulously.

Alfred scoffed at the ludicrous accusation. He *never* cried.

But then he felt it again – something rolling down his right cheek – and there could be no doubt. He watched a teardrop as it leapt off his face and fell to the forest floor. He didn't know what to think, so he simply tried to recall the last time he'd cried. Surely it hadn't been that day eleven years ago when he'd vowed to never again speak to his father? It couldn't have been that long, could it? He didn't know, didn't want to face the answer. All these endless questions and answers were pushing him toward insanity.

"What's the matter?" Franz asked.

"Nothing," Alfred said and put his Luger pistol back in its holster.

"Don't give me that," Franz said. "What the hell is your problem? Why are you always putting that damn gun to your head? It's the third time today. And now you're crying too."

"I'm not crying. Something got in my eye, that's all."

"In *both* of them?"

Alfred, at 32, was over a decade older than Franz, a foot taller, and at least fifty pounds heavier. He glared at Franz with his practiced stare, both eyebrows furled tightly toward the bridge of his nose and low over his eyes. "Yes," he said, "in *both* of them."

"Why do you even have a pistol?" Franz asked. "I thought only officers got them."

Alfred ignored the question and watched the two deer lazily rip grass from the ground while a squirrel chattered from somewhere in the treetops.

The Polish forest they stood in was similar to the ones Alfred knew and loved in the Fatherland. Alfred grabbed his rifle and began marching once again. Franz hesitated a moment, then followed.

Alfred had so many unanswered questions today. They surrounded him, swirled about, taunted him. And even when the answers came, they defied any attempts Alfred made to match them with a question. Instead, they joined in on the fun. Some even mocked him.

"Is it about tomorrow?" Franz asked.

"Is what about tomorrow?"

"Whatever's bothering you."

"Yeah," Alfred answered, "and about the day after that, and the day after that, and the day after that." He regretted answering already. He never should have told Franz what he'd overheard that morning – that they'd be attacking the Soviet Union tomorrow at sun up. He should have ended the conversation with Franz before it even started. He had learned, by repeated failure, that his fellow Germans – soldiers or not – weren't interested in hearing any contrary viewpoints.

"What's there to fear?" Franz asked rhetorically. "You see how poorly defended their borders are. The Poles put up a harder fight than the Russians will. We'll be in Moscow before the leaves turn color."

Alfred remembered when he was Franz's age and how he'd been just as arrogant.

"We were outnumbered in the last war," Franz continued, "and we still annihilated them. I just don't understand you. We have all of Europe now, and who wants that miserable little island? The Brits can keep it as far as I'm concerned."

Alfred knew history well, and he understood perfectly what had happened to the last army to conquer the whole of Europe and then forge on to Moscow. That army had been led by one of the greatest military leaders of all time, and yet Napoleon and his army had been devastated by their attempted conquest. They had been destroyed slowly and methodically, day in and out, by the cold, the hunger, and the shrapnel ripping through their backs as they desperately retreated.

"And besides," Franz said, "we need living space ... and natural resources. That means going east."

Alfred remembered reading how in 1814, only two years after Napoleon had retreated, victorious Russian armies and their allies celebrated the fall of France by marching down the Champs-Elysées and through the Arc de Triomphe in the center of Paris.

"We'll be doing the world a favor, you know," Franz continued, "by taking Russia and slaughtering all the communists. They're not human."

"I suppose they think the same about us," Alfred said and stopped to look around.

"Well, they're wrong. And we'll prove it to them real soon." Franz looked at his watch. "In eight and a half hours to be exact."

Alfred studied his compass for several seconds, and Franz opened his canteen and took a drink of water, being careful not to spill a single drop.

"Are you sure we're not lost?" Franz asked. "Shouldn't we be close by now?"

"I know exactly where we are. We're right on schedule," Alfred replied and put his compass away.

The border to the Soviet Union was three miles ahead, Leningrad, more than700 miles to the north, and their native Germany, so very far behind them. When Alfred thought of Dresden and his beautiful brick home with its little garden out back, the despair and the helplessness once again threatened to overwhelm him.

"It's not like Russia is going to cease to be anytime soon," Franz said. "We'll never be safe with these monsters on our borders."

"You're right," Alfred said sarcastically. "The killing isn't going to cease anytime soon."

Franz studied Alfred's face for a moment before answering. "That's not what I said," he replied.

"We were promised *peace*," Alfred countered. But of course he knew better now. The wars would continue, and the Third Reich wouldn't stop until it brought about the destruction of everything that Alfred held dear.

"We don't need peace, we need oil," Franz said, stressing the last word.

"That argument is entirely illogical. First of all, there's . . .," Alfred stopped in mid-sentence, suddenly deciding that he'd had enough of arguing. There was no point to it. He wasn't going to convince Franz, or anyone else for that matter, of the error of their views.

Alfred wiped down his bald head with the green rag he always kept in his pocket and then placed his right hand firmly around the handle of his pistol. He thought how nice it would be to cry some more, if only his tears hadn't dried up already. It was time for him to make a decision: to continue living in a world of destruction, hatred, and fear, where death was waiting impatiently around every corner; or to put the gun to his head and end his suffering.

"What's today?" Alfred asked.

Franz eyed him nervously. "It's June twenty-first," he replied.

"Hmm, so it is. Have you ever seen the incredible palaces in Leningrad?"

"No, never," Franz said and stepped closer to the wide trunk of a neighboring tree.

"What a pity," Alfred said and pulled his handgun out of its holster. "They're works of art – very majestic."

* * *

It was a few minutes past 8:00 p.m., but the northern sun was still shining brightly. Misha Borisov focused his binoculars in on the lone German plane gliding lazily through the blue sky. The plane veered wide left for several minutes, then wide right for a few minutes, and then climbed straight toward the sun before diving back to its former altitude.

Misha set down the binoculars and lit one of his precious few cigarettes. His duty had only started five minutes ago, and he knew that having a cigarette so early meant he'd have to be extremely conservative to make the remaining three cigarettes last until the end of his shift.

He wondered if it was the same plane as two days ago. It probably was. That plane had done the same maneuvers – most likely out of boredom, Misha guessed. There wasn't anything new in this area that the Germans hadn't already seen.

It was the same routine every time: the German planes would cross the border into the Soviet Union (about 50 miles from the airbase where Misha was stationed), then fly over military installations, cities, rivers, lakes, roads, railroads, and whatever else they wanted to, and then return to their base on the other side of the border. Misha leaned back in his chair and concentrated on his cigarette. It was one of the few pleasures he had at his disposal while on duty. His job – from 8:00 p.m. to 2:00 a.m. – was to guard the 93 planes that lined the sides of the runway and to be on the lookout for any enemy planes. It was a boring job and one entirely unsuitable to a 19-year-old who knew exactly how things should and should not be in the world. The planes were chained to the ground to prevent anyone from stealing them, and Misha hadn't seen so much as a stray dog near any of the planes.

He ground out his cigarette. From the corner of his eye, he saw his commanding officer and another soldier coming his way. His commanding officer, a captain, was a tall, slender man who was inordinately quiet. His dark skin suggested he was from either the far North or the far South, but he spoke perfect Russian, with no trace of an accent. Misha didn't recognize the man walking next to the captain. He was wearing the same uniform Misha was, so he definitely wasn't an officer. He walked with an air of indifference that only came with connections or stupidity. He had no expression on his face, and for some strange reason, Misha found himself wondering how long it had been since the man had last smiled or frowned.

Misha rose to his feet, cursing himself for not reporting the plane sighting yet. It would be within eyesight now, and as he quickly stole a glance in that direction, he saw that it was. He cleared his throat and prepared to inform the captain of the German plane sighting but saw the captain had already noticed it himself.

"Comrade Private, why haven't you reported that plane?"

"I was just about to, Comrade Captain. It's another German reconnaissance plane."

The plane descended abruptly and was suddenly less than 75 feet off the ground. The three men stood together and watched as it approached. The captain took out his pistol but did not aim it, and just before the plane roared over their heads, it tilted to the right, and the pilot waved at them. Misha waved back.

"What the hell was that? Do you want to get twenty-five years?" he yelled at Misha.

"But, Comrade Captain," Misha protested, "surely waving cannot be considered a provocation? We see German planes deep in our territory everyday. We're not allowed to shoot them. What else is there to do?"

"You're a lunatic. You're going to get yourself killed or sent to Siberia one day."

"Siberia? But Stalin loves me. He only sends provocateurs and kulaks and Trotskyites to Siberia. Not workers like me." The soldier next to the captain arched his eyebrows at this, though in amusement or consternation, Misha couldn't tell.

"Shut up, Borisov!" the captain yelled. His demeanor struck Misha as odd. He wasn't usually so quick to anger. Misha studied the captain's nose yet again. It was the flat, crooked nose of a brawler, and it didn't fit the captain's personality at all. No matter how many times Misha had asked him about it, though, he never got a straight answer.

"I've been patient with you because you're new," the captain explained. "You can consider yourself warned. Your insolent remarks won't be tolerated." He glared at Misha for several seconds, as if to emphasize the point.

Finally, he turned to the soldier who accompanied him and introduced him as Comrade Stepanovich. "I want you to show him the ropes," the captain explained. "You two will be working together from now on."

The captain left without another word. Stepanovich watched him walk away and then turned his head slowly from the far right to the far left, seemingly looking for something that wasn't supposed to be there. Misha could smell garlic on his breath and perhaps alcohol, though he wasn't sure about that.

Stepanovich looked intently at the rows of planes ahead of them. He poked his pinkie in his ear and twisted his wrist slowly one way and then the other. Misha couldn't help but notice what disproportionately wide and flat fingernails he had. Never in his life had he seen such large fingernails. It was grotesque.

Stepanovich seemed to survey his surroundings forever, and Misha started to wonder if he had forgotten that he was standing next to him. To remind him, Misha scraped some dirt under his boot and cleared his throat. But Stepanovich still paid no attention to him.

"So, where you from?" Misha asked meekly.

Stepanovich turned toward him with a look of surprise on his face. "What?"

"Where are you from?" Misha repeated.

"Moscow."

"Ahh, I thought so!" Misha said and smiled. "A fellow Muscovite! You've definitely got that Moscow look about you. It'll be nice to have someone with half a brain to talk to – not like these simpletons from the villages. The guy before you was a complete idiot. We couldn't talk about anything. He believed anything anyone told him. One time I told him that the Earth was the center of the universe. Another time I told him that the moon was actually the old sun that had burned out five hundred years ago, and he believed me!"

Stepanovich looked grimly in Misha's direction but said nothing in response.

"Don't you just hate people like that?" Misha asked, forcing himself not to stare at those inhuman fingernails. "They're not like us, you and me. We're from the city. We know Jupiter from Saturn, and geometry from geography. But these people from the villages, you have to tell them what's what."

To escape the sweltering heat of the late-day sun, Stepanovich stepped off to his right and into the long shadow of one of the hangars. He pulled a rag from his pocket and wiped the sweat off his forehead.

"You know the kind, right?" Misha asked, casting a hopeful glance. "The ones who can't think for themselves, who buy everything the Party sells them."

A short silence made Misha uneasy, and he recalled the warnings his mother had given him about his "dangerous habit" of always saying what was on his mind.

"I hate those fuckers from the villages," Stepanovich finally answered.

"Ha-ha," Misha laughed nervously, but Stepanovich neither laughed nor smiled.

"You know today is my three month anniversary," Misha said.

"What?" Stepanovich said.

"Today – June twenty-first – is my three-month anniversary of being stationed here."

"So."

"So, I just thought I'd tell you. It's nice being able to talk to someone without having to worry about every word you say." Misha cracked his knuckles as he stretched his arms. "Have you heard anything about the war? They tell us that Hitler's going to invade England, but I'm not so sure. If they're going to do that, then why are they flying all these reconnaissance flights over us?"

"I guess Hitler doesn't trust us," Stepanovich replied and then scratched his crotch.

"Maybe," Misha said as he swatted a fly away from his ear. "Back in March, a German reconnaissance plane made a forced landing here. I figured we'd arrest him, but instead we received orders to tow his plane in, give him dinner, refuel his plane, and then send him on his way. Makes no sense to me."

Stepanovich grunted and looked Misha in the eye for the first time.

"It's true!" exclaimed Misha. "Ask anybody."

Several gnats began flying around Stepanovich's head, but he made no effort to swat them away. Misha watched as one of them landed on his bushy left eyebrow.

"So, you want me to show you what we have to do for the next five and a half hours?" Misha asked.

There was no response – not even an acknowledgment that his words had been heard. Misha continued anyway. "Every seventeen minutes, we have to do rounds and check the hangars and planes, and . . ."

"Why?" Stepanovich interrupted.

"Why? Because that's what we have to do, that's why. Sure it's stupid, but you and I both know that that doesn't matter. If you ask me, it's because there's only one damn viewpoint allowed. Don't get me wrong, I was in the Komsomol in school, I just think that this top-down order is bad for us. I mean, you can't even take a leak around here without permission."

"Is that so?" Stepanovich said and smiled for the first time. It was a strange smile and made Misha uneasy. Stepanovich looked satisfied, like he had just finished an exam and done well.

Misha decided he wouldn't talk anymore. He'd said too much already. His mother had taught him that honesty was a virtue, but in this day and age, it was sometimes a crime.

* * *

Alfred's hand trembled ever so slightly as he pointed his pistol at Franz's chest.

"I said, put your gun on the ground," he repeated slowly and in no uncertain terms.

Franz did as he was told. "What the hell are you going to do?" he asked.

"Shut up. Put your hands on your head and get on your knees." Alfred removed a rope from his backpack, forced Franz to sit up against a tree, and tied his arms around behind it.

"What have I done to you to deserve this?"

"You didn't do anything."

"Then you're simply insane? Is that it? Do you know that you've gone crazy?"

"I'm through arguing with you."

"So you agree with me then? You actually know that you're crazy?"

"Enough with the questions!" Alfred screamed.

"Or else what? You'll tie me up and leave me to die?"

Alfred became light headed for a moment and felt as though he was floating away from his body. He pictured himself up above everything, looking down on all the busy people below. The thought calmed him and the world stopped spinning.

"You'll be all right," Alfred said. We're close enough to the road that someone will find you."

"Nobody travels down that road, and you know it," Franz shot back.

"Not true. There's at least two or three vehicles a day . . . and besides it'll probably be overflowing with tanks and jeeps soon enough." He picked up his backpack and put it on.

"Where are you going?" Franz demanded.

"I'm going to stop this war before it starts."

"What? What are you talking about? You can't do anything to stop it. It's the will of the German people – their God-given right to defend themselves."

"You don't defend yourself by starting a war," Alfred replied and started walking away.

"We're not *starting* anything. We're protecting the Fatherland."

Alfred continued on his way, stepping over a large fallen tree and ducking underneath the low hanging branch of a giant evergreen.

"You're no German!" he heard Franz yell after him. "You're a coward! A traitor!"

Alfred ignored him and contemplated once again what his father had told him so long ago. It was right before his father had divorced his mother, and Alfred was 18 years old. His father had said that there would come a time in Alfred's life when he would become wise enough to listen to his own wisdom. It might be a small change or a dramatic one, but in either case, a voice inside would yell *enough is enough*.

On a large, flat rock next to a small stream, Alfred sat down and reflected on his decision. It was just as he always thought it would be. It was irrevocable. It meant being ostracized – or even death. He knew that it would forever weigh upon his mind if he failed to act. And he was sure that it would bring solace, an absoluteness of right and wrong, and a comfort, rather than a regret, on his deathbed.

Alfred thought he'd heard that voice scream *enough* on the day he stopped speaking to his father. But now, he understood that had been a mistake. The point in his life when he was wise enough to listen to his own wisdom was occurring right now. He would never again see his home in Dresden, never again enjoy his aunt's homemade spaetzel, never again taste the splendidly bitter lager beer brewed by the old farmer up the road. That was the price he'd have to pay. And maybe, just maybe, he could prevent Germany, the country of his birth – the country he loved with all his soul – from making what he was sure was a tragic mistake.

The Soviet guardpost stood at the foot of the bridge. It was nothing more than a tiny wooden shack. One soldier sat inside it – his head down, his weapon leaning against the wall. Another soldier sulked outside, shifting his weight from one foot to the other at ten second intervals. It had taken Alfred a little longer than he thought it would to find it, considering he'd been part of the scout team that had tracked up and down the river marking down every bridge, guardpost, and potential crossing.

After trekking through the Polish woods in the heat and humidity of late June, Alfred's army fatigues were drenched. He tried to wipe down his hairless head, but his green rag was already too soaked with sweat to do much good. The back of his neck and his muscular forearms were dotted with tiny, red mosquito bites that he scratched absent-mindedly from time to time. But his blue eyes – those sparkling blue eyes that were the first thing anyone ever noticed about him – were still intense, still burning with desire.

As he watched the Soviet soldiers smolder in their boredom, he gently laid his gun on the ground and took his army-issue knife from its sheath and clenched it in his left hand. He squatted behind some bushes for several minutes doing nothing more than taking deep breaths.

As he kneeled in the bushes, images came to him of that day eleven years ago when he had finally gathered the courage to confront his father about the miserable childhood he'd had. The conversation hadn't gone the way Alfred had rehearsed it in his mind. Instead of the expected sympathy and regret from his father, he received recriminations and denial. He could still see his father standing near the fireplace, his arms folded, his fists clenched, his face red. "You ungrateful bastard. You don't appreciate anything!" he'd yelled. "I fed you and clothed you and put a roof over your head, and all you can do is complain." Alfred had wanted to tell his father how he'd always criticized him, how he never spent any time with him, how *he never seemed to give a damn* for him. But he didn't say any of that. Instead, he'd stood there facing his father – arms folded, fists clenched, face red – and said nothing. After his father had finished his tirade, Alfred went home, broke three of his knuckles punching the wall, and vowed never to speak to his father again.

The sun was coming in at such a low angle in front of Alfred that he had to look straight into it if he wanted to see the guardpost. It was almost nine o'clock and the sunset would be complete in a few more minutes. He watched as the Soviet soldier who had been standing, went over and kicked the other soldier to wake him up. Alfred (who understood Russian fairly well but could only speak it in short, broken phrases) heard the soldier tell the other that he was going somewhere to do something – exactly where he was going and exactly what he was going to do, Alfred couldn't make out. As he started walking in Alfred's direction, Alfred hid further behind the bushes that, just a second ago, he'd been positive made him all but invisible.

The soldier approached with his rifle haphazardly hanging from his shoulder. When he got to the bushes where Alfred was, he stopped, set down his rifle and began to take a piss. With one quick move, Alfred could jump him and slit his throat. But Alfred hadn't come to kill, he'd come to surrender. He wasn't going to sit idly by this time. He wasn't going to regret his inaction again.

When the man finished, Alfred stood up with his arms over his head, startling the Soviet soldier so that he took a quick step back, and fell over a stone. Alfred simply stared straight ahead. He didn't move. He didn't speak.

The End Of Sorrow

When the Soviet soldier got to his feet, he pointed his gun at Alfred, and motioned him toward the guardpost.

Though a mere 40 yards, the walk seemed much longer to Alfred. Doubts about his decision fought valiantly in his mind, but Alfred crushed them one by one. He reminded himself that nothing really mattered; indeed, *he* didn't matter. He was small, insignificant, almost entirely inconsequential. When he died – just as everyone in this whole bloody conflict eventually would – he'd be judged the same as they would. With that in mind, he marched in pride, in belief, and in trepidation and fear toward the guardhouse and his destiny.

As Alfred lay on his stomach, with a guard's foot pressing hard between his shoulder blades, he listened and tried his best to understand what the other guard was saying into the phone. "That's correct. I said that I have a German soldier here who has surrendered."

After a short pause and an exasperated sigh, he heard, "Yes comrade, you are correct that he could not have surrendered when we are not at war. That was my mistake. We have a German soldier here who has *deserted*. He says that the German army will commence an assault tomorrow at 4:00 a.m.. What shall I do with him?"

Alfred again heard muted mumbling from the other end of the line, then another sigh from the guard and a response. "Yes Comrade Captain, I understand that any provocations against Germans will be dealt with severely, but he came up to us with his arms in the air and said he had something important to tell us. He says he's a member of the 222nd Infantry Regiment of the 74th Infantry Division. And he says he heard his commander, a Lieutenant Schultz, state the date and time of the attack. He has also observed troops being deployed for the attack."

All was quiet for several seconds, and then Alfred heard the guard explain, "No sir, he doesn't speak Russian. He speaks German, and no, I don't think it's a trick."

The longer the conversation went on, the more distinctly Alfred could hear the irritation in the guard's voice. "I learned how to speak German at the university, sir. It's in my records if you care to check."

After the guard finished the conversation and disconnected, he whispered into the other guard's ear, "Ohn durak."

Alfred understood that he was the one being referred to, and understood all too well what the guard had said, *"He's a fool."*

* * *

In the center of Leningrad, the Cathedral of Our Lady of Kazan sits quietly on the main thoroughfare of the city. The proud, Romanesque structure, more commonly called the Kazansky Cathedral, has held a quiet authority over the city ever since the first stone of its foundation was laid by Tsar Alexander I on August 27, 1801. Stretching its massive wings out to the east and west, it always seems to be ready to fly away to the more perfect place it surely must have come from. But it never leaves, and perhaps that's why it holds such a special place in the heart of so many Leningraders. It's always there, in repose, patiently watching the cars, buses and pedestrians as they move in steady streams up and down the stately Nevsky Prospekt.

In 1931, the cathedral was shut down and transformed into the "Museum of the History of Religion and Atheism." But for Felix, it would always be known as Kazansky Cathedral. He'd fallen in love with it the first time he saw it and promptly learned every detail of its storied history.

It was now after 11:00 p.m. and the setting sun colored the sky beyond the cathedral with soft pastel hues of violet, gold, and crimson. Felix and Katya walked slowly by the rose bushes in front of the cathedral. It had been a long, but fun day, and Felix hated to see it come to an end. He was walking Katya back to her apartment building, trying to squeeze every minute he could from the day. He reached his arm out and pulled her close as they walked. He loved to run his hand slowly up and down her side, feeling how her waist seductively curved into her hips. Leaning over to give her a quick kiss on the cheek, he suddenly changed his mind, dropped the picnic basket and took her in his arms. He kissed her on the lips and squeezed her body tightly to his – delighting in the firmness of her breasts as they pressed against him. She wrapped her arms around his neck and kissed him back.

After a few seconds, Felix heard a mother with small children approaching and he reluctantly pulled away. As he and Katya prepared to cross the street, he switched the picnic basket to his left arm so he could hold her hand as they crossed.

He smiled at Katya, then looked back one last time at the cathedral and the dozens of giant Podoust stone columns that marked the front facade, wondering what it must have been like to be part of the Romanov royal family and been married within Kazansky's majestic confines.

"Did you talk to your father?" he asked Katya.

"About what?"

"You know perfectly well what," he said, annoyed that the pleasure of a minute ago was gone so quickly. "Don't make this into an argument again," he added.

"Don't talk to me like that," she said testily.

"Like what?"

"In that tone. You talk to me sometimes as if I'm a child and you're the parent, and I hate it."

Felix reflected for a second. "You're right," he concluded. "I'm sorry. It's just that I get tense even thinking about this subject. Have you talked to him yet?"

"What's there to talk about? I know what his answer will be – the same as last time."

"So you're not even going to try anymore?" Felix stopped and turned to face her.

She shrugged her shoulders.

"But Katya, why do you need his approval? We're both eighteen now."

"Why do you ask questions like that? It's annoying."

"Come on, so what if he sits on the City Soviet. He's only one man."

"Felix," she said, the volume of her voice climbing a notch. "He's *friends* with Party Secretaries. He doesn't just *know* powerful people – he plays chess with Kuznetsov; he has *tea* with Zhukov."

"But you can't tell me he's going to ruin the life of his only child out of mere spite. He may not act like it, but I know he loves you. He wouldn't hurt you."

"You don't understand, Felix. You don't know him. He thinks he knows what's best for me and it doesn't matter what I think. He'll never change his mind."

"But he can't do this. It's *your* life."

"He *can* do it. And he is."

"*No*, he can't. I'm going to have a talk with him."

"Felix, no. Please, don't do that. He could have you arrested if he wanted to."

"Arrested for what? For talking to him?"

"I'm serious. Don't do it. I know him, and I know you. You're both pigheaded, and if the two of you go into a room, probably only one of you will come out."

"Oh come now, Katya. You underestimate me. I'm not violent."

"Just promise me you won't try to talk to him."

"Promise you? First, promise me you'll marry me one day – with, or without, your father's approval."

Katya stared at the ground for several minutes, wringing her hands from time-to-time, before finally answering. "Can't we talk about this some other time?" she asked with an air of resignation.

Felix nodded yes and they walked the remaining three blocks to Katya's third floor apartment in silence. Her neighbor Petya was smoking a cigarette and leaning over the railing looking down on them as they walked up the stairs. "You certainly picked a beauteous day for your picnic, Katya. Any leftovers?"

Felix and Katya looked above at Petya's portly figure – pot belly hanging over his belt, shoulders slouching forward over his chest, cigarette held limply in his right hand. He stood with his weight disproportionately on his left leg. "Hi Petya," Katya said, "I thought you usually took a nap about now, so you could write all night."

"Who could sleep on a day like this?" He said it sarcastically, and Felix glared at him in response.

After they reached the third floor, Felix set the picnic basket down and

Katya started looking through it. She had some strange connection to Petya that Felix didn't understand. She said she considered him a friend, though Felix wondered if it was out of pity. Felix didn't much care for Petya. He thought him fat, lazy, and conceited, and hated it when he used big or unusual words. In particular, he didn't like the way the twenty-seven year old writer constantly stared at Katya. But Petya's disfigured right leg (it was shorter than his left and he walked with a limp) and Katya's assurances convinced Felix that he was harmless.

"Sorry, Petya," Katya said as she closed the picnic basket, "there's nothing left over except a couple of boiled potatoes and a pickle."

"That's fine. I'll take them."

Katya dug them out and handed them over to him. "So did you go outside and enjoy this *beauteous* day, Petya?" Felix asked.

"I went to the store and bought some paper this morning," he said, but instead of looking at Felix, he looked at Katya as if she had asked the question.

The entrance to the building creaked open and then closed and footsteps echoed in the stairwell. Felix and Katya glanced over the railing, but you couldn't see who it was until the person reached the second floor.

"It's Dmitry," Petya said.

"How do you know?" Felix asked.

"I know," he said confidently.

As the person rounded the corner onto the second floor, Felix and Katya saw a familiar small head with short, dark hair and a cowlick and knew that Petya was right. It was Dmitry Shostakovich.

"How do you do that?" Katya asked, her face full of amazement.

Petya smiled for the first time and said in a mock humble voice, "It's but one of my innumerous talents."

Shostakovich had likely come to visit his friend, the old painter, Alexander Guzman. Guzman lived next door to Petya and Katya and had a beautiful piano, but couldn't play a note. He admitted to keeping the piano only because Shostakovich loved it and frequently came over to practice or compose.

"Good evening, Dmitry," Katya said.

"Ahh, Katya. How's my favorite poet?"

"Fine. I heard you playing something new yesterday. Have you started on your Seventh Symphony?"

"Oh, those were just some random ideas," he said, wiping his round black-rimmed glasses on his shirt. He laughed nervously.

"Did you know that it's Felix's birthday? He's eighteen today," Katya said.

"Is that so? Happy Birthday, Felix. And to think, only last year I was *twice* your age. Say, why don't you go to the soccer game at Dynamo Stadium with me tomorrow. My treat. I got two tickets today, but I saw my friend just a minute ago and he said he can't make it."

"I'd love to, except I promised my friend I'd help him move tomorrow."

"Ok. How about you, Petya? You want to go?" Shostakovich asked.

"No, that would make me too happy. I can't write when I'm happy."

"Did you write today?" Shostakovich asked.

"No."

"Are you happy today?"

"No."

"I think you need a new hypothesis. If either of you change your mind, you know where to find me." Shostakovich walked down the hall to Guzman's apartment, knocked, then slipped inside. Katya kissed Felix on the cheek and wished him happy birthday once more, before she too disappeared into her apartment.

On his way home, Felix enjoyed the cool night air and the sweet, salty fragrance from lilacs and the Neva river. Just as he reached his apartment, a bell chimed twelve times, signifying the end of June 21st and the beginning of June 22nd. For a reason he couldn't explain, he suddenly felt out of breath, and a strange shiver went up his spine.

* * *

Day 2: June 22, 1941

Vanya Chetvernikov swayed ever so slightly from side to side as he listened to the music. Though it was already early Sunday morning in Leningrad, the band on the hotel's ballroom stage was still full of energy. Vanya had just finished his fourth shot of vodka, and was nothing if not a happy drunk. As he put his arm around Iosif Rosenberg, he exclaimed that of all the places in the world he could be right now, he would choose to be exactly where he was at and exactly who he was with.

"What about Paris?" Iosif asked.

"Paris? The Nazis have Paris!" Vanya yelled over the music.

"True, but it's better in Paris than Siberia, which is where we're liable to be soon enough, ha-ha."

"In Siberia with Russians is still better than in Paris with Frenchmen!" Vanya laughed heartily.

"What about New York then?"

"New York?! With the Capitalists and Profiteers? Never!"

"That's the right answer my boy. You've learned well," Iosif jested. "To be perfectly honest Vanya, I'm glad you are where you are at this particular moment myself."

"Comrade, that calls for a toast!"

With their left hands they clinked their glasses of vodka, and with their right hands they saluted one another. "Nazdarovye!" – To your health! – they said in unison, and slammed back their drinks.

The band started playing the now familiar chords of the hit song, 'We'll Meet Again in Lvov, My Love and I.' "I love this song!" exclaimed Vanya. "Let's go ask those girls over there to dance," he said to Iosif as he pointed to the other side of the dance floor. "I saw them earlier, they know the foxtrot."

Vanya blazed a path straight through the dance floor to the girls. He knew he had to be quick or else the gregarious sailors would ask them to dance first. From the way the girls were giggling, smiling, and enjoying themselves, it was obvious that they were relatively new to the scene. Most girls who were *veterans* of the balls always did their best to look bored and unapproachable.

"Good evening, ladies," Vanya said as he swooped in and kissed first the blonde's, and then the redhead's hand. "May we have the next dance?"

The girls – no more than 17 years old, but who had done their best to look at least 19 – accepted the offer. Vanya gave his arm to the blonde, and couldn't resist a long glance at her as he escorted her to the dance floor.

Though she had light skin to begin with, she had applied her makeup so that her face was just as pale as her ivory blouse. The effect was that her bright blue eyes and the scarlet-red lipstick she wore provided the only color to her face. Vanya thought it a stroke of genius.

Out on the dance floor, Vanya and Iosif laughed and tried their best to outdo each other. Neither of them was very adept at the foxtrot, but they both kept the beat quite well. Iosif tried to mix in a few waltz steps he knew, but it only confused the girl. Still, she was laughing and having just as good a time as Iosif. Vanya saw another couple do a promenade step and tried it himself, but they ended up on the right-hand side of the stage. With the limited footwork Vanya knew, he couldn't get them back out on the dance floor. Finally in desperation, laughing, he picked up his partner and carried her back out to the middle of the dance floor.

As the last few notes of the song trailed off into the warm Leningrad night, Vanya invited the girls back to their table for a round of vodka and pickles. And no sooner had they arrived at their table when a high-ranking naval officer walked on to the stage and yelled for everyone's attention. When the crowd had quieted, he announced that a 'Number One Alert' had been sounded and that the ball was over. The Number One Alert meant that all sailors were to return to their ships, and all soldiers to their bases. The music must have prevented them from hearing the siren and the call over the city loudspeakers.

"Beautiful woman, I don't even know your name," Vanya said to the blonde he'd just danced with.

"My name is Anna," she replied.

"Oh what a beautiful name! It's the same name as my mother. Anna, you must give me a kiss before we part," he implored. "You've stolen my heart, and if this is war, we may never see each other again!"

Iosif laughed heartily at Vanya's audaciousness and nearly choked on the pickle he was eating. Vanya, knowing that Iosif knew his mother's name was really Alexandra, looked over and gave Iosif a quick wink. Anna giggled, pursed her scarlet lips, and closed her eyes. Vanya wrapped his arms tightly around her and did a dramatic dip while he kissed her long and hard. When he was through, he thought the four of them would never stop laughing. And when they finally did, he was sad for the first time that evening. He jokingly proposed a toast "to the defense of Leningrad!" The alert was just another practice, he reassured the girls. It was common knowledge that Germany wouldn't attack the Soviet Union.

But Vanya wasn't so sure. An immense gloominess hung over him like a menacing storm cloud. He wanted nothing more than for it to go away and hoped that some more vodka would do the trick. He poured one last shot for everyone, saving the biggest for himself.

The journey from the hotel back to their base was a long one, and Vanya's head had started spinning only a few minutes into it.

"We were absolutely *charming* back there," Iosif said. "If it weren't for that damn alert, we might've had a truly enchanting evening with those two lovely maidens."

Vanya put his arm around Iosif's shoulder, partly out of friendship and partly for physical support in his drunken state. "A minor setback, my friend. We'll be singing a different tune tomorrow," he said, slurring his words slightly.

They walked through a park where the only sounds they could hear were from the hundreds of invisible crickets and the falling water of a nearby fountain.

"It's such a beautiful night," Iosif said. "I wish every night could be like this."

"If every night were like this, it'd be heaven," Vanya replied.

"Heaven, huh," Iosif said, paused, then asked. "Do you really think there's a heaven? Someplace where there's eternal peace, where there's no hate – nothing but love? Could there really be a place like that?"

For Vanya, the word heaven was irrevocably linked to religion and always set his mind racing. Instead of harps, clouds, bliss, and angels, he saw absurd, tortuous scenarios of impending war. He was shot by a sniper he couldn't see. He was stabbed in the back by a bayonet. A machine gun nearly cut him in half. A dozen scenes played in his mind in horrific detail, each of them having one thing in common – he always died.

"Don't be stupid," Vanya said. "Of course there's no heaven. There's no heaven because there's no God. If there was a God, I would've gotten lucky tonight."

The night air was sweet and fresh, and the darkness was a cushion that enveloped them. Off in the distance, they could hear someone strumming a guitar.

"But can't you feel it on nights like tonight?" Iosif persisted. "I don't know, maybe it's the vodka, but every once in a while on nights like this, I feel like God is everywhere – all around us. In the trees, the grass, the water, that guitar, . . . even inside us."

Vanya concentrated on the sound of the guitar in the distance. It really was quite charming. A perfectly played G chord could bring a tear to his eye. He loved music more than anything in the world. To him, it was a window to the soul and gave him peace and joy and the belief that there was something greater than the self – something that united all men, no matter their color or language. If there is a heaven, he thought, it's *filled* with beautiful music.

"You definitely had too much to drink," Vanya said. "Tell you what though, why don't we do an experiment right now. We'll pray to God that this alert is just another drill and that there won't be a war. And if it comes true, I'll give God a second chance. How about it?"

Iosif agreed, so they stopped next to a park bench, looked around to make sure no one was watching, then got down on their knees and folded their hands in front of them. Vanya prayed as intensely as he could, squeezing his eyes shut and clenching his teeth together tightly. "Please God," he said silently over and over, "I'm too young to die. My life just started."

After they finished, they were quiet, and walked the rest of their journey in an uncomfortable lull. The possibility of war continued to haunt Vanya. To keep his mind off of it, he sang bits and pieces of songs he knew. In his head, he replayed some of his favorite melodies. Over and over, saxophone solos, balalaika melodies, and tambourine rhythms floated through his head. But no matter how hard he tried, he couldn't get them to replace the sadness and fear. Instead, they merged together, creating a sickening symphony that grated on his ears.

* * *

Misha Borisov cursed the devil under his breath as he shuffled wearily from the latrine to his barracks. His legs moved so slowly, it was as if they were already in bed and asleep. Each and every muscle felt numb with drunkenness, though he'd had nothing whatsoever to drink.

These *attacks* inflicted him from time-to-time, and he'd never found a defense against them. It was more than being tired. It was a relaxation so intense that he could barely command his muscles to move, and the sensation could last for eight miserable hours.

He felt somewhat fortunate this time, because the onset had occurred shortly after midnight and near the end of his duty guarding the planes. It was much harder to bear when it happened during the day and robbed him of what little time he had to himself.

It was 2:15 in the morning now, and Misha looked forward to nothing more than deep, unrelenting sleep. His body demanded it. And so it was no surprise that after a mere four minutes of lying on his bed with this lava-like relaxation coursing through his veins, that Misha fell into the sleep of the dead. He did not move. He had no dreams. Time did not exist.

Fifteen minutes later, he was awakened by a firm hand squeezing and shaking him by the shoulder. A gravelly voice calling him by his formal name demanded he wake up immediately.

"Mikhail Borisov?" the voice asked impatiently.

"Yes, he is," Misha replied, not sure if he was dreaming the whole thing.

"What? I'm speaking to you, asshole. Are you Mikhail Borisov?"

"Who? Oh. Yes, yes, that's me." The glare from the flashlight hurt his eyes and Misha used his hand to ward it off the best he could. Through his squinting eyes, a fat, square face came into focus. The man's forehead sloped heavily over his eyes so that they could hardly be seen. Below his head was a grapefruit-shaped body that had outgrown the uniform he wore.

"Get dressed then. You're coming with me. You're under arrest."

"No, there must be some mistake. Who are you looking for again?" Misha was confused and tried to will himself awake.

"Mikhail Borisov! Is that you or not?"

"Yes, that's me. But why would I be under arrest? I haven't done anything."

"You have ninety seconds to get your clothes on. I suggest you get started now."

"But it has to be a mistake! What are you talking about? What's the charge?"

"You're only wasting your own time. You have less than sixty seconds now."

"What?! You just said I had ninety seconds!" Misha jumped out of bed and frantically grabbed his uniform and boots from his locker. He saw that another soldier, skinny and pale, had accompanied the fat one.

"What am I being charged with?" Misha asked as he put his shirt on.

The fat one ignored him, but the skinny one began to answer, "Comrade, we don't know. We're just following orders, but it's most likely..."

"Shut up!" the fat one shouted, and then turning to Misha added, "Just get your damn clothes on, Borisov, and stop wasting our time."

Misha finished putting his uniform on without saying a word, but he couldn't locate his socks and was still barefoot. Socks were a luxury to soldiers in the Red Army, as the standard issue were *portyanka* – cheap, square rags that one wrapped around their feet. Misha's mother had given him socks only the month before, and he was especially protective of them. Anything of value left behind probably wouldn't be there when he came back. Frantically, he searched for his socks inside his locker and on his bunk.

"Your sixty seconds is up," said the fat one. "Let's go."

"But I can't find my socks!"

"Too bad, let's go," he said and grabbed Misha by the arm.

"Let him get his socks for goodness sake," the skinny one said. "Comrade, where do you usually put them?"

"Next to my boots," Misha said. "I always put them next to my boots!"

The skinny guard looked around and then pointed to a small lump of dark clothing in the corner between Misha's locker and the wall. "What's that over there by your locker?"

"Ahh yes, that's them," Misha wriggled free from the fat soldier's grip and grabbed his socks.

As he put his boots on, he snatched his last two cigarettes and a couple of matches from the bottom of his locker. If they were taking him to the cells, he knew he wouldn't be allowed to bring them, and so he tried to do it discreetly. The skinny soldier watched Misha stuff the cigarettes in his boots, but only looked away as if he hadn't seen it.

Misha found himself in a tiny, damp room with an old man who stank. At one end of the room was a small, dingy window with black metal bars covering it. At the other end was the heavy oak door where Misha now paced back and forth (six small steps one way and six small steps the other).

"Be grateful you're not here in the winter," the old man said. "You get ten days here in the winter, it's a death sentence. You don't die in those ten days, you die soon enough because your health'll be destroyed."

"What are you here for?" Misha asked.

"Don't know. Been five days and they still won't tell me."

Misha lit one of his cigarettes and continued pacing. He could tell from the old man's accent that he was Estonian

"If you gotta piss, there's a bucket in the corner," the old man said, pointing to the floor left of the window.

Misha looked at the bucket and then at the old man, trying to decide which of the two was making the room stink.

"Can you read?" the old man asked.

"Can I read what? Estonian?"

"No, no, it's Russian. I got a bible my wife brung me, but I can't read. She's the one that usually reads to me, but I was hoping maybe you could. Not now, but maybe a little later."

"I'm not gonna be here for long. This is all a big mistake."

"Well, for your sake, I hope so. They don't treat you so nicely here."

"Look, I don't want to talk right now. I need to think."

"All right, I'll be quiet. It's time for me to say my prayers anyway. I can say one for you if you want me to."

Misha inhaled deeply on his cigarette, hoping it would decrease his suffering in some small way. He looked at his hands and saw they were trembling.

"Well?" the old man asked.

"Well what?" Misha yelled. The old man irritated him. And that god-awful smell! He couldn't get away from it.

"Do you want me to say a prayer for you or not?"

"No, I don't! If there was a God, I wouldn't be in this mess in the first place! Now leave me alone!"

Misha continued his pacing until the cigarette had burned down to his fingers. Then he stubbed it out and sat in the corner opposite the old man. He tried to figure out what exactly he was doing there. What could they possibly have arrested him for? Had his commanding officer ordered it? If he had, why did he wait? Why wouldn't he have had Misha arrested while he was on duty?

Of course Misha had heard of the stupefying number of officers arrested, but he was sure they had all been arrested for a good reason. His arrest *had* to be a mistake. It was only a matter of time before they came and apologized to him.

But after only a few more minutes, Misha started to cast doubt on his own view. Perhaps there had been no mistake in his arrest. He started to recall all those things he'd said to Stepanovich last night. And then the realization sunk in. He was just like the rest of them – just like the thousands of others who'd been arrested. Misha saw things clearly now. He was in this stinking cell because of his big mouth. If it wasn't Stepanovich, then it was one of the countless, faceless others. He put his face in his hands and started to weep like a child, without shame.

The old man stood now and put his arm around Misha. "There, there my boy. You won't suffer long. They'll be here soon and it'll all be over with."

"*Who* will be here soon?"

"What? I thought you could hear them. Isn't that why you're crying?"

Misha held his breath and tried his best to hear something out of the ordinary, but all he heard was a pair of soldiers chatting in the distance. "I don't hear anything."

The old man shuffled back to his corner. As he knelt down, his knees cracked loudly. He began making the sign of the cross in an unbroken pattern and reciting the Lord's Prayer aloud.

Misha was still straining to hear anything out of the ordinary. He heard some sort of buzzing and looked around the room to see if there wasn't a small bee trapped inside somewhere. But Misha quickly realized that this buzzing was coming from some distant place, and it was growing louder and starting to sound more like a deep hum.

"What on earth *is* that?" Misha asked of the eerie sound.

"It's the savior! I told my wife he wouldn't forsake us. All you Russians will pay now – he'll make you pay for your sins."

"Pay for what?" Misha asked incredulously. "I'm only nineteen I haven't done anything!"

Misha's grandmother had told him about the Apocalypse when he was young. It had both terrified and intrigued him then. Now, it only terrified him. Legions of angels with swords drawn descending from the sky filled his mind.

The low, distant hum began to be accompanied by far-off thunder and Misha ran to the window to look out. It was still dark and he couldn't see anything, but he realized now the only thing that could make that peculiar humming sound – dozens and dozens of incoming planes.

"It's the fucking Germans!" Misha yelled. "They're attacking us!"

The thunder was getting closer and the old man had started clapping. When Misha looked at him, he saw tears streaming down his face and a gratifying smile on his lips.

"The Germans have come! I knew Hitler would save us!" the old man yelled.

"You traitor!! I'll tell them what you said! They'll shoot you!" Misha strained to see out the tiny, dirty window. Three soldiers ran by in a complete panic, muttering obscenities.

"Why aren't our planes firing up? The pilots should've been in their planes five minutes ago. No, *in the air* five minutes ago!"

An entire wave of German planes flew high overhead, and not a single gun from the Soviet anti-aircraft artillery fired at them. Even when the bombs started falling on the airfield and the fighter planes swooped in low and the bullets rained down like hail; even then, Misha couldn't hear anyone firing back.

"Those idiots! They still won't let us shoot at the Germans!"

Explosions filled the air and shook the ground. Misha watched as the building across from him was flattened by an assembly of bombs. Figuring his building would probably be next, Misha ran to the other end of the room and pounded on the door.

"Let us out! Let us out!" he screamed.

"Old man! Help me break down this door! We've got to get out of here."

But no sooner had Misha said this when an explosion threw him against the wall. His ears were ringing, dust filled the air, and pieces of brick lay all around him. To see if anything was broken, he tried to move his hands and feet. His left leg was twisted awkwardly underneath him, his right arm was stretched high over his head.

The dust settled, and he could see that the wall with the window was no more. Relieved that everything seemed to work correctly, Misha got to his feet and looked for the old man. It took him a few seconds, but he finally saw a head sticking out of the rubble, blood running down its face.

"Help me," the old man mouthed, and more blood trickled from his lower lip.

Misha studied the situation for a second. He could help the man get free, but he was scared of another bomb dropping on the building and wanted to ensure his own safety above all else. "Go to hell, Judas," he said, then clambered over the remains of the wall to the outside.

Spotlights searched the night sky. Fires raged out of control in nearly every building. Smoke stung Misha's eyes and the continual explosions were so painfully loud, he was sure that if he lived, he'd be deaf. Everything around him seemed to move in slow motion. He'd never seen such tremendous fires before. The flames rose higher and higher, looking as though they wanted to escape the destruction. The big red brick building that housed the officers looked like it was about to collapse. An orange and white cat leapt off of its third floor balcony, and Misha watched as it landed awkwardly near a large unexploded bomb. The cat took a few steps, then fell over on its side, its legs clawing at some invisible foe.

Misha was mesmerized by the devastation and stared blankly at the fires consuming the buildings and the planes crisscrossing the sky unleashing their fury on the ground below. The entire area was lit in beautiful, wicked shades of red and orange. Another loud explosion and a terrifying scream shook Misha from his stupor.

A man ran out of the building next to his. A small fire was perched on his back, biting and clawing at the man. The burning man swatted at it, spun in circles, and ran in dizzying directions in an attempt to get it off. *Someone should smother it*, Misha thought. But there was no one else around. It was only him, the burning man, and two blood-smeared corpses near a bomb crater.

The burning man ran faster and screamed louder, but it only seemed to incense the fire's rage. It grew bigger, climbed up his back and onto his shoulders. Misha took a few steps toward the man and yelled for him to roll on the ground. From somewhere behind them, a giant blast went off, shaking the ground. The burning man ran in his frantic zig-zag toward Misha. Straining his voice above the thunder, Misha yelled at the man to roll on the ground. But the man didn't drop to the ground, he continued running toward Misha. Not wanting to catch on fire himself, Misha ran away from the man. Screams for help didn't slow him down, neither did the cluster of bombs that ripped apart the hangar on his left. The only thing that stopped him were his own clumsy feet. He tripped and tumbled into a large crater.

Bombs fell all around Misha. Dirt fell like rain. He tried to burrow into the ground to protect himself. He hoped that the bombs would, at the very least, put the poor burning man out of his misery.

Only when the bombing ended did Misha leave the security of his crater. As a fighter plane made its last run through the base, looking for anything left to shoot at, Misha finally heard some anti-aircraft guns firing. They missed their target, and the fighter plane quickly climbed to safety and joined the rest of the planes heading back to their bases to rearm and refuel.

The sun peeked above the horizon. Misha wiped the dirt from his face and hair. Ahead of him, in their same neat rows, were the Soviet planes. Each and every one of them was smashed to pieces and burning. There were ninety-three planes in all. Ninety-three planes still chained to the ground.

*　*　*

A scrawny pigeon with ruffled feathers and only one eye stood several feet away from the half dozen other pigeons feasting on the bread crumbs being tossed their way. Each time the one-eyed pigeon attempted to join the gathering, he was chased away. And so he paced back and forth underneath the shade of the park bench – forced to watch from a distance as the others ate.

The next breadcrumb unexpectedly landed a few inches from him, and he quickly snatched it with his beak and retreated before the others moved in. The next bread crumb again landed only a few inches from him, and again he was the first one to get to it. But the other pigeons closed in anyway, several viciously attacking him. The melee ended when bread crumbs were tossed in front of the next park bench over. The one-eyed pigeon limped out from under the bench and flew away to the safety of the Pushkin statue twenty feet away. He settled on top of the great Russian writer's head.

A light breeze rustled the young green leaves of the numerous trees in the park. A streetcar full of people passed by. In a small clearing off to the left of the Pushkin statue, three boys excitedly kicked a soccer ball back and forth. And leaning forward on a park bench, tearing crumbs from a loaf of bread, was Felix. It was almost 9:00 a.m. now and he had been sitting on that same park bench for the past three hours.

Just across the street in front of him was the yellow, two-story city government building where Katya's father worked. It was customary for Katya's father to work late and come home in the early morning hours, even on weekends. The trait had evolved from Stalin, but 9:00 a.m. was exceptionally late – even for night-owl party officials.

Felix had already decided that he would wait as long as he had to. He was supposed to help Dima move at noon, but Dima had others helping him so Felix could skip it if he really had to.

The episode with the ragged, one-eyed pigeon reminded Felix of his father and how he had been continually undermined and ultimately chased away from the university where he'd taught in Ukraine. Those were the darkest days Felix had ever known. His father had started drinking daily and almost anything would set his temper off. But things had changed so much for the better since then, and all due to the kindness of Ivan Petrovich Pavlov. The Nobel Prize winning scientist admired Felix's father's work in the field of physiology and took him under his wing – bringing him to Leningrad to assist Pavlov with his experiments. Felix's father had gained enough stature to become a leading scientist in the field of physiology, surviving even Pavlov's death in 1936.

At long last, a bear of a man wearing a wrinkled white dress shirt and black pants emerged from the building. He started walking quickly down the street and Felix had to run to catch up with him. "Might I have a word with you?" Felix asked.

A stern, arrogant man by nature, Katya's father looked strangely nervous. His shoulders were tensed up toward his ears and his lips were pursed and void of color. "I don't have time, Felix. I have to get home."

"Then I'll go with you."

Felix walked along beside him the rest of the block, trying to figure out how to broach the topic gracefully. After they crossed the next street, he gave up on that approach and decided to go straight to the heart of the matter. "I want to know why you won't let your daughter marry me," he said.

Katya's father cast a dubious sidelong glance. "Because she's too young, that's why."

"She's the same age as her mother – may she rest in peace – when you married her."

"That was different."

"How?"

"It just was. Besides, Felix, it's not a good time right now. Things are very tense in the world."

Katya's father was walking extremely fast and Felix found it difficult to keep up. Felix had always known him to be a fairly slow walker and found it odd that he was walking so quickly now.

"I think you're hiding something," Felix said. "You don't want to tell me the truth. We're both men – tell me the real reason."

Katya's father stopped walking for a second and looked Felix in the eyes, then resumed his frantic pace once again. "All right," he said, "I'll tell you. It's because you're a Jew."

"Aha," Felix said.

"You're a Jew and nothing in the world is going to change that. Do you think you'll ever be more than a second-class citizen here?"

"In Socialist societies, there are no classes, no distinctions between . . ."

"Don't give me that. You've got two eyes. You see what's going on around you. Tell me, in your heart, do you really believe that a few decades of Communism is enough to wipe out a thousand years of anti-Semitism? You think people will just conveniently forget who killed Christ?"

Felix looked away. He focused on the spot in the sky where he had seen the moon the night before. He tried to comprehend its vast distance from the Earth.

"Felix, I like you," Katya's father said and stopped walking. He rested his hand on Felix's shoulder. "I don't care that you're Jewish. But these other people *do* care. They may pretend that they don't, but I know them. I know what they say behind closed doors. Do you think it would be fair to Katya to be married to you? What kind of a life would she have? If you truly love her, then you'll put her interests above yours and do what's best for her."

Felix stared at Katya's father's brown shoes until he noticed them walking away. Felix went in the opposite direction. His thoughts strayed once more to the moon. He remembered reading that when meteorites and asteroids enter the Earth's atmosphere, they usually burn themselves into oblivion before ever reaching the surface. The moon, however, doesn't have the luxury of an atmosphere, and so is defenseless against such attacks. Its surface is barren and dotted with deep craters from the constant bombardment. Scientists speculated that life probably could not exist there; only the strongest and most resilient of life forms could possibly withstand such harsh conditions.

For over four hours, Felix roamed the streets of Leningrad. Though nothing in particular occupied his thoughts, a general melancholy filled him to the tip of his unmistakably Jewish nose. Lost in his own world, he took long, slow strides along a particular canal for an hour, then followed the Neva river for another hour. He walked past the tall golden needle spire of the Admiralty, past the Winter Palace, past the elevated, imposing statue of Peter the Great. Under the hot summer sun, he walked and walked and walked through the expansive city until one image came to dominate his thoughts and he could think of nothing else. The image was of the sculpture of Saint Andrew the Apostle that flanked the huge bronze doors in front of the Kazansky Cathedral. The look of desperation and abandonment on the statue's face haunted Felix and he had to go to the statue, to see it with his own eyes, to sit next to it in silence and commiseration.

Like the dying elephant that travels to a designated graveyard it has never been to, so too Felix arrived, without particularly knowing how, at the Kazansky Cathedral. A crowd – much larger than usual for 1:10 in the afternoon on a Sunday – had gathered in front of the building. So many of the people seemed unreal to Felix, as if they were thoughts that had escaped from his mind. Everywhere he turned, he saw these people who looked so familiar, but who were in fact strangers to him. A big man with a beard yelled in anger as tears streamed down his face. School girls huddled around one another with looks of horror in their young eyes.

As he walked through the strange crowd toward the statue of Saint Andrew the Apostle, Felix heard bits and pieces of conversations that confirmed his belief that his thoughts were not his own, but open for public mocking and ridicule.

"What did you expect?" said a tall man with a gaunt face and hollow eyes. "I said all along they couldn't be trusted. They'll pretend like they're your friend, and then stab you in the back."

A young woman with a summer hat pulled low over head hissed, ". . . the whole thing was just one big lie. They've played us for the fool."

Felix hurried by, unable to look at them. *Fear* was alien to him and its presence now confused him.

"You know she won't last long. This will be too much for her," muttered a pale man with wavy gray hair. "It's probably best to just move on now. Take what you got and get out."

"Death," an old woman sighed. "That's what will come of this in the end. Maybe not today, maybe not tomorrow, but mark my words, death *will* come."

It was getting to be too much for Felix. He wanted to scream. He made it through the crowd to the statue, but he couldn't escape the voices.

"With bayonets!" the man standing next to Felix shouted. "That's how we'll welcome them."

Since the word bayonet had never entered Felix's mind, this last statement made him stop and consider.

"Welcome who?" Felix asked the man.

"What are you talking about? You haven't heard?"

Felix shook his head.

"The Germans!" the man replied. "The damn Germans attacked us this morning. Molotov just announced it."

The significance was slow to sink in, but Felix finally understood that it meant war. He thought of his mother and father and how they would be out of their minds by now if they knew. He left the cathedral and quickly headed for home.

As he ran along Nevsky Prospekt, he saw people with wads of paper rubles in their hands running into grocery stores that were already packed to capacity. People leaving the stores had their arms full with sugar, flour, butter, groats, sausage, and canned goods. Felix recognized a Party official's rotund wife. She was balancing over a dozen cans of caviar and four bottles of vodka in her plump arms.

At the State Savings Bank, the line was around the corner and halfway down the block. Everyone in line was pushing and shouting and demanding their money "*immediately!*" A fight between two women broke out near the front of the line, and, for a moment, it looked like the whole block might erupt into a riot.

A dozen men stood together in a tight circle arguing amongst themselves, while small boys tried to squeeze between their legs to see what was happening. A group of teenagers – mostly boys, a few girls – started marching down the middle of the street singing the Internationale, their voices rising briefly above all the shouting and commotion. ". . . We peasants, artisans and others / Enrolled among the sons of toil / Let's change the earth henceforth for brothers . . . the last fight let us face / The Internationale / Unites the human race . . ."

On the corner, an old man with a long beard and black cap waved his cane wildly in the air. "Comrades," he roared at the top of his lungs, "we didn't ask to live through this, but by God we'll make it! They'll see how strong we are!"

~

Глава Вторая — Chapter Two
A Dream Incomplete

The unhappy clock could tick and it could tock,
    but missing from its life seemed the key to its lock.
High and low it searched in defeat,
    for its logic and reason left it incomplete.
How to fill the void inside, it knew not,
    but secured in that lock was the answer it sought.
The key it so yearned for really did exist,
    but the time on its face could no longer twist.
There is truth in deception, success in defeat,
    but a premature death is always a dream incomplete.

The pain in his ribs spread outward in all directions with each breath he took. The only remedy seemed to be not to breathe or not to think about the pain. Alfred chose the latter.

Although the Soviet interrogators let him sleep for just a few hours at a time and fed him day-old black bread and stale water, the only things that really bothered him were his bruised ribs and that he hadn't been able to bathe in so long. The bruises were courtesy of one of the guards after Alfred had turned his head away for the fifth time in a row just as they'd tried to take a photo of him. From the sheer number of people and the way they were fussing over how the picture was to be taken, he knew it was going to be used for propaganda purposes and wanted no part of it.

When they finished with the photo, his suspicions were quickly confirmed. They wanted him to issue a statement calling on German soldiers to overthrow Hitler and his government. They were prepared to inflict further physical punishment, but Alfred surprised them and cooperated on that. He was all in favor of banishing that madman from power.

All that had happened eighteen days ago, and now the pain in his ribs never left him. If he focused his attention and energy on something else, then he didn't notice it. And he went to extreme lengths not to think about the pain. He recalled boyhood memories, relived tragic episodes with his father, and speculated on what the world would be like in 50 years. He played incredible movies in his head where he was alternately the hero and then the villain. All these things occupied his mind relentlessly, and yet whenever the slightest pause occurred, he realized without a doubt that the pain was still there. So he started up his movies and his memories and his thoughts about the future once again.

The guards would be coming for him soon. They never went longer than four hours between interrogations. Let them come, Alfred thought. Let them spend his time however they wished.

He stretched his arms over his head and walked to the end of his cell. The window there was set unnaturally high and Alfred had to stand on his tiptoes to peer outside. In between the iron bars, he could see the guard standing in the wooden tower in the far corner. He was always there, either pacing back and forth with his rifle resting in his arms or standing stock still and looking down at the people walking below. Alfred watched a bee drop off the edge of one of the pink roses and then buzz out of sight over the high brick wall that surrounded the complex. He'd spent hours contemplating that rose bush. Why would anyone plant roses in a prison?

Outside his cell was a dark windowless hallway that led to two places – to the sun and the sky outside, and to a thick wooden door that opened into a tiny room with just enough space for a desk and three chairs. Alfred had walked down that hallway 20 times the past two weeks, but he had yet to see the blue sky.

He could hear them coming down the hallway now – the unmistakable jingling of the keys and the echo of a pair of heavy footsteps. Quickly, but carefully, he spread the green bed sheet over the edge of his bed so that it almost touched the floor. He pulled one side a little higher up from the floor than the other, and then rumpled the parts of the sheet that laid on top of the bed. He stepped over to the doorway and looked at the bed and wall behind it closely. It wasn't perfect, but it did the trick – the drooping sheet hid the loose bricks in the wall.

Alfred had started chipping away at it earlier that day after he discovered that the plaster practically crumbled with the slightest touch and the bricks behind were loose.

Stern Face appeared in the dirty oval window of the door to Alfred's cell. "Prisoner! Step away from the door," it instructed him in broken German. Stern Face said that each and every time he came for Alfred, whether Alfred was, in fact, near the door or at the other end of his twelve-foot cell.

The door swung open swiftly, smacking the wall behind it. Alfred watched as more plaster fell to the floor. That was what had given him the idea in the first place, but he didn't like that the door kept doing that now. He was afraid it was only a matter of time before the guards had the same thought.

Two men entered Alfred's cell: Stern Face, and a new face. New Face wore small oval glasses that rested on a short, thin nose. He had eyes the color of slate, thick dark hair that was combed impeccably straight back, and a thin mustache that barely reached the corners of his mouth. He was short, only coming to Alfred's chin, and his posture was perfect.

"Why does he stink so bad?" New Face asked Stern Face in Russian.

"He's a Nazi," Stern Face replied matter-of-factly.

"I want him bathed this evening," New Face said. "That smell makes me sick."

Though they had spoken in Russian, Alfred understood everything that was said, and quite involuntarily, a slight smile crept across his face. As soon as he realized it, he reverted back to his usual blank expression, but he was concerned that New Face had already caught his tiny blunder.

"Does he speak any Russian?" New Face asked Stern Face.

"None," Stern Face said. "He's an idiot."

"Hey German," New Face said slowly in Russian, "I've come to take you out back and shoot you." New Face watched Alfred closely, but Alfred simply stared back blankly.

If New Face had meant to scare Alfred with his statement and provoke a response or some sign of comprehension of Russian, then he had miscalculated. Alfred did not fear death. Telling him he was going to die that afternoon was no different than telling him it was going to rain that day. Alfred was a strong believer in fate, and if he was supposed to die that day, then so be it.

Alfred never let on to anyone that he understood some Russian. There had been a few close calls, like the time his first interrogator asked the translator if he wanted some water, and Alfred said yes and nodded his head because he thought he was the one being asked. He'd gotten out of that one – just barely – by turning his *yes* into a yawn, and his nod into a neck stretch. He had been much more careful since then. If a question or command was said in Russian, Alfred was careful not to answer it nor do as he was instructed. He did his best to look as uninterested as possible in what people were saying, and only responded when something was said in German.

New Face surveyed the plaster on the floor where the door had struck it. Then he looked at the bed.

"Were you sleeping?" he asked in impeccable German.

"No," Alfred replied, then immediately thought he should have said yes.

"Then why is your bed sheet hanging over the edge like that? Why isn't your bed made?"

Alfred made no response. He was impressed with how well the man spoke German. He thought he might be a new translator, but decided he couldn't be because he had an air of authority about him, and besides, translators never visited him in his cell unless an interrogator was present.

"Get your shirt on and come with us," New Face said and led the way out of the cell and down the hall. Alfred put on his smelly brown t-shirt and followed. Stern Face, his pistol drawn, went last.

At the end of the hallway was an iron gate. New Face called out to the guard on the other side to unlock it so they could pass through. As they waited, Alfred smelled the freshly polished leather of Stern Face's gun holster and closed his eyes tightly in an attempt to hold on to the sensation.

When New Face turned right after he passed through the gate, Alfred's heart began to race. Could they be letting him go outside? But when Alfred reached the intersection, he was directed once again into the small stuffy room on the left.

Alfred went in and sat down. New Face sat across from him with his arms resting on the table and his hands clasped together, just like Alfred's previous two interrogators. The chair for the translator was empty.

"So, Private Liskof, can you explain to me why you surrendered yourself to the Soviet Border Guards?"

"I've explained that twenty times already."

"Well, perhaps twenty-one will be your lucky number, because quite frankly your answers to this question have been unsatisfactory so far."

"You mean the truth is not to your liking?" Alfred said with more than a hint of sarcasm. He wondered how long this interrogator would last before they sent yet another one.

New Face twisted in his chair and brought his right hand up to support his chin. "I'd prefer that we don't get off to a bad start. Both of our well being depend upon a successful outcome."

Alfred arched his eyebrows slightly, surprised at New Face's frankness. His comment about *well being* confirmed Alfred's fear that an inauspicious ending awaited him soon.

New Face took a cigarette out from a small tin case and offered it to Alfred. Alfred's first thought was that it might be laced with some sort of chemicals meant to inebriate or asphyxiate him, but he decided he'd take the risk. After all, they had more forceful means at their disposal for getting him to ingest something.

The tobacco was harsh, obviously Russian, but tasted good all the same. Alfred became a little light headed after a few inhalations. It was probably because he hadn't eaten anything in so long.

"When's the last time you had a cigarette?" New Face asked.

"The day I took my leave of the German army and came here."

"Yes? And what day was that?"

"June 21st of course."

"I'm curious. What prompted you to, as you put it, 'take leave of the German army'?"

"I left because I thought they were making a terrible mistake and I wanted to do something about it."

"How patriotic of you."

Alfred inhaled on his cigarette and meant to reply, but found himself subject to a coughing fit instead.

"You'll have to excuse our Soviet tobacco," New Face said. "I'm afraid it's not very high on our list of priorities. Probably your German tobacco is much more to your liking."

New Face reached into the desk drawer and retrieved a rolled-up poster. "I'd like to show you something," he said as he unrolled the poster and spread it out on the desk.

It was a picture of Alfred dressed in his German army fatigues. He knew which picture that was – the one taken right after he'd received the blow to the stomach. In the picture, Alfred had a dour expression on his face. At the bottom of the poster were the words: "A mood of depression rules among German soldiers."

"What do you think?" New Face asked.

Alfred shrugged his shoulders. "I don't think it's true."

"But you see, that's where you're wrong, Private Liskof. It *is* true. It is printed quite distinctly on the poster."

Alfred eyed New Face warily, and then blew smoke out his nose like he used to do when he was a teenager.

"We need to work together, you and I," New Face said. "We need to work together to ensure that the Soviet people clearly understand your story. And it's my job to help you."

Alfred was so damn tired of being in this tiny room with its stale air and greenish-gray walls. He examined New Face and calculated how quickly he could kill him. It wouldn't be difficult. He could just smash his nose up into his face and then jump over the desk and put him in a choke hold.

"You see," New Face continued, "if you were to get up in front of a crowd,

THE END OF SORROW

we would want to be sure that your message was conveyed correctly. The people of the Soviet Union need to understand that you *deserted*. They need to know that you left because you were treated badly, and that you had no desire to take up arms against your *brothers in labor*. Soviet citizens must know how *desperate* the situation is in the German army. Are we beginning to understand one another?"

Alfred cracked his knuckles and then folded his arms in front of his chest. "I understand that I'm a prisoner here," he said, "that you're my interrogator, and that our two countries are at war."

New Face never took his gaze from Alfred, never moved or stretched. He was like a bronze statue situated in a perfectly erect position opposite Alfred. "That's precisely why I was sent here," he said calmly, "to help you with your *understanding*. You are a prisoner here only in the sense that we can't let you just walk away. I would like us to think of each other as partners, or allies, if you will. If we work together, we can each get something very important to us."

"The only thing I want is an end to this insidious war and to go home."

"There, you see, we have more in common than you think. I, too, want an end to the war and to go home. And I would like you to help me put an end to this war. Will you help me do that?"

Alfred thought he understood New Face well enough, he just hadn't expected this and didn't know how to react.

"That's okay, I didn't expect an answer just yet," New Face said. "We don't have to discuss this anymore right now. I just wanted us to meet and try to reach an agreement to work together. I want you to think about it for a while and be sure of your answer. Ok?"

Alfred nodded. He had a strange thought that everything was a dream, that nothing was real. He wasn't really in a Soviet prison. There wasn't really a war engulfing the entire world. Indeed, nothing was as it seemed. It brought Alfred a sense of relief and he tried to hold onto it. But it refused to be grasped and slipped away just as quickly as it had come.

New Face got up and opened the door. Alfred had taken his place to return to his cell when New Face turned to him suddenly and asked if he would like to go outside for a brief walk. Puzzled by the sudden generosity, Alfred couldn't answer. Before he knew it, he found himself outdoors in the slightly humid, yet thoroughly refreshing air of summer. Without a cloud in the sky, the sun was exceptionally bright and hot. Alfred, with his blue eyes, bald head, and fair skin, normally despised weather such as this. The sun was his enemy, he frequently said. But not today. Today, the sun was his childhood friend that he hadn't seen, nor thought about, in ages. Today, he was grateful just to be able to breathe the air and walk in the light of day.

* * *

Felix had been near the end of the line and when his turn finally came, he had a choice between a shovel, a hand axe, or a hunting knife. Though the shovel wasn't as lethal as the other two, it did have more length, so he could fight from a greater distance. He picked it up, and, gripping it with both hands, lunged it forward like a bayonet. Then he moved his hands closer together on the handle and swung it like an axe. He set it down and picked up the hand axe. It was short – no more than 18 inches long. He gripped it with his right hand and swung it up over his head and down in front of him. He set it down and picked up the hunting knife. It was even shorter – about ten inches long. It was old and rusty and hadn't been used in a long time, but he could easily sharpen it. He didn't know how to throw a knife and had no training in how to fight with one.

The ten men still behind Felix were getting restless and yelled for him to hurry up. He made a quick decision to go with the hand axe, picked it up and started walking away. After two steps, he had the thought that if they found themselves under attack – be it from bombs or bullets – the shovel would come in very handy to dig a quick trench. He turned around and put the hand axe back, and took the shovel instead.

He walked over to Dima, who was sitting on the ground, busily inspecting the twenty-five year old rifle he'd gotten. Dima had been near the front of the line.

Dima looked up at his friend and the shovel he carried with him. "Good. You got a shovel. You can dig a trench with that. Those guys who took picks and axes don't know the first thing about modern-day warfare. Do they think it's going to be like Vikings doing hand-to-hand combat with their enemies on beaches or open fields?"

Felix sat down next to his friend. He couldn't help but notice that those who were still in line for a weapon all had the same Jewish nose that he did.

"Your rifle looks a bit old," Felix said. "Does it work?"

"It's actually in decent shape. It's pretty much the same rifle my father used in the Civil War, and I feel like I already know everything about it. He used to talk to me for hours about the battles he was in and how his rifle never let him down."

Felix knew that Dima understood a lot about fighting and strategy and such, certainly much more than he did. Dima's father was well known for his exploits in the Civil War, and he had drilled Dima from an early age on the do's and don'ts of battle – everything from how to dress a wound to how to respond to attacks by tanks or planes.

"You know," Dima said, looking at the shovel once more, "you could sharpen the handle and make a nice bayonet out of it."

"Good idea," Felix said, and retrieved the small knife he always carried with him. He sat down beside Dima and began whittling the end of the handle.

The 1st Volunteers Division, of which Felix and Dima were a part, was a motley collection of nearly 11,000 men with little or no military background or training. The average age of the men was much older than the regular army. Some men were approaching 50, while others, like Felix and Dima, were still in their teens. About a third of the division consisted of Party members or Young Communists.

Felix and Dima were part of a company that consisted almost entirely of men from the same furniture factory. Most all of them knew one another, and instead of using military language, those in command would politely say, "I beg of you . . ." or "Please do so and so . . .." Only a small percent of the division's officers had any command experience or formal military training. Some of the men in the division wore uniforms from the Civil War of twenty-five years ago – likely given to them by their fathers or uncles. Most of the division's officers had on regular Red Army uniforms, but not all, and the vast majority of men simply wore their everyday clothes.

The division had only about a third of the machine guns they were supposed to have and hardly any artillery at all. Some of the men, like Felix, had no rifles and carried only picks, axes, shovels, or knives. More than a few men were armed with nothing but their own courage.

Felix and Dima had joined the People's Volunteers shortly after the war started. They went into training the night of July 3rd, and used the playgrounds of the Fifth School on Stachek Prospekt as their drill field. Katya came by every evening with tea, a loaf of bread, and a large hunk of cheese.

They were supposed to receive a month's worth of training, but the rapid advance of the Germans had cut that short and they were now preparing to head to the front to help hold the Luga line. It was the morning of July 10th, and the mood of the men preparing for battle was overtly upbeat. They acted especially macho – making black humor jokes about their weapons and readiness, mixing a vast array of obscenities and profanity into every sentence, and talking much louder than necessary.

Felix, amazed at first at how brave they all acted, joined in with them. But he eventually realized the insincerity of it, and that for the men to honestly admit to the absurdity of it all would be a betrayal. The division was forming into a column now, and a man at the front carried a red and gold banner, presented by the Kirov factory workers. A band assembled behind the man, and within a few minutes they were on their way to the Vitebsk freight station.

The man marching next to Felix had a thick white beard that covered all of his neck and most of his face. He wore a gray jacket with a black belt around the outside of it, and knee-high leather boots. There were five medals pinned to his jacket and a solemn expression on his face. Felix, with his white dress shirt, clean-shaven face and black pants, wondered how he must appear to this old veteran. Probably like someone who'd just finished visiting a museum for the day, he thought.

As the band played and they marched through the streets, crowds of families, friends, and onlookers cheered and waved from the sidewalks. Felix tried, but he could not share in their enthusiasm. Plastered on a building they passed, he saw the now familiar poster of a German soldier with a dour expression and the caption, "A mood of depression rules among German soldiers." The posters had gone up shortly after the war began.

"Dima, have you seen those posters?"

"Of course, they're all over the city."

"What do you think about it?"

"I think it shows how desperate the situation is in the German army."

"But they're winning. There's talk they may even take Leningrad before the Fall."

"They'll *never* take Leningrad!" Dima said angrily. "Not in a million years will a Nazi boot step on this ground!"

"But Dima," Felix protested, "we're being sent to the front to defend the city and you have an antique gun and I only have a shovel."

"It doesn't matter. It's only a matter of time before the tide turns. The Red Army was simply taken by surprise. Hitler's treachery caught us unprepared, that's all. Once we regroup, we'll drive the Nazis all the way back to Berlin. They're winning now, but it's only momentary. The German soldiers are being pushed to their limit by their bourgeois officers. That's why the Party put those posters up, to remind us what's at the root of this aggression. The German soldiers won't put up with much more. They'll rise up against their officers and demand to go back home. And then they'll overthrow Hitler and his sham government and the Revolution will spread. Things may look a little bleak right now, but trust me, it's just a matter of time before the German army starts to fall apart and the Red Army gets reorganized."

Having listened to Dima, Felix felt more confident and upbeat. He was reassured by Dima's words on how things would turn out. He saw the poster again on another building and wondered about the man in the picture. Felix heard that the man had deserted to the Soviet lines and he admired that. He admired the man's courage and thought that if the situation had somehow been reversed that he would not have been able to do the same. Felix could never leave the loves of his life – Russia and Katya – behind. He was much too attached to them. He wondered how many more German soldiers were like the man in the poster, how many more felt the way he did?

* * *

Back in his cell, Alfred dropped onto his bed like a dead man. He was hungry and tired, and wanted nothing more than to sleep. But he couldn't help thinking about his fate. What were they planning for him? Did they mean for him to give some sort of public speech denouncing Germany and the capabilities of the German army? What would happen if he didn't cooperate?

He stared up at the ceiling and contemplated the light in his cell that seemed to hang in the air, floating up toward the ceiling rather than dispersing in equal measure throughout the room. The pungent smell of his sweaty clothes permeated the air. He dozed off for a few minutes before the two familiar thumps on the door announced the arrival of the guard who served his late afternoon meal – a combined lunch and dinner.

"Nazi criminal," he said in Russian. "I have your dinner for you."

He was a skinny man, probably around 55, and did everything at the pace of a snail. He spoke in slow, lazy Russian that made it quite easy for Alfred to understand him. He liked to ramble on about things, and most of the time held complete conversations with himself – asking questions and then providing the answers as if someone else had asked it. Though Alfred was never sure why, almost every day the man would test him in some small way to see if he understood any Russian.

As the man shuffled in the door, Alfred looked up at what he'd brought. The well-worn wooden tray held a large bowl of something steaming, the usual stale black bread, and a glass with a small crack that descended like lightening from the top to the bottom.

"Here's your food." The man set the tray down on the bed next to Alfred. "That little commissar has made me bring you beef stew and English tea. It's better than I eat, and yet you, an enemy of the people, get it." He leaned against the door frame and looked at Alfred. "But what do I know? I'm an old man putting in my time until they let me die."

He always came unarmed and alone – unlocking the door, bringing in the food, then waiting until Alfred finished so he could take the tray and its contents back with him. The last several times he'd come, he'd spoken at length about how poorly the war was going for the Soviets. Alfred didn't understand how someone like him could know so many details about the war, but he found himself believing the man and his strange stories.

"General P__ complained again that his tanks on the front are all quite old and in need of repair," he said. "'And the planes ain't much better!' he yelled. They didn't like that none. Complaining don't ever go over too well."

Alfred sat on his bed and listened, all the while staring at the wall or the dusty floor and pretending as if he didn't understand a word.

"And what happened to those twenty-five front-line divisions?" the man asked, glancing over at Alfred.

"I'll tell you what happened to them," he continued, "they've been obliterated by the Panzer tanks and the Luftwaffe – those demons from the sky. Tell me, how is it that the great Soviet army is being routed? How is that possible?" he asked.

Alfred turned his attention to the food on his tray and noticed that the bread wasn't moldy or stale for once, and the stew looked quite fresh. He simply didn't know what to think about the tea. He usually just got water.

"Perhaps it's all a lie," the man replied to his own question. "Perhaps some of the reports sent in from the front are the work of German propaganda. Or maybe provocateurs." Then the man rejected his own theory. He leaned against the wall, watched Alfred drink the tea, and patiently explained how many of those who had been in command at the start of the war had already been replaced.

While Alfred listened to him ramble on, he looked beyond him at the hallway. It seemed that it would be so easy to escape – break the man's neck and run down the hallway to freedom. But he knew there was nowhere to escape to. There was the locked iron gate at the end of the hallway, and even if he somehow got the keys or picked the lock, there was still the pistol-clad guard stationed on the other side. If he made it through the door and managed not to be shot dead, there was still no place to go. The entire building was surrounded by a fifteen-foot wall with barbed wire, and of course there was that guard tower and its search light.

Alfred doubted that the building, the entire complex really, was ever meant to be a prison. In fact, he'd never seen another prisoner. Perhaps he was the only one. If the complex was not a prison, that would explain the rose bush, the lack of a slot in the door to his cell, and the fresh mortar holding the bars in place on his window. The security seemed quite lax to Alfred. Why, for instance, didn't an armed guard accompany the man serving his food? Alfred sometimes wondered if it wasn't some game they were playing with him. It seemed that they were constantly playing little games to which Alfred hadn't been taught the rules.

The man watched Alfred eat the bread. "Hey German, you want in on a little secret?" Alfred ignored him, and prepared to take a bite of the stew. He thought the man was testing him again – trying to catch him off guard. "That stew's been poisoned," the man said and stared at Alfred.

The spoon was already on its way to Alfred's mouth when the man said it, and Alfred knew he had to think fast. Was he serious? Or was this another one of his tests? Or maybe he just had a strange sense of humor? If Alfred didn't take the bite of stew, or even if he paused, then he would give himself away as understanding Russian.

Perhaps it was time to die, Alfred thought. Poisoning shouldn't be too painful. Perhaps he'd just fall asleep and never wake up. He'd be okay with that.

But he wasn't ready to die just yet, and he knew it. His mind and body both told him that there was some last step that he had yet to take. But what could he do now?

Alfred decided he'd put the spoon down and end his charade, but then he looked at the man and somehow knew that he was bluffing. He couldn't explain it, but he knew without a doubt that it was a trick. He took the bite of stew. It tasted a little funny, but then everything he ate in this country tasted funny to him.

"So you're going to eat it anyway, huh? That's the problem with you Germans – you're too trusting."

Alfred continued to eat the stew, and found – much to his surprise – that he enjoyed it immensely. If it was the last thing he was ever going to eat on this earth, he might as well enjoy it. He closed his eyes and ate slowly, chewing every bite thoroughly before picking up his spoon for another bite. He wished he'd eaten every meal of his life this way.

The man wiped his nose with the back of his hand and looked at the bits of plaster that had fallen to the floor behind the door. "I remember," he continued, "we had about a dozen of you Germans pinned down in the last war, and my commander – Kalinovich – told you to put your weapons down and surrender, which was a joke because there was only five of us. Somehow he got you all believing that we were a full battalion and had you surrounded. And every damn one of you believed him. Damn fools. As soon as you all walked out into the open with your hands up, Kalinovich ordered our machine gunner to fill you full of bullets. Still makes me sick, every time I think about it – seeing all those bloody corpses lying on top of one another. After it was over, one fella was still alive, had his guts hanging out of him and screaming at the top of his lungs. It took four more bullets to finally shut him up. And that smell! I'll never forget that as long as I live . . . ."

The more Alfred ignored the man, the more he talked. He rambled on and on about anything and everything. Even after Alfred had finished eating and went to the corner of the room to take a piss in the can, the man continued talking.

"That little commissar is going to eat you up, you know. He's probably got your trust already," the man said, shifting his weight to his other leg. "Yes . . . he's very disarming in his thoughtfulness. Everyone knows about him though. Well, everyone but you, I guess. He ain't got no friends I hear, but he sure does seem to know everybody. Don't like to joke none – I know that for myself. No, the only time I ever heard him laugh was when I told him that story about Kalinovich shooting all the Germans after he'd tricked them into surrendering."

"Comrade Surikov!" a voice yelled from down the hall, "What is taking you so long?" Alfred recognized the voice as Stern Face.

"Nothing comrade," the man replied. "I'm leaving now." And with that, he took Alfred's tray and closed the door behind himself.

Alfred listened to the man's heavy footsteps fade away. He moved his bed away from the wall and carefully removed the four bricks that he'd already managed to loosen and set them off to the side. He was halfway done – another four bricks and he'd be able to squeeze through the opening to the outside. The mortar was very old and had been done carelessly. Alfred had little trouble coaxing the bricks out of it with the long rusty nail he'd pulled out of the bed frame.

As he dug and chiseled and pushed and pulled on the remaining bricks, he thought of many things. But more than anything else, he thought about his father. He remembered a particularly violent spanking he'd received from him because his mother had told him to do something and he'd said no. It had all happened so suddenly. He'd been in a bad mood because he'd had to work all day. And then, just after dinner, when he thought at long last he'd get to play, his mother told him to do something. Alfred couldn't remember what it was, but it didn't matter. He was sick and tired of working. When he said no, he hadn't really meant it. He knew he had to do whatever his parents told him. He'd said it to be rebellious. As soon as he'd said it, his father flew out of his chair, grabbed him, ripped his pants down to his ankles, and beat his bare buttocks with all his might. And when it was all over, Alfred choked back his sobs, pulled his pants up, looked his father straight in the eyes, and said, "I hate you." He'd braced himself for another blow, but it never came. Instead, his father said, "I don't care if you do or not, but you'd better do what your mother and I tell you to or you'll be sorry," and then turned and walked away.

Alfred finished his work on the hole in two hours, and then laid down to take a break for a few minutes. He wanted to work on his escape plan, but he was so incredibly tired. He was so tired that he wondered if maybe they really had poisoned the stew. He decided he'd rest for just twenty minutes or so, and then get to work.

Within thirty seconds of this decision, Alfred was fast asleep. He had strange and vivid dreams. In one dream, he was a clerk in charge of filling out racial purity forms for SS officers who wanted to have children. After he had finished interviewing each officer and had filled out the form, one of his fingers would fall off, only to somehow grow back and fall off again after finishing the forms for the next officer.

In another dream, he was a young boy, six or seven at the most, who was a soldier in the German army. He had *three* legs – the third one was small and without bones and hung limply from the middle of his back. He spent most of the dream trying on different uniforms that he hoped would somehow hide the abnormality, so he could be just like everyone else. But no matter how many he tried on, the lump on his back was obvious. He eventually gave up trying to be like the others, quit the army, and went home. In his little bedroom on the second floor, he laid on his stomach and cried his eyes out and beat his fists on his pillow. His father opened the door, but instead of comfort and words of encouragement, he was told he'd better stop his crying because crying was for sissies and girls. To drive the point home, his father clenched his fist and shook it at Alfred.

* * *

There were crowds of people at the freight station and from somewhere in the sea of people, a man yelled Felix's name. Felix searched the figures and faces, but couldn't locate the man. Both Felix's and Dima's parents saw them off at the start of the march, so he knew the voice wasn't either of their fathers. He searched the groups of people: young boys and girls no taller than Felix's shovel, old men with canes, plump babushkas, tearful wives, and proud mothers and fathers. They all gathered in circles around men – some young, like Felix, and some twice his age – who were about to board the waiting train for the front. Before Felix could find the man, he saw Katya, and then realized the man yelling for him must be her father.

Katya ran up to Felix, wrapped her arms around him and kissed him on both cheeks. She was wearing a sleeveless dress that bared her thin, slightly tanned arms and shoulders. A few seconds later, her father arrived and shook Felix's hand. He looked perplexed when he saw Felix's shovel. "Where's your weapon?" he asked.

"*This* is my weapon," Felix grinned as he held forth the shovel. "And here is my bayonet," he added, pointing to the sharpened end of the handle.

"Are you serious?" Katya's father asked, arching his eyebrows. "They told me we were short on weapons, but I had no idea it was this bad. What are you going to do with a shovel?"

"He'll dig their graves for them, that's what," Dima said.

Katya rolled her eyes at the statement. "Oh father," she pleaded, "can't you do something? This is sheer insanity."

"Don't worry about me," Felix said. "We've been told we probably won't even see any Germans. And if they do show up, we'll ask them to wait until we finish our training. Ha-ha."

Katya smiled at his joke, but didn't laugh. "Aren't you terrified of going into battle with only a shovel?" she asked.

"We're not afraid of anything," Dima declared, "least of all the Germans."

"Show me a man without fear, and I'll show you a man without a pulse," Katya's father said.

Dima and Katya's father then began arguing about the role fear plays in man's life, and Felix used the opportunity to slip away with Katya. They held hands and walked toward the end of the train.

"Your father doesn't look so well," Felix said. "He's so pale."

"Yes I know, he looks awful," Katya said, her smile receding into concern. "He works non-stop now. He doesn't get any sleep and he's losing weight, and of course the war isn't going well. Every time I see him, he tells me about someone new who's been 'relieved of his duties.' I keep begging him to slow down, to take at least one night off a week to rest. And of course he agrees and promises to do it, but always comes up with an excuse at the last second."

Felix stopped and took both of Katya's hands in his. "Well, he's always been strong as an ox. He'll be all right." Felix half believed what he said. Her father *was* a vigorous man, but Felix had honestly never seen him look so old before. His hair, usually a mix of grey and black, was now entirely grey.

"Listen Katya," Felix continued. "We don't have much time left. They'll be calling us to form ranks any minute and . . ."

"Don't go," Katya interrupted.

"What?"

"I'm serious," she said. "Don't go. It's not right."

"Katya," Felix said, bringing her hands up to waist level and squeezing them a little tighter, "we've been through this before. If nobody goes to fight, then the Nazis win. We'll be slaves."

"Let the others fight," she said. "You don't have to."

"I do," he said. "I do have to fight."

"Why?"

"To protect people like you," he said, brushing the back of his hand alongside her cheek.

Her hands started to tremble.

"Now I know that nothing's changed so far," Felix said, "so I'm not going to ask you to promise to marry me one day." He pulled a ring out of his pocket. It had a small ruby in the middle and a petite diamond on each side. "My mother gave this to me. She said it was my grandmother's ring. I want you to keep it as a promise that you won't forget me – you know, should anything happen . . . ." Felix looked into her sad brown eyes and saw tears forming.

"Oh Felix, this world is so crazy," she said. "Maybe that's why you fit in so well." She then started laughing as she cried. "To hell with your forget-me-not. When you come back, I want to marry you – with *or without* my father's permission."

"Don't joke about such a thing," he said. "It's not funny to me."

"Who's laughing?"

"*You* are."

"Ok, so maybe I am, but not about that."

Felix's face lit up. "You're serious?"

She nodded her head. "Yes, I decided life's too short to play by someone else's rules."

"Kirov Division of Volunteers! Fall in!" an officer shouted.

Felix kissed Katya quickly on the lips. "I've got to go," he said. He started to walk away, but then went back and kissed her again, this time longer.

"You'll be careful, won't you?" she asked.

The laughter was gone, as quickly as it had come, and Felix saw tears streaming down the sides of her nose. "Oh my Katya, I'll be careful," he said. And then, brushing her cheek once more, he added, "I promise." He ran to join his comrades in formation, but then remembered he still had the ring.

"Katya!" he yelled.

She turned toward him, and Felix tossed the ring over the young girl walking between them and Katya caught it with both hands. He blew her a kiss, admired her slender neck and bare shoulders, then hurried to line up next to Dima.

Fifteen minutes later, they were aboard the train and on their way to the front. Felix stared out the window for most of trip, thinking of Katya and how precious life was. That he could die in battle seemed preposterous. Life had always been fair to him, and God, or whoever was in charge, surely wouldn't do that to him. There was doubt, though, in the back of his mind because of the mystical experience he'd had when he was twelve.

It was after he had awakened from a nap. In his room, a strange being had appeared out of nowhere. Felix didn't understood who or what the being was, but it introduced itself as Ariel. It was mostly just a bright white light, but Felix could also make out the edges of what looked like a human form. It spoke with a feminine voice, telling Felix a prophecy about his life. Felix had chosen, Ariel explained, a *challenging* path for this lifetime.

Then, strangely enough, Felix actually remembered doing just that. He didn't know if Ariel was helping him recall it or not, but he had a fuzzy recollection of agreeing beforehand to the circumstances in which he would live his life. And he remembered too, being cautioned that the path he had decided upon was deemed high risk. It was a gamble, and there was no guarantee that he would be successful in what he wanted to do. In fact, the odds were against it.

Ariel echoed the same message to him now, saying, "If you are not strong enough, diligent enough, my love, this life will not turn out as you hoped. You will succumb to a great bitterness, loneliness, and contempt."

"And if I am successful?" young Felix had asked in response.

"If you are successful," Ariel said, shining brighter than ever, "then you will undergo a great transformation in your life under the most trying of circumstances. You will have found what you've been searching for for a very long time."

Climbing down from his bed and stepping closer to Ariel, Felix had asked, "And what is that?"

The light that was Ariel suddenly expanded, encompassing the entire room, Felix included. He was suffused with an immeasurable sense of peace and love.

"You will have found the end of sorrow," Ariel answered.

A hand-painted sign had been nailed to a tree for all to read as they disembarked from the train. It read: "Our cause is just, the enemy will be beaten, victory will be ours." Felix – one of the last ones off the train – had just finished reading it when the force of a tremendous blast knocked him to his knees. He escaped any shrapnel, but the man behind him hadn't been so fortunate. Dima grabbed Felix by the arm and jerked him to his feet. Felix was dizzy and confused for several moments and simply ran along as best he could with this familiar figure who had helped him up.

The train ride to Batetsk had been so uneventful that the chaos they now found themselves in seemed surreal. They had been unloading from the train when they'd heard planes, and then a minute later, gunfire and explosions. German Divebombers and fighter planes were welcoming the new Soviet troops, and the men scattered to find shelter from the lethal rain of shrapnel.

Dima and Felix kept running until they reached a small house. They ran to the back side of it and leaned against the wall listening to the shouts, screams, gunfire, and explosions behind them. Once Felix caught his breath, he realized where he was and who the former stranger was.

"Dima, what do we do now?" he asked.

"We've got to get to that," Dima answered and pointed to a small hill with several trees and bushes.

Felix looked at the hill and the open field they would have to cross to get there. Katya's words rang in his ears, *"You'll be careful, won't you?"*

"Perhaps we should stay here until the planes leave," Felix said. "It seems a bit dangerous to cross that open field."

"We can't stay here," Dima said. "It's only a matter of time until they start shooting up this house. The trees and bushes on that hill will shield us from the sight of the planes."

Four more men rounded the corner of the house and joined them. One of them was wounded, bleeding badly from the shoulder. One of them carried an ax, another a pick, and a third held a rifle. The wounded man had no weapon.

Dima took a piece of cloth out of his pocket and handed it to the man. "Here," he said, "put some pressure on the wound."

The man, who had a long nose and looked to be in his thirties, did as he was told. "We've got to get him to a medic fast," Dima said to the group.

"It's nothing," the wounded man said.

Dima looked at the man's blood-stained shirt once more and reiterated that they needed to get him to a medic right away.

"We're going to have to make a run for it," Dima said. "I'm going to count to five, and then you guys go. Be sure to spread out. Don't bunch up and give them a target."

"Are you going with us?" one of the men asked Dima.

"No," he replied. "I'm going to find a medic."

Felix grabbed his shovel and wondered if he should carry it like a bayonet or just with his right arm the way he'd been carrying it.

"One," Dima began counting. Felix looked across the field – one hundred yards of open space, no houses, no trees, no bushes, no hills, no ditches.

"Two."

A plane flew high overhead – the roar of its engines building, and then fading away.

"Three."

Felix heard a whistling sound, and then a gigantic explosion that shook the ground they were standing on.

"Four."

Thick black smoke drifted past them, and Felix took a deep breath while he still could.

"Five!"

Felix waited for the others to start running before he himself left. He ran to the far right of everyone else, putting as much distance as he could between himself and the next person. Felix was the fastest runner of the group and reached the midway point well before the others. The sun shined brightly, the black smoke drifted aimlessly, and Felix ran desperately. He could hear the planes overhead, but didn't dare take the time to look up. He was much too focused on reaching his goal.

When he reached the small hill, he hid behind a tree and watched the others as they came in. The wounded man arrived last – holding his wound with both hands. He crumpled to the ground shortly afterward. While they waited for Dima to arrive with the medic, they watched the planes machine gun and bomb the train they had traveled in. Every couple of minutes, a few more men would join them on the hill. Felix hated them because he worried they would attract the planes.

Eventually the planes ran out of bombs and bullets and left the area. Any excitement or fervor the men had felt in Leningrad had vanished, and the wounded man had long since died before Dima finally returned.

"Where's the medic?" Felix asked him.

"Dead," Dima replied, and sat down on the ground next to him.

Gnats flew around Felix's head, and he found himself uncharacteristically annoyed and unable to block them out. The voice in his head that usually reassured him, instead whispered softly: *I don't want to be here; I don't want to be doing this.*

After the chaos subsided, the 1st Volunteers Division assembled to assess the damage. Over a dozen men had been killed and fifty more wounded. The train and the tracks were badly damaged, but that wasn't a major concern of the Volunteers. Their primary objective was to get to the eighteen-mile section of the Luga line that they were to protect. There, they would be able to finish their training so they would know what to do the next time they were attacked.

The long march to the front didn't go well for the Volunteers. They lost nearly twenty percent of their men – not to opposing enemy forces – but to physical exhaustion. Besides being considerably older than regular army troops, many of the men were terribly out of shape and unprepared for such a hike.

When they did finally make it to the front, they had only two days to rest and train before a surprise attack by German Panzer tanks and infantry. The

Volunteers had just been given a hand grenade and a Molotov cocktail each and were learning how to throw them when gunfire and explosions in the distance interrupted their training. They were informed that the Germans were attempting to break through the line near Lake Ilmen, and they were sent there to repel the attack.

Felix and Dima's company was sent to a small village and told to dig in and prevent the Germans from coming through there. The sky was clear. It was warm and the sun was shining, and Felix felt sad that he had to spend the day like this. It was the kind of day he'd love to spend swimming in the Neva and then laying on the shore to dry off and soak up the sun.

When they got to the village, there was no fighting, though they could hear it all around them. Their commander, an engineer who had never been in a battle before, instructed them to take up positions at the end of the town. Dima pointed out that the Germans would likely attack from the other end of town and that it made sense to set up there instead, but Dima was asked to kindly keep his mouth shut and do what he was told. Felix put his shovel to use, digging a trench for Dima and himself next to a row of raspberry bushes. And there they waited with forty-two other Volunteers.

The village consisted of two dozen small houses and an old church that now served as a post office and general government building. Some of the families who lived in the houses were still there. A small group of Volunteers went around to each house ordering the men to come out and help fight. The men, mostly farmers, carried axes or old hunting rifles out from their houses and settled in with the rest of the Volunteers.

Felix and Dima had a good view down the main road of the town. The lake was to their left, and Dima said they didn't have to worry about the Germans trying to go through the narrow tract between their position and the lake.

"Where do you think they'll attack?" Felix asked.

"If they decide to come this way," Dima said, "they'll probably come down this road. It's the best terrain for their tanks."

Felix was going to ask what they were supposed to do if a tank came down the road, but Dima hushed him and pointed at the other end of town. Emerging from the trees along the side of the road were German troops. When Felix saw them, his heart dropped into his stomach and he felt nauseous. A German tank came into view and started rumbling toward them. Felix could see a black emblem with a skull and crossbones painted on its side. A few soldiers rode on the back of the tank and several more jogged along behind it.

About two dozen German soldiers, including those who had been riding on or behind the tank, moved quickly behind a couple of houses at the far end of town. The tank continued its trek down the road toward Felix and Dima and the rest of the Volunteers.

Felix looked around at the men and realized he wasn't the only one that was terrified. He saw Pavel, a tall, lanky Siberian, crouching behind an old outhouse. Pavel was one of the lucky ones with a gun, but even so, he hadn't been taught to use it. He'd never even shot it before.

As the tank drew nearer, their commander ordered them to shoot at it.

"That fool!" Dima muttered under his breath to Felix. "It's a waste of ammunition."

Several Volunteers stood up and shot at the tank. The bullets merely ricocheted off, and a few seconds later the tank pounded their position with its guns. The ground erupted like a volcano, and several men were killed instantly. At least a dozen Volunteers dropped their weapons and ran to the safety of the nearby forest.

Ahead of them, Felix and Dima watched as a man jumped out from behind a house with a lit Molotov Cocktail in his hand. As he stood facing the oncoming German Panzer tank, he hoisted the cocktail over his head in preparation to throw, and was promptly gunned down.

On the other side, three men stepped out from their hiding spot and threw a grenade each at the tank. Two of them had thrown the grenades too high into the air, and they landed well short of the tank. The third had thrown his underhand, along the ground, in an apparent attempt to get it to bounce its way underneath the tank. It too landed well short and exploded harmlessly in the middle of the road. Again the tank fixed its guns on the men's hiding spot – a dilapidated brick fence – and blasted it to pieces.

The battle had barely begun and already Felix had seen at least half a dozen of his comrades killed and many more wounded.

"We've got to flank that tank," Dima yelled.

Felix didn't know what he meant, but he was all for leaving the spot where they were.

"Follow me," Dima yelled to the men around them, and then leapt out of the trench for the back wall of the nearby house. Felix followed him, but the others stayed where they were. Felix understood them – too afraid to fight and too afraid to run.

Felix and Dima ran down an adjacent alley to the main road. When they passed the third house, they turned back toward the main road and stopped at a house on the corner. Dima readied his Molotov Cocktail and Felix stole a glance around the corner. They were now behind the tank and could see it slowly making its way up the road, decimating the Volunteers that remained.

Dima lit the cocktail, stepped out from behind the house, threw it at the tank, and quickly stepped back behind the safety of the house. Felix, looking around the corner, saw that Dima hit the tank. It was covered in flames. After a few seconds, the men inside scrambled out. One of them was on fire and died a few feet from the tank. Another ran to the opposite side of Felix and Dima and disappeared behind the houses.

There was gunfire throughout the small village now.

"Good," Dima said, "that means we must be fighting back. I saw a good spot to fire from on our way here. Let's go back there."

Dima led as they made their way back down the alley. Felix's legs felt like rubber and he cursed the fact that he didn't have a gun.

As they ran around the corner of a small house covered with grape vines, they surprised three German soldiers on the other side. Two of them were kneeling on the ground and had just finished setting up a machine gun; their rifles were lying on the ground next to them. The third soldier was standing, rifle in hand, on guard for anything. He'd been looking the opposite way when Felix and Dima rounded the corner. He turned around quickly now, but it was already too late. Dima stopped, took aim, and fired a shot into the man's chest before he had a chance to shoot at them.

One of the other Germans tried to swing the machine gun around and shoot at Felix and Dima, and the other lunged for his rifle on the ground, but Dima and Felix were already too close. Dima charged with his bayonet at the soldier on the right, and Felix gripped the handle of his shovel and swung it like a club at the soldier on the left. The man didn't have enough time to get out of the way, and put his arm up to block the blow. The edge of the shovel hit his forearm, cutting deeply into his flesh. He staggered to the right, his helmet fell off, and he tried to run away, but Felix swung his shovel again, this time over his head like an ax. He struck the man on top of the head and then watched him collapse to the ground, face first, blood gushing from the back of his skull. Felix raised the shovel over his head again to strike a final blow. But as he did, the man turned over and looked up at him, and Felix couldn't do it. He couldn't kill him. He brought the shovel down to his side and rested it on the ground.

A terrifying scream brought his attention to Dima. Felix looked over just in time to see Dima thrusting his bayonet into the stomach of the other soldier. The man fell to his knees, and then his side, and then gasped for air. Dima kicked the man's rifle away from him so he couldn't reach it, and then looked at Felix. Dima's eyes grew large instantly, and he yelled, "Watch out!" Instinctively, Felix took a step back, but not before he felt a sharp pain. He stumbled backward a few steps and then made his way slowly to the ground. He'd been stabbed with a knife.

Dima rushed over and thrust his bayonet into the ribs of the German soldier. "Why didn't you finish him off?!" Dima chastised Felix.

Felix was in shock and couldn't reply – not that he knew the answer anyway.

Dima's bayonet stuck in the dead man's ribs and he couldn't get it out. After a few attempts, he abandoned the effort and dragged the dead German soldiers in front of the machine gun and stacked them on top of one another. Felix then watched as Dima swung the machine gun around and fired at several German soldiers trying to cross from one side of the road to the other. Of the four Germans that made the attempt, only one reached the other side.

The pain from the stab wound was the most intense thing Felix had ever experienced. All the blood coming from the wound compounded the nausea he'd already been feeling and he had to turn his head and vomit on the ground next to him. The voice in his head that had been saying, *"I don't want to be here; I don't want to be doing this,"* was through whispering.

Now it just screamed.

* * *

It was early morning when Alfred woke up. He'd slept for over ten hours straight. He was covered with sweat. The bed sheet snaked around his arms and legs. Alfred untwirled it and threw it across the room. *Damn this country,* he muttered. He'd come here to prevent a catastrophe, but they hadn't listened to him. And what happened to that shower he was supposed to get? Probably just another lie, he told himself.

He scratched two of the half dozen mosquito bites on his arms, legs, and neck, but then stopped because he knew that it only made the discomfort worse in the long run. He rose slowly and walked over to the window. It was hot and the room was stuffy.

The window was dingy, and he noticed that it was cracked in one of the corners. He tapped it a few times until it broke and then stuck his nose as close to it as he could to breathe the fresh air. He could smell lavender from somewhere and it reminded him of his mother's garden – that wonderful garden where she grew everything under the sun. He recalled how he used to pick strawberries to eat and how his legs would itch from the leaves. Strawberries had always been his favorite and he thought of how good one would taste right now. But then a quick boiling anger erupted within him and he struck his fist against the wall. As if his jailers didn't torture him enough – he had to torture himself as well!

He felt better after they served him his breakfast. Again, he'd gotten English tea, and was grateful for it. When they came to take him to the interrogation room, he felt up to the challenge. For the first four hours, they discussed Alfred's scheduled "speech" and Alfred argued with New Face over every assumption and nuance in their conversation. He wouldn't give an inch.

"So, in principle, you agree with me," New Face said as he leaned back in his chair and interlaced his fingers behind his head.

"In principle," Alfred replied," I believe in right and wrong, good and bad, and truth and lies."

New Face arched his eyebrows. "And where has this misguided philosophy got you in life?"

"This *misguided philosophy* has landed me in a Soviet prison where I spend my days either in a tiny cell by myself or in a tiny cell talking to you."

"And do you like spending your days this way?"

"It's great," Alfred said sarcastically, and watched New Face for his reaction.

New Face almost smiled, but didn't. "Do you like talking to me for hours on end?" he asked.

"Oh yes, it's fascinating," Alfred said and started to laugh, half out of delirium and half out of exasperation. But he couldn't laugh completely because it hurt his ribs too much.

"Alfred," New Face said, "it's time to be honest with yourself. Don't you think it's about time you do something different?"

Alfred held his aching ribs with his right hand and shrugged his shoulders.

"You're a soldier," New Face said, "what would you do if you were going into battle and your gun didn't work?"

"I'd try to fix it."

"And if it still didn't work?"

"I'd get a new one that did work."

"Precisely! So throw away these anachronistic views of yours and adopt some that work! These are not the old times anymore. The *truth* is what the people need to hear – it's that simple. Here in the Soviet Union, the Party makes the decisions and . . ."

"The Party doesn't decide for *me*," Alfred interrupted.

New Face frowned at Alfred's statement. He leaned forward in his chair, bringing his face close to Alfred. His slate-colored eyes taking on a duller shade of grey. "I think it's helpful at times like this," he said slowly, "to remind ourselves of why we're here and why we're both interested in a successful outcome." He sat back in his chair, but kept his gaze fixed on Alfred.

"What is it that I want?" he asked rhetorically. "*I* want to get away from this miserable little outpost and return to Moscow. And *you* . . ., I suppose *you* would like to continue living, yes?"

Alfred didn't respond, instead he focused his attention on how New Face's dark hair was always combed straight back so perfectly. He wondered how much effort that took. As long as he focused on that, he wasn't really in that room – wasn't really in the situation he was in.

New Face didn't wait for Alfred's answer. "Now then," he continued, "let's review once again the important points of what you're going to say and where you'll stand on the stage."

Another hour went by and things started to seem futile to Alfred. He felt his will slowly breaking. New Face never quit. Even when Alfred had succeeded in getting him to acquiesce on a particular point, it would only be a matter of time until New Face returned to the same point and started from the baseline. It infuriated Alfred. He couldn't argue like that. Once a point was won or lost, you had to move on. Those were the rules when one was debating. You couldn't go back to a point and start again as if you hadn't already discussed it. But that was exactly what New Face did, and Alfred was through being angry about it. He was resigned.

After another half hour, Alfred was back in his cell. He laid on the bed and wondered what the point of anything was. He felt so out of place in this day and age. Nobody wanted to try to understand anyone else. Nobody was interested in the truth or honesty or good intentions. No matter the country, leaders all seemed to prey on people's fears. It was a game of "you're either with us or against us." Independent thinking was frowned upon. It was dangerous. To question authority was to question life itself, and no mere soldier or citizen was qualified to do that. No, to question those in power was to risk your life. Alfred felt like crying, but again no tears would come. Where were they? Where were all those tears that he never allowed to see the light of day?

He longed for freedom, for the time when man was free to speak his mind and live as he pleased. But when was that time? Had it ever existed? History had always been one of Alfred's passions, and he strained his mind to think of a time when man was truly free. He thought of the ancient Greeks, the Romans, the Egyptians . . .. But none of them. Not a single one of them had ever allowed man to be free!

Freedom. The thought weighed heavy on his mind. What exactly was it? And why did he need it? There was freedom from hunger, freedom from pain, freedom from suffering, freedom from death . . .. But no, there was no freedom from death. No one could escape it – not the rich man, not the holy man, not even the one with the heart of gold. Perhaps true freedom is merely acceptance, he thought. Acceptance that to live means to suffer and to eventually die. Wasn't that what everyone was fighting for? A vain attempt to decrease their suffering. Thinking that more military victories or more land will somehow make them happy.

But if people accepted suffering – accepted it as a part of life – then wouldn't that change something?

He didn't know the answer. He was filled with despair and wanted nothing more to do with the world. He was through with it. He was through fighting to ease his suffering. And if death was ready for him, he was certainly ready for death.

"Nazi criminal," a voice announced from the hallway, "your dinner is here."

Alfred didn't answer, didn't move. He thought of home, the lavender in the garden, the
fresh strawberries in June . . ..

The man opened the door and walked in. "Well, General P__ was shot last night," he announced as he set the tray down. "Too many complaints and not enough victories, I guess."

Alfred looked at the man and was filled with hate. He sprung from his bed and put him in a choke hold before the man could utter a sound. Then he used his weight to swing the man around and smash his head into the brick wall. He only had to do it two times until the man's body went limp, then Alfred laid him down on the floor. He was still alive, just unconscious.

Alfred took the man's Soviet army fatigues off and put them on. They fit rather tightly, but at least they fit. He quickly and quietly moved his bed away from the wall, removed the bricks to his hole, and set them off to the side. He squeezed through the opening head first, and found himself on the other side behind a small bush with sharp thorns.

He looked around and saw the guard standing in the tower in the far corner. It was the same tower he could see from the window in his cell. A light breeze brought him the scent of lavender again. The sun was high in the sky. White clouds drifted by aimlessly. Everything was remarkably quiet. The colors around him seemed brighter than usual. There was a strange familiarity to it all, like he had seen all this before, only a long time ago.

Two Soviet soldiers walked out the door of the building on his left. They were chatting and both stopped to light cigarettes, then continued on around the corner of the building in front of Alfred. He didn't know what was on the other side of that building, but he hoped that the complex's exit was there.

Alfred looked around again, and seeing no one, stood up and started walking. After a few seconds, he glanced up at the guard in the tower and saw he was looking at him. Then that image from his dream came back to him – he, a small boy, screaming and crying on his bed and beating the pillow with his fists, and his father walking in and telling him to stop crying, telling him to "grow up and be a man." Alfred had stopped crying, wiping the tears from his eyes and coming to an understanding with his father that crying was something boys – and ultimately men – did not do.

He was nearing the corner of the building and could hear some men having a conversation. They were talking about a long forgotten song that their parents used to sing and were trying to remember some of the lyrics. "The willow tree whispers my name," one of them hummed, "and the wolf searches for the water, but the stream has dried up . . ."

"No, it wasn't a willow tree," one of the others interrupted.

Alfred pulled his cap down tighter over his head. When he turned the corner, he saw the three of them congregating in front of the exit that led to the outside. One seemed to be the guard on duty; he was standing with his back to the exit and holding a semi-automatic rifle. The other two had their backs to him. The exit to the outside of the complex was about six feet wide. There was a giant wooden door that could be closed, but it looked as if it was permanently propped open.

Through the exit, Alfred could see a narrow dirt road and lots of open space. There were jeeps and motorcycles parked in front of a small building about 50 yards away. Alfred hoped to make it there and hop on one of the motorcycles. He'd grown up with motorcycles and knew how to start one without the keys. But first, Alfred would have to get through the exit.

As he approached, he bowed his head and crossed his right arm in front of his face, pretending to scratch his left eyebrow. Alfred wasn't sure if he would be questioned as he went through. He thought of what he might say if he had to speak. It had to be something short, a word or phrase that was used often, so that he could mumble it slightly so they wouldn't recognize any accent. With his limited Russian, if he had to speak more than two words, he was doomed.

Just as Alfred approached, an officer walked through from the outside. Upon seeing the man, the guard stopped talking and stood at attention. His two companions left abruptly. The officer stopped in front of the guard, looking him up and down. "Are you supposed to be socializing while you're on duty?" he asked him. Alfred recognized New Face's voice. "No, comrade," came the response.

Alfred was too close to turn away without drawing attention to himself. He passed within a few feet of the two men as he walked through the exit. He was then outside the complex and walking toward the motorcycles. From behind him, he heard someone sniffing loudly. "When's the last time you bathed?" New Face asked the guard.

"Just last night, comrade."

"Then why do you stink so bad?"

"It's not me. It must be him."

Alfred was sure he was being pointed at, and that both of them were staring at him as he walked away.

"Comrade," New Face yelled in Alfred's direction, "may I have a word with you."

Alfred kept walking.

"Who was that?" New Face asked the guard.

The guard said he didn't know, then yelled at Alfred to stop.

Alfred knew that if he turned around, it was the end. He pretended he didn't hear anything and kept walking away.

New Face ordered the guard to fire a warning shot.

"Halt!" the guard yelled again and shot his gun into the air.

There was a thick evergreen tree next to the motorcycles. If Alfred could get away with a few more steps, then he could run and make it to the tree.

"I know that smell," Alfred heard New Face say. Then, in German, New Face called out, "Stop! Or you will be shot!"

Alfred decided to make a run for the tree. His heart was pounding furiously and he took off like a charging bear. He could be at the tree in only a few seconds.

"Shoot him!" New Face yelled to the guard.

Bullets whizzed past Alfred, striking the ground around him and kicking up little clouds of dust. He felt something sting him in his left forearm and knew he'd been shot. Before he made it around to the other side of the tree, he felt something else penetrate his chest through his back. It didn't hurt, but he could instantly feel that it was harder to breathe.

He sat on the other side of the tree with his back against it. The sound of gunfire quickly faded, and all was quiet again. He closed his eyes and the image from his dream was there again. But then he remembered something else, something he'd never remembered before. He remembered the look on his father's face – that look of exasperation, of anger and despair. And then Alfred had the strange feeling that he'd had these issues and these confrontations with his father many, many times – more than just this one lifetime.

He opened his eyes and looked at the clouds again. Big white cotton balls floating through the sky. They were so beautiful. He tried to suppress a cough, but couldn't and blood came up into his mouth.

Alfred had the realization that he and his father were continually *choosing* each other in that place between death and rebirth in the hope that they could transcend their differences and help one another move one step closer to the Light. He thought back to his childhood and the violence that had been inflicted on him in the name of religion and tough love. He thought of the constant criticism and the indifference with which his father had regarded him. He felt so angry about it. So many vile things he'd always wanted to say to his father.

"Alfred!" New Face called out. "Come out from there."

Alfred wasn't coming out. He was dying. He could barely breathe.

He wondered what was at the core of all that bitterness his father had held. A strange idea occurred to him. The thought was that his father's attitude and behaviors had *nothing at all* to do with Alfred. Perhaps his father acted the way he did because *he* was suffering. Maybe all his criticism, cursing, and anger were all misguided attempts at satisfying some need of his? Some need for respect, for understanding, for love?

The idea astounded him. For the first time in his life, Alfred had stopped thinking about himself and what he'd went through, and thought solely about his father instead. His father couldn't have been happy. To have acted the way he did, he must have been miserable. *I shouldn't hate him*, Alfred thought, *I should feel sympathy for him. My God, how much he must have suffered to be that miserable!*

And as Alfred opened his heart, all the black hate in it poured out and drained into the earth. He wanted to see his father so badly, to tell him that he'd forgiven everything, that he was no longer angry. He wanted to tell his father that he *loved* him. If he could only do that, then he could die without regret.

But it was getting even harder to breathe, and he couldn't help coughing. He could taste blood in his mouth even stronger now. He could hear men approaching, and New Face urging him to come out with his hands up. But it was too late for that. It was too late for everything. Perhaps in his next lifetime he'd get it right.

He took his last breath, felt the earth with his hands, and as he felt himself float up and away from his body, three words floated along with him. They were like miniature light blue clouds, and Alfred reached out to try to touch them. But as Alfred moved his hand toward them, they only moved further away – floating farther and farther from him until the words – Forgive Me Father – coalesced into a small bright star in an infinite black sky.

~

Глава Третья — Chapter Three

The Greenfinch's Song

I am caviar and fireworks,
    and music too loud for your ears.
I am your opiate,
    the master of your hopes and fears.
You'll know me when I enter you.
    you'll moan with the deception deep inside of you.
Feels so good, between your thighs,
    feel the meaning of life explode in lies.

Misha Borisov watched the train go by, hoping it would stop so he could get on, but knowing that it wouldn't. His legs felt like rubber, and every muscle in his body pleaded to lie down and rest. He thought back to the last time his legs had felt like this – that horrible night of his arrest at the airbase. But Misha was not under another one of those attacks that rendered him so relaxed and useless. Misha was exhausted this time because he'd been walking all day long – not only today but for the past six days.

The train was traveling slowly around the sharp bend in the tracks, and Misha noticed that it wasn't well protected. There were no anti-aircraft guns, and only three soldiers that he could see. After the second train car went by, he realized why. Children. The entire train was full of children. They stood or sat with their faces pressed up against the windows and waved at Misha and Igor. Misha waved back – holding his arm up high and swinging it slowly back and forth.

"Where are they going?" Igor asked. He stood to Misha's left and did not wave back at the children. Igor was a twelve-year-old boy with big ears, a pug nose, and in desperate need of a bath and a haircut. He'd begun traveling at Misha's side two days ago – much to Misha's dismay.

"I heard they're evacuating Leningrad and sending children to live on the other side of the Ural mountains until the war is over," Misha replied.

Some of the children on the train were quite young – no more than three or four years old. A few looked to be Igor's age, but the vast majority were between five and ten years old. A group of older boys yelled out the window to Misha and Igor asking where the Germans were. Misha pointed behind himself. "How far?" they asked. "Dolga!" – a long ways – Misha yelled.

Eventually, the whole train had passed by. There was nothing except the clack-clack of the rails as the caboose vanished into the thick green foliage of the forest.

"Why would they leave the city? My father says the war will be short – a few weeks or months at the most," Igor said.

Misha felt uncomfortable whenever the boy talked about his father in the present tense. "The only way the war will be that short is if the Germans win," he replied.

"You're a liar!" the boy yelled. "My father says Stalin will lead the Red Army to victory. He's not a coward."

Misha didn't know if the last statement was meant to refer to the boy's father or to Stalin. It didn't really matter though. Misha wasn't going to argue with him. The boy had been through enough already.

Wiping the sweat from his brow, Misha opened his canteen and took a drink of water. When he finished, he saw the boy holding out his hand and passed the canteen on to him.

Only a few days ago, the boy watched his parents die on the side of the road. The three of them had been living in a rural area in a small house when the Germans came. Igor's father had told Misha how they were forced to stand by while the soldiers burned their crops, stole their animals, and looted their home. When they finished, one of the Germans used a flame thrower to set their house on fire. Igor's father had tried to stop them, only to be laughed at and beaten to the ground with the butts of their rifles. Misha thought that seemed to be the hardest part for the boy to take – them laughing at his formerly invincible father.

After that, Igor and his parents made their way to the nearest village only to find that it, too, had been burned to the ground. Then they resigned themselves to joining the mass of refugees on the roads east, not knowing where they were going nor how long it would take to get there. That's where Misha had met them.

A week into the journey, Igor's father suffered a heart attack and died a miserably slow death in the heat and dust of an overcrowded road. The boy's mother, a soft-spoken woman with acute arthritis in her knees, kneeled by his side and held his hand the whole time. Igor had done his best to make himself useful, offering to fetch water or anything else that might save his father. But nothing could save him and he passed away.

Three miles further up the road, Igor's mother was struck by a truck that veered off the road. Before she too died, she asked Misha – who had already been traveling next to them for several days at that point – to take her son to Leningrad where he had an uncle. She gave Misha all the food and money in their possession, kissed the boy on the cheek, then took her last breath.

Misha still couldn't get that image out of his mind, of the boy pounding on her lifeless body with his tiny fists, tears streaming down his face as he kept asking, "Why? Why?" Misha didn't have an answer for him back then, and was still looking for one now.

Igor tugged on Misha's pack. "How long before we get to Leningrad?" he asked.

"I don't know."

"Some Soviet you are," Igor huffed. "My father would know."

Misha could have said no to Igor's mother's request. Several times already he wished he'd said no. He got especially irritated with the boy's constant questions. But Misha said he would take care of Igor and get him to Leningrad and he was intent on honoring that no matter how much Igor annoyed him.

Misha thought again about what the boy had said about the war being short, that the heroic and mighty Red Army would push the German invaders out in short order. That was certainly the official position of the Party. Misha didn't buy it. He'd seen first hand how inept the resistance had been. He'd seen how organized and fast the Germans were. He'd seen the roads jammed with refugees and retreating Soviet troops. He'd been on those roads himself, walking alongside young women carrying newborns, elderly and crippled with their walking sticks, dogs and cows and horses and confusion. Misha had evidence walking along next to him of who was winning the war.

Igor tugged on Misha's pack again. "How many Nazis have you killed?" he asked.

"Enough," Misha said and ducked under a low lying branch.

Igor ducked as well but then grabbed the branch and bent it back until it broke. "You can *never* kill enough Nazis," he said.

Sometimes Misha found it hard to believe he was only seven years older than Igor. He felt at least a decade more mature. He looked at Igor now. The index finger of his left hand was up his nose and he had a furious expression on his face. The two of them had nothing in common, but Misha appreciated that the boy hated the Nazi invaders just as much as he did. Misha couldn't comprehend the point of burning a peasant's house and crops or bombing a tiny village. Did these things count as military victories? He shuddered to think what life would be like with the Germans in power. Would Misha and Igor even be allowed to live?

"When we get to Leningrad, I'm going to join the Red Army and kill a thousand Nazis," Igor said. "Stalin will give me the Order of Lenin."

Misha was convinced that things couldn't get any worse militarily and so held out a sliver of hope they would eventually get better. The big question in his mind was whether or not the improvement would come in time. If the Red Army finally became the fighting machine it was supposed to be as the Germans marched through the streets of Leningrad and Moscow, then it would be far too late.

"Let's just hope we make it to Leningrad before the Nazis do," Misha said.

He wasn't going to Leningrad solely to place Igor with his uncle. Misha's mother also lived in Leningrad, and he wanted to get her out before the Germans overtook the city, and by his estimates he didn't have much time.

His mother was the only person he cared about in this world. The only person he loved. But it was a love built on sorrow, on pity. Fate had not been kind to her, taking her husband shortly after Misha was born, and inflicting disease after disease on her ravaged body as she grew older. Her physical and mental condition regressed to the point that Misha stopped going to see her. The pain and grief he felt were too much to bear. Every moment spent with her simply watered seeds of resentment and bitterness in him toward the world.

"Look!" Igor shouted and ran off toward a large fallen tree. He got down on his hands and knees and started gathering something from the ground.

"What the hell are you doing?" Misha asked.

"There's mushrooms over here!"

"They're probably poisonous. We can't eat them."

"No, they're not! Don't you know how to tell good mushrooms from bad ones?"

A city-dweller since birth with a cosmopolitan mother, Misha had no idea how to tell which mushrooms were edible. He sat down on the ground to wait and surveyed his surroundings. He was on a small treeless hill, surrounded by fields and forests. Up ahead of him was a grove of birch trees and he looked forward to walking through them.

Misha had decided not to travel on the roads anymore. Not only was the going slow because of the vast numbers of soldiers and refugees, it was also dangerous because Misha could be caught again. He left his initial posting at the airbase after it had been annihilated by the German Luftwaffe. Then he'd been rounded up along with other lost soldiers and forced to fight with another division. He'd narrowly escaped with his life when the new division was also annihilated by the Germans, this time by hundreds of Panzer tanks.

He'd heard a rumor that Zhdanov had issued a decree on July 14th stating that anyone leaving the front regardless of rank or responsibility would go before a field tribunal and be shot on the spot. Misha wasn't sure if it applied to him though. The front had been following him every step of the way toward Leningrad.

Two gray planes suddenly zoomed over Misha's head.

Igor ran back from where he'd been picking mushrooms. "Are those our planes?" he asked.

Misha had seen the black iron crosses on them. "No," he said. He guessed they must have broken off from their formation to search for targets of opportunity.

"What are they doing out here? Are we near a military base?"

Misha was just as puzzled as Igor. There was nothing that he knew of out here but young trees and old foxes.

The sound of the planes' machine guns filled the air. Misha watched them loop around for another strike.

"What are they bombing?" Igor asked.

"I don't know," Misha mumbled. *Was there a small village buried in the forest? A secret military base that he didn't know about?*

"I bet they're shooting up that train," Igor said.

"That's ridiculous," Misha replied, "the train's full of children. Why would they attack it?" Then Misha had the thought that the German planes didn't know what, or even who, was on the train. *Igor was right! They were attacking the trainload of children. Oh God, no!!*

Misha screamed. "No! Stop!" he cried. But he knew they couldn't possibly hear him.

"*Do* something!" Igor pleaded. "They'll kill all those kids."

"Shut up!" Misha snapped. "What the hell can I do?!"

"Shoot the planes!" Igor shouted. "Shoot the planes down!"

Misha knew that trying to shoot the planes with his Mosin-Nagant rifle was futile. He estimated his odds of hitting a plane at one in a hundred and his odds of causing any significant damage, if he did hit it, at one in a hundred. So overall, his odds were one in ten thousand.

The planes were completing their loop and settling in for another strike.

"You're a Soviet soldier!" Igor yelled. "You can't just do nothing. If my dad were here, he'd shoot them."

You don't have a chance, Misha told himself, but he agreed that he had to do *something*. He began silently reciting a short prayer, just as he used to do as a boy, but then caught himself. *Stop it, Misha! You know you don't believe in God.*

Misha aimed his rifle at one of the planes as it approached for its second attack. He held his breath as he squeezed the trigger. The bang startled Igor and he stumbled backward a step. Misha then fired again, and again. He shot three times at the plane, but nothing happened. Both of the planes completed their attack and began to circle around for another strike.

"You missed them," Igor said dejectedly.

"Igor, shut up. You're an idiot," Misha said. He felt powerless to do anything about the attack on the train. Right then he hated Igor and his ridiculous big ears just as much as he hated the Germans. "It's nearly impossible to hit a plane from this distance and do any damage," Misha explained.

"My dad would've hit them. He could shoot a rabbit from over two hundred yards away."

Misha wanted to yell at Igor that his father was dead and to get over it, but he didn't say it. He held his resentment and leveled his rifle on his left arm.

When the planes descended again, Misha fired three more times at the plane on the left. Again, the planes completed their attacks and began to circle around. But then, the plane on the right – the one Misha had not shot at – started spewing black smoke from its engine. The smoke thickened quickly, and both planes aborted their strike and ascended to the safety of a higher altitude.

"Hoorah! Hoorah!" Igor exclaimed, jumping up and down. "You did it!"

"Not bad, huh?" Misha said.

"How did you do it?"

Misha glanced over at Igor and felt pleased about the smile and awe on the boy's face. "I shot its engine," he said. "It's the only place where they're vulnerable."

They watched the planes fly higher and higher. The damaged plane spewed out more black smoke by the second. Before long, it started to lose altitude. As the other plane continued to fly away, Misha and Igor watched the pilot of the damaged plane jump out and launch his parachute. His plane continued to lose altitude until it eventually disappeared from sight and crashed with a loud thud in a far off field.

Misha took his cap off and held it out in front of him to shield his eyes against the glare of the hot sun. He'd gotten the cap from a fallen comrade several weeks earlier. In addition to protecting his head from the sun and rain, the lieutenant's insignia on it had come in handy a few times. He watched the German pilot drift through the sky toward the ground, an early autumn leaf. A gust of wind caught his parachute and pushed him slightly toward Misha and Igor. In the distance, humongous gray and white smoke clouds ascended from the train, slowly dissipating into the atmosphere.

Misha tucked the cap inside his pack and began running toward the pilot, pausing every once in a while to allow Igor to catch up and to look up through the treetops and adjust his direction. When the pilot finally dropped from sight behind the pine trees over the next little hill, Misha and Igor were less than a hundred yards away.

When they arrived, the pilot was still struggling to free himself from the large oak tree he'd landed in. Misha raised his rifle to shoot him but then decided it would be too hard to search him if he was stuck in a tree.

Pine cones and brown needles covered the forest floor, and the whole area was infused with the sweet, fresh scent of pine. The oak tree the pilot was stuck in was old and dying and was also the sole non-evergreen tree around. Misha kept his rifle on the pilot as he waited for him to untangle himself and make it down to the ground.

Igor tried grabbing Misha's rifle away from him. "Let me shoot him," he begged. "Let me shoot him for my pa."

Misha pushed the boy to the ground. "Don't you ever grab my rifle," he yelled.

The pilot wore a brown leather jacket. A pair of goggles hung from his neck. As he made his way down the tree, he glanced at Misha and Igor and said something in German. When he swung from the last branch down to the ground, he smiled and raised his hands. Igor took a step behind Misha, and Misha again aimed his rifle at the pilot, preparing to shoot him.

The pilot stood a head shorter than Misha and was probably twice Misha's age. He had thin blonde eyebrows that were barely visible against his pale white skin. His face had a certain natural sereneness and harmless quality to it that Misha found galling. Misha jerked the barrel of his rifle upwards, and the pilot raised his arms from his chest level to up above his shoulders.

The great clouds of smoke in the distance started to turn from light gray to dark gray. "You know that train you just bombed was full of children," Misha said, looking intently at the pilot's face.

"Shoot him in the knee first," Igor said. "My pa told me it hurts like hell, but won't kill a man. He said he and his buddy used to do it to the rich farmers during the Civil War."

"Shut up," Misha said. He was looking for a quick reason to shoot the pilot dead, half hoping the man would lunge at them or turn and run.

The German pilot looked at them both with a blank expression on his face, obviously not understanding a word of Russian. Misha made him lie on the ground and held the rifle a few inches from his head while Igor went through his pockets. Igor found a pistol, a half-eaten slab of bread, and a photo of the pilot with his family. His wife was young and beautiful, his son still a baby, and his daughter a smiling two year old with big dimples and curly blonde hair.

The smoke in the distance was getting thicker and blacker, and Misha thought he could hear people screaming. He recalled with fondness the curious boys on the train who'd waved to him and asked him where the Germans were. That they might all be dead infuriated him. He hated the fucking Germans, this one especially. Why shouldn't he shoot this Nazi? He deserved to die for what he did.

As the pilot laid on the ground in front of him, Misha put his boot on his neck and pushed. He placed the tip of his rifle against the man's head and started to squeeze the trigger.

"Yeah, shoot him! Blow his brains out!" Igor yelled.

But Misha didn't pull the trigger. Not yet. The pilot had to see what he'd done first.

They marched along the railroad toward the smoke around the next bend in the tracks. The closer they got, the louder the yelling and screaming became. The screams were high-pitched, too high to be coming from adults. The pilot turned back toward Misha several times with his thin eyebrows arched, his jaw hanging down, a look of confusion on his face.

Misha could just make out some of the words the adults were yelling: fire, evacuate, why, children, God, hurry, dead, why. The screaming coming from the dozens of young voices was all the same: unintelligible high-pitched shrieks, wails for "mama."

When they could at last see the train, Misha's heart sank. He'd hoped that the damage would be small and the injuries few. The reality was much uglier. He could already see several small lifeless bodies on the ground next to the train, and it had only been a little over ten minutes since the attack. A short distance away, dozens of children huddled together, hugging and holding hands as they watched the smoke and flames grow thicker. The German pilot whimpered, crossed himself, and started reciting a phrase over and over. When he turned to look at Misha again, his hands trembled and his eyes were full of tears.

The last car of the train was on fire and smoke poured out of its smashed windows. The back of the car was being devoured by flames while three women frantically carried children out the front exit.

The July heat was intense and Misha hated it. He cursed the bright sun and held his hand above his eyes so he could see better. His stomach felt queasy and his mouth dry. Igor walked beside him. The German pilot was in front with his hands in the air. The pilot's arms dropped slowly toward his waist with each passing step. As soon as they were within fifty yards of the train, he started running toward it. At first, Misha yelled for him to stop and thought to shoot him. But the pilot wasn't running away. He was running toward the train, so Misha gave chase.

When he got to the train, the pilot leapt up the stairs into the car that was on fire. By the time Misha and Igor got there, the pilot was already leaving the car, carrying out a small girl who had a pink bow in her hair. Misha wasn't sure how to react. The pilot set the visibly frightened girl down by the others, watched her cough for a few seconds, then ran back into the car. Misha followed. A few seconds later they both came out with injured children.

Igor tried to help, but Misha told him to stay out of the way. The flames roared out the back of the car, and Misha didn't want to go back in there again. The smoke stung his eyes, and he found it difficult to keep them open. He felt a tug on the back of his shirt and was about to yell at Igor to leave him alone, when he saw that it was the little girl with the pink bow in her hair. She had such a look of terror on her face that Misha thought to pick her up and hug her. "My brother," she said with great effort, "he's still in there." She pointed at the burning train car.

"Are you sure?" Misha asked.

"I don't see him," she cried, "and he was on the same car as me."

"He's probably already out here somewhere. Go ask some of the other kids if they've seen him," Misha said and pointed to the groups of children huddling together in the distance. "I'll go see if he's still in there," he yelled over his shoulder and jumped back in the car. The smoke was now twice as thick, and he could barely see a few feet in any direction. He walked down the aisle yelling for any children who needed help. Hearing no responses, he turned back toward the front to search under the seats. He passed by the German pilot who was going further back into the train car. Misha began to tell him that there was nobody back there, but then realized the pilot couldn't understand what he said anyway.

Misha couldn't see under the seats, so he just reached his arm in and felt. Under the fourth seat he checked, he came upon a small bare leg and pulled it toward himself. He didn't know if it was a boy or girl, dead or alive. He carried the child out and laid it next to the motionless others.

His eyes were red and burning from the smoke, and he closed them for a minute for relief. When he opened his eyes again, he saw that the child was a little girl. She had long blonde hair and a small doll tucked inside her dress – the head of it peeking out near her shoulder. There was no noticeable blood on her, but she wasn't breathing all the same.

Misha looked up and saw a giant of a man in a Red Army uniform run up to the burning car and almost stumble headfirst into the side of it with his giant-sized feet. He was out of breath and his big, flat face had beads of sweat streaming down it. For some reason, he had only half of his right ear. Before he jumped in the car, he asked Misha if there were any more children inside. He spoke with a heavy peasant accent, and Misha immediately thought him an idiot.

"I already got all the children out," Misha said.

The man then proceeded to unhook the car from the one in front of it. Misha had thought of that earlier too. If the burning car wasn't separated from the one in front of it, then the fire would eventually consume that one as well. Though it was possible to unhook them from one another, it would be impossible to move them away from one another, Misha reasoned since he'd heard that each car weighed over fifty tons.

Misha thought to tell half ear that it was pointless to unhook them since they couldn't be moved apart, but he decided to let him figure it out for himself. Those peasants always had such thick heads.

Half ear began trying to push the burning car back, and Misha watched him. The flames at the back of the car rose higher and higher and half ear grunted and groaned and dug his heels in. Then – inch by inch – the car began to move. Misha could hardly believe his eyes. The giant moved the car about eight feet in all.

As half ear bent over to catch his breath, the pilot came out of the burning car carrying yet another child. The body of a boy rested limply in the pilot's arms, and half ear stared in astonishment as the German walked past.

Misha recognized the lifeless body that the pilot was now laying on the ground. It was one of the boys who'd waved to him earlier. Misha remembered him because he had a long scratch on his cheek that hadn't quite healed yet.

The pilot coughed for a long time, then kneeled at the boy's side and put his ear next to the boy's nose. Misha saw that the pilot's blonde hair and eyebrows had been singed from the heat of the fire.

"What's he doing?" Igor asked.

"He is listening to see if boy still breathes," half ear said.

Misha could see from where he was that the boy's shirt was soaked with blood around his belly.

"I thought I saw two other soldiers with you on the train earlier. Where are they?" Misha asked half ear.

"Dead," came the reply.

Misha watched two young women and a *babushka* – an old woman with a kerchief tied around her head – as they treated the wounded children. They tore strips of cloth from bed sheets and used them as gauze to wrap around wounds. Misha counted over a dozen bodies on the ground with white sheets covering them and another two dozen or so children who were wounded. He wanted to do more to help and felt sick that there was nothing left to do. All the children that could be saved from the fire had already been rescued, and the women were tending to all the wounded.

Looking at the pilot, half ear asked, "Is he the one that jumped out of plane?" He spoke slowly and enunciated each syllable, as if he was a child still learning the language.

Misha nodded his head yes.

The wounded boy was unresponsive to any of the pilot's efforts to save him. The pilot used his hands to push down on the boy's chest, but it only caused more blood around his midsection. He pulled the boy's shirt up and saw why. There was a bullet hole in his stomach and any pressure on his chest just pushed more blood out of it. The pilot sat back on his knees and coughed some more. He wiped his hands on his shirt and pants to try to get the blood off. When that didn't get it all off, he poured water from his canteen over his hands and rubbed them together furiously. He used every drop of water he had, but the blood wouldn't go away.

"Murderer," Misha muttered under his breath.

"What do we do with him?" half ear asked.

Off in the distance, Misha saw the little girl with the pink bow in her hair coming toward him. He wondered if she found her brother or not.

"Let's cut his stomach open and pull his guts out like they used to do in the old days," Igor said.

"Are *you* going to do it?" Misha asked sharply.

"No," Igor said, dropping his gaze to the ground.

"I know," Misha said. "We could tie him to a tree and each give him a pop to the nose!"

"Yeah," Igor said, echoing Misha's excitedness. "Let's bloody him up and then leave him out here for the bears to find! We could even smear him with honey!"

Misha laughed a brief, derisive "ha," then told Igor to shut up. The little girl with the pink bow was calling out her brother's name over and over again, "Seryozha! Seryozha!"

"I think we turn him over to authorities," half ear said.

"*Who?*" Misha asked sharply. "You want us to track down General Zhukov so we can give him a Nazi pilot? Zhukov would shoot him on the spot. That's what he'd do."

"It is right thing to do," half ear said. "It is not our place to judge and sentence him."

"You should have shot him when you had the chance, Misha," Igor said.

"Shut up," Misha said. He studied half ear's face. He wondered if he was born with only half an ear or if he'd lost it in some accident.

"Are you blind? Don't you see what he's done?" Misha said. "He deserves to die for what he did."

"It is not for us to decide," half ear repeated, stuttering a few times on the last word.

"Then whose right is it to decide?"

Half ear opened his mouth to speak but then hesitated. He looked back at Misha with his mouth agape and a puzzled look on his face.

"Russ-ian," Misha said, sarcastically pronouncing each syllable. "I'm speaking Ruusss-iian. Do - you - un-der-stand - me?"

Igor erupted in jeering laughter. "Do you un-der-stand Russ-ian?" he repeated, trying to mock as well as Misha had.

Half ear's face became crimson red. He turned from Misha to Igor, and then back again, looking like he would blurt out an obscenity or two, but choking on his own rage instead.

"It is not for us to decide," he stammered again.

"Then whose right is it?!" Misha yelled. He couldn't tolerate this villager's insolence. "Is it *God's* right?" he asked, studying half ear's face once more.

"He's a Jew!" Igor yelled.

"I am no Jew."

"Then what are you?" Misha asked. "Are you a *Christian*? . . . Or are you a *Soviet*?"

"I," he said haltingly, "I . . . am . . ."

"*What?*" Misha asked impatiently. "What are you?"

"I am a man."

"He's a coward!" Igor yelled.

Half ear turned toward Igor with an angry stare. Igor took a step back and fixed his gaze on Misha.

"As Soviet soldiers, we have an obligation to the Motherland to defend our country," Misha said.

"The German risked his life to save child," half ear said and pointed to the little boy lying on the ground in front of the pilot.

"That boy would still be alive if it weren't for the German!" Misha said.

"He did not know what he was doing. He did not know that train was full of children. Look. He cries," half ear said.

Misha looked and saw tears streaming down the pilot's face. The little girl with the pink bow was only a few yards away now, still calling out her brother's name. "He's not crying," Misha said. "That's just from the smoke. It got in my eyes too."

Half ear offered the German his handkerchief, which he accepted and used to dry his eyes. Misha continued to watch the pilot, feeling uncomfortable being in the presence of another man who was so openly crying.

"It's all an act," Misha said, feeling reassured by his own words, "he probably understands what's going to happen to him."

"He made mistake and knows it," half ear said. "Why you don't understand that?"

"He's a soldier," Igor yelled. "It's not his job to understand things!"

"Shut up, Igor," Misha said. "I stopped trying to *understand* things," Misha said to half ear, "when this war started because none of it makes any sense to me. I only know that the Nazis invaded our country and are killing our children, and *you* are the one who doesn't understand that."

"Give him to me," half ear said. "I take him to prison in next town. They serve justice there."

The little girl's call for her brother suddenly changed from a plea for an answer to a scream of panic. "Seryozha!" she cried and ran to the dead boy lying in front of the pilot. She knelt down by him and saw that he wasn't moving. "What's wrong with him?" she asked.

No one answered her.

Misha felt his rage start to flow over the edges of the small container he tried to keep it in. He took a deep breath and did his best to keep from exploding into a thousand lethal pieces. "We're going to serve justice *here*," he said calmly, "right here and now." He looked over at Igor. "Take the girl over to the women who are treating the wounded," he said, "and then bring me my pack."

Igor picked up the little girl, who continued to ask what was wrong with her brother, and carried her away. Misha switched his hostility from the pilot to half ear. *Who did this peasant think he was to argue with him?* When Igor returned, he set Misha's pack down at his feet. Misha retrieved the cap from it and pulled it down over his head. "In fact," Misha said, looking at half ear, "you're going to help us." Misha pulled a rope out of his pack and handed it to Igor. "Help Igor tie the German to that tree over there." Misha picked up his rifle and pointed it at the pilot.

Half ear continued to sit where he was, leering at Misha.

"That's an *order*," Misha said and adjusted his cap with the lieutenant's insignia on it.

Half ear stood up, but didn't take his eyes off Misha. Misha was sure he was the biggest man he'd ever seen. He towered over him, but Misha wasn't afraid of a half-brain peasant. He knew how to be tough with them. You had to show them who's smarter and put them in their place.

Misha motioned for the German to get up and go over to the tree behind them.

"Come on. Let's go," Misha said to half ear and Igor. "Igor, show half brain how to tie a knot."

"I know how to tie knot," he said, clenching his fists.

"Then what are you waiting for?" Misha looked at him and scowled. "Does it take that long for your brain to tell your legs to move? Get over there and tie him up."

Igor and half ear started walking over to the tree while Misha stood watch with his rifle. Misha smiled to himself over his last remark about the length of time for half ear's brain to tell his legs to move. He thought that was pretty ingenious, associating this giant peasant with a dinosaur.

The air was hot and sticky, and drops of sweat rolled down Misha's forehead to his eyebrows. The leaves of the trees were a dark and somber shade of green against the bright July sun. Igor and half ear tied the pilot's arms and legs tightly behind the tree. The pilot didn't resist in any way. He looked straight ahead at nothing in particular, that same harmless look about him that aggravated Misha to no end. When they were nearly finished, he said something in German that sounded like a question.

"What did he say?" Igor asked, looking to Misha.

Misha shrugged his shoulders. "Who cares," he said. "Just finish up."

The German repeated himself, emphasizing the last word – "tah-bak."

"I think he wants cigarette," half ear said.

"Shut up," Misha said. "You don't know that."

But then the pilot looked at half ear, nodded his head yes and repeated the same word, "cigarette."

"I do not smoke," half ear said, looking at Misha. "You have cigarette?"

"Of course I have a cigarette," Misha said. "I'm a man." He took out a half-smoked cigarette and lit it. "He ain't getting one though."

Misha wiped the sweat from his forehead and glanced at the still burning train. The fire was going stronger than ever and the crackle of the flames filled the air. He looked again at the dead boy that the pilot had tried to save. He found it was so hard to accept that the boy was dead, that his life was over before it had really begun. Misha felt that familiar constricting in his chest and stomach and wanted to scream as loud as he could to let it all out.

"We got him tied up, Misha," Igor announced. "He can't get away. Are you going to hit him now?"

Misha leaned his rifle against his pack and stepped in front of the pilot. He stretched his arm over his head, then swung it around in circles to loosen it up. He inhaled the last bit of his cigarette and flicked the butt to the ground. Then he blew smoke in the pilot's face as he cracked the knuckles of his right hand one by one. He was going to make this Nazi pay for what he'd done.

Igor giggled. "Break his nose, Misha!" he yelled.

Misha, who had never actually been in a fight, who had never actually hit a man in the face before, clenched his fist and flung it wildly at the German's face. He hit him just below the left eye – squarely on his cheekbone.

"God damn it!" Misha yelled, shaking his hand in agony. The pain was so intense that he was sure he must have broken a bone. He held it still for a second to look at it, but saw nothing out of the ordinary.

Behind half ear, a group of boys and girls had gathered round to watch what was going on. Misha looked their way as he shook his hand. He was surprised at how big one of the boys was and decided he must be Siberian. He was almost as tall as the pilot and had arms bigger around than Misha's. From his chubby cheeks and hairless face, Misha guessed he was about twelve years old.

Misha looked back at the pilot, expecting to see a big bruise and feeling angry when he didn't. The pilot had his eyes closed tightly and seemed to be reciting something. His lips moved at a feverish pace, but no sound came out.

"Children," Misha shouted, "would you like to get some revenge against the Nazi pilot who attacked your train?"

None of the children said yes, nor did any say no. They made no response at all to Misha's offer.

Misha scanned the twenty or so children standing by to see which of the boys were big enough and old enough to step up and let the Nazi have it. He didn't want to hit the pilot again – his hand was already starting to swell – and he doubted he could get half brain to hit him, though *he* more than any of them had the strength to inflict some serious pain. Misha was fairly sure he could get Igor to hit him, but the boy acted a bit scared, and besides, then what? That would be the end of it. No, the Nazi wasn't getting off that easy.

"It's time you older boys became men," Misha said. "Who wants to be a Soviet soldier and defend the Motherland? Raise your hand."

A short girl who was cross-eyed and had her hair in pigtails raised her hand determinedly. Three of the oldest boys followed suit, and then another half dozen younger boys raised their hands.

"He said *boys*, Masha. Put your hand down," one of the older boys said to the girl.

"No, that's all right," Misha said. "She was the first to put her hand up. She can keep it up. Now, which of you are brave? Step forward."

Again, the girl was the first to step forward. She wore a plain brown dress and carried a small piece of driftwood that she had fashioned into a toy pistol. The boys followed her lead and stepped forward as well.

"Excellent. That was your first test. Only the brave can be soldiers in the Red Army. Stalin would be very proud of each of you." Misha paused to look each boy in the eye for emphasis. "Now, by the power vested in me as a lieutenant in the Red Army of the Union of Soviet Socialist Republics, I hereby designate each of you a volunteer soldier in the Red Army. Raise your right arm and repeat after me."

Standing tall, faces solemn, the children raised their arms. The girl still clutched her driftwood gun – pointing it harmlessly to the sky.

"I, a citizen of the USSR, stepping forth in the ranks of the Armed Forces," Misha said and paused while the children repeated it, "take the oath and solemnly vow to be an honorable, brave, disciplined, diligent fighter, strictly guarding military and state secrets," he continued. He only knew part of the actual oath, so made the rest up as he went along, ". . . and defend the Motherland – the glorious birthplace of socialism – with every drop of my blood."

Half ear stood off to the side with his massive arms folded in front of his chest. From time to time he would shake his large head slowly from side to side, then look down at the ground and kick at the dirt.

Misha finished giving the children the oath and saluted them. "I congratulate you, citizen soldiers, and welcome you to the Soviet army," he said. The children saluted back, proud expressions emblazoned on their young faces.

"Now line up here," Misha said. "Your first duty as Red Army soldiers is to serve justice against this Nazi pilot."

Misha looked over at half ear pawing at the dirt. "Good idea, huh half brain?" he taunted.

A small boy with bleach-blonde hair ended up at the front of the line. He wore glasses that were too big for him and kept sliding down his nose. Whenever he tried to move back, the older boys would push him to the front again.

"No," Misha said to them, "you older boys go first so you can show the younger ones how to do it. Line up from oldest to youngest. You there," Misha pointed to the largest boy who'd caught his eye earlier, "you go first."

The boy wore suspenders and pants that had been stitched together one too many times. He came forward and stood in front of the pilot, but didn't do anything. He swatted a fly away from his ear and glanced over at Misha repeatedly.

"Come on!" Igor yelled. "Let's go. Punch him in the face."

The boy made a loose fist and threw it lamely at the pilot's face. The pilot opened his eyes momentarily, but then closed them again and resumed his silent recitation.

"Harder!" Misha yelled. "Hit him again!"

The boy threw another punch and hit the pilot on the nose.

"Again! Hit him again!" Misha yelled.

This time the boy clenched both fists and threw sharp punches that struck the pilot's face on both sides. Each successive blow seemed to strike harder than the one before.

Misha and Igor and the children in line cheered. Half ear frowned and folded his arms even tighter.

"Excellent job, comrade," Misha said to the boy. "That's exactly the way to do it."

As the boy walked away, those in line patted him on the back and shouted, "Good job, Sasha!" He smiled awkwardly at the kudos, revealing a large gap between his top front two teeth.

"I want to go next!" Igor yelled. "Misha, let me go next."

"You'll get your turn. Don't worry," Misha told him.

Blood started dripping from the pilot's nose. It trickled over his lips and down his chin where it pooled slightly before dripping to the ground. The blood looked luminous against his pale, white complexion. He said something – curses, Misha guessed – and spit off to his left side.

"Comrade, I beg of you," half ear said, "stop this."

"Shut up," Misha said. "Who's next? Get up there!"

Next in line was the girl. She was at least half a foot shorter and weighed a third less than the first boy.

"Masha, you're too small," the boys behind her said. "You can't hit him."

Masha crossed her arms in front of her and stood her ground. "He said line up oldest to youngest," she said, pointing her finger at them, "and I'm older than all of you."

Misha thought about telling her to wait, to let the biggest boys go first, but he was intrigued to see what this dark haired girl with the thin lipped grimace could do. Her face and posture had an expression of determination and contempt that he liked.

"Go ahead, little girl," Misha said. "Make him sorry he ever crossed the border."

"I am *not* little," she told Misha, putting her hands on her hips. "I'm twelve years old!"

Misha laughed. "Forgive me, comrade," he said, and bowed to her.

Masha was too small to reach the pilot's head, so she tried jumping and throwing her tiny fists at his face at the same time. She had limited success. She could do it, but it wasn't hurting the pilot in any way.

"She's too small," Igor said. "She can't hurt him."

"Kick him!" Misha shouted.

Masha kicked the pilot in the shin, but her shoes weren't very hard, and again she wasn't able to inflict any noticeable pain.

Igor walked over to the railroad tracks, picked up a fist sized rock, then handed it to her. "Here," he said, "throw this at him."

Misha nodded approvingly. Half ear shook his head and walked off toward the front of the train.

The girl took a few steps back and the others made room for her. Looking at the pilot, she squinted her eyes and bent forward slightly. She looked to be so cross-eyed that Misha wondered how she could possibly aim at anything. Gripping the rock in her right hand, she quickly wound up and threw it sidearm. Though the rock had tremendous velocity, it missed the pilot as well as the tree completely.

The boys in line burst into laughter. "I told you girls can't throw," one of them said.

Masha, undeterred by the teasing, ran and retrieved the rock and got set to throw it again.

"Masha," a boy yelled, "you couldn't hit the train if you were standing right in front of it!"

She seemed not to hear what the boys said or else had learned to block it out. She squinted, aimed, and threw again.

This time she was on target. The rock hit the pilot near the groin. Igor laughed a high-pitched, "ha-ha!" The pilot screamed in pain. Several of the smaller children who were watching began walking away.

Misha felt pleased to see that the pilot's face – eyes closed tightly, nose bleeding, eyebrows furled – was no longer so annoyingly placid. "Good job, comrade," Misha said to the girl. She walked past the boys in line, sticking her tongue out and pointing her driftwood pistol at them one by one.

Misha couldn't help smiling to himself now that he had everything under control: the pilot was getting his due, the children were learning how to be tough, he was the undisputed leader, and Igor was in awe of him.

The boy with bleach-blonde hair was next in line. His skin was pale, like the pilot's, and light freckles dotted his cheeks. He inched closer to the pilot, more by the pushing of the boys behind him than his own volition. Judging by his place in line, Misha guessed he was probably eleven, maybe even twelve years old, though he looked to be nine at the most. Several seconds went by with him just standing there staring at the pilot, and the pilot with his eyes closed busily reciting something that only he knew. Misha grew impatient. He was afraid of losing momentum. "Hurry up!" he yelled. "Hit him with the rock." The boy just stood there, looking as though he would burst into tears at any second. "Come on, Vanya," the boys behind him said. "Don't be a sissy." He picked the rock up and raised it behind his head and held it there. "Throw it," Misha yelled. "What's the matter with you? He killed your friends!" The boy then threw the rock straight down at the ground and ran away in tears.

Misha was disgusted with the bad example set by the boy and wanted to move on quickly. "All right, Igor, it's your turn now. Come on. Hurry up," he said. "And make it hurt!" he added.

Igor walked up to the pilot with a malicious grin and picked up the rock.

The older lady who wore the kerchief on her head and had been tending to the wounded children now came down. "What's going on here?" she demanded. "Who screamed? Is somebody else wounded?" She looked to Misha first and then saw the German pilot tied to the tree, blood running down his face, Igor standing in front of him with a rock in his hand. She gasped and covered her mouth with her hands. "You monsters," she said under her breath.

"Babushka," – old woman – Misha said to her, "this isn't for women. Go back and tend to the wounded."

Half ear was now on his way back from the front of the train. He held his right hand in his pocket. "Boris!" the woman yelled to him. "Boris, do you know what's going on here? Come stop this madness."

He heard her and quickened his pace.

"Half brain isn't in charge here. *I* am," Misha said.

She ignored him and kept her gaze on half ear, who stumbled over a large tree root and fell to the ground with all the grace of a wounded buffalo. Misha and Igor laughed spitefully, and the children joined in as well. The woman hurried down to help him.

"Ignore them," Misha said to the children. "I'm in charge here. Igor, we're waiting for you. Hurry up."

With his left hand, Igor brought the rock back behind his shoulder and then threw it awkwardly. It wasn't thrown very hard, and it was obvious he didn't know how to throw. The rock bounced harmlessly past the pilot's feet.

The children all laughed. "You throw like a girl!" the boys teased him.

Igor's big ears turned beet red. "Shut up!" he yelled back.

"He throws *worse* than a girl. Masha can throw better!" they shouted.

Misha watched Igor's face contort in anger and rage and found it amusing. "Are you going to let them tease you like that?" he said with a smirk.

As half ear and the woman approached, the children continued to taunt Igor. "Masha, come show him how to throw. He can't hurt the Nazi," they shouted. Igor glared at them all – lips downturned, fists clenched, back arched. "I'll show you," he said and pulled a knife from his belt. He ran up to the pilot – the blade sparkling in the sunlight – then plunged it into the side of the German's neck. Bright red blood started trickling down his chest and the pilot bent his head over the deadly wound, trying to stem the flow of blood.

Several girls screamed and ran away. Half ear ran to the front of the line and pushed Igor and the rest of the children away. "All right, that is enough!" he yelled. "That is enough!"

"What are you doing?!" Misha shouted. "It's not over. Children! Stay here! The Nazi isn't dead yet."

Half ear pulled a pistol from his pocket, and Misha dove to the ground.

The End Of Sorrow

He was facing away from half ear when he heard the gun fire. When he didn't feel anything, he knew that half ear must have missed him. He rolled toward his rifle, grabbed it, and turned back toward half ear to return fire. But he saw that half ear had already put the pistol back in his pocket and was walking away. Behind him, the German pilot slumped from the tree – a gunshot wound to his chest.

"Boris!!" the woman screamed and covered her mouth once more.

Head bowed, arms hanging loosely at his sides, Boris slowly walked over to her. He dropped to his knees and leaned forward into her arms. She held his large head in her bosom, stroked his bushy brown hair, and said, "Boris, my Boris, what has happened? I don't understand anything anymore. I just don't understand."

Misha's mind went blank momentarily, and then his contempt and rage turned to bewilderment. The German pilot looked like a gory scarecrow, his head lying limp and bloody over his right shoulder. Misha looked briefly at the woman holding half ear's head against her breast, and then he closed his eyes. He heard the wounded children whimpering softly to themselves, the crackle of the flames as the train continued to burn, the woman whispering, "Oh, Boris, my Boris. This is madness. What have we done? What have we done?" And beyond it all – like it wasn't even real – he heard a bird singing in the distance. It was a Greenfinch. He knew because he recognized its high-toned "schkeeee" and "chichichichit" song. When he was a child, the pretty green and yellow birds used to sit outside his bedroom window and serenade him as he awoke.

Misha let go of his rifle and held both hands over his ears. He hated that bird and its song right then like he'd never hated anything in his life. He squeezed his hands tighter and tighter over his ears, but it didn't help. The Greenfinch's song went on and on and on.

* * *

Katya set her notebook aside, laid flat on her back and stared up at the night sky, smiling at the thought of God looking back at her. She'd been writing poetry for the last three hours, working and re-working lines until she was sure that they couldn't be improved.

Much of her poetry was optimistic and inspirational, because that's who she wanted to be. To her and her friends she was *idealistic*. To her father, she was *naive*.

She had a childlike quality about her that she consciously tried to cultivate. Whether it be skipping down the sidewalk on a sudden impulse, doing arts and crafts, singing that nursery rhyme she was so fond of, or just being silly and laughing at every little thing. She didn't want to grow up, didn't want to face the cruel world the adults had created.

It was her grandmother who had nurtured that side of her. Katya's mother had died when Katya was nine years old, and her father took her out to the countryside the week after the funeral to live in the small house on the edge of the woods with her grandmother. He came and visited often, but as the years piled up, Katya began to view him mostly as a generous stranger – someone who stopped by once in a while, brought food and gifts, and then disappeared again the next day.

Though her father clearly loved and respected his mother, the two of them had a strained relationship and bickered often in front of Katya. They argued mostly about God and religion and what Katya should and should not be taught. Her grandmother, Katya came to understand, was a rebel. Someone who was a threat to the 'Powers That Be.' That was why her father had made her live out in the countryside by herself all those years, instead of in the city with the two of them. Her grandmother believed in some very dangerous ideas. She was a Mennonite.

She'd become a member of the historic Christian church at age 67 by undergoing adult baptism. While Katya lived with her, her grandmother taught Katya all the church's essential teachings: that one's loyalty was ultimately to God and not the State, that people should be voluntarily baptized as adults rather than involuntarily as infants, and most heretical of all – pacifism. Mennonites, Katya learned, believed more than anything that Jesus taught peace, that one should 'Love thy enemies.'

It wasn't until Katya got older that she realized just how revolutionary the teachings were. Since the war with Germany had started, she frequently found herself in conflict, either outright with other people, or internally. She was finding that living what you believe was not always an easy (or even safe) thing to do.

She never understood completely who had taught her grandmother to be a Mennonite, but she did understand that her grandmother had been the last one left. The rest had emigrated to Canada as soon as it became obvious that the Bolsheviks would be victorious in the Civil War.

Her grandmother had died two days after Katya's thirteenth birthday, and her father took her back to Leningrad to live with him. He loved her dearly but it became clear that his mother's teachings had had a profound effect on her. Katya and her father argued repeatedly, and he often told her how worried he was about the things she'd learned while living with her grandmother. When he discovered that he couldn't 'undo' the teachings, he resorted to threats, pleas, and warnings for her to be careful in what she said and did in front of others.

The night air was warm and comforting, and Katya watched the fat anti-aircraft blimps sailing silently high above the buildings. They looked like oblong meatballs. Their floating in the sky would catch her off guard sometimes and she would have to ask herself if she was dreaming.

Sometimes she would "wake up" within her dreams at night. She always loved it when that happened. She would rise up out of her body, turn and look down on it laying in bed, then spread her arms and start flying to wherever she wanted to. She would fly high into the sky and back down again. She would do somersaults, and flips, and dance ballet with the clouds. One time she flew straight up as far as she could fly until there was no more sky, no more birds, no more anything. She stayed there looking down at the shiny blue and white marble below until she had the thought that there was no oxygen in space and that she shouldn't be able to breathe. The thought startled her so much so that she promptly woke up and found herself back in her bed, disappointed to be in the mundane reality of her physical existence.

But she wasn't dreaming now. It was sometime between two and three in the morning, and she was on the roof of her apartment building, alone, and on guard for fires from the German planes that never came. It had been six days since Felix had left for the front. She had no idea if he was dead or alive. She worried about him incessantly, and then chastised herself later for expending so much energy on such a useless task. Life without him was unimaginable, so in her mind he was of course always alive. She pictured him on the front courageously rescuing a fallen comrade or rallying the men around him – telling them to be brave, to stand their ground and hold the line to protect the citizens of Leningrad. She never pictured him killing enemy soldiers. The image was too barbaric for her sweet Felix.

The door to the stairwell creaked open. In the dim light, Katya saw her neighbor Petya appear next to all the fire fighting equipment. He accidentally kicked one of shovels, and it knocked over an ax which then fell between the water buckets and sand pails. He limped toward her, his bad leg lightly scuffing the spilled sand on the roof. A moth fluttered in front of him and slipped inside the door before it closed.

"What a prodigious evening," he said.

Katya watched him approach, curious why he was there, but also grateful to have some company. She wasn't interested in him romantically, but she did consider him a friend and someone she wanted to get to know better. He seemed to know so much about the world, and he had a dark side to him that deeply intrigued her. She found she could 'figure out' most people, but not him. He seemed to have a thick shell around himself nearly all the time, and she enjoyed the challenge of trying to break through it.

He sat down beside her, tilted his neck back, and looked up at the stars. "It's always so peaceful up here," he said. "I used to come up here for inspiration all the time. Just to lie back and stare at the stars and listen to the sounds of the city. But now, of course, it's so quiet. No cars, no people, nothing."

"Why did you stop?" Katya asked.

"I'm not sure. There are so many quiet activities in our lives that we love to do and give us pleasure, but we stop doing them for some reason. It's strange. We decry all these *busy* activities that we claim we *have* to do everyday. But the truth is, we *choose* to do them. We choose to do them instead of the quiet activities. I've done it all my life, and I see others do it, and it's never made any sense to me."

He sighed and his arm brushed against Katya's as he stretched. The hairs of his arm tickled her skin and gave her a pleasant shiver.

"It's all because of Original Sin," she said to him.

"I knew religion had to play some role in it," he sneered. "Tell me more."

"Original Sin taught us that we're inherently flawed beings. Adam and Eve were kicked out of the Garden of Eden for failing to control their urges, their curious nature. They were made to feel guilt and shame for who they were and learned they weren't good enough 'as is.' Ever since then, we've expended a good deal of energy trying to prove that we *are* good enough, and *deserve* to be allowed back into the Garden of Eden."

"Hmm, that's interesting," Petya said. "So you're saying that we do all these things we don't like doing because we think they're the way to prove our self-worth? That's probably why the Germans are invading our country – out to prove to the world they're not the culprits they were made out to be after The Great War."

"I hadn't thought of that," Katya said, "but I think you're right."

"And what about you, Katerina Selenaya? What do you expend your precious energy on?"

"On silly, bourgeois things, like worrying about my Felix," she half-joked.

"Oh yes, he went to the front, didn't he? Have you heard from him?"

"No, I haven't heard from him. And it's driving me crazy."

Katya scratched an itch on her shoulder and then ran her fingers through her hair. She thought she smelled cologne.

"Yes, it's no fun being in love with a soldier. You shouldn't get too attached to him."

Katya turned her head to look at him and even before she said anything, Petya was already backtracking on his last statement. "I mean you shouldn't get too attached to him being around you very much. I've said it crudely, but I mean that as a friend. He's a great guy, and war is a difficult time for lovers. I just want you to know that if you ever get lonely and want someone to talk to, I'm available. I'm always around you."

The last sentence made Katya a little uncomfortable, but she brushed it aside. "Thanks," she said meekly.

They sat in silence for a while and stared up at the sky.

"They say the Germans will use gas," Petya said.

"Yes, and they also say Leningrad will be taken in a month. These rumors fly all around the city like pigeons. I've learned not to put too much faith in any of them, except for the ones about a potential famine."

"You mean you don't believe our diligent, honorable officials and their assurances of massive food supplies?" Petya said sarcastically.

"I remember my father telling me about the food shortages here in the 1920's," Katya said. "I hope we don't have to live through anything like that."

"Did you also hear the Germans are planning a paratroop attack on our fair city?"

"Yes, the Supreme Command announced it just last week, right?" Katya brushed a mosquito away from her bare arm. "Do you think we'll wake one morning and see Nazis falling from the sky like hail?"

"Boy, I hope so," Petya said, "maybe that would enkindle my creativity."

Katya didn't laugh.

"I'm only kidding," he said.

"I know. I guess I'm just not in a joking mood. It feels inappropriate to laugh when our men are dying on the front defending us."

Katya smelled cologne once again and stole a glance at Petya. His chubby face was clean shaven. He was wearing a fashionable shirt she'd never seen before. His dark hair was freshly washed and neatly combed.

"Your shift is about over, isn't it?" Petya asked.

She nodded.

"Who gets the glorious job of defending our building from those cursed Nazi planes next?"

"Guzman," she answered.

"Really? I saw Shostakovich going to visit him earlier," Petya said. "He was telling me how he and other musicians were sent to dig trenches beyond the Forelli Hospital. He said one pianist came in a new suit and was later covered in mud up to his thighs. Another one came with a briefcase and kept slipping off to a shady bush to read some thick volume of musical history every few minutes."

"You can't expect musicians to be very proficient at those kinds of things," Katya said. "They can do so many amazing things with their hands, but wield a shovel? The authorities really should have done a lot of the preparations like that beforehand."

"That's what he said too," Petya said. "He went on and on about how Tukhachevsky was the only one to have started preparations, how he was such a brilliant man, the best marshal the Red Army could have asked for."

"So he doesn't believe Tukhachevsky was a German spy?"

"No, he thinks it was all made up," Petya said. "They were close friends, you know."

A mosquito landed on Katya's arm and she pursed her lips and blew it away. "Did you know Shostakovich is applying for the Volunteers?"

"Yes," Petya said. "Dmitry's quite the patriot, and after all he's been through too."

"I doubt he'll be accepted," Katya said. "Even *he* seems to think they'll probably assign him to air-raid duty."

Petya ran his hand over his hair, patting down a spot that was sticking slightly out of place. "You know," he said, "I've never understood why they've never arrested him – that evil *formalist*. They brand him an enemy of the people, and yet he's allowed to walk around and write new symphonies as if everything's fine."

"I certainly don't envy him," Katya said. "He told me he keeps a bag packed and ready to go should they come and arrest him in the middle of the night. He said he's been expecting that knock on the door every night for several years now. It must be tremendously stressful, living like that."

Petya slapped his arm, killing a mosquito. "What do you think of the charges? That he's a formalist," he said. "Some of my friends say that Stalin himself wrote the articles in Pravda condemning his work."

Katya heard her father's voice inside her head telling her to be careful of what she said on contentious political matters, and her first reaction was to not answer Petya's question. But she was tired of doing that. Silence felt somehow dishonest. Besides, she trusted Petya.

"I think calling him a formalist," she said, "is just another useless label. We seem to be so fond of labels these days. 'He's a counter-revolutionary.' 'She's a Trotskyite.' 'He's a formalist.' It's just a way of dumbing down complex issues. You don't have to examine the specifics of anything. Labels make everything black and white. In reality, they're gray."

Petya smiled. "Beautiful," he said. "Honesty seems to have gone out of style. It's refreshing to hear it once in a while." He stretched his neck around in a slow circle. "Do you ever feel intimidated around him – Shostakovich?" he asked.

"Intimidated? Why?"

"What do you mean, '*Why?*' He wrote his first acclaimed symphony when he was just eighteen, and he's a star, not only here, but throughout Europe and America. They've played his symphonies in Rome and London and . . ."

"No, I'm not intimidated by his success," Katya interrupted. "I'm inspired by him. His music is so moving."

Petya said nothing, and Katya sensed she had erred in her response. "Do you feel jealous because you'd like the attention and recognition he's getting?" she asked.

"Absolutely, I feel jealous," he said. "But the thing is, I know I could be just as successful as him if only I could apply myself and simply write more. I wish some of his productivity would wear off on me."

"You need to be patient. I think . . ."

"No," Petya interrupted, "that's one thing I don't need. Things have been expected from me for a long time now. You're still young and there's no pressure on you to make something out of your life yet. When you get to be my age in another eight years, you'll understand."

Katya looked up at the night sky. "My father's always telling me," she began, then jokingly imitated her father's deep, gruff voice, "'You think you've got it all figured out at your age. You know everything. But just you wait, every year from now on you'll realize how much you *don't* know.'" She paused, then added, "That scares me for some reason."

"My uncle used to tell me that when we're adolescents that that's what we need – answers," Petya said. "After adolescence, what's important in life is the opposite of answers – it's the mystery of it all. He told me that most people never make it out of adolescence, that a vast majority of the world was stuck there. Stuck in the things that are important to humans of that age: sex, violence, being right, being 'cool.' I remember he always used to say, 'If people don't start growing up pretty soon, they're going to destroy the world.'"

"Looks like he was right," Katya said. "I fear this war might leave a scar that can't be healed."

They were quiet for a time, then Katya asked if Petya still kept in touch with his uncle – an ambassador to Turkey.

"No, he's too busy for me," Petya replied. "He always has been," he added bitterly.

Like Katya, Petya had lost a parent as a child. In his case, *both* of his parents had died – killed before his very eyes. Katya couldn't imagine the immensity of something as traumatic as that and felt an endearing sympathy for Petya. She knew he'd built a lot of walls around himself so that no one could ever hurt him the way his aunt, uncle, and the other kids at the orphanage had.

He'd written a story once that still brought tears to her eyes when she recalled it. The main character was a young boy who was not well-liked at the orphanage where he lived. One day some of the bigger kids decided he needed to be 'taught a lesson.' They'd held his arms while other kids took turns hitting him with their fists. The boy took every punch, every kick, every laugh. It was only after they'd broken his collarbone that he couldn't take it anymore and collapsed to the ground, crying and instinctively curling into the fetal position. Katya found out later it was a true story, and that Petya was the little boy who'd been beaten up.

Katya hated those kids, hated that the world could be so ugly and mean. What had Petya done to deserve having his parents killed, his aunt abuse him physically and emotionally, and those kids at the orphanage beat him up? She shuddered to think of the scars he must have from those experiences. If those things had happened to her, she was sure she would have been broken, crushed by the cruelty of it all.

She often learned more about Petya through his writing than by talking to him. He let her read drafts of his stories and asked for her feedback. She loved his writing, loved the honesty and sincerity of it. With a little support and encouragement, she was sure he could overcome everything that had happened to him and become one of the country's top writers.

"How's your novel coming?" she asked. "Last we spoke, you were on the third chapter."

A brief look of surprise flashed across Petya's face. "Yes, of course," he said, "the third chapter." He began to sigh again but then cut himself off and answered quickly, "Well, that's nearly finished. I mean it *is* finished. Well no, it's got a ways to go. Katya, can you keep a . . ." Petya finished his abandoned sigh, then said resolutely, "It will be done this week."

"That's good news!" Katya said and squeezed his arm reassuringly. "When can I read some?"

"Soon. Soon."

"You've said that for the past two months."

"All right, all right," he said, his voice trailing off peevishly. "I'll give you something next weekend."

Petya's company and the warm Leningrad night gave Katya a wonderful sense of peace and communion. She looked up at the sky again and tried to connect the points of the constellation Ursula Major. When she was halfway finished, a shooting star streaked across the black sky.

"Petya, did you see that?"

"Yes," he said. "Pure resplendence."

"We get to make a wish now," Katya said. She closed her eyes and made a heartfelt wish for Felix's safety. She smiled at the thought of him – his curly hair, his iron-grey eyes, how courageous he'd been at the train station when he had only a shovel to defend himself on the front.

She turned to Petya. "Did you make a wish?"

"Yes," he said. She noticed for the first time how close they were sitting next to one another. A light breeze massaged the hair on the back of her neck.

"I wished for your happiness," Petya said.

"You're not supposed to tell!" she said and playfully punched his arm. "Now it won't come true."

"Oh. Then, we'll just pretend I didn't say anything." He stretched his arm around Katya's shoulder, squeezed her, then let go.

The door started to creak open again, and Katya made her way to her feet. Dmitry Shostakovich walked toward them in careful, measured steps.

"Katya?" he said in his tenor voice. "Is that you?"

"Yes, Dmitry. It's me."

"Your father just called Guzman's place. He's been trying to reach you."

Her father never called for her at home. It had to be an emergency. "What is it? What happened?"

"He told me Felix was wounded at the front."

Katya gasped and stared at him with her mouth open.

"He's on a train on his way to a hospital here in Leningrad."

She covered her mouth with her hands and struggled for something to say. Petya got to his feet and stood next to her. "How bad is it?" Petya asked.

"I don't know. I don't think her father knows either or else he would've told me." He walked a few steps closer to Katya. "Your father said he'd be home in three hours to take you to the hospital."

She wanted to say thank you, but couldn't get the words out. Crossing her arms in front of herself, she fell into Shostakovich's arms and he held her. Petya mumbled something to himself and lit a cigarette. The stars that made up the constellation Ursula Major continued to shine no brighter and no dimmer than usual.

~

Глава Четвёртая — Chapter Four

The Last Line

Once there was nothing,
    no thought could be found;
But things soon changed
    when "life" was unbound.
Along came logic,
    shortly after time
Something from nothing
    has no right to define
Out of touch
    but in control,
Who are they
    to sell my soul?
Thinking is dangerous
    for we all just might find
Not the answers we seek,
    but a void in the mind.

Petya Soyonovich sat at his tiny desk staring at a sheet of paper with one sentence written on it. It read: *Ivan chimed the bell three more times than he was supposed to and he knew there would be hell to pay from the other monks.* Petya couldn't think of the next line.

He had written that first line forty-five minutes ago. Since then, he had stared out the window for five minutes, organized his small library of books by author (he had sorted them by title just the day before), made a grocery list, shaved, written his friend in Moscow a long-overdue letter, and stared at the empty page once again for ten minutes. For such a supposedly gifted writer, he wasn't the least bit productive with his time. *For such a supposedly gifted writer*, he thought bitterly, *he wasn't worth a damn.*

His room was small, a perfect square except for a *shkaf* – a large wardrobe closet – that hogged the corner opposite the door. The room was intimate in a claustrophobic kind of way. The lone window overlooked a dirty red brick wall and the sun never shined through it and a breeze never blew through it. The room was stale, not meant for those who enjoy living.

Petya felt he was cursed. By what or whom, he didn't know. He knew only that he couldn't meet people's expectations. Try as he might as a young man, he couldn't live up to the standards of success that had been set in his childhood.

When Petya was only twelve years old, he wrote a short parody of Pushkin's famous poem, "Eugene Onegin." He had been informed on that day that he was a mere step away from being a genius – a step away from being the next great writer of classic Russian novels. It had been fifteen years since that day, and Petya was still struggling to take that step.

On many days, today for instance, Petya felt that not only had he not taken that last step forward but had actually taken a step (or two!) backwards. The excuses were endless: not enough time, too much time, no inspiration, too tired, too alert. Each day that he couldn't write, he came more and more to believe he was an imposter, a fluke. He told himself that if he couldn't write something good before his next birthday, February 23rd, then he would accept his fate: he wasn't a writer and would quit writing forever.

He threw down his pencil in disgust and went out into the stairwell of the building to smoke. He shared the small apartment with two other people: Boris, a plumber originally from Novosibirsk whose wife and two-year-old daughter had already been evacuated, and Oksana Petrovna, an older lady with a finicky black cat. Oksana didn't smoke and she forced both Petya and Boris to go outside or to the hallway to light a cigarette.

The stairwell was only a little dark now since it was daylight out. At night it was pitch black because someone kept stealing the lightbulbs. The entire stairwell smelled of rotting food, and at least a hundred flies now made their home there. It wasn't usually like that. It was a nice building, but someone had spilled some garbage and for some reason neither they, nor anyone else, had cleaned it up.

Looking at the potato peels on the floor, Petya realized that he hadn't eaten in quite a while. Everyone thought he was fat because he ate too much, but in reality Petya ate no more than others. His excess pounds were a result of a slow metabolism and an inactive lifestyle. The majority of his days were spent sitting at his desk tapping his pencil against the side of his head.

After he finished his cigarette, Petya thought about what else he could do before getting back to writing. Since he was running low on tea, he could go see his friend and buy some from him. Then he imagined his friend might not have much left. Perhaps he had traded most of his tea to stock up on flour or canned meat? After all, that's all he heard everyone talking about – how the stores were running out of everything. Perhaps his friend had *already* run out of tea. The thought made him panic. How could he survive without tea? He cursed the Germans for taking so long to capture the city and restore order. With the Germans in command, he was sure the city would never run out of tea. He went back inside his room to comb his hair and get some money to go see his friend.

As he retrieved the money from his secret hiding place behind the radiator, he heard a knock at the front door. To improve his writing skills, he had trained himself to pay attention to details, such as the way people knock on doors. He knew everyone's knock – from the "takity tak tak" of Guzman, to the "duk duk" of his artist friend, Vladimir. The current knock – "tump tump tump" – didn't fit anyone he knew.

He stood at the door a minute and listened to the voices on the other side.

"Damn, it stinks out here," a male voice said. "You'll fit in perfectly if this is the right place."

"I don't think anybody's home," another male voice, much younger, replied. "Let's go get some food. I'm hungry."

"We just ate a few hours ago."

"It's *my* money. Give it to me. I'm hungry."

"We used up all the money your parents gave you a long time ago."

Petya opened the door and saw before him a young soldier in army fatigues and an adolescent boy with big ears and a pug nose. Petya was about to ask them what they wanted when Oksana's cat appeared out of nowhere and bolted out into the hallway.

"Get that cat," Petya yelled. "It's not supposed to be out."

The young man in army fatigues quickly maneuvered to pin the cat against the wall with his leg. Then he grabbed it by the back of the neck and threw it inside the apartment. The cat landed on its feet, shook its head, then sat down and licked its fur as if nothing had happened.

"Thanks," Petya said. "There would have been hell to pay had that cat gotten out."

"No problem, comrade," the taller one said. "My name is Misha, and this is Igor. We're looking for Grigori Selenii. Does he live here?"

Petya stared blankly for a moment, wondering what they wanted with Katya's father. "Do you have an appointment to see him?"

"He's my uncle," Igor announced.

"His parents died," Misha said, jerking his head toward Igor. "Before his mom died, she asked me to take him to her brother in Leningrad."

Petya knew that Katya did indeed have an aunt who lived in the country. She had spoken about her a few times. Apparently Katya's father refused to speak to his sister because of some terrible event that occurred a decade and a half ago.

"Did you knock on the door down there?" Petya asked, looking down the hallway toward the entrance to Katya's apartment.

They nodded yes.

"Well, then they're not there," Petya said. "Katya is probably busy at the hospital, but she should be back in an hour or two. Check back then."

"Who's Katya?" Misha asked.

"Grigori Selenii's daughter."

"Oh," Misha said, peeking over Petya's shoulder into the apartment behind him. "Are you going somewhere?"

"Why?"

"I was hoping maybe Igor could stay here with you until Katya gets back."

Petya looked at the boy and felt sorry for him. He knew what it was like to lose one's parents. Petya's parents had been shot – murdered by the Bolsheviks – right in front of his eyes when he was four years old. It was an image that he expended a great deal of energy on trying to block out of his mind every minute of his waking life.

"Don't worry," Misha said. "He'll be quiet and won't bother you." Misha elbowed Igor. "Right, Igor?"

Igor shrugged and looked at the floor.

"Ok," Petya said. "He can stay with me until Katya returns."

"Great," Misha said. "Stay out of trouble," he said to Igor and patted him on the head like a dog. Then he pushed Igor toward Petya's door, turned, and walked down the hallway.

Igor watched Misha until he descended the staircase and was out of sight, then he thrust his hands in his pockets and looked down at the floor once again.

"Come in," Petya said, directing the boy to his room. He decided not to go out for tea just yet since he didn't know when Katya might return.

Igor shuffled his feet into Petya's room, still studying the floor. "He didn't even say goodbye," he mumbled, just loud enough that Petya heard him.

"Who? Misha? I'm sure he meant to. He probably just forgot." Petya sat down at his desk. "You can relax on my bed until Katya gets back."

Igor jumped on the mattress and scooted over to the mirror on the wall. Petya watched him stare at the ceiling for a few minutes and then turn his face toward the mirror and begin scratching and popping the numerous pimples on his nose, forehead, and chin.

Petya's right cheek began to twitch involuntarily. It frequently did that when he was nervous or irritated. He was quite particular about keeping his room clean and orderly, and he worried about the effects this foul-smelling, juvenile boy would have.

"Would you like to take a bath or a shower?" Petya asked, desperately hoping he'd say yes.

"Nah," Igor replied. "I don't like taking baths." He was holding his face inches away from the mirror as he methodically squeezed one pimple and then the next.

Petya's cheek twitched even more. "I'd prefer you don't get the mirror dirty."

"I won't," Igor said.

Petya turned so he couldn't see Igor and decided to try writing again. It was probably best to ignore the boy as best he could until Katya got back. He picked up his pencil and thought what the next sentence of his novel should be. As he concentrated, he alternately chewed on the pencil and twirled it with his fingers. After a couple of minutes, Igor started humming, softly at first, but then progressively louder.

"Stop that, please," Petya said, the twitch returning to his cheek. "I need to do some work." He didn't have much experience with children, particularly twelve-year-olds, and started questioning his decision to take the boy in. He tossed a newspaper on the bed. "Here, you can read that if you want."

For the next ten minutes, Petya contemplated one idea after the other for the second sentence. Nothing seemed to fit. He kept wondering why he had to choose writing as a career. It was an impossible profession – trying to create perfection when he knew damn well that perfection was unattainable. Perhaps he should have been a street sweeper. That seemed like a nice occupation – nothing to think about, no pressure, no lofty goals. It sounded so enticing not to deal with all the bullshit he put himself through every day trying to write.

Igor had moved so that his back was on the mattress and his legs were stretched up against the wall. At first he slapped his hands on the mattress, then he began tapping his feet against the wall.

"Stop that," Petya said, exhaling loudly.

"I'm bored."

"I gave you the newspaper to read."

"There's no pictures in it."

Petya's friend, Vladimir, had somehow got his hands on a French magazine a few years back. It was full of advertisements and pictures of stuff to buy. Petya dug it out of his desk drawer and gave it to Igor. "Here, this one has pictures."

Petya sat back down and returned to contemplating the next line of his novel. When nothing came to him, he began cursing God for creating him in the first place. He didn't ask to be born. It had been forced upon him. He would much rather not exist. If he didn't exist, he wouldn't have any worries, or discomfort, or insomnia. He wouldn't have to try to write. If he didn't exist, then those damn voices in his head wouldn't exist either. He thought how nice it would be to have never been born. It would be total bliss for sure.

But once you *are* born, that's it. You're stuck in this world whether you like it or not. Even if you killed yourself, Petya was convinced you couldn't get away. You'd just be in some kind of holding tank for a while until you were shipped back to earth, reborn to live another life of sorrow.

"I'm hungry," Igor announced.

Petya's first reaction was one of rage. He wanted to whip the boy for being interruptive and annoying. But he knew where that came from. That was how Petya's aunt had raised Petya as a child.

After his parents had been killed, he was sent to live with his aunt and uncle. He loved his uncle, but he was always traveling and rarely ever home. His aunt was an ardent Baptist who made Petya study the Bible, and beat him mercilessly for every sin he committed – and even some he didn't. As a result, he tended to feel guilt or shame for half of everything he ever said or did now.

He didn't want to pass that wretched legacy on to anyone. Nobody deserved that.

He went to the kitchen and grabbed a bowl of black sunflower seeds off the table. When he returned, he handed them to Igor, stressing that he didn't want any empty shells on his bed. "Now could you please stop talking and making noise for a little while?" Petya asked. "I like to work in quietude."

"You like to work in what?"

"Just shut up for a while. Ok?"

"No problem," Igor said. "You won't hear a peep out of me."

Petya went back to his desk, read the first sentence again, and then – much to his surprise – began to write:

> But the Lord had confided his wishes to Ivan. And who was he to argue? God had explicitly stated that he was a chosen one, and Ivan, though humbled, accepted his fate.
>
> He retreated to the green onion-domed church and knelt before a painting of John the Baptist. It showed the man's disembodied head on a silver platter, and Ivan felt a capacious void in his bosom. "There's nothing without love," he said aloud. "I am your lamb. Lead me, oh Lord." He then began reciting a prayer as . . .

"Hey," Igor interrupted. "Why ain't you in the army?"

At first, Petya thought he might be able to get away with ignoring him, but after ten seconds, Igor simply raised his voice and repeated himself.

"I *ain't* in the army because of my leg," he answered. "Now will you leave me be? I'm trying to . . ."

"What's wrong with your leg?"

Petya clenched his jaw tightly to try to stop his cheek from twitching. What could he do to get this boy to leave him alone so he could write? When Boris' daughter had started bugging him, his trick was to tell her a scary story. She'd usually be so frightened that she would leave before the end. Igor was considerably older, but he was from the countryside so Petya thought he was more likely to still believe in folk tales and superstitions.

Petya moved over to the bed and sat next to Igor. "Ok, I'll tell you," he said in a low whisper, "but you have to promise me you won't tell anyone. Cross your heart and hope to die."

Igor's jaw dropped slightly as he nodded his head yes and moved in closer.

Petya tried to look as serious as possible and fixed his gaze on Igor. "A couple years ago," he said slowly, "my cousin and I were walking out in the country at night. I guess it must have been around midnight. I remember there was a full moon and it was really quiet for some reason. We were walking to the next house over when something started making noise from the sunflower field next to the road. The noise was a cross between a dog's growl and a bear's heavy breathing. Whatever it was, it followed us for a long time."

Igor swallowed a few times and his eyes grew bigger. "Eventually, we started running," Petya continued, still in the same low whisper, "and then it burst out of the field and started chasing us. We ran as fast as we could, but it caught us. It got my cousin first and ripped his throat out. I looked back and saw it was huge, whatever it was. It had dark gray fur and a huge head – much bigger than a bear's. I kept running and almost made it to the house when it caught me too. It bit my leg off and would have killed me had not an old man come out of the house and fired a gun in the air. The beast picked up my leg with its giant jaws and ran back into the sunflower field."

Igor held his arms tightly across his chest, a look of terror on his grimy face.

"So, since my cousin was dead, they cut off his right leg and gave it to me. The only problem is that my cousin was a couple inches shorter, so my left leg is a bit longer than my right. That, and sometimes when I feel irritated, I get this urge to bite people's legs. It's happened a few times – the people had to go to the hospital and get stitches – so I have to be careful not to get irritated."

Igor stared at Petya, eyes still wide open, jaw hanging even lower.

Petya went back to this desk, feeling smug and smiling to himself. He heard someone coming up the stairs and listened intently for a few seconds before accepting that the footsteps belonged to his roommate, Oksana. He had so hoped it was Katya. He began dwelling on his disappointment but then caught himself and returned to writing.

> *. . . a young woman walked in wearing a short dress and a veil over her face. She knelt beside Ivan. There was a softness and lightness about her that he could feel by her mere presence – a maddening grace about the way she moved through the air. Her arm brushed up against his. It sent a tiny shiver up his spine. He knew she wanted him. She wanted him violently but just couldn't bring herself to admit it.*
>
> *Ivan slid his arm over, slowly pulled her dress up and stroked the smooth tan skin of her thighs. She arched her back and moaned in pleasure. Her beauty was flawless, angelic. Ivan leaned over and kissed her neck. "Katya," he moaned. "Oh Katya, I can't take it anymore . . ."*

"Damn it!" Petya yelled. He thrust his face into his hands, then threw his head back in frustration. He ripped the piece of paper in half, then wadded it up and threw it across the room.

"Damn it. Damn it. Damn it," he cursed.

"I didn't do anything!" Igor pleaded. "Please, don't get irritated."

Petya went over to his shkaf and began searching for the clear glass bottle he kept there. When he found it, he pulled the cork out and drank two large gulps of vodka. He caught Igor's reflection in the mirror and wondered how he could possibly be related to Katya.

"Don't worry," Petya said. "You didn't do anything." He put on his black beret and grabbed his apartment keys. "Come on," he said to Igor.

Igor looked at him suspiciously. "Where are we going?"

"I need to go see my friend to get tea."

Igor hopped off the bed. "Tea? Who cares about tea?" he said. "You should buy some food before it's all gone. Misha told me the city will run out if the Nazis surround it."

Petya sighed, disappointed that the alcohol hadn't taken effect. "I can live without food. I can't live without tea," he said as they walked out of his room. He closed and locked the door behind him and limped down the hallway. The vodka warmed his throat and stomach. More than anything he hoped it would help him forget about Katya for a while.

"So what's my cousin like?" Igor asked as they descended the stairs.

"Katya? Well, she smells considerably better than you, but other than that you two have a lot in common," Petya said.

"Really?" Igor said excitedly.

"Yes, she has this certain quality about her – just like you – that makes one wish he were somebody else."

* * *

Felix sat up in his bed and took the bandage off his wound to see how it was healing. The skin was still covered with the scaly, dark-red scab, and it looked exactly the same as the last time he'd checked. Disappointed, he put the bandage back on. In his first ever combat experience, he'd been stabbed between the thigh and groin, and not a day went by when he didn't curse the Nazis for his suffering.

He looked at the calendar on his bedroom wall for the fourth time that day, still amazed that it was August 28th already. Nearly the entire month had slipped into yesterday. Where had all the time gone? It seemed like only yesterday he was celebrating his birthday with his friends, but it had been almost *ten* weeks since then.

Without warning, a wave of pain made its way forcefully from his left leg, through his lower back, past his shoulders, up his neck, and into the base of his skull. He tried not to grit his teeth, to focus instead on the pain and give it a color and a frequency. But the pain was so mixed up with the story about how he was wounded that he couldn't do it. He couldn't stop thinking about how they had tried to kill him. It was war, and he knew the thought was preposterous, but every time the pain from his leg peaked, he experienced that same outrage he'd felt when the Nazis started shooting at him. As the first bullets whizzed by his head on that day in early July, he'd felt such rage he'd wanted to scream, and kill, and set the whole God-damned world on fire.

But he hadn't screamed then, and he wouldn't scream now. The pain pulsated and pounded and his body was one gigantic knot of tension. And then it was over. The pain receded, and he was alone again in his room, the sun shining faintly through the windows, a fly buzzing on the ceiling.

That's how it always was. The throbbing pain from his leg would come on without warning, torture him for ten or twenty seconds, and then dissipate.

He prepared to get out of bed, which was no longer a thoughtless task. His entire left thigh was black and blue and he could only bend his knee with difficulty. To get out of bed, he had to put his right foot under his left leg and lift it over the edge of the bed, and then swing his torso up quickly before too much pressure was put on the knee.

Felix did it all in one swift motion, then limped to the kitchen and retrieved the open newspaper from the table, careful all the while not to wake his napping father. Back in his room, Felix sat on the bed, rested his left leg on a pillow, and started suspiciously scanning the headlines. He marveled at what they said about the war, especially since he knew better.

Before he'd been released from the hospital, Felix started making inquiries about a different position, one that would keep him closer to Katya. Every job seemed to require the individual to do a lot of standing or walking, neither of which Felix could do with his injured leg. If he waited until his leg was healed, he was sure they'd opt instead to send him back to the front where they needed men the most.

Katya had asked her father for help, but he insisted there weren't any positions a one-legged man could do. Katya kept pressuring him until he finally gave in and told her about an army clerical position that was opening. "They'll be interviewing candidates tomorrow," he'd said.

"Can't you just tell them you already have somebody?" Katya asked.

"No, the commanding officer is quite particular and wants to get the person who's the best qualified. He's got some test that each candidate has to do."

"Test? What kind of test?" Katya asked warily.

"Oh, nothing special . . . just a short typing test."

"What?! Father, you know Felix doesn't know how to type!"

"Oh really," he'd said. "I thought he could. Too bad."

When Katya angrily recounted the story to Felix at lunch that day, he was unfazed. He had her borrow Petya's typewriter and then spent twenty hours straight learning how to type. It was grueling and he went the entire time without food or sleep, but he knew what he wanted and nothing could stop him. Out of the six people they interviewed the next morning, Felix had typed the least number of words per minute, but was the only one who hadn't made a single mistake. The commanding officer had been impressed with Felix's meticulousness and selected him for the job.

Typing orders to commanders on the front gave Felix a good picture of how the war was going. While the newspapers weren't necessarily printing lies, they weren't giving citizens a complete picture either. A heroic handful of factory workers holding off an entire German company for two days was a nice story, an inspiring story, but Felix thought it confused people. If the story was an indication of how the war was going, then how was it that Leningraders heard the shelling getting closer and closer every day?

The newspaper accounts certainly didn't match what Dima told him, and Dima had been on the front lines since the beginning of July. Everyone in the city seemed to know the war was going badly. Felix feared that the vague accounts of the losses in the newspapers only heightened the frustration and distrust of all things 'official.'

He set the newspaper down and looked out the window to the east. There was a large apartment building that blocked the view of what lay beyond, but he frequently saw the moon rise from behind the building. It was always a mystical sight. In a few more days, it would be September and the Harvest Moon would return to bathe the city in its peculiar orange tint. When Felix lived in Ukraine, autumn had always been a time for rest and gratefulness – the harvest rush was over, food was plentiful, and people enjoyed the remnants of the summer weather. But here in Leningrad at war, Felix felt nothing but anxiety. He knew all too well what came after the Leningrad autumn – the Leningrad winter.

He had to make sure Katya left the city now. He couldn't bear the thought of her here in the winter if the Germans surrounded the city. It didn't matter how close he was, there was only so much he could do to protect her.

The front door of the apartment creaked open, and Felix listened intently for a sign of who had arrived. Then his father's voice sounded from the hallway, yelling those three words he'd been anxiously awaiting all day, "Felix, Katya's here!"

He hobbled out of bed and made his way to the front door, joy and anticipation crowding out any remaining pain from his leg.

His father was talking to Katya, gesticulating wildly the way he always did when he was excited. He worked so much these days that he rarely ever saw Katya. "Oh you're a sight for sore eyes," his father said to her. "So young! So beautiful!" Felix looked at Katya. She was dressed in a sleeveless silk blouse with black and gold stripes. Her brown hair was short and curled up at the ends. Her long, graceful neck was seducing him already. Sometimes he just couldn't believe that her heart belonged solely to him.

"Father's been working a lot of hours lately," Felix said as he approached her, "staring at beakers and vials for days on end."

"Oh, you can't imagine. Every time the anti-aircraft guns start firing, those dogs howl like there's no tomorrow, and Tolya curses them like an old sailor. But that's besides the point, Felix. Isn't she the most beautiful thing you've ever seen?"

"Without a doubt, father." He kissed Katya on the lips and wrapped his arms around her. "Hello gorgeous," he whispered in her ear.

"I'll leave you two lovebirds alone," his father said and walked down the short narrow hallway back to his room.

Felix took Katya by the hand and led her to his bedroom where they embraced and kissed once more. It was a warm day and Felix swung open the large windows at the foot of his bed. Katya loved to sit in the windowsill and read, draw, or just look out over the city. On a clear day like today, you could see the Neva river and even the Spire of the Admiralty in the Peter and Paul Fortress on the other side.

"How's your leg?" she asked.

"Much better now that you're here." He kissed her on the cheek, a big grin on his face. He saw her nearly every day, but it didn't make a dent in his affection for her.

"You're so adorable," she said. "Everybody thinks you're so tough and strong, but I know the truth. You're a puppy dog."

"Only for you," he said.

"Is Dima coming by for lunch?" she asked.

Felix nodded. "Yes, he should be here soon."

"You must be excited. You haven't seen him since you were wounded, right?"

"Yes. Did I tell you he was made a commander shortly after that?"

"Our Dima? A commander? I guess it was only a matter of time."

"Yes, apparently the first one was deemed incompetent – I can certainly vouch for that – and then the second one was killed only a week later."

Katya went over to the open windows, propped her arms up on the windowsill, and leaned out to look around. Felix admired the ravishing curves of her body and the smooth, slightly tan skin of her legs. He wished they had more time to be alone together.

"Did you remember to bring yesterday's newspaper?" he asked.

"Yes, I have your *precious newspaper*," she teased, retrieving it from her bag and handing it to him. "How did you manage to miss yesterday's news?"

"Father gave the paper away before I had a chance to read it."

Katya grabbed a pencil and pad of paper and situated herself, catlike, in the windowsill. She used the pencil and paper to either draw the city's skyline or write poetry, and Felix wondered which it would be today. The sun, which had been behind one cloud after another for the entire day, finally broke free and shined directly on her. Felix wasn't surprised. She had that effect on most people. Why should Mother Nature be an exception?

He set the newspaper aside and wondered how best to bring up the subject of his desire for her to leave the city. He was fairly sure she wouldn't like the idea, but it was something that needed to be talked about. Deciding on the direct approach, he took a deep breath and said, "Katya, I want you to evacuate Leningrad."

She had closed her eyes and now opened them with a start. The pencil and paper fell to the floor.

"I think it's for the best," he continued. "You'll be safer someplace else."

Katya stared at him, then turned and looked out the window. "So you want me to leave too . . .," she said.

Felix heard the "too," but it was slow to sink in that someone else might have already advised her to evacuate. "Well, it seems like the best decision at this point and time," he said.

"I think the 'best decision' is for us to stay together," she said. "I thought you might be of the same opinion."

Felix felt a tightness in his throat and a flush of blood to his face. He knew this wasn't going to be easy.

"I don't *want* you to leave, I would like you to stay with me," he said. He got up from the bed and limped over to her.

"I'm so sick of this damn war," she said, and buried her face in his chest. "Why are people so stupid? Can't they find any better way to prove who's right than by killing one another?"

Felix disliked anything even approaching an argument with Katya. It was a tremendous struggle for him whenever they didn't agree on something. He felt like crawling inside his shell like a turtle now, but he overcame the urge and took her hand. "What do *you* think, Katya?" he asked. "What do you want to do?"

"I wanted to stay with you, but now I'm not so sure you want me to."

"Nothing would make me happier," he said, squeezing her hand, "than to spend every day of the rest of my life with you."

"You mean it?"

"Yes," he said, putting his arm around her.

"But if I go," she said, "I may never see you again."

"We can't think that way. We have to trust and believe," he said. "As long as we keep our faith in one another, nothing can come between us, not even this war."

"I do believe," Katya said, wrapping her arms around his waist. "I just want us to be together."

"We need to think about what's best for the future," he said. "It will be painful to be separated in the short term, but it makes the most sense in the long term for you to go live . . ."

"In Moscow," she said, finishing his sentence.

"Sure," Felix said. "Maybe your father could pull some strings and . . ."

"He already has," she interrupted.

Felix remembered the "too" she'd said earlier and then put the pieces together. "Your father has already arranged for you to be evacuated, hasn't he?"

She nodded. "I was going to tell you after lunch," she said. "The train leaves tomorrow at 3:00 p.m.."

"So, the decision's been made already?" Felix felt a sinking feeling in his stomach, but also a sense of relief.

"No, the decision hasn't been made. It's not made until *I* make it."

Felix looked out the window, past Katya, at the tops of the buildings below them and the thin ivory-white clouds drifting through the sky. "I want you to be safe," he said. "I'm terrified of something happening to you."

"And *I'm* terrified of something happening to *you*," she said.

He stretched his arms around her and they squeezed tight against one another. They stayed in that position, neither saying a word, for a long time.

"It won't be for that long, right?" Katya said, breaking the silence. "The unbeatable Red Army is just off to a slow start, that's all," she joked.

Felix looked her in the eyes and smiled. "You agree then?" he asked.

"Da," – yes – she said and kissed him softly on each cheek and then on the lips.

He could hardly bear the thought of her leaving tomorrow. He started to say something several times, but no words came out.

"Felix!" his father's voice rang out again. "Dima's here."

Felix kissed Katya on the top of the head and started to leave to greet his friend.

"Wait," Katya called out.

He stopped and turned back toward her. She was staring at the ring he gave her.

"I don't want . . . ." She pulled the ring off her finger and held it in her hand. "I mean this was a promise . . . ." She slid the ring back on. "What I want to say is, let's get married tomorrow before I leave. I know we've been making all these plans for our wedding, but let's just the two of us go to the bureau tomorrow morning and get a marriage license."

She raised her head, and for the first time he could recall, the sorrow in her chestnut-brown eyes disappeared completely. As his eyes met hers, he felt again that he held the entire world inside his heart. He whispered, "Konyeshna" – of course – then lingered in the doorway smiling at her, his heart so full he couldn't speak another word.

He made his way to the front door, feeling light. One of his dreams was a step closer to becoming reality. The voice inside congratulated him but also sent a word of caution that it hadn't happened *yet*.

His father was standing in front of his best friend inquiring about the sling that held Dima's left arm.

"Oh, it's no big deal," Dima said. "The German fascists tried to take me out with their cannons. They got lucky and a piece of shrapnel hit me in the wrist. I'll be back in action soon enough, and *then* the Nazis will be sorry!" he laughed.

Felix was surprised at how different his friend looked. Though it had only been two months since he last saw him, Felix couldn't help but notice how straight he stood and how hard his body looked under his uniform. He seemed to be all muscle now. Felix had been confined to bed for weeks and had no doubt who would win a pushup contest if they were to attempt one today.

"I see you're limping still," Dima said to Felix.

"Yes, the healing hasn't been so smooth, but it's a hundred times better than just a few days ago. Once I walk for a minute or two, it's okay. It's just when I've been sitting or laying around for a long time that it gets so stiff. In another week or so, I think it'll be healed completely."

They hugged and then Dima patted Felix on the stomach. "I see your mother has fattened you up like a goose," he said gaily.

"Yes, and it seems you're as strong and lean as a tiger," Felix replied. He laughed and slapped Dima on the back.

"Well, they definitely put me to work. Food doesn't seem quite as important when you're in battle. I tended to completely forget about it, and only remember at the end of the day when I was completely exhausted. I would have a few bites and practically fall asleep before I finished my meal."

"Well, I hope you're hungry today," Felix's father said warmly. "I'll go get lunch ready."

"Where is your wonderful wife?" Dima asked Felix's father. "I was hoping for some of her delicious borscht soup."

"A friend of hers called. She heard that a store on Vasilevski Island was selling butter, so the two of them went over there to see if there was any truth to the rumor."

"Yes, I've heard the food situation has gotten quite out of hand," Dima said. "It's all these panic mongers and hoarders that cause so much trouble."

"Yes, some food items are hard to come by, but there's no shortage of rumors!" Felix's father started toward the kitchen. "You're in luck on the borscht," he said over his shoulder. "She knew you were coming and made some beforehand."

"Excellent! Cold, I hope."

"Of course. She never makes hot soup in the summer."

Katya came out and gave Dima a hug and kiss on the cheek. "So how's our commander?"

"A little tired," he said, "but no worse for the wear." He retrieved a small booklet from his pocket and handed it to Katya.

Katya looked it over, thumbing through a few pages. "It's in German."

Dima nodded. "Yes, it's a Leningrad guidebook. I found it in the pocket of a dead Nazi."

Katya handed the booklet to Felix who started looking through it as well. "Why can't they just leave us alone?" she asked. "This war makes no sense to me. The Germans come to our country and bomb our roads and bridges and cities and kill people – old, young, doesn't seem to matter. And for what reason? No matter how many times it's explained to me, I'll never understand it. I mean the Germans are human too."

"They're not human," Dima scoffed. "They're Imperialists. And that's all you need to understand."

Felix set the booklet down and winked at Katya. "They're not only Imperialists," he said, a sly smile on his lips, "they're *efficient* Imperialists – the worst kind."

Katya laughed, but Dima didn't. Since the war began, their friendship had started to change. Felix noticed how serious Dima had become and how he rarely laughed at jokes anymore. He pushed Dima toward the kitchen, and he and Katya followed. His father was busy slicing a loaf of dark bread. "Sit, sit," he begged them. "It'll be ready in a minute."

The room smelled of fresh dill. Dima took a seat at the end of the table while Felix and Katya retrieved soup bowls and spoons from the cupboard.

"So Katya," Dima said, "Felix tells me you have a new roommate."

"Oh you mean Igor? Yes, he's quite a handful – always getting into things, curious as a cat. But my neighbor, Petya, has just been wonderful with him, keeping him occupied so he doesn't drive me crazy."

"Igor is your cousin? Is that right?" Dima asked.

"Yes," she said, setting four white soup bowls on the table. "I'd never met him before, though. He's from the country, and my father and his mother never talked. Igor told me the Germans burned their house and bombed the neighboring village, so he and his parents were refugees and just wandered for a long time. His parents ended up dying on the journey, and a Soviet soldier brought Igor all the way here to Leningrad and found us."

Felix set a spoon next to each person, then sat down himself. The windows next to the small table were open, and a slight breeze carried in the sound of children playing in the courtyard below.

"How old is Igor?" Dima asked.

"Twelve."

"Then he should be helping out on the front or at least doing something here in the city."

"Oh believe me, he wants to," Katya said. "The problem is he has the maturity of a ten-year-old. Whenever he tries to help, he usually makes things worse."

Felix's father began filling each person's bowl with a bright pomegranate-red colored soup. Katya used a match to light a burner on the stove, then set a pot of water on it.

"Dima, you've no doubt heard about the retreat from Tallinn," Felix's father said. "Practically the entire fleet's been sunk. It's such a crime the way the whole affair was handled."

"What do you mean it's a crime?" Dima asked.

"It's a crime there was never a plan to evacuate. So many lives and so many ships could have been saved. My friend – one of the few to survive – told me all about it. They were trying to navigate the harbor with its thousands of Nazi mines while being bombed by Nazi guns from the shore and swarms of Nazi planes in the air."

"The real crime is those Estonians taking up arms with the Germans," Dima said, clenching his fist. "We must all get behind the Party and be united with a single focus. If we're divided, the Germans will beat us. We *never* should have retreated from Tallinn."

"But, Dima," Felix's father said, "the rules of war dictate that sometimes you attack and sometimes you retreat. To never retreat when you've been beaten is suicide. Surely you understand that?"

"Retreat is something I hope never to understand," Dima said. "Tallinn would have kept the Germans busy for a long time. Now all those Nazi troops will be joining the battle for Leningrad."

"Do we have sour cream?" Felix asked his father.

"No, I'm afraid not. Your mother hasn't been able to find any. I have some dill though," he said and retrieved a small bowl from the counter.

"Dima, do you remember Katya's neighbor, Petya?" Felix asked. "Katya said he told her he doesn't think it's necessary to stock up on food because the city will have to surrender soon."

Katya grinned and poked Felix with her elbow. Felix glanced at her and winked, waiting for Dima's reaction.

"He's a traitor," Dima said. "If the Party weren't so busy preparing for the defense of the city, then people like him would be dealt with. Anyone who thinks of surrender should be shot."

Felix's father was oblivious to his son's mischief until he noticed Katya having difficulty suppressing a giggle. "If we had a whole army of people like you, Dima, we'd never lose a battle," he said, joining in.

"Well, I don't know about *every* battle," Dima said.

Katya burst out laughing, and Dima looked at her quizzically.

"Oh, I'm sorry," she said. "I just remembered a joke someone told me."

Felix turned toward her, a glint in his eye. "Well, we could all use a little humor. Why don't you tell us the joke?"

She raised her bottom lip, directing a fake scowl at Felix. "No, I'm terrible at telling jokes," she said. "Let's eat. I'm sure Dima's starving."

"Yes, let's eat," Felix's father said.

Each of them sprinkled some of the fresh dill on their soup, took a thick slice of black bread and began eating.

"Delicious," Dima said. "It sure beats what they give us on the front."

A small bee flew in the window and buzzed around the table until Felix's father chased it back outside again. Felix, normally a fast eater himself, was surprised at how much quicker Dima was eating than he. Dima's bowl was nearly half finished in a matter of seconds.

"Katya, how is the work at the hospital going?" Felix's father asked.

"Oh, I don't want to talk about it," she said, dropping her shoulders. "These poor old men and these young boys keep pouring in. It's awful, just awful."

"I agree. Let's not talk about that," Dima said. "We mustn't concentrate on the negative: the retreats, the traitors, the wounded, the food situation. We need to focus on the positive – on the news and stories that inspire us, not deflate us. We should be talking about the Colonel Podlutskys of the war."

"Podlutsky," Katya repeated. "I know him. He's in our hospital. All the men speak so highly of him. What did he do?"

"He was in the artillery unit of the 70th Division," Dima said. "They fought the Germans with everything they had but were badly outnumbered and ultimately encircled. With the division in shambles, Podlutsky led his detachment out of encirclement 125 miles behind enemy lines."

"Yes, I heard about that," Felix said. "But don't you think the Soviet people deserve to know the truth about how the war is going? The newspapers often hide disappointing news, and it only feeds the rumormongers."

"The truth is what history writes," Dima said. "If the Party is wrong, then it will be so judged. But the Party is not wrong. You'll see. Speaking of which, how is your father, Katya?"

"Overworked as usual. I think he suffered a minor heart attack two weeks ago, but he won't admit it. He was having difficulty breathing and kept holding his hand to his chest complaining of pain and tightness. I couldn't get him to go see a doctor though. He said, 'The doctors are busy with the wounded. I won't have them wasting their time on an old man with indigestion.' I fear he'll do himself in before the Germans ever do."

Felix's father used a piece of bread to soak up the remaining soup in his bowl. "I tell you what I'd like to ask him," he said while eating the bread. "I'd like to know about these rumors of people being evacuated – particularly children – right into the path of the Nazis."

"I'm afraid you'll have to wait to ask him that," Katya said. "He's in Moscow now."

"Moscow? When did this happen?"

"He left on the train yesterday morning."

"So the city's not surrounded yet? That's one less rumor to believe," Felix's father said.

"Father, I told you the Northern Railroad was open and that trains were still going to Moscow. You trust Katya but not me?"

"Don't be cross, Felix. I'm a fool for a beautiful woman." He held his hands over his heart and looked intently at Katya across the table. "If Katya told me the sky was green, I'd believe her."

"Why can't you listen to me like your father does?" Katya said to Felix, elbowing him in jest once more. "Actually, Igor and I will be joining my father in Moscow tomorrow."

"So you'll all live in Moscow?" Felix's father asked.

"No, father's supposed to return September 1st. Igor and I will stay in Moscow until this madness is over with."

Felix sensed both his father and Dima looking at him, waiting for an answer to a question that hadn't been asked.

"Yes, my father's set it all up," Katya continued. "And Felix quite agrees with him."

"I think it's for the best at this time," Felix said. He was wary of Dima's reaction and didn't have to wait long.

"I don't think anybody who can help should leave," Dima announced. "Now, more than ever, it's important for us to stick together. United, we can win, but if able-bodied people evacuate the city, we're digging our own graves."

"Don't try using your twisted logic with this, Dima," Felix said, no longer amused by his friend's intransigence and arrogance. "It's the Germans who are digging our graves, and you know it. It's not right to blame the people of Leningrad for needing some safety – for wanting to protect their loved ones."

"It's precisely that kind of thinking that will doom us," Dima responded. "That's the most dangerous type of thinking there is, because it hides behind those antiquated notions of the individual having more importance than the collective whole. That's sentimentality masquerading as logic."

Felix felt a flash of anger but held it in. Most of the arguments he had with Dima usually ended like this: Dima belittling individual needs and desires, Felix feeling uneasy with a rebuttal.

Dima continued eating as though there had been no emotion in the conversation. "Felix, don't be angry," he said. "I don't hold your misguided thinking against you. You just need more time for the Party's teachings to sink in. That's why I'm so patient with you, and you should be patient with yourself as well. It takes time and courage to change these beliefs that have been ingrained in us for so long."

Felix clenched his fists and was just about to tell Dima what a conceited, presumptuous ass he was when Katya put her hand over his left fist and squeezed. Felix saw her smiling so calmly his anger immediately softened. He could tell by the look on her face she understood that it was pointless to argue with Dima. She had squeezed his hand to remind him of that as well. Felix took a long, slow breath and knew that he didn't have to react to Dima's instigation. "Thanks, Dima," he said. "And I'll do my best to be patient with you as well."

Dima looked puzzled for a moment but then continued eating.

After lunch, Dima, Felix, and Katya went for a walk, while Felix's father stayed behind awaiting his wife's return. It was another warm, sunny day and the air was thick with the scent of the Neva river and turning leaves. Fall was fast approaching.

After a few minutes, they came to the Kazansky Cathedral. The cathedral's dome was set against a tepid blue sky, and they walked around the cathedral under the shade of a row of linden trees whose leaves had turned yellow. Katya picked one of the leaves and admired it up close, then stuck it in Felix's hair. He was busy telling a joke to Dima and so let her do it.

They turned down a small street that was blocked off to traffic. Coming toward them from the other end was a man who staggered from one side of the street to the other, barely able to keep his balance. They watched him stumble and fall to the ground. When he got back up, he began yelling and cursing and the people who passed by him veered toward the far side of the street. His speech was slurred and some of his words were incomprehensible, but most of his blasphemous rant was quite clear.

"The Germans are coming!" he shouted. "They're going to take over. And the Soviets can't stop them. Nobody can! They'll slaughter all the commissars . . . every last one of them. Do you hear me?!"

As they got closer, they saw the man was wearing a badly tattered Red Army uniform. Felix glanced at Dima and saw his face contorted in fury, his arm reaching for his pistol.

"Down with the Soviets! Down with the Commissars! Down with Socialism!" he continued shouting to anyone within earshot.

Felix hurried ahead of Dima and Katya, going as fast as his hurt leg would allow him. "Comrade," he said, trying to get the man's attention by standing right in front of him, "you need to be quiet now – for you own good."

"I ain't your *comrade*," the man shouted. His forehead had a scrape on it and blood trickled down his left cheek. "I ain't nobody's comrade. I'm autonomous. Do you understand?" The man saw Dima approaching – hand on pistol – and shouted loudly in his direction, "I'm autonomous I said!!"

"Look at me," Felix said, wrapping his fists around the man's shirt and pulling him close. Felix wasn't afraid of the man hurting him. He was exceptionally good at up-close fighting, having studied the Russian martial art, Sambo, for three years and being the best in his class.

The man had trouble focusing. He looked everywhere except at Felix – at Dima, at Katya, at the people starting to gather around. "Look me in the eyes," Felix commanded. The man reeked of alcohol, and Felix could tell by his breath that he was drunk on cologne. "You need to stop talking *now*," Felix said. "You've had too much to drink and you're going to get in big trouble if you keep talking. Do you understand me?"

"I ain't afraid of nobody!" the man shouted. "Kill the commissars!"

"Listen!" Felix shouted in his face. The man finally looked Felix in the eyes, though his head kept swaying from side to side. "Do you see that man coming toward us?" Felix asked. "The one with the army fatigues and hand on his pistol?"

The man looked at Dima again. "Yeah, I see him," he slurred. "I ain't afraid of him."

Felix gripped the man's shirt even tighter. "Well, you should be afraid of him," he said. "He's going to kill you if you don't shut up."

The man suddenly seemed to sober up. He fixed his eyes on Dima, who had now arrived and was standing five yards in front of him. A crowd of six or seven people had gathered at a distance to watch. The man used his forearm to wipe some of the blood from his cheek and forehead.

Dima withdrew his pistol from its holster. "It's alright Dima," Felix said. "He didn't know what he was saying. He's done now."

"You bastard," the man growled, still looking at Dima.

"Stop," Felix whispered and placed his hand over the man's mouth. "Stop talking."

The man pulled Felix's arm away. "You're just like the bastard who shot Vitya in the back!" he shouted at Dima. "Let me go!" he said to Felix, struggling to free himself from his grasp. "I'll say whatever I damn well want to say! I ain't afraid of nobody!" He turned toward the crowd of people. "The Germans are coming! They're going to slaughter every commissar and communist they find. Down with the Soviets!"

Dima pointed his pistol at the man, but Felix still had him by the collar. "Felix, move away!" he ordered.

"Dima, he's drunk," Felix said.

"I don't care," Dima said. "Move away."

"Don't do this, Dima," Katya said. "Please."

"He ain't gonna shoot me," the man said. "Down with the Soviets!" His shirt ripped and he broke free from Felix's grasp. He made one step in Dima's direction and a shot rang out. The bullet struck him in the chest and he collapsed to the pavement.

Katya let out a high-pitched scream. "Oh God!" she said. "You didn't have to do that, Dima. You didn't have to do that!" She rushed over to the man, inspecting the wound and checking his breathing. Two policemen ran out of a nearby alley and quickly approached.

"Leave him be," Dima said to Felix and Katya. "Let the traitor die."

"I need something to stop the bleeding," Katya said to Felix.

Felix took his shirt off and handed it to her. She wadded the shirt into a ball, pulled Felix down next to her, then told him to put pressure on the wound. "If we can get him to a hospital quickly, he has a chance," she said.

The policemen arrived. While one questioned Dima, the other talked to the people in the crowd. After only a few seconds, they approached Felix and Katya and told them to move away from the man.

"He's dying," Felix said. "I need to keep pressure on the wound. Is there a stretcher nearby?"

"I said *move away*," the taller policeman repeated.

"I'm a nurse," Katya said. "We need to get him to a hospital right away."

The other policeman grabbed Katya by the arm and lifted her up. "Let him be," he said.

"No, leave me alone!" She tried to break free, but he just gripped her arm tighter.

The taller policeman moved closer to Felix. "If you don't want to get arrested," he said, "I suggest you move away now."

"I told you," Felix said angrily. "He's dying. Can't you see that?!"

The policeman grabbed Felix by the arm and forcibly pulled him to his feet. Felix quickly broke his grasp and then gave him a blow to the stomach that sent him reeling backwards. The other policeman let go of Katya and withdrew a small black club from his belt. Felix prepared to fight him, but Dima quickly jumped in front and wrapped his arms around Felix in a tight bear hug. Felix continued to struggle but he didn't want to hurt his friend, and eventually Dima managed to pull him away to a safe distance.

Katya came over and started to cry. Felix took her in his arms and held her as he brushed away something he felt in his hair. The linden leaf floated to the pavement.

The dying man had long since taken his last breath by the time Dima persuaded the two policemen not to arrest Felix. During this time, Felix and Katya had done their best to convince a shaken little girl who'd witnessed the scene that the dead man was a German spy disguised as a Soviet soldier. The girl's father was in the army and she couldn't comprehend how a Soviet soldier could kill another Soviet soldier when the Germans were the enemy.

When they were finally allowed to leave, the three of them walked back to Nevsky Prospekt. There was a knot of tension between Felix and Dima, but neither of them wanted to discuss it. The stately Nevsky was filled with a strange mix of citizens and soldiers. They passed a young mother and her three children sitting on the curb enjoying Eskimo pies, then a company of soldiers in tight formation, then two young boys carrying gas masks. Felix found it hard to believe there was a war going on. Somehow it didn't all seem real yet. Young women still wore their summer dresses and cast curious sidelong glances at admiring young men. And despite all the talk of a food shortage, you could still buy Eskimo pies.

Dima was the first to break the uncomfortable silence. He grabbed Felix by the arm and came to a stop on the sidewalk. "Felix, let me give you a word of advice," he said, narrowing his eyes. "You better decide who's side you're on, and you better decide damn soon."

Felix yanked his arm out of Dima's grip. "I know what side I'm on," he said. "I'm on *my* side. The side that knows right from wrong."

"That's your problem," Dima said. "You think that you're somehow *qualified* to decide. But it's Moscow that determines what's right and what's wrong. The Party is the one with the knowledge of history. The Party is the collective wisdom of the Proletariat. Who are you to think you know better?"

Felix took a deep breath, looked at Katya, then back at Dima. "You know we've been best friends ever since we were kids, so let me say as a friend..."

"We are not friends," Dima interrupted. He held his hand in front of him, pointing his finger in Felix's face. "There's no room in these times for quaint things like friendship. We are *comrades* – nothing more, nothing less."

Felix stared back, a tight frown on his lips. "I see. Then there's nothing more to say, is there?"

"No," Dima said, "there isn't." He was about to walk away when he added, "Let me give you one last piece of advice. You have this habit of crossing lines that shouldn't be crossed, and one of these days you're going to be very sorry. One of these days, you're going to cross the last line." He turned his back to Felix and walked to the other side of the street. Felix watched him leave, wondering if he would look back and say goodbye. He didn't.

Dima had always been Felix's closest friend, and Felix recalled their times together now with a great sadness. As kids, they'd shared dreams of becoming pilots, explorers, and Olympic athletes. When they were nine, Felix had saved him from drowning after Dima had broken his leg on a sharp rock. In those simpler days, Dima had made a blood vow to return the favor one day. In those simpler days, they could forgive and forget so easily.

Felix was sick of this war. It was insatiable. It took and took and never gave anything back. And now it had taken his best friend.

* * *

Katya cursed out loud after she tripped on the uneven sidewalk. She managed to keep her balance and not fall, but she certainly startled both herself and Igor with the profanity. Only with tremendous effort had she been able to make it this far. Her feet felt like lead and each step was torture. She didn't want to leave her beloved Leningrad. She didn't want to leave Felix. She didn't want to go to Moscow. Yet here she was, heading to the train station, suitcase in hand.

That morning, she and Felix had gone to the bureau to get a marriage license. A smiling, happy couple had just been leaving when they arrived. With nobody else in line, Felix and Katya stepped up to the counter to announce their intention. They hadn't gotten far before the clerk informed them they needed two witnesses in order to get married. They were dejected and about to leave when Felix asked the clerk if they had to know the witnesses. The clerk said no, and Felix went outside and persuaded two strangers to take a few minutes out of their day. Next, the clerk reviewed their papers, disappeared into another room for a few minutes, then reappeared and told them the office had run out of forms. They'd have to wait until a new supply came in. Felix was furious and demanded to know why, if that was the case, the clerk hadn't told them in the first place. Why had he made them get witnesses? Why had he checked their papers first? The clerk's ambiguous answers incensed Felix even more, and they'd left the office seething.

Katya felt suspicious about the whole situation, but what could she do? Nothing made sense anymore. She was convinced the entire world had gone mad. They were both heartbroken about not being able to get married but decided as they walked not to let it alter their plans for Katya to evacuate the city.

Igor walked a pace or two ahead of her now, trying his best to impress her by carrying three of their bags, including both heavy ones. He was infatuated with her, and she knew it. Katya normally thought it cute when he tried to act twice his age around her – how he would be so serious and try to come off as brave and knowledgeable. But she was too preoccupied now with her thoughts to pay him any attention.

"I bet Felix couldn't carry all three of these bags," Igor said.

Felix was on duty, but he had a lunch break in fifteen minutes and would be meeting them at the train station to say goodbye.

When she didn't respond, Igor repeated himself a little louder.

"We'll test him later," she said curtly. "He'll be at the station to see us off."

Ahead of them, a long military column moved slowly through an intersection. They shuffled along haphazardly, in no hurry to get where they were going. It was nothing like the boisterous mood most of the troops had been in when they'd initially set off for the front. Felix had told Katya that most of the men you saw moving through the city like this were the remnants of forces that had survived some battle and had been hastily regrouped for redeployment to the latest "hotspot." They were constantly moving troops around trying to plug holes in the tenuous line protecting the city from the Nazi assault.

"Those men aren't in formation," Igor said. "They should be marching in step in close ranks."

A few of the soldiers glanced in Igor and Katya's direction but seemed to look right through them. They neither smiled, nor frowned, nor even talked to one another.

"What do you think is wrong with them?" Igor asked. "They look so sad."

"How should I know?" Katya said. She watched a shirtless soldier walk by, wiping his bandaged forearm across his sweaty forehead. "I don't think fighting a war is exactly fun," she added.

The sun was bright and high overhead, and the scuffing of the soldiers' boots on the pavement reminded her of a funeral procession.

Once they were well clear of the soldiers, Igor turned to her and said, "They should be *happy* to kill Nazis."

Katya shook her head. "Well, so far, the Nazis seem to be doing a better job of killing us, than we of them," she said.

Igor spit over his right shoulder. "If I were on the front," he said, "I'd kill a thousand Nazis."

As they rounded the next corner, a new mass of people blocked their way – this time women, children, and old men standing in a queue. Katya looked for the front of the line to see what they were waiting for, but it snaked all the way around the corner of the next block.

"What are you in line for?" Igor asked an elderly man standing at the end.

"I don't know," he said. "Hopefully something good." A young woman in line four spots ahead overheard, and said, "I heard they're selling sugar."

Katya squeezed by the people in line and Igor followed. She was in a hurry, and after they crossed the next street, she turned left to take a shortcut through the park. Like all the other parks, it was filled with trenches, but at least this one you could still walk through with ease. The leaves on the trees were a jumble of red, gold, and green, and a pair of squirrels chased one another into the empty trenches and then back out again.

"There's a few benches over there in the shade," Igor said. "Do you want to take a break from the sun for a minute?"

Katya shook her head no. She was caught in her thoughts again. She tried to figure out how exactly she had come to be in the situation she was in. She'd told herself numerous times to never get so wrapped up in a man as to think she couldn't live without him. But that was exactly what she found herself thinking now. *How could she possibly live her life without Felix?*

"You must be getting a little tired by now," Igor said. He set the bags down and panted for a few seconds. "Would you like me to stop so you can rest?"

"No, I'm fine," Katya replied and kept walking.

Never in her life had she met anyone quite like Felix, someone who was so comfortable with who he was, who never felt a need to hide anything or pretend he was something he wasn't. Since he didn't seek the approval of others to validate his self worth, he didn't have lofty goals. He wasn't anything like Dima, who wanted to be Party Secretary one day. What Katya appreciated most of all about Felix was how much he enjoyed life, how he was genuinely grateful that he'd been born. That separated Felix from Petya more than anything, she thought. Petya cursed the fact that he'd been born while Felix reveled in being alive.

"Are you sure you're not tired?" Igor persisted, dropping the bags once again. "It's no problem for me to wait a minute if you want to rest."

Katya wanted to get to the station quickly so she could spend as much time with Felix as possible. "No," she said. "I already told you, I'm fine."

She started walking again, but Igor called her back.

"Come here," he said. "You've got to see this." He was leaning over, hands on knees, breathing heavily.

She went back to where he was. "What is it? Is everything okay?"

"Look at that," he said, pointing off to his left at an old tree. Its crimson leaves glimmered in the afternoon sun, and under its thick, knotty branches was a carpet of mushrooms – more than Katya had ever seen under one tree.

"Igor, we don't have time to pick mushrooms now," she said.

"No, it's not that . . .. Those aren't edible anyway."

"Then what?"

"It's a very bad omen," Igor said.

"What is?"

"The babushkas in my village had a saying: 'Many mushrooms – many deaths.' They said it's a warning about the coming winter, that it will be hard."

Katya studied Igor's face, hoping he was joking, but saw that he was not. "There's lots of old sayings," she said. "That doesn't mean there's any truth to them." But her own words didn't provide her with much reassurance. She wasn't superstitious, but she did have a great respect for folk wisdom. She'd always been amazed how some of the old timers from the villages could predict the weather, how well the crops would do that year, or what gender a baby would be. Their predictions had no scientific basis, but more often than not turned out to be true.

But Katya had no time now to dwell on fate. She picked up her suitcase and one of the bags Igor was carrying and started toward the train station again. Igor protested that the bag she took from him was too heavy for her, but when she offered to give it back, he complained that his shoulder was hurting him – an old injury from taming a wild horse, he said – and that he wasn't sure he could continue carrying it.

When they arrived at the train station, they found it overflowing with evacuees. Two young girls pushed bags off the back of a truck to their mother who then swung the bags down to the ground. Mounds of boxes and bags covered the walkways, with anxious mothers and uneasy children standing between and around them. Katya and Igor wove their way through the crowds and eventually found their train's platform.

The train had not yet arrived but would soon. Katya set her bags down and looked around for Felix. Since she didn't know the train platform ahead of time, they couldn't pick a specific spot to meet. Instead, they decided they'd each find the right platform and then meet at the sixth train car from the front.

Katya hoped that Felix would already be there, but it was still early. She was five minutes ahead of the schedule she'd set for herself.

While they waited, Igor paced back and forth behind their bags. There was a scraggly bush with sharp brown leaves growing there, and a sheet of white paper was caught in its branches. Igor picked it out and started reading the text aloud to Katya.

"Beat . . . the . . . Jews." He read haltingly, unsure of each word he pronounced. "Beat . . . the . . . ." He held the leaflet in front of Katya. "What's this word?" he asked.

"Commissars," she answered.

"Beat . . . the . . . Commissars," he continued. "Their mugs beg to be bashed in. Wait for the full moon. Bayonets in the Earth! Surrender!"

Igor, mouth agape, curled his thick furry eyebrows down toward his pug nose. "What does this mean? Are we giving up?"

"No, we're not giving up," Katya said. "The Germans dropped those leaflets from a plane. They're trying to scare us."

Igor wadded the paper up and threw it back in the bush. "I'm not scared," he said, his voice sounding more nasal than usual. "I was just worried about you, that's all."

Katya thought to smile and say that she appreciated it, but she was too anxious about Felix's arrival. The train was now making its way to their platform and would be boarding people in another five minutes. It was a long train and was backing in slowly. The passenger cars were all dark green and nearly every window was open.

"I thought Felix was meeting us here," Igor said.

"Yes, he's supposed to." Katya continued scanning the crowds for him, wondering if he had to work late or if he couldn't find the right platform.

"Is he a Jew?" Igor asked.

"Who? Felix?"

"Yes. My father always told me to stay away from people with names like Iosif or Felix. He said people with those names were always Jews."

"And what did you father tell you about Jews?"

"He told me you should always hate them and should never confuse a Russian with a Jew. He said you could tell a Jew by his big nose and beady eyes. He said Jews were bad people – that they made human sacrifices to the devil and only cared about money."

"Well, you've known Felix for a while. What do you think? Is he a Jew?"

Igor wrinkled his forehead in thought. "I'm not sure," he said. "That's why I asked you. He seems like a Russian . . . and he's always nice to me. He even bought me an Eskimo pie one time." He crossed his arms in front of his chest, then added. "But his nose is kind of big."

"If I told you he was Jewish, would you hate him?"

He shrugged his shoulders. "Does he make human sacrifices to the devil?"

Katya took Igor by the hand and looked him in the eyes. It saddened her that Igor had never known their grandmother and thus none of her wonderful teachings on peace and tolerance. She decided she'd be the one to pass them on to him. He was still young and impressionable, so there was still hope. "Igor, I bet your father was a very wise and knowledgeable man. He probably taught you a lot of things, right?"

He nodded.

"But I think your father might have had a bad experience with someone who happened to be Jewish, and then he probably thought that all Jews were like that. Jews are no different than you or I. We all experience joy, and we all experience sadness. We all make mistakes. We all get mad sometimes, and do or say things we regret. We're all humans."

Igor looked at her intently, then asked, "Why do the Nazis hate the Jews so much?"

"I don't know for sure," she said, "but I think most of them have been taught by Hitler to hate Jews. He wants to use them as a scapegoat – someone to blame all their problems on."

"I hate Hitler," Igor said. "I'd kill him if I could."

People had now started boarding the train. Katya guessed it would take them at least fifteen more minutes to get everybody boarded. They had to check everyone's papers, and then check them again, and then argue for a minute, and check them one last time. Felix definitely should have been there by now.

"Igor, could you go walk around quickly and see if you can find Felix? Don't take too long though."

Igor walked down the platform and disappeared into the crowd. Katya watched a fat, dark gray pigeon walk up to her bags, pick up a small stone with its beak, then drop it and keep walking. There was a large clock behind her and she saw that the train was scheduled to leave in nine minutes.

There was a man on the other side of the platform with his back toward her. He had the same build as Felix and was walking in the opposite direction Igor had gone just a minute ago. She could see curly dark hair sticking out from under his hat. She wrung her hands and took a step toward him. "Felix!" she shouted, but he kept walking. "Felix!" she shouted even louder. He stopped and looked back and she saw a forty-year-old man with sunken cheeks and a thin black mustache.

The intensity of her disappointment startled her. She wondered how it was that Felix had become so integral to her life. She had always thought of love as something that opened one's eyes, but now wondered if love didn't also blind one. There were so many people and things in the world to love. How had she become so wrapped up in loving this one person so much?

The line to get on the train was empty now. Katya looked around and saw that the only people left on the platform were those who had come to say goodbye or those waiting for the next train. A grey bearded man with a brown cap and a nervous smile came up to Katya and asked

The End Of Sorrow

if she needed help with her bags. Katya shook her head no, and the man shuffled down the platform to the next person.

She was on the verge of crying and felt angry that she and all these other people had to leave, angry at the Germans for starting the whole bloody mess in the first place. She imagined that her grandmother never got angry or hated anyone – no matter what they did – but Katya found herself on the edge of hate so often now. All she had to do was open the newspaper or listen to the radio and she'd be confronted with the latest Nazi atrocity and would feel her chest tighten. She used to be so sure that she understood her grandmother's Mennonite teachings, but not anymore. Perhaps she had understood them theoretically, but *living* those teachings was a different matter altogether.

She closed her eyes and saw her grandmother in her little garden with its cucumbers and tomatoes and carrots and dill. There was a particular scene in the garden that Katya had always remembered. It was a beautiful summer day and Katya was picking and eating green grapes from a vine that ran up the side of the house. Her grandmother, in her big pink sun hat, was tending to her precious roses and singing one of her favorite Bible verses over and over, "♪ And I will grant peace in the land, and you shall lie down, and no one shall make you afraid . ♪"

Katya opened her eyes now and thought how strong and full of faith her grandmother had been. That was how Katya wanted to be too.

When Igor came back without Felix, Katya knew what she had to do.

"Igor, help me with the bags, please," she said. "The train's about to leave."

"But Felix isn't here yet," he protested.

"Yes, I know."

They boarded the train and quickly found their seats. Katya sat next to the window and continued to search the crowds for Felix. Igor sat down beside her and awkwardly put his arm around her shoulder. "Don't worry," he said. "I'll take care of you."

When she heard that, she felt an immense sadness settle over her. She wanted *Felix's* arm around her shoulder, and *his* voice telling her not to worry. She wanted to run her fingers through his curly hair, put her lips to his skin, feel his strong hands on the small of her back. The thought that she might never see him again was unbearable. She was ready for the tears to start. She was ready for that familiar feeling of mourning to set in.

She stopped looking out the window and stared at the ceiling instead. When the tears started to come, she felt no relief. What good are they anyway, she thought. They can't change anything.

If only she knew what to do – how to live a life of peace and pacifism

– then things would be all right. If only she didn't constantly question her beliefs. If only she knew how a lamb was to survive when wolves were roaming the world so freely. If only she had her soul mate with her so they could lean on one another.

Suddenly Igor yelled, "It's Felix!" He pointed toward the back of the train. "Look! There he is!"

Katya stuck her head out the window, scanning the platform frantically. She finally saw him running alongside the train, jumping up every few steps and yelling to the passengers on each car, "Katya! Katya!"

She waved her arm at him. "Felix! Down here!" He saw her and started running toward their car. Katya rushed out of the compartment. "You can't get off," Igor yelled after her. "The train's going to leave!"

Katya fled down the aisle and Igor chased after her. When she got to the exit, Felix was already there and she leapt from the stairs into his arms. He squeezed her against himself and swung her around in circles, her feet never touching the ground. "I'm so sorry, Katya," he said, his voice cracking. "I couldn't find you. I just couldn't find you."

Katya felt her breasts tight against his chest and his strong hands around her waist. She wrapped her arms around him, buried her face in the side of his neck, and inhaled deeply the scent of his skin. "I can't do this, Felix," she said, the tears now flowing like a river. He pulled his head back and began showering her cheeks and forehead with kisses. "I can't leave you," she said. "I can't do it."

With a loud rusty groan, the train lurched forward and began inching down the tracks.

"Katya!" Igor yelled, pulling on her arm. "The train's leaving! Come on, let's get on!"

Katya heard Igor, and she heard the train as well. But nothing was going to break their embrace. Felix held her as tightly as ever, and she watched the train pull away, overjoyed that she wasn't on it. Overjoyed that her lover once again held her in his arms.

* * *

Misha was caught in another dream from which he couldn't awaken. He kept trying to yell, but the only sound he could get out sounded like the bleat of a baby goat calling for its mother.

In his dream, he saw a dozen people march single file down a dark hallway. They all looked familiar, but Misha couldn't place a single one of them. It was the same feeling he got after he'd had a few drinks and suddenly thought he knew each person he saw. Everyone would stir some distant memories in him. But the people in his dream were different in one significant way – they were all dead. Misha didn't know how he knew this, but there was no doubt in his mind about it. They all acted very strange, very freakish. They were indifferent to everything and only looked straight ahead at the door of the room they were progressing to. Each had a stoic expression on their face, and they all wore the same dark robes.

Misha felt an irresistible urge to join them but knew he couldn't. He couldn't join them because he wasn't one of them. He was not dead yet.

But if he wasn't dead yet, then why was he there? And who were these people? What were they doing? And why did he feel this urge to join them? The dream wasn't so much frightening as it was confusing.

The dead were oblivious to him, and Misha followed a few steps behind. There were no windows in the hallway and the walls were made of wet, jagged rock. He wondered if they were underground. The door at the end of the hallway looked like something from the last century. It was made of warped, unpainted wood and black iron hinges. It creaked loudly when it opened. The dead disappeared through it, and after a few seconds, Misha snuck in after them. He wanted to catch them somehow, to expose what they were doing. This seemed to be very important.

The room was similar to the hallway, cramped and without windows. Wooden torches jutted out from the cold, stone walls, but the light they provided wasn't nearly enough for the room. From the doorway, Misha watched as the dead gathered into a circle at the front of the room, surrounding a young woman there who was very much alive. They held hands and bowed their heads but said nothing. The only sound came from the crackle of the torches.

Misha looked at the young woman closely, recognizing her as his mother in her twenties – around the time when he was a young boy. She was radiant and had a calm, serene look on her face. Misha wanted to go to her, to be with her and feel that wonderful sense of peace and tranquility that he had only ever felt wrapped tightly in her loving arms.

Now was the time, he thought. Now was the time to yell to let them know they'd been caught and that neither he nor his mother belonged there. But again, all he could manage was a weak "bleawww" sound.

His mother strained to see through the darkness. "Misha," she called out. "Misha, is that you? Where are you? What are you doing? Come home, Misha. Come home."

Misha tried to go to her, but something grabbed his legs and wouldn't let him. He looked down at the floor and saw that it was covered with people, both dying and already dead. There were German soldiers, Russian soldiers, old men, women, and children.

The man holding his legs had thin blonde eyebrows that were barely visible against his pale white skin. He had goggles around his neck, his nose was bleeding, and he had a gunshot wound to the chest. Misha recognized him as the German pilot he'd tortured.

"Let go of me, you bastard," Misha shouted, striking him with the butt of his rifle. When he still couldn't free his legs from the man, he fired several rounds into his chest and head. But still the man held tightly to Misha's legs. Only after Misha fastened his bayonet and plunged it into the man dozens of times did he finally release his grasp.

He looked up to the front of the room for his mother, but she was gone. He was furious. "Damn you," he muttered and prepared to stab the German pilot again. But the bloody corpse at his feet was no longer the German pilot. It was his mother.

Misha was startled back into consciousness. He awoke gasping for air.

He was alone, swaying slightly from side to side, and sitting on a wooden seat that folded out from a wall. He had trouble catching his breath and convincing himself that it had all been a dream.

A rifle leaned against his left leg. He could see houses and trees passing by the window to his right. Yes, he was starting to remember now. He was on a train, and he'd sat down to rest between stations. That's when he must have fallen asleep.

Feeling relieved, Misha tried to put more of the pieces of the puzzle together. He had to do this a lot lately. It seemed a part of him wanted to forget, wanted to deny what was going on all around him. A part of him wanted to pretend that it didn't know who he was and what he'd done in his life. Misha struggled against this part of himself more as an obligation than a desire to truly be rid of it. He would gladly forget, if he could.

He didn't have to think very long before it all came back to him. It was August 30th and he was a guard on a train on the Northern Railroad. He remembered he'd been in Leningrad dropping off Igor. Then, while he was trying to find his mother, they'd demanded to see his papers, and he'd been rounded up with the rest of the deserters, the refugees, and the merely lost. They herded everyone before tribunals where they were either sent to a firing squad, a construction battalion, or reassigned to another infantry unit.

The deserters were mostly sent to the firing squad, and Misha was thrown into that group. He tried explaining to the tribunal how he hadn't actually deserted – how his air base had been annihilated by the Luftwaffe – but they had no interest in his story. At that tribunal, suspects were guilty until proven innocent, and Misha had no evidence to back up any of his claims. Right after that, a high-ranking officer came in and interrupted the proceedings. He stated to the tribunal that he needed twenty-four men to perform duties as guards on the trains evacuating citizens from the city. Misha had heard about the big push to get as many people out of the city as possible, and hoped he would be selected. But then the officer stated he'd take anyone except deserters, who, he added, should be hung from Leningrad's lampposts for all to see what cowards they were.

The tribunal began sorting through men looking for the best candidates. It was a small, overcrowded room, and in the brief chaos of men switching groups, Misha slipped out of his group and joined those being selected.

They counted heads at the end and found twenty-five men, instead of twenty-four. Misha was afraid they'd find him out, but then one of the men coughed and wheezed for a long time, and the officer pulled him out of the group and sent him back to the tribunal.

Misha was proud of his ability to survive but also felt that fate had destined him for something. If the officer had walked in five minutes later, Misha was sure he would've already been marched off to the firing squad.

He went over to the train car door now, opened it, and stood in the doorway for a few minutes. The sun was bright, and the wind blasted him with the scent of smoke and buckwheat. They were passing by a blackened forest that was still smoldering. Bomb craters filled with brown water dotted the landscape, and four smashed train cars lay helplessly on their sides next to the tracks.

Sitting back down, Misha wondered how many more times he could cheat death. He knew that it always won in the end. One of his mother's favorite sayings was, "Everyone you love and everyone you hate, everyone who tells the truth and everyone who tells a lie, will all eventually die."

Misha wanted to live. He wanted to live at any cost. That was what life was about – surviving. You survived any way you could. You lied, stole, and cheated your way, if that was what it took. People who didn't understand that were stupid..

The way to survive against the Nazis was to meet them on the same level. They were animals, and animals had no moral dilemmas or remorse about killing. You had to stoop to that level to beat the Nazis.

The door coming from the next train car opened, and Olga, the woman who collected passengers' tickets and checked their papers, walked in. She held no military rank, but there was no doubt as to who was in charge on this particular train.

Misha jumped to his feet.

She looked at the open door, then back to Misha. "Comrade," she said, "I see you have disobeyed me once again by opening the door." Sunlight shined on her face like a spotlight, and her gold tooth glinted when she spoke.

Misha saw no point in responding. He'd been caught red handed and awaited the usual venom to pour from her lips. Olga was a forty-five year old mother of three grown sons who were in the navy. She was from a small village in the north, had an accent to match, and a thick body that was not unlike the T-26 tanks that defended Leningrad from the Germans. Her face seemed to have a permanent scowl etched into it. With her on the train, Misha often wondered why guards like him were even necessary to keep the order. He had heard many accounts, and even personally witnessed her push, kick, and punch people – men, women, and once even a child – who dared cross her.

She stepped closer to Misha, and he thought he might be the next one to be on the receiving end of her blows. She bared her menacing gold tooth in preparation to either say something or bite him. Misha wasn't sure which.

"You're going to get what's coming to you one day, you little weasel," she said. Her breath smelled like moldy tea. She started to say more, but the train jerked them both forward a step as it began to slow unexpectedly – its brakes squeaking and squealing the long column of cars to a crawl.

"We can't be at Obukhovo yet," Olga said. "Why the hell are we stopping?"

Obukhovo was the first station on Leningrad's outskirts, and Misha could tell from the scenery that they were indeed not there yet. He leaned out the doorway and saw three men on the station platform ahead. They were signaling for the train to halt. "There's an officer and two other soldiers up ahead waving for us to stop," he said. The name of the station was written on white-painted stones nestled among red and white petunias. Misha read it aloud, "Mga."

"Let me see," Olga said, pushing him out of the way.

Mga was a small station about twenty-five miles southeast of Leningrad. It was the last of the numerous sleepy little stations in between Moscow and Leningrad, and they didn't usually stop there.

When the train at last came to a standstill, Olga, Misha, and the eleven other guards on the train jumped down and started walking toward the Red Army officer who signaled impatiently for them to gather around him. Anti-aircraft guns thumped in the distance, and judging from the loudness, Misha guessed they were only a few more miles up the tracks. He walked a few steps behind Olga, gripping his rifle tightly, expecting to see German warplanes any second.

A few of the guards had already gathered around the officer, and he began pointing to a spot in the sky up ahead of the train. Everyone looked in that direction, and Misha quickly saw what he was pointing at. There were at least three dozen paratroopers gliding through the sky and many more who'd already landed on the ground.

Once everyone had assembled, the officer addressed them. "Comrades, I am Major Leshchev. We are in a very dire situation. As you can see, the Germans are attacking. We have very few men here to fight back. What do you have on this train? Any weapons?"

Olga spoke up. "We have nothing of use, comrade. We've been evacuating citizens from the city and were just now returning to get more."

Leshchev shook his head and cursed. "All right then, we'll have to make do with what we have. I need all the men I can get. How many soldiers do you have on this train?"

"Just these men," she said, pointing at Misha and the others. "They're the guards for the train. But they will stay and fight."

Leshchev paused a minute, looking pensively over the men. "Very well," he finally said. "Bring every weapon and cartridge you have. We have to prevent the Germans from taking this station."

"You heard him," Olga yelled. "Get going!"

Misha moved quietly into the shade. He didn't have anything else to get, so he stayed where he was and scratched at the earth with his boots. The recent rain must have just missed this area as the ground was quite dry. When a breeze came, it picked up clouds of dust and rolled them along the ground.

"Comrade Major," Misha overheard Olga say in a low voice. "I wish to stay and fight as well."

Misha saw that Leshchev didn't even raise an eyebrow. "Can you handle a rifle?" he asked.

"Yes, I've had training."

"Very well," he said. Then, turning to one of the men with him, "Lisovsky, go tell the conductor the tracks ahead have been bombed. He'll have to go back to Volkhov."

The man saluted and left for the front of the train. "And one other thing," Leshchev said to Olga, "tell your men to bring all the food, water, and blankets you have on the train." Then, leaning over to her and whispering, just loud enough so that Misha heard, "We've been fighting the Germans all the way from Novgorod. We have no artillery, very few cartridges, and my men are exhausted."

Misha watched Olga hesitate. He wondered if she grasped the full meaning of what Leshchev had told her. Did she comprehend the futility of the situation? That an additional twelve men and one woman weren't going to make a difference in this battle? "I will stay and fight," Olga responded. "And so will my men."

He nodded his head somberly. "Someone told me this is the last railroad in and out of Leningrad. Is that true?"

"Yes," Olga said. "This is the last line."

Leshchev glanced in the direction of Leningrad and sighed. "These are dark days, comrade," he said. "Long, dark days."

Misha watched the remainder of the German paratroopers land on the ground and form up at the far end of the field. He wondered what would become of Leningrad if the Germans took this station. Without this railway, the poor city would be cut off from the rest of Russia, and then the Germans could lay siege and force its inhabitants to surrender or starve.

The train reversed course and began pulling away from the station. The breeze picked up again, and a solitary brown leaf twirled by him. Misha tried to keep track of it as it scurried along the ground – past the hurried footsteps of his fellow guards, past the retreating train, and eventually past the tiny station of Mga that had quite unexpectedly become the key to the battle for Leningrad.

~

ДВА — Part II

We two form a multitude. - Ovid

Глава Пятая — Chapter Five

All that Matters

Dragged,
    by well-fed ignorance
Down,
    into subtle lies
That can't disguise
    this ruse,
    this fuse,
    that goes
Tick-tock, tick-tock, tick . . ..
Meet me down by the railroad
    where the tracks curve west.
Meet me before the realists
    steal the youth from my chest.
Meet me while this righteousness
    still burns on my breath.

Hitler's war plan for the Soviet Union, code named Operation Barbarossa after the Holy Roman Emperor who marched east in 1190, had as a general objective the destruction of the Soviet Union's military capability and control of the country's vast agricultural, oil, and raw-material resources. With a total of three million German troops, Operation Barbarossa was to culminate in an assault on Moscow. German forces were to attack from the north and the west in a giant pincer movement. The capture of Leningrad was critical to Hitler's plan. Only after Leningrad was taken could the forces from the north march on Moscow.

Field Marshal Ritter von Leeb, the 65-year-old commander who had triumphed over the Maginot Line in France, was in charge of the forces from the north. His army, Group Nord, was to have taken Leningrad by July 21 – a mere month from when the invasion of the Soviet Union began.

Now, in early September, von Leeb's forces consisted of about twenty divisions, including Panzer and mechanized corps, and numbered around 500,000 men. The fall of Mga had effectively closed the circle around Leningrad. The only remaining connection with the "Russian mainland" was by air or over Lake Ladoga to the east.

Men, women, and children still living in Leningrad at this time numbered about three million. Though the Soviet forces facing the Germans were nearly equal in numbers, they were anything but equal in terms of artillery, rifles, machine guns, ammunition, and organization. The German forces had every advantage, including two tank divisions to the Soviet's none. In addition, the German Luftwaffe controlled the skies.

After winning the battle for Mga, von Leeb consolidated his forces in preparation for a new offensive against Leningrad on September 9. It was designed to be the final blow that would break the spirit of the Russians and lead to the city's surrender. If the ground assault did not succeed, then Leningrad would be annihilated by air and artillery bombardment just like Warsaw and Rotterdam had been. Von Leeb and the German Supreme Command anticipated a quick victory over Leningrad, so they could then move on to Moscow and perhaps end the war in October – only slightly behind schedule.

* * *

Petya held the envelope a few inches above the whistling teapot. He was a self-taught professional at opening letters and then resealing them so that recipients never suspected. He'd already finished with the first envelope and was now steaming the seal of the second one.

He'd actually stopped reading other people's mail about a year ago because he found their letters (not to mention their lives) so boring. But he was very eager to read the two letters he was opening now. Katya's father,

Grigori, had asked Petya for a favor before he'd left for Moscow. He knew there was a chance he might not return to Leningrad. He told Petya he was worried about the Germans cutting off his return route, but Petya had a feeling that was only part of his fear. Considering how badly the war had been going so far, Petya wondered if Grigori had been picked to be one of the many scapegoats. He knew that when senior Party leaders were called to Moscow these days, it usually wasn't to congratulate them on their achievements. There were two groups for those deemed guilty in the Party's blame game: the lucky ones, who were reassigned to new positions in different, less desirable regions of the country; and the unlucky ones, who were shot after they got off the plane.

Grigori had asked Petya to be on the lookout for a letter with a return address of the Bureau of Archives and Records. It was "of the utmost importance" that Petya intercept the letter if, a.) Grigori was "unable to return from Moscow for any reason," and b.) Katya was still living in Leningrad. When – and if – that letter arrived, Petya was to mail an envelope that Grigori had already sealed and addressed. Under no circumstances was Petya to open the letter from the bureau nor let Katya know of its existence. To ensure compliance, Grigori had reminded Petya that a certain region in the far north was still terribly short of workers for its mining operations. Petya had gotten the hint and vowed his loyalty.

With the precision of a surgeon, Petya pushed his special not-too-sharp but not-too-dull knife under the seal and carefully slid it the length of the envelope. Then he removed the letter from the bureau, postmarked yesterday, September 3rd, and read it.

> *Comrade Grigori Selenii,*
> *As you requested, this is a notification that the specified individuals, Felix Varilensky and Katya Selenaya, visited our office. They arrived in the morning on August 29, 1941 and requested a marriage license. Per your instructions, they were denied.*
>
> *- Stepan Rostovich*
> *Bureau of Archives and Records*

"Petya," Oksana Petrovna's weary voice rang out, "are you making tea?" She was in her room, yelling through the closed door.

Petya tucked the letters and envelopes under his shirt. "Yes," he replied, waiting to see if her door was going to open. "But I just used all the water. I'll put some more on." He was startled that she was home. He'd listened at her door for a minute before starting the process and concluded that she was at her job. She worked at the Mariinsky Opera Theater as a technician on the set. Since the war had started, all the technicians had been reassigned to making artillery guns and tanks out of canvas and plywood. They scattered the props around the city to fool the Germans.

"No, don't bother," she said.

Petya went to his room, closed and locked the door, and read the letter Katya's father had written.

> Dear Nikolai Semyonovich,
>
> I know you are busy fighting the war and I apologize for taking your time. But if you are reading this, then my fears have come true and I have been separated from my daughter, Katya. You know from our many late night talks that she has been seeing a certain Jew originally from Ukraine – Felix Varilensky. It has always been my belief that their misguided courtship would be short-lived, that it was merely a phase she was passing through. I have tried to be patient, waiting for their eventual break up, but I fear the war may have brought them closer together for the time being. I am greatly concerned that she may make a terrible mistake in my absence and so I would like to speed up the process, so to speak, of their going their separate ways. I know you too would be alarmed if your daughter was seeing a Jew. So from one parent to another, I ask for your help in seeing that F. Varilensky is reassigned from his clerical duties back to the front, where we desperately need more men anyway. If you can do me this favor, I will forever be in your debt.
>
> Your friend and comrade,
> - Grigori Selenii

Petya grinned as he put the letter back in the envelope and resealed it. What a pleasant surprise to learn that Felix would be leaving for the front again. He combed his hair straight back, put on a clean shirt, and set out to mail the letter that very afternoon.

He glided down the stairs, whistling a whimsical tune that he'd picked up, quite involuntarily, from his roommate Boris. As he exited the building and felt the sun on his face, he whistled even louder. He saw Katya and Igor in the distance, examining an apartment building that had been struck by a German shell. The side of the building had crumbled, exposing the interiors of several apartments – yellow wallpaper, hanging pictures, toys on the floor.

Petya walked over to them. "Bon jour, mademoiselle," he said to Katya, bowing regally.

"What did he say?" Igor asked.

"He said hello in French," Katya answered. "Hi Petya."

"It's so lovely to see you this afternoon," Petya continued. "You look absolutely ravishing, as usual." He admired the low cut neckline of her dress and the glimpse of the top of her breasts it offered.

"In this outfit," she said, looking down at her faded dress. "You must be kidding."

"Au contraire," he responded. "You wear it very nicely. Those comely flowers on your dress must be terribly jealous though. They simply pale in comparison."

Katya wasn't one to fall easily for compliments. Most of the time she'd laugh them off, but Petya knew he'd succeeded this time. He wondered if she'd been feeling a bit vulnerable and he'd caught her at the right time. In any case, Petya's day was getting better and better.

She was blushing slightly and gave him a sidelong glance. "You're a sly one, Petya Soyonovich," she said, grinning.

"Why are you in such a good mood?" Igor asked Petya.

"Well, my little lummox," Petya said, "war makes one cogitate on the meaning of life, and appreciate it more. I'm just grateful that I'm alive, that you and Katya are alive, and the sun is shining."

"That's a good point. I've done nothing but worry lately," Katya said. "Thanks for the reminder."

"Happy to return the favor," Petya said.

He couldn't stop looking at her. She was like an exquisite work of art in the Hermitage. No matter how long he looked, he never got tired or bored. He was transfixed by her beauty.

"What's a lummox?" Igor asked.

Petya ignored his question. He was studying Katya's childlike ears, those delicious pink lips, and the thin brown eyebrows that gracefully arched over her chestnut-brown eyes. It was such a shame that social rules dictated that he not stare at her for a prolonged period of time. That he had to look away seemed so unfair.

"Did you hear Shostakovich on the radio on Monday?" Katya asked.

"Yes," Petya said, "he's quite the worker-bee – completing new scores, serving as a fireman during air-raids . . . ."

"Wasn't he just brilliant?" Katya said. "One part in particular nearly made me cry. He said, 'Remember that our art is threatened with great danger. We will defend our music. We will work with honesty and self-sacrifice that no one may destroy it.' I just loved that."

Petya didn't want to talk about how great Shostakovich was. It was yet another painful reminder of his days spent in the orphanage. There had been another kid there, Alexander, who was just as smart as Petya. The two of them were similar in many ways and became friends. But the one big difference between them was that everyone loved and praised Alexander, while Petya was constantly picked on by the other kids and criticized by the adults.

Petya changed the subject. "Were you able to read any of my novel yet?" he asked Katya.

"Oh yes! I almost forgot. I was going to tell you how incredible it is. I finished it this morning. It's so unlike any of the other stuff you've given me. I'm amazed at your diversity. I think this one is going to make you famous for sure."

Katya's last sentence was like balm for his jealous heart. If only others could know how great he was, then life would be worth living. "I'll take you on my publicity tours to Paris and America one day," he said and laughed.

"I'm going to hold you to that, you know," Katya said and pinched him playfully.

Petya felt so happy just to be near her. She was so enticing. "Well, I'm pleased you like it," he said.

"Just one thing though that was rather strange," Katya said. "The chapters were really short."

Petya had been afraid of disappointing her that he actually didn't have three chapters done yet, so he'd divided up the chapter and a half he had into three. "Yes, I'm trying a different approach," he said.

"I see." She looked thoughtfully from Petya to Igor. "Oh, before I forget, I wanted to ask if you'd be willing to have Igor stay with you on the night of the eighth – that's this coming Monday. Felix is coming over that night."

"Certainly, certainly. It would be my pleasure to have Igor's company again," he said. "Perhaps we'll tell some more ghost stories," he added, winking at Igor.

"Thank you, Petya. I really appreciate all the time you spend with Igor. It's important for him to be with other men – especially someone as educated as yourself."

"Perhaps I'll teach him a few words of French," Petya said. "Parle vous Francais, Igor?"

"I don't need to learn no stupid French," Igor huffed.

Petya laughed, then noticed that Katya was looking at the two envelopes in his hand. He shifted them to his other hand and made sure the blank side of the envelopes was facing her. He tried to do it as naturally as possible – as if he hadn't noticed her looking at them.

"What are those letters?" she asked.

"Oh, nothing special," he said, "just a couple of letters that I need to mail."

Katya continued looking at the envelopes. "You know," she said, "the handwriting on that one envelope looked just like my father's."

"Oh really?" Petya said, holding up the envelope so he, but not Katya, could see the address. "No, that one's from Oksana. She asked me to mail it for her. Actually I better get going . . . .. Need to mail these before the Germans take over the city." He laughed again and started to step away. "We'll talk later," he said, doing his best to move his large frame quickly without limping too much. "Bye, Katya," he shouted over his shoulder. "Bye, Igor," he said without looking back.

* * *

Katya sat at the table alternately taking tiny sips of her tea and trying to smooth some of the million wrinkles in the white tablecloth. Felix sat across from her, eating his food and staring out the window.

"How are the potatoes?" Katya asked. "I fried them with lots of garlic just the way you like them."

"Good. They're very good," he said, forcing a smile and glancing at her.

Katya took another sip of her tea. "The weather's been so nice. It hardly feels like autumn. I guess summer is making up for its late start."

Felix made no reply. He continued looking out the window, though at what, Katya had no idea. It was 6:40 p.m.. She saw the sun still floating high in the western sky and was comforted by the fact that it wouldn't be setting for nearly another two hours.

Katya had been trying to make her tea last as long as possible, but she now finished the last sip. She pressed even harder on a patch of wrinkles in the tablecloth to try to smooth them, but it made no difference. "Would you like more potatoes?" she asked. "It's no problem for me to make more."

At first, Felix looked at her like he didn't understand the question, but then he shook his head no.

"Well how about some tea then?" she asked. "Would you like me to make you some tea?" She stood up, wringing her hands, anxiously awaiting his answer.

"No, thank you. I don't want any tea," he said.

She picked up her empty teacup and tapped her fingernails against it. The silence was maddening. The only sounds she could hear were Felix chewing his food and his fork clinking against the plate. She sat down again and joined Felix in staring out the window. Then she got up and put a kettle on and lit the stove anyway.

"Why don't you just not go?" she finally said.

"If I don't go . . .," he said, putting his fork down and watching Katya drum the side of her teacup. "If I don't go, they'll shoot me."

"But your clerical duties are very important to the war effort," Katya said. "You told me your superiors think very highly of you and your work."

"They don't want to see me go. The decision is out of their hands."

Katya sat down, reached over the table and put her hand on top of his. "I'll ask my father to pull some strings and see if you can stay in your current position."

"You haven't heard from your father since he left. You don't know where he is and you have no way of getting in touch with him. And besides, I don't think he'd lift a finger to help me," Felix said frankly.

"That's not true," she said defensively. "Someone left that note a few days ago saying my father wanted to let me know he was okay and still in Moscow. I think it's just a matter of time before he comes back."

"Time," Felix said, "is something we don't have."

"Oh, don't say that! I can't stand it when you talk like that – like it's the *end*."

"Katya, we need to face reality. There's no use hiding from it. We're going to be separated for a while." He brushed the back of his fingers against her right cheek. "But, my love, know this: I *will* be back for you. We will be together again, and we'll be married one day."

Katya frowned thinking about their failure to get married. They'd finally found time two days ago to go down to the Bureau of Records again. Katya had brought two of her friends from the hospital to serve as witnesses, and they were cautiously optimistic they'd be able to get a marriage license this time. But when they got to the building, they found it in ruins – a pile of rubble with deep craters all around it.

Felix's efforts since then to find out if the office had been relocated were all met with annoyed responses. "Don't you know there's a war on?" they would say, or "The Nazis are threatening to take the city any minute and you're concerned about getting a marriage license?" The reprimands hadn't deterred him, but neither had he been successful.

He squeezed Katya's hand now and then finished his last bite of fried potatoes.

"Well if you're going to the front, then so am I," Katya said. "The hospital director is always saying how they're short of nurses there."

"I'd prefer you don't do that," Felix said, fixing his eyes on her. "I've heard that nurses on the front suffer higher casualties than the men fighting." He leaned toward her and kissed her on the forehead. "Katya, just stay here please. I'll be able to get leave to come and visit once in a while. And we'll write."

Katya was seething about the unfairness of it all. She hated the Germans for laying siege to her city and she hated the Soviets for taking Felix from her. She thought of the Bible verse her grandmother always used to say, "Love your enemies, do good to those who hate you, bless those who curse you, pray for those who abuse you." How did that make any sense? How could she possibly love those she hated?

"Yes?" Felix asked. "You'll stay?"

She stood up, brushed crumbs off her dress, and nodded yes. She'd stay. It was the least worse out of all the wretched options she had. "Let's not talk about it anymore tonight though," she said. "We're together right now. That's all that matters."

Felix stood up and leaned forward into her arms, and she suddenly understood how difficult this was for him too. They held one another for a while, then headed to the balcony.

Katya leaned against the railing, and Felix put his arms around her, resting his head on her shoulder. Her apartment was on the third floor, and the sun was hidden behind the buildings surrounding her balcony. There was a nice view of the wide avenue in both directions, and Katya liked to spend hours just watching the people and cars go up and down the street.

The street was quiet and empty now, as was the case everywhere in the city these days. The usual traffic had been replaced by soldiers and policemen and barricades. A thick wall of sandbags erected by citizens of her block stood at the far end of the street – a crude reminder that there was nothing to fall back on, nowhere to retreat to.

"Petya told me this morning the Germans have been dropping flyers giving an ultimatum to the city to surrender by September 9th," Katya began.

"Tomorrow?"

"Yes, they . . ."

She was interrupted by wailing air raid sirens.

They both looked to the sky but saw nothing out of the ordinary, just the usual deep blue sky of autumn with an occasional pale, borderless cloud.

"Should we go down to the shelter?" Katya asked.

"Let's wait a few minutes," Felix said. "It might be a false alarm."

Katya thought she saw a shiny object in the sky, but then it disappeared. A few minutes later they heard anti-aircraft guns firing and then tremendous explosions. Massive clouds of dust erupted into the distant sky. The explosions were far away but seemed to get closer and louder with each passing second.

In the street below was a woman hunched rigidly over her cane shuffling from one building to the next asking to be let in before the bombs came. Felix and Katya both recognized her; *everyone* in this neighborhood knew her. She was Evgenia Pitskova, once a feared informant for the secret police, personally responsible for sending twenty-three people from this block to gulags, torture chambers, or early graves through her insinuations and, sometimes, outright lies. She was bitter and old and despised by everyone in the neighborhood. Since she had fallen from favor with both the secret police and the Party, people now hated her openly, unafraid of her threats of reprisals.

"Hurry!" Katya yelled to her. "They're coming this way. You have to get off the street."

"Don't you tell me what to do!" she hollered back, shaking her cane at Katya.

Across the street two teen-aged boys and their mother were hurrying into their apartment building. Evgenia tried to squeeze in with them only to be kicked out the door and pushed to the ground by the boys. She fell hard and didn't get back up. "You won't get away with this!" she shouted. "All you kikes won't get away with this!"

The thunderous explosions and massive clouds of dust and debris were like an angry tidal wave forcing its way further and further inland. Katya watched it moving toward them at ever increasing rates of speed.

"I'm going to go get her," Felix said. "Meet me in the basement."

"No, it's too late," Katya said, grabbing him by the arm. "The bombs are already falling."

"We can't just leave her out there to die," Felix said, tearing himself away and hurrying out of the apartment.

Katya ran to the kitchen and shut off the stove, grabbed her diary from her room, and fled to the stairwell. Before she reached the next floor down, she ran back to the apartment to close the curtains. If the explosions shattered the windows, she didn't want tiny shards of glass all over the floor.

As she pulled the first curtain closed, she saw Felix emerge from the building into the street below. As she pulled the second curtain closed, she felt the building tremble and saw the end of her street disappear in a thick fog of grey that gradually swallowed the old woman lying in the street and the brave young man running to save her.

Katya was frantic. She ran out of the apartment, down the two flights of stairs, and opened the door to the outside. The dust was so thick she couldn't see the other side of the street. She called out Felix's name. Another explosion shook the earth, and she stumbled a bit as she made her way toward the street.

She heard Evgenia's voice, though she couldn't see her. "What are you doing? Put me down! You'll pay for this." And then Felix appeared out of the dust. He was carrying Evgenia in his arms, and she was struggling against him. Relieved, Katya held the door open. They went down to the basement, Evgenia uttering threats and curses all the while.

The shelter was dimly lit and cramped, the air cool and smelling of tobacco smoke. A small baby near the entrance let out a high-pitched scream. Katya winced and her ears rang for a few seconds afterwards.

"Make some room please," Felix said and set Evgenia down on one of the long benches that lined the walls. Evgenia cursed Felix a few more times, then demanded he go back out and get her cane.

"Why did you bring her here?" Katya's neighbor Oksana Petrovna said roughly, spraying spittle all over Katya's arm.

"You should have left her where you found her," another woman said. "She deserves to suffer."

The air in the shelter was tense as people jostled for space, and the woman's comments only made it worse. Children outnumbered adults two to one. Babies and toddlers screamed and cried as they clung to their mothers. Anti-aircraft guns pounded relentlessly, and the ground continued to tremble with each explosion outside. It was the first time Katya had been in the shelter, and she thought it little safer than her apartment. She looked around for a place she and Felix could sit, but all the seats were taken. Evgenia quieted down and didn't appear to be greatly injured. She hummed to herself now and rocked slowly back and forth.

"Hello, Katya," a voice said from the darkness.

She turned and saw Petya and Igor sitting in the corner. Igor was hugging his knees to his chest with his eyes tightly closed. Petya, looking calm and relaxed, was smoking a cigarette.

"This is quite the revelry, isn't it?" Petya said.

"Oh, hi Petya," Katya said. "I'm glad to see you two are all right."

"You and Felix certainly took your time getting down here," Petya said, blowing smoke over his left shoulder above Igor's head. "You must have been busy, huh?"

"Petya!" Oksana yelled. "I'm warning you for the last time. You better put that damn cigarette out!"

Petya took one last long drag and snubbed out the cigarette on the wall. Then he tucked the butt in the crease of his rolled-up left pant leg. "Hey Felix," he said. "How's the clerical work for the army going?" He smiled smugly, dropping his head forward and revealing his double chin. "That is what you do, isn't it?"

"I've been reassigned," Felix said. "I'll be going back to the front tomorrow."

"No, you don't say," Petya said. "What a shame."

A large explosion rattled the entire building, shaking dust from the ceiling of the shelter.

"This is hell!" Oksana shouted. "Damn those Germans! I swear if I ever get a chance to pay them back, I'll make damn sure they suffer twice as much as we are now."

Katya saw many of the women cross themselves and recite prayers, even the ones she knew to be members of the Communist Party. It didn't surprise her that in such situations Party ideology and antireligious propaganda paled in comparison to the comfort of an omnipotent God and eternal life in heaven. She felt pleased to see their gestures and felt closer to them.

"They kept telling us Leningrad was impregnable," a woman mourned.

"They were all lies," Oksana responded. "They told us our anti-aircraft defenses were a giant wall. They said our borders were secure, that the Red Army was unbeatable. Then they said the Nazi soldiers would revolt against their commanders. Lies, lies, lies!"

The End Of Sorrow

Katya waited for someone to argue or reproach her, but nobody did.

It seemed like an eternity before the All Clear sounded and everyone left the shelter. Felix and Katya went out into the street to see how bad the damage was.

The word 'shalom' kept going through Katya's mind. It was a Hebrew word that her grandmother said was how one should one live one's life: in a good relationship to God, to yourself and your body, with your neighbors and other people, and with the earth as a whole. To live a life in shalom meant to be in balance and relate to the world around you with a peaceful spirit.

Katya so desperately wanted to live her life in shalom, but looking at the wreckage the German bombers had inflicted on her block, she felt nothing but rage. One apartment building near the end of the block had been obliterated. Usually there would be a wall or two left standing, something to remind you that people once lived there, people once ate and slept and argued and made love there. But there was nothing. Just a pile of bricks.

* * *

Felix lit a small candle and poured vodka into two yellow teacups. The cup with a chip in it was Katya's favorite, and he reserved it for her. The insides of both cups were stained brown from many years of holding scalding black tea.

It was nearly 10:30 p.m., and he went over to Katya's bedroom window to look outside. Hers was the only apartment on the floor whose windows hadn't been shattered by the earlier bombing, and that was an extremely lucky break. There was no glass available to replace broken windows and the other apartments would have to have plywood installed.

All the windows in the building had been taped for some time to try to prevent them from shattering. Felix found it curious that Katya's windows had been the only ones with tape in the form of a cross, rather than the usual, safely secular, X.

Every once in a while, Felix could see a vague blue light on one of the streets below signifying a moving military vehicle. In the apartment buildings across the street, everything was dark. It seemed the city was deserted, but Felix knew better. There were people behind those dark walls – people who were tired and scared and filled with fear about what tomorrow would bring. Those same people were also brave and resilient and intensely protective of their beloved city. He knew they would rather see it wiped from the face of the earth than let Nazis occupy it.

Felix reflected on how strange it was to feel so calm and serene. Not long ago, a quiet like this might have driven him into a bout of melancholy. Now, he found it comforting. There was no where to go, nothing to do.

He didn't have to be in a hurry. He could just enjoy what was alive in him here and now. And what was alive in him was a feeling of peace. He didn't have to be anywhere other than where he was or be anybody other than who he was.

He took a sip of the vodka and savored the burn as it coated the inside of his throat, then took a deep breath to extend the feeling. And then he let it go. The bathroom door opened and closed, and he knew Katya would be back in a moment. He heard her laughing at something and smiled to himself. He was quite fond of the way she laughed so suddenly and unexpectedly at little things, the way a child does. When she did that, it brought out the kid in him as well. That's what he appreciated about her – her wonderful ability to take them both back to the basic goodness of childhood, to feel the joy that is always there inside, but so often in adulthood imprisoned by anger, jealousy, and fear. He never imagined loving someone so much. Nor had he ever thought it possible to be so afraid of losing someone.

Katya returned with a mischievous grin on her face. She was wearing his favorite dress, the yellow one with the purple flowers. Felix liked how nicely it conformed to the seductive curves of her body. She opened her hand to Felix, revealing two small dark chocolates. "My father was hiding these in the tea jar for a month. I think he must have forgotten about them," she said. She started to say something else, but the air raid sirens interrupted her. Felix looked outside and saw the sky crisscrossed by searchlights.

"Should we go back down to the . . ."

Felix didn't let Katya finish her sentence. He wrapped his arms around her and pressed his lips to hers. He kissed her for a long time, running his hands gently from her hips up past her waist, then back down again. When he was finished, he held her close and whispered in her ear, "I love you, Katerina Selenaya."

Her big brown eyes shined and then *she* kissed Felix for a long time. When she stopped, she jumped on him and wrapped her legs around his waist, laughing contagiously.

"And do you love me?" Felix asked half-jokingly. He frowned and did his best to look like a sad little puppy.

"Comrade, you should be ashamed of yourself," Katya said, doing her best imitation of a pretentious Dima. "That's sentimentality masquerading as logic."

Felix laughed. "You know, somehow I'm not mad at him," he said. "Despite what happened and what he said at lunch that day. It's strange. I think he's wrong and even though my head can't make any sense of what he says, I think in my heart I understand what he's after."

"My grandmother always said that's the most important place to have an understanding of anything," Katya said. "To have an understanding in your head means nothing. It won't get you any closer to God – no matter how much stuff you cram in there."

Felix kissed the underside of her wrist. "Seems like you've got everything figured out," he said. They could hear explosions now, but they were muted and distant.

"Oh definitely," she answered, "I know everything. Go ahead, ask me anything."

She had a playful smirk on her face and Felix felt so incredibly fond of her and her ability to be light and fun.

"What's the square root of 143?" he said.

"Oh that's too easy," she said. "You sure you don't want to know something a little harder, like, 'What's the meaning of life?'"

"Who cares about the meaning of life when we have chocolate and vodka," he said.

He turned her hand over and kissed her fingers. "Promise me you won't change," he said. "Promise me you'll stay forever young and beautiful and happy. That's all I want."

Katya laughed. "That's your problem, you want too much. You need to want what you have."

"I do want what I have. I *have* you," Felix said, pulling her closer to him, "and I *want you*." He kissed her softly below the ear, and she bent her head to the side so he could kiss more of her neck. She imitated the sound of a cat purring, and he whispered "nice kitty" in her ear.

"I remember," Katya said, "when we first met you said you weren't sure you believed in love."

"Yes," he said, "but I was a boy then. Now I'm a man."

Katya pinched him playfully. "Don't be in such a hurry to grow up."

"Ok, I won't grow up," he said, caressing her shoulders. "Just for you, I'll defy the laws of science."

She laughed, and Felix gave her the yellow tea cup with vodka. "Let's stay kids forever," she said, grinning from ear to ear. "How about it? The first one to grow up has to eat a raw worm."

Felix grasped her hand and shook it. "Deal," he said. Then he fed the chocolate to her and she chased it with a drink of vodka.

The light from the candle cast shadows against the playful designs on the yellow wallpaper, and through the thin walls they could hear Guzman's piano. Shostakovich must be over there, and they too must have decided not to go down to the shelter.

Shostakovich was playing something new. Perhaps he was writing another of his popular marches. Or perhaps it was part of the new seventh symphony he was working on. Whatever it was, it was strange. Felix couldn't decide if it was a melancholy concession or profound righteousness. It was hypnotic in its sudden key changes, its mounting tension, and unexpected pauses. It was uplifting and sorrowful all at the same time. The distant explosions and anti-aircraft fire provided a kind of perverse percussion to the piece.

Felix sat down on the edge of the bed, pulling Katya onto his lap. He brushed his lips across the tiny hairs on the back of her neck and wished he could stay in this moment forever. Let the candle flicker but keep burning. Let the piano pause but keep playing. Let time come to a stop right now, and he would be eternally happy.

The lovers kissed and embraced and trembled with each touch. Outside, air raid sirens echoed endlessly and German planes dropped payloads of death and destruction on a besieged city – a city with people who refused to give up. A city with some who even refused to stop loving.

* * *

Felix awoke early, before the sun had risen. Katya's arm was draped across his chest, and he gently lifted it and placed it by her side. He dressed in the dark, careful not to wake her.

Before he left, he watched her for a while as she slept: curled up on her side, right hand under her head, bangs hanging over her face, chest rhythmically rising and falling. He preferred to remember her this way, rather than wake her and confuse things with a bunch of useless words. He kissed her softly on the forehead, then slipped out the door and down the hallway.

He climbed the stairs to the roof where he and Katya had spent many a cool spring and summer morning watching the sun rise. The city was shrouded in darkness now, but Felix could still see a great deal because of his exceptional nighttime vision, and also because of the light from a great fire in the distance. The air was chilly. He could see his breath when he exhaled. There was a faint scent of caramelized sugar in the air that puzzled him. He stared at the bright orange fire, wondering what the Germans could have bombed that would burn for so long.

For the first time in his life, he craved a cigarette, but he let the sensation pass through as quickly as it had come. In the river of thoughts that flowed through one's mind, Felix had learned it best not to pull them to shore but to let them just keep flowing. He left the rooftop and went out into the street. The light was low and crept surreptitiously around the buildings and dark figures walking to and fro. Shadows were indistinguishable from one another, all blending together to create an impossibly inky collage. He pulled his collar up and walked down the sidewalk. People and buildings appeared and disappeared like ghosts – images of a time and place he'd seen many times before but might never again.

When he reached the Neva, the sun started peeking over the horizon. The waters of the familiar river were calm. On the other side he could see the golden spire of the Admiralty glittering in the early light of dawn. He

THE END OF SORROW

wondered if Lenin ever appreciated what a beautiful city it was. Or had he been so caught up in his politics that all he ever saw were "repressed masses" and "Bourgeois excess." Felix studied the far shore of Vasilevski Island. The buildings there were black and murky and it looked more like a giant castle of a foreign kingdom than another sector of Leningrad.

Blue-gray clouds hovered just above the rooftops and over the river. The sky was vast and without edges, extending forever in every direction. Leningrad was endless, and that was what Felix loved most about the city. He felt boundless and free walking along the wide avenues, catching the scent of the sea, watching the ripples of the Neva make their way from one distant side to the other. The sweeping vistas reminded him of the countryside in Ukraine, only he wasn't in the country but in the middle of a large cosmopolitan city. It was the best of both worlds.

He kept walking, letting his heart guide him, passing the grandiose Winter Palace, the Hermitage museum, and the eloquent Palace bridge until he arrived at the statue of Peter the Great on his rearing stallion. It was Peter who had carved this great city out of the woods and stone and swamp. It was he who had built the imposing Peter and Paul Fortress and the massive Kronstadt naval base. It was Peter's inspiration for a lavish capital second to none that had lived on through all the years as the city grew and matured. Saint Petersburg, as it was originally called, was his window on the West, his showcase of the mighty Russian Empire. It was regal, elaborate, stately, and even in its current crisis, Felix still believed in it. He believed in its music, its ideas, its arts, and its vision. It wasn't just the city's inhabitants the Germans were up against. It was the city itself, and it had a soul of its own.

He looked in disgust at the piles of sandbags surrounding Peter the Great's statue. He wanted to tear them off and let the "bronze horseman" ride again, to have him point the way and lead his countrymen out of the hopelessness and siege they found themselves in. They needed Peter's will of iron more than anything. To make it through this crisis, they'd have to believe in themselves unconditionally. They'd have to withstand great hardship, and only stubborn souls and firm convictions would enable them to do that. Where the spirit led, the body would follow.

Felix turned back toward Nevsky Prospekt, his beloved Kazansky Cathedral calling him. He doubted it had changed like the rest of the city. It was much too proud to compromise itself, no matter the circumstances. He saw the cathedral from afar, looking as dignified as ever. When he reached it, he walked under its immense left wing and strolled among the giant stone columns, gently touching each one as he passed by it. Kutuzov, the great field marshal who was so instrumental in the Russian victory against Napoleon, was buried on these hallowed grounds. Who would be the Kutuzov of this war, Felix wondered.

He came to the forlorn statue of Saint Andrew the Apostle and thought back to the last time he'd visited it – that fateful day, June 22nd, when the Germans had begun their invasion and irrevocably interrupted his life. Things could never be the same again, and it was time he accepted that. He pulled himself away from the cathedral and took a deep breath. He was through resisting the way things were. He had been preparing himself, mentally and physically, for the rigors of battle. He was ready.

It was time to report to the front.

Streetcar No 9 lumbered down the tracks, its front-mounted machine gun sleeping soundly, nose pointed lazily over the passing buildings. The motorman looked suspiciously at Felix and the two other men waiting to board. At first Felix thought he was going to drive right by them, but he stopped abruptly and the three of them got on. The car was nearly full, even at this early hour, mostly with soldiers, but a few civilians as well. Two officers sat in the back, eyeing everything that went on and whispering back and forth to one another.

The red trolley moved slowly down the wide expanse of Stachek Prospekt. The street was littered with cars, some simply parked along the side, some in pieces and burned out, and some still burning. Felix saw a charred corpse laying in the street, not far from an anti-tank gun.

The entire city had been transformed since the early days of the war. Sandbags lined the ground floor windows of many buildings. Windows on upper floors were boarded over or taped with large X's. Everywhere one looked were firing points and anti-aircraft guns. Huge silver balloons nested on the ground, ready to go up each night to stave off low-flying German planes.

Manholes and sewer openings had "extermination" points for firing at German tanks should they break through. Corner buildings had reinforced concrete "pillboxes" – designed to withstand the floors above them collapsing so soldiers could keep firing. Huge steel anti-tank "hedgehogs" and sandbag barricades with barbed wire blocked many streets from motorized entry. In the distance, Felix could hear the warships of the Baltic Fleet firing their tremendous guns endlessly into the German lines.

He moved down the aisle to the back of the streetcar, pleased that his injured leg felt strong and healthy once again. A 60 ton KV tank drove along the street beside them. Felix listened in as the officers near him talked about the fierce bombing of the night before. "You've no doubt heard about the Badayev warehouses?" one said to the other.

"I heard there were some enormous fires in that sector. They bombed Badayev?"

"Yes, with incendiary bombs."

"And the food reserves? The flour, sugar, canned meat . . ."

"It's still burning now. They haven't been able to put it out."

"You mean it's *all* gone?"

The other officer nodded his head gravely.

At first, Felix felt furious. How could the authorities be so negligent as to put all the food for the city in one place? It was either treason or stupidity. Everyone in Leningrad knew about the Badayev food warehouses. With all the German spies in the city, no doubt the pilots knew exactly where to drop their bombs.

Felix thought of Katya and was filled with regret that he hadn't forced her to get on that train out of Leningrad. He found out later it had been the last one to leave the city. Now he reflected on the consequences. He knew she had a good supply of food, but that was before Igor started living with her. Who knew how long it would last now.

He was angry with himself. Why hadn't he been able to let go of her? Why did he have to hold on so tightly? He cursed and stamped his foot on the floor. The officers paused their conversation and looked at him. He ignored their curious stares and went on thinking.

What could he do about it now? There was no point in torturing himself about the decisions he'd made in the past. He couldn't waste his time on that. He had to put his energy into surviving. That was the main thing now, to stay alive. If he could stay alive, then he and Katya could still be together in the future. He clung to the thought that he and Katya *would* be together again and be able to live their lives in peace.

The Kirov works were up ahead. That meant he'd be at the front soon.

He'd been reassigned to the 2nd Regiment of the 1st Volunteers Division – or what was left of it. The 1st Volunteers had lost about two-thirds of their strength and had very little of the arms and equipment they'd started out with. Felix knew they were in rough shape.

He wasn't thrilled about the prospect of rejoining his former comrades and was particularly anxious he might be put in a platoon under Dima's command. Though Dima was probably one of the most competent commanders out there and would be more efficient than others in battling the Germans, that didn't necessarily mean his men would be safer. Dima, more than anyone Felix knew, was the most likely to sacrifice his life (and others') for a cause.

There was a steady stream of soldiers and workers walking toward the Kirov works. It was the largest engineering sector in all of Russia, with hundreds of shops and thousands of laborers. On the other side of it was the enemy – two and a half miles away. The Germans were a mere ten miles from Leningrad's Palace Square.

A steady stream also moved in the other direction from the Kirov works – women and children carrying bedding, clothes, bags, and milk tins. They were evacuating to safer parts of the city, the Petrograd and Vasilevski Island districts.

When the trolley reached the Kotlyarov streetcar barns, the motorman announced to everyone onboard, "Last stop. Everyone off. This is the front." Felix jumped down with the others and followed them. He wasn't sure where to go. The officer who'd given him his orders didn't know where the 2nd Regiment was. The 1st Volunteers had been in Pushkin a week ago. His best guess was they'd fallen back to the front just beyond the Kirov works. That was all the information Felix had.

As he walked toward the front, he asked several people along the way if they knew where the 1st Volunteers were. Most didn't answer. The ones who did simply shook their heads.

He walked for half an hour, passing by military trucks, barricades, and tank traps. Then he took a break to wipe the sweat from his face and adjust his pack, and continued walking for another half hour. The sounds of the front grew nearer. He passed by dozens of dugouts and machine gun nests. A pair of stretcher bearers went by carrying the body of a badly wounded soldier. The man was moaning and thrashing his head from side to side. Lying next to him on the stretcher was his right arm – dirty and bloody, no longer attached to his shoulder. Felix asked the stretcher bearers where the trenches were. One of them motioned over his right shoulder. "Beyond that cemetery," he said.

High in the sky there was a dogfight between a Soviet and German fighter plane. Felix watched them for a minute while he took a drink of water from his canteen. The Soviet plane was being chased and made a sharp turn to the left and dove toward the ground in an attempt to escape. At the last second, it pulled up and barely avoided crashing into the earth. It was a desperate attempt, Felix thought, but that was what it would take to defeat the Germans.

He'd found the 2nd Regiment of the Volunteers and a young, fresh-faced officer assigned him to the 1st Platoon. Felix asked who commanded the platoon, but the officer didn't seem to know and had neither the time nor inclination to find out. After spending the rest of the morning looking for the 1st Platoon, Felix finally found it. His next task was to find its commanding officer and report for duty. He'd checked several trenches already with no luck and was now making his way to the next one.

The fighting was heavy in this area. There was a constant din of machine gun fire and exploding mortars, and occasional screams of agony. Houses stood in ruin, trees burned, the stench of rotting flesh filled the air. Despite all the sounds of fighting, Felix couldn't see the enemy. They were somewhere up ahead – behind houses, or camouflage, or in trenches of their own. Every now and then, he would see a man in green run from one spot to another, crouching all the while and taking a few shots at the Russian lines as he did so.

Felix jumped into the trench he'd been directed to. He thought it would be empty since he hadn't seen anyone firing back at the Germans. But there were twelve men in there, all sitting with their backs to the incoming fire. Each man had a rifle, but it was either lying harmlessly at their feet or resting against the wall. On Felix's right, at the far end of the trench, was a dead Soviet soldier. Dark red blood covered his right side from the neck down, and his face was sunk into the orange-colored earth. A dozen tiny black ants congregated near the dried blood on the side of his neck.

Only a couple of the men turned their heads to look at the stranger who'd just dropped into their trench. The rest of them continued staring at the dirt wall in front of them. Having just arrived at the front, Felix was alert and on edge and found their detachment incomprehensible.

None of the men had showered or shaved in at least a week and a half – the strong body odor that hung in the trench and the thick stubble on their cheeks testified to that. As Felix watched their behavior, he wondered if any of them had even *slept* in a week and a half.

A mortar round exploded in front of the trench and dirt fell like rain on top of them. Felix was startled by the deafening sound of the blast and pulled his helmet down as low as it would go. The other men hadn't even flinched. Their reactions were identical to the man who was already dead.

Felix reached into his pocket and pulled out the pack of cigarettes he'd brought. He didn't smoke himself, but figured they would make a nice gift for his new comrades. He'd heard that cigarettes were sometimes hard to come by on the front. After he opened the pack, he offered one to the man nearest him, then told him to pass it down the line. Every man took at least one, looked down the trench at Felix, and nodded appreciatively. When the nearly empty pack made it back toward Felix, he waved it off.

The sun was hot. Felix wiped some sweat from his forehead, then opened his canteen and took a drink. When he finished, he noticed several of the men staring at him, an unspoken request in their eyes. Guessing they had all run out of water, Felix then passed his canteen down the line. Again, all the men took some and nodded to him appreciatively. One of the men even summoned up the strength to speak. "Thank you, comrade," he said.

Someone suddenly jumped into the trench, startling Felix. He turned his head to the new person next to him and was flabbergasted to see Dima looking back at him. "Ahh, Varilensky," Dima said, "so nice of you to finally join us."

Felix was taken aback by Dima's formality. He couldn't recall Dima ever calling him by his last name before.

"We expected you yesterday," Dima said.

Felix noticed how different Dima's demeanor was from the other men. He had the same short beard as the others, but his movements were quick and sharp. His forehead was wrinkled into a scowl as he awaited a response from Felix.

"My orders were to report today," Felix said.

Dima laughed. A sharp, derisive taunt. "That's not what I was told," he said. "I don't want to waste time arguing though. Where's the ammo? We need to get it distributed."

"Where's the what?"

"The bullets," Dima said irritably. "They said you'd be bringing a crate of ammunition with you. We're nearly out."

Another mortar exploded nearby, and again none of the men reacted. What a pitiful bunch, Felix thought. How can you fight a war like this? "I had no such orders," he said to Dima. "And I have no ammunition to give you."

"Devil take it!" Dima muttered. "Do you even have a rifle?"

Felix shook his head. "I was told I'd be assigned one when I reported," he said.

Dima opened his mouth but said nothing. He turned to the rest of the men in the trench. "Comrades!" he said. "We're going on the offensive again. We're going to retake the area south of the school."

None of the men moved nor showed any sign they'd even heard him.

"Dima, I realize that I just got here," Felix said, "but it doesn't seem to me like these men are in any shape to mount an offensive."

"First of all," Dima said, scowling once again. "You will address me as Comrade Lieutenant. Secondly, if I want your opinion, I'll ask for it." Dima quickly checked his rifle to see how many rounds he had left. "My orders are to attack," he added, "and I will carry out that order. The enemy must not have a moment's rest."

"Have we any artillery?" Felix asked.

Dima didn't respond. He was peeking his head over the shallow clay ditch at the German lines.

"Have we any machine guns?" Felix asked.

Again, Dima didn't respond. He hollered to the other men in the trench, asking how many grenades they had left.

"Comrade Lieutenant," Felix yelled. "Do you have a weapon for me? Or will I be sent out with a shovel again?"

"Enough of your provocations!" Dima yelled back. "You'll get your weapon from the enemy or when one of us has fallen." He turned to the others. "Men! Be ready to move out when I give the signal. Kazinsky and I will take out the machine gun on the left flank first, and then we'll move up that side."

Felix studied the blank expressions on the men's faces, the complete lack of emotion, and wondered how far their "offensive" would make it.

"Where's Kazinsky?" Dima shouted over a series of thundering explosions.

One of the men pointed at the end of the trench. Dima turned and looked at the corpse with its face pressing against the dirt, then addressed Felix. "Grab his gun. You and I will take out the machine gun."

"He just got here," the man who'd thanked Felix earlier said. "You're trying to kill him already, lieutenant?" He said the last word contemptuously.

"Perhaps *you* would like to go in his place?" Dima retorted.

"It's all right," Felix said. The man looked away, and Felix made his way down the trench and slid the gun out of the dead man's hands. It was a strange rifle and had a scope on it, and Felix understood that Kazinsky must have been a sharpshooter. Dima took the rifle from Felix, quickly inspected it, then gave it back to him. Felix realized why the rifle seemed strange to him – it was German.

Felix peeked over the red dirt of the trench to get a glimpse of the target. He could barely see the machine gun off to his left. The Germans had chosen a good spot next to the corner of a building. They had an excellent angle to fire on a wide expanse of the Russian lines, but it wasn't easy for the Russians to return fire. Felix only saw a narrow gap where the nest was vulnerable.

Dima waved his arm at Felix. "Let's go," he shouted.

They jumped out of the trench amid the angry spitting of the machine gun and the sound of bullets slicing through the air all around them. They ran to the safety of an old brick schoolhouse. There were bomb craters and unexploded shells in the playground. Two swings moved slightly from side to side in the light breeze. Through a window, Felix could see into one of the classrooms. Tiny desks were scattered about the room, most of them tipped on their sides. On the chalkboard was a crude map of the area, a swastika, and, in Latin, the words, "Veni. Vidi. Vici." In the far corner of the room, a German soldier lay sprawled on a group of desks. His head and neck were wrapped in bloody gauze, his right arm hung limply over the edge.

Felix tugged on the back of Dima's shirt and pointed to the classroom. Dima looked and nodded. "They took it last night, but we drove them back again this morning."

Dima pointed to his right. "You see that bomb crater on the side of that slope in between those small bushes?"

"Yes, I see it."

"When I run from here to that next building, you run to that crater."

Felix looked at the building Dima was referring to. "Dima, that's wide open. That machine gun will cut you down before you get three steps."

"That's the idea. I'll draw their fire so you can make it to that spot. You should be able to get off a good shot from there and take the machine gunner out. They've only got one guy manning it for some reason, so that'll make things a little easier."

Felix couldn't tell if he'd be able to get off a shot from the bomb crater Dima had pointed to. If he couldn't, he'd be a sitting duck once they saw him. There was little cover there and nothing to run to. The plan seemed so desperate to Felix. Either one of them, or maybe even both, might be killed before they even got close.

Dima crept to the edge of the wall and prepared to run. "Varilensky!" he shouted. Felix turned. "Make them count. There's only two bullets left in that gun." Then Dima dashed into the open and the machine gun followed him. Little clouds of dust rose from the ground all around him.

Felix took off running for the crater, and though it seemed like an eternity, made it there in just a few seconds. He looked through the scope and saw immediately that he didn't have the angle to get a shot off. He'd have to move further to his right, but there was absolutely no cover there. When he got up and started running, another German soldier arrived at the machine gunner's side. He was carrying more ammunition for the machine gun. When he saw Felix, he alerted the machine gunner, and Felix knew he had only a second or two before the machine gun swung around and started spitting its poison at him. He found the machine gunner's head in the center of the scope, aimed for the man's nose, and fired. The bullet went high and hit the man's helmet just above the eyes. The man was stunned for a second, but then quickly finished swinging the gun around and started spraying the ground around Felix with bullets. Felix took aim again. He knew he had to hit the man with this shot. His life depended on it.

He blocked everything out, carefully aimed two inches lower than last time, then squeezed the trigger. The bullet smashed through the man's right cheek and he slumped forward.

The other soldier immediately started pulling the dead man away from the gun so he could fire it. Felix was out of bullets and had no choice but to try running back to the schoolhouse. He doubted he could make it in time. Out of the corner of his eye, he saw someone running straight at the machine gun. It was Dima. He had a grenade in his hand and when he was close enough, he lofted it high in the air and then dove to the ground. The grenade landed just behind the machine gun's nest and exploded. The German soldier crumpled into the sandbags just as he fired his first round.

Dima jumped to his feet and ran up to the machine gun. He fired an additional bullet into each of the fallen Germans, then picked up a rifle and some ammo, and ran over to Felix. "Here," he said, handing the rifle to Felix, "those German guns seem to suit you."

At first, Felix thought Dima's remark a provocation, but then he saw him wink.

"Let's get the others and move out," Dima said.

They ran toward the trench and when they were within shouting distance, Dima yelled, "Comrades! Let's go!"

Nobody responded.

"Fedushkin! Ivanovich! Let's go!" Dima repeated.

Still no response.

They ran to the trench and jumped in. Felix expected them all to be gone or dead, but they were still there. They sat in the same position as when he'd left, staring blankly ahead.

"Come on, men! For the Motherland! For Leningrad!" Dima shouted.

Two of the men started to move, but the others remained motionless. Dima withdrew his pistol and pointed it at them. "Cowardice is no different than treason," he said. "Those of you wishing to remain here will be joining Kazinsky in *permanent slumber*."

The men still hesitated, and Felix thought Dima had erred by threatening them with eternal sleep. That probably sounded quite appealing to most of them.

"Listen!" Felix said to the men. "You're exhausted. You want some rest and water and food." A mortar whistled over their heads and exploded 50 yards behind them, sending mounds of dirt flying into the air. "You didn't ask for any of this. You don't want to be here. But we are *not* going to die in this miserable trench from a German shell launched a mile away." Felix had to shout to be heard above the din of battle. "If we are to die today," he continued, "then let our deaths have meaning! Let us die defending our wives, our children, our parents." Every man had now turned their head to look at Felix. He went down the line, looking them each in the eye as he said, "We don't fight for the generals. Or for the Party. We fight for ourselves and our family, for our right to exist!"

There was a pause while his words sunk in, then one by one, the men slowly picked up their rifles and tumbled out of the trench. Dima was out in front, leading the charge, but the men stayed close to Felix. There were no shouts of "hurrah."

In three hours of heavy fighting, the combined Soviet offensive drove the Germans from their second line of trenches. For Dima's men, the price of this success was steep. Of the forty men under his command at the start of the offensive, only eighteen now remained. The fighting had been like that of 1916: inch by inch, trench by trench. With very little ammo, Dima and his men had to work their way in close to the German lines, fasten their bayonets, then charge. The ensuing hand-to-hand combat was bloody and intense.

Now, Felix and the others were in a large warehouse that the Germans had occupied only a short time ago. There were cigarette butts, tin cans with German labels, and pages from a German newspaper scattered across the floor. It was mid-afternoon and most of the eighteen men remaining were sprawled out on the bare floor catching an hour of sleep.

Felix and Dima were about to begin their shift as lookouts on the roof. Dima was lamenting their ammo situation once again. Each man had an average of nine bullets left. Felix had more bullets than any of them since he was still using a German rifle. Another crate of ammo and grenades, as well as additional troops had been promised, but they were to have been there over two hours ago.

Felix felt frustrated with the lack of organization and resources. "If we don't get that ammo soon, we *have* to pull back," he said. "It's only a matter of time before the Nazis rearm and bring in some reinforcements."

There were several crates of mineral water stacked up next to them, and Dima was looking through them checking for an unopened bottle. "We're not going anywhere," he replied casually.

"Are we to fight the Germans and their tanks with our bare hands?" Felix asked sarcastically.

In the last crate, Dima found one glass bottle that still had some water in it. It had clearly already been opened, but Dima poured its contents into his canteen anyway. He pulled one of the crates toward the wall, sat down on it, and lit a cigarette. "Don't you understand, Varilensky? We can't let them rest. We can't let them plan, strategize, and regroup. We have to fight them with everything we have right here, right now, or else we're finished. By going on the offensive, we've tricked them into thinking we're stronger than we are. We can't let them know we're hanging on by a thread. Every battle counts now, no matter how big or small. We've got to hold on one hour at a time. We've got to destroy their tanks one at a time, and kill each fascist one by one. There's no other way." Dima took a long drag on his cigarette. "Every platoon's in the same shape we are. I know it's bleak, but I would rather die than see the Nazis take Leningrad. Do you understand that?"

"I do understand that," Felix said. "I want to beat the Germans just as much as you. We only disagree on how to go about it. Sacrificing ourselves isn't going to defeat the enemy or make Leningrad any safer. Heroes and martyrs don't win wars; only those who stay alive win wars. The smarter one – the more cunning one – stands the better chance of coming out the victor. It's not glamorous, but that's how you win."

"Well, when you're in charge one day, you can decide on the best way to go about it. For now, I'm in charge, and we're staying here." Dima exhaled a cloud of smoke, then started walking away. "Come on. Let's get up to the roof."

They climbed up and relieved Fedushkin and Ivanovich. The roof was flat, with a three-foot wall running all the way around it. Dima used his binoculars to pan back and forth where the Germans used to be. "I know you're there," he said. "Where are you?"

"What do you suppose they're doing?" Felix asked.

"I wish I knew," Dima said. "I can't see them anywhere now. We used to be able to see them just over that long, rolling hill. But they seemed to have disappeared."

They had an excellent vantage point and could see nearly a mile in front and behind. There were no buildings or trees nearby blocking their view. In fact, the only object around besides the warehouse was a bombed-out Soviet army truck that sat dejectedly fifty yards away.

Gunfire and explosions continued to echo in the distance. Felix had gotten used to it now and actually found it comforting. Only when it stopped and silence took over did he get nervous.

Felix took his rifle from his shoulder and wiped both ends of the scope. After the first rifle Dima had given him ran out of bullets, Felix took the scope off and mounted it on this new one. He used the scope now to check on the other Soviet forces next to them. Dima's platoon had been part of a broad offensive and had moved up to this location with the help of other, better equipped regiments. Felix couldn't see any of them now and wondered if their platoon was out here all alone.

When he looked farther over to the right, he was shocked to see a dozen blurry vehicles moving across the horizon. He squinted and saw they were tanks – surprising, since Soviet tanks were in terribly short supply. He steadied his arm and focused again and saw a black and white Death's Head emblem on the side of one of the tanks. He could hardly believe it. Something told him to turn and look in the other direction, and when he did, he saw the same thing, German tanks pushing their way past the Russian lines. They were using their favorite means of encirclement – the pincer movement.

"Look over there!" Felix shouted to Dima.

Dima looked to the right with his binoculars.

"And they're on the other side as well," Felix said.

Dima took his time, slowly turning to the left, then focusing his binoculars in that direction as well.

"I don't see any of our comrades. They must have fallen back already," Felix said. "We need to get moving ourselves. We don't have much time."

Dima lit another cigarette. "We're not going anywhere," he said, and sat down on the short wall running around the roof.

Felix's ears turned bright red. "We have no ammo!" he yelled.

"Doesn't matter. We're not retreating," Dima said. He tilted his head back and blew smoke into the air. "We're going to stand our ground."

"Damn you!" Felix said. "Either we retreat or this warehouse will be our grave."

"This warehouse," Dima said, scratching his chin, "is just as good a place as anywhere else to die." He looked Felix in the eyes, then added sarcastically, "Perhaps our deaths will have meaning here."

The rest of Felix's face turned beet red and he clenched his fists. In a fury, he stepped toward Dima and swung at his face. Dima had no chance to get out of the way, and the punch hit him squarely in the jaw. His head snapped back, and then he wiped blood from his bottom lip with the back of his hand. "That's good," he said. "*That* is what we need to win this war – a little more hate and fear, and a little less desire to *understand*." Dima said the last word with contempt.

"Consider this your final warning," he added. "Any further insubordination – I don't care how small – and you'll find yourself in front of a firing squad." He spit off to his side and a bloody tooth fell out and bounced on the roof. "Even," he said, "if I'm the only man left to do it."

Word of impending doom spread quickly among the men, and they began to curse Dima openly when he wasn't around. A tall Siberian led the accusations against their commander. "Who is he to decide we should all die like rats?" he asked. "Why should we be sacrificed to appease a madman's ego?" When some of the men nodded their heads in agreement, he became even bolder. "We need a change of command!" he roared, clenching his fist and driving it into his other hand. "The Lieutenant isn't going to stop until each and every one of us is dead!"

Mutiny seemed imminent as nearly all of the men murmured their agreement. Felix, who had been trying to rest, now gave up on that idea and listened to the conversation swirling around him.

"Comrade," someone said to the tall Siberian, "you should keep your voice down. Sound travels a long way in a warehouse."

"I don't care if he hears me!" he shot back. "He's threatened me for the last time. I'm leaving. If he tries to stop me, he'll get a bullet in the face."

"What do you mean, you're leaving?" someone asked him.

Felix watched as the man began stuffing items into his pack. His eyes were bloodshot from lack of sleep, and his face would sometimes become blank as though he had forgotten where he was and what he was doing.

He looked puzzled for a second, like he didn't understand the question, but then quickly regained his senses. "I'm getting out of here. That's what I mean. I'm going back to our side of the line," he said. "If any of you have half a brain, you'll come with me." He stood up, towering over the men near him, and slung his rifle over his shoulder.

"I'm going too," someone said.

"Me too," another said.

Felix saw several men start to pack their things and get ready to leave. He sat up and faced them. "Comrades, don't be foolish," he began. "We have to stay together. It's the only way we have a chance."

"How about you take over?" An unusually quiet and reserved man turned to Felix. "I trust you," he said. "I don't trust the Lieutenant."

A few other men echoed the man's sentiment.

"*Dima* is the commander," Felix responded without hesitation. "We follow him."

"But he's lost his senses," the man countered. "We could easily arrange for the Lieutenant to have a little *accident* and for you to take over command. I'd stay then. If not, I'm leaving too. I won't sacrifice myself."

"Neither a mutiny nor a sacrifice will accomplish anything," Felix said. "Staying here is not a sacrifice. It's the best chance there is of getting out of this alive. We're already surrounded, and it's certainly safer here than in the wide open space out there. Our forces might repel the Germans. The reinforcements and ammo might still arrive. Any number of things could happen. We just need to stay put until things play out more. If we can hold on until nightfall, we might sneak back then, but to go out now in broad daylight is suicide!"

"Staying *here* is suicide! At least we have a chance out there," the tall one retorted. "It'll be too late if we wait until nightfall. We have to go now!" He went to the door and opened it. Bright yellow sunlight streamed into the warehouse, and the ever present din of battle grew louder. "We're sitting ducks here. Now, who's with me?"

At first, no one moved. Then one man walked to the door, then another, and then several more. Ten men in all had gathered around the door when footsteps echoed through the large chamber. Everyone turned and watched as Dima strode toward them from the other end of the warehouse. No one moved or spoke. The men standing near the doorway gripped their rifles tighter and fixed their eyes on their emerging commander.

"Comrades," Dima said calmly, "could you tell me what's going on here?"

The tall one closed the door and stepped forward. "We . . . We're . . ." he stuttered. "We're geaving." Then he cleared his throat and pronounced it correctly, "We're leaving."

"Is that so?" Dima said, looking genuinely astonished, though Felix knew it was an act.

"Yes," the tall one said, "and you're not going to stop us."

"Well, you're all smart men," Dima said. "I'm sure you've thought this over and are aware of the risks. You've no doubt already figured out how you're going to get past a few thousand Nazi soldiers, and how you're going to make it to the Soviet lines without your own comrades shooting at you. And I'm sure you've already rehearsed the story you'll tell the commissars explaining why you're falling back toward the city you've sworn to defend."

The men near the door exchanged nervous glances with one another.

"What an interesting conversation that will be," Dima added.

"We'll tell them the truth," the tall one said, "that our commander went out of his mind."

"So you'll tell them that your commander – following his superior's orders – ordered you not to retreat, not to cede an inch of ground to the enemy?" Dima asked.

Felix watched the men shrink before his very eyes. Their necks twisted one way to look at Dima and then the other way to look at the tall one. The tall one had nothing to say.

Dima looked at the men who were not standing by the door and addressed them. "We have lots of work to do," he said. "The first thing I want us to do is strengthen our firing points." He stopped and looked back to the men near the door. "You might as well be on your way," he said.

The men stood motionless until the tall one opened the door once again. "Davai," – let's go – he said. "Who cares what the Lieutenant says anyway. He'll be dead soon . . . dead and rotting along with everyone else who stays here."

"Or," Dima said loudly, "if any of you have changed your minds about this treason to your country, you are welcome to stay and fight with us. And if we perchance die, we die with glory and honor, instead of shame and cowardice. But mark my words, once you step through that door, you will have become traitors, enemies of the people."

"It's better than certain death!" the tall one yelled and walked out the door. Five more followed him, including Fedushkin. Four remained inside.

Felix looked at the small group standing outside the doorway. Their faces were dusty and pale. Most of them stared at the ground or some other direction rather than into the warehouse. Besides the tall one, only Fedushkin looked back at Dima and his comrades who were staying. That Fedushkin was leaving surprised Felix and he studied his face for a clue why. But rather than a clue, Felix got a strange premonition that Fedushkin was going to die that day. The feeling made no sense to him. He had nothing to base it on. Each of them had absurdly high odds of dying on any given day at any given hour. Yet Felix couldn't shake the sense that Fedushkin would not live to see tomorrow. He found the whole incident disturbing and made a conscious attempt from that point on not to look closely at anyone else's face.

The tall one waited a few more seconds, then let go of the door. It slammed shut with a loud, reverberating thud.

"All right then," Dima said, addressing the men once more. "I want you two manning the southern firing points, and we need to have four men serving as lookouts on the roof. We'll rotate every three hours. Those on the . . ."

Felix waited patiently for Dima to finish giving his orders, then approached.

"Comrade Lieutenant," he said, "permission to look around the warehouse? Maybe there's some weapons stashed somewhere or . . ."

"Permission denied," Dima said without looking at him. "I just went through the entire warehouse. I want you on the roof with your scope. We don't know which direction they'll be coming from, so we need to be sure we've got them all covered."

"But if I could . . .," Felix started to say.

"Shut up!" Dima yelled. "Shut the hell up and do what you're told for a change."

Felix stood still and stared at him a second, then said, "As you wish . . . *Dima.*" He walked away slowly, wondering if he'd made the right decision not to participate in a mutiny.

Felix never made it to the roof. He gave his rifle and scope to Ivanovich and then wandered the large warehouse looking things over and mulling his fate.

The warehouse was mostly empty. Nearly everything had already been evacuated by the Russians or plundered by the Germans. In the middle of the warehouse was what used to be a workshop. There were scraps of rusty metal in the corner, a long workbench with a vice, boxes of nails, and an old drill press. Felix was surprised at first to see the drill press, but after he looked closer he saw how old it was and understood why it had been left behind. In the other corner were half a dozen large black barrels. Two of them stood in front of a small door and Felix went over and kicked them. They were empty. The other four were arranged in a diamond formation. He kicked the outer three and found them all to be empty too. Then he moved those out of the way and kicked the fourth. There was something still in it, and he searched for some markings on the barrel indicating what it was. When he didn't find any, he opened the plug at the top and smelled. It was turpentine.

He moved the barrels away from the small door, but found that it was locked. Taking a step back, he lowered his shoulder and then rammed the door open. Inside was an ancient generator covered with dust and cobwebs. Felix opened the tank to see if there was any diesel fuel in it. There wasn't.

He looked around some more, and finding nothing of note, went up to the roof to think things over. There was the turpentine which they could use for Molotov Cocktails, but they didn't have any glass containers. Then he remembered the empty cases of mineral water he'd seen Dima looking through. Those would work. And what about those nails? Those would make excellent bullets, if only they could fire them somehow.

While he worked out some of the details in his head, the men on the roof gathered around him. Ivanovich was the first to speak. "A lot of us stayed because you said you'd lead us back to our lines come nightfall."

Felix was about to say that he'd made no mention of leading them, that he wasn't their commander, and that it was just an idea anyway. But he stopped himself from saying these things because he knew he had to be careful now. Morale was tenuous, and the slightest misstep might just start the downward spiral that would condemn them all.

"Well . . . yes . . . maybe," Felix said. "But we can expect a German attack before then. We'll have to be prepared."

"How can we fight? We barely have any ammunition and only a couple of grenades."

"We'll make our own weapons," Felix said. "I found a bunch of turpentine and dozens of glass bottles. We'll make Molotov Cocktails with them."

"Oh come now," one of them scoffed. "What good are a few Molotov Cocktails going to do?"

"We'll make bombs too," Felix said.

"Out of what? The empty tin cans the Germans left behind?"

"I saw several boxes of nails. We can use those," Felix said.

"What are we going to do? Throw them with our hands?"

"No," Felix said calmly, suddenly realizing how they could use the nails. "I counted at least five unexploded artillery shells outside – some German, some Soviet. Ivanovich, you told me you worked in a factory that made shells, right? So you can tell us how we can get the gunpowder out. Then we'll make one hell of a bomb with the nails."

The men liked the idea. "That would be quite a bomb, huh?" they said. "Those nails would fly in a hundred different directions. The Nazis wouldn't know what hit 'em."

Once everyone heard Felix's plan, they were eager to help out. Those who weren't on duty as lookouts or at firing points helped build the improvised weapons. They worked feverishly in preparation for the eventual Nazi assault. The production of Molotov Cocktails went smoothly. They filled the mineral water bottles with turpentine, then stuffed some gauze from their medical supplies into the end to serve as fuses.

Making the nail bombs was a bit more involved. Ivanovich wasn't entirely sure his plan to get the gunpowder out would work and kept repeating that the German shells might not be the same as the Soviet ones he built. They needed to drill into the shell, which meant they somehow had to get electricity to the old drill press and hope it still worked. Felix went outside to see if he could siphon some diesel fuel out of the bombed-out truck. When he checked the tank, he saw it was empty, as he expected. Either the Soviets or Germans had likely already siphoned the remaining fuel out. But Felix didn't need much – a gallon would do – so he hoped that whoever had already sucked out the fuel had been lazy about it. And he was right. It took him a while, but he was able to get three-fourths of a gallon out.

Felix was pleasantly surprised when the generator started easily and the old drill press still worked. But the good fortune didn't last. They had just started to drill a hole in the first shell when it quit working. They traced the problem to the generator, whose large, well-worn belt had broke in two.

They searched frantically for a replacement belt but couldn't find one. Felix suggested they try the bombed-out truck for a belt they might use. They checked, and it did have a belt, though no one knew if it would work. When they put it on the generator, it was plain to see that it wasn't a perfect fit, but with a little coaxing they were able to get it to work. The smell of burning rubber told them that it wouldn't last long, so they worked as quickly as they could to drill the holes in the shells before it gave out. Since they weren't absolutely sure that the shells wouldn't go off as they drilled into them, they had the bare minimum number of men do the job – one to hold the shell and one to drill the hole. The rest of the men stayed as far away as possible, nervously smoking cigarettes and talking among themselves.

All during this time, no one could locate Dima. Felix went through the warehouse calling his name but received no response. A few looked around outside but couldn't find him there either. The men began speculating. Dima had snuck out. He had a secret plan of escape all along. One man even suggested Dima was in cahoots with the Germans and had agreed to lead his men to this warehouse and have them conveniently run out of ammunition.

In Dima's absence, the men began taking orders from Felix, though Felix didn't pose them as orders. He asked questions and then hinted at the solutions. The men themselves came up with the answer, and volunteered to do it. Every man wasn't needed to help in making the weapons, but Felix made sure that everyone played some role, no matter how minor. Though it was critical for them to construct the improvised weapons, it was even more critical that they regain their confidence.

Felix could see the gradual shift in their demeanor. The despair at their situation lessened, replaced by a determination to fight for their survival. By getting them involved in the preparations and listening to their ideas, Felix bought their trust and, more importantly, restored their belief in themselves as capable and resourceful fighters.

When they were nearly finished, Ivanovich began fretting that the length of the fuses on the nail bombs was too long. Felix assured him they could shorten them quite easily on the spot. Then Ivanovich feared that the turpentine had somehow "gone bad" and wouldn't light. He wanted to test one to make sure they'd work as intended. Felix talked him out of it because he feared the Germans might see the smoke. Since they had so little going for them, it was imperative they maintain the element of surprise – if it existed at all.

As they started making the last two nail bombs, Felix again went to look for Dima. Walking through the warehouse, he heard a thump that seemed to occur every twenty to thirty seconds. He followed the sound to a small room and saw Dima inside throwing his knife into the soft wood of a big bulletin board. There were two things that Dima was never without:

one was the pocket watch his father had given him, and the other was this small knife that he folded and hid in his right boot.

Felix knew now without a doubt that something was bothering Dima. The only time he ever practiced throwing that knife was to blow off steam. There were several cigarette butts on the floor around Dima. He was facing away from the door, smoking yet another cigarette and looking out the window. "What is it Varilensky?" he said without turning to see that it was indeed Felix. "Are the Nazis coming yet?"

"No, not yet," Felix said. "Is everything okay, Comrade Lieutenant? We've been trying to find you for the past two hours."

Dima made no reply. He tilted his head back and blew smoke into the air.

"I found some turpentine and glass bottles and we've made Molotov Cocktails to use against the Germans," Felix said.

Dima turned and looked at him. "How did you find this stuff if you were on the roof?"

Felix didn't answer. He felt the anger bubbling up inside him, but tried to breathe his way through it. He didn't want this to turn into another confrontation.

"So you disobeyed a direct order?" Dima added. "Are you testing the warning I gave you earlier?"

Felix wasn't about to answer either of Dima's questions. He wouldn't allow himself to be drawn into that discussion. "We've made some other things too," he said, wiping dust off his pants. "Would you like to come and see?"

Dima closed his eyes and dropped his head. "Why not," he said and sighed. He folded his knife and put it in his boot. "Show me all your *glorious* weapons."

Felix led him to the front of the warehouse where the men were finishing the last nail bomb.

"What are you making there?" Dima asked them.

"A nail bomb, Comrade Lieutenant," Ivanovich answered, beaming like a young boy who'd just caught his first frog. "We got the gunpowder from some unexploded German shells, and now we're packing it together with the nails."

"We made Molotov Cocktails too," another man said. "We have thirty-six – that's three per person, Comrade Lieutenant."

The men waited eagerly for Dima's reaction. Felix saw the fire in their eyes and hoped Dima would be pleased, but he seemed rather indifferent.

"The only problem is . . .," he began, looking around at the men. "The only problem is that they'll surely come in with their tanks first. The nail bombs won't do any good against a tank, and how are you going to get near enough to throw a cocktail at them. The tanks will cut you down with their guns before you get close enough."

The men looked to Felix for his rebuttal, but Felix had none. He had no idea how they could get close enough. He hadn't thought of that. In their previous encounters with tanks, there were things to hide behind, ways to sneak up on the them. But there was nothing around the warehouse except open space.

The downward spiral started. There was no hope after all.

From time to time Felix looked out over the small wall that ran around the roof, but mostly he sat and contemplated how the Germans were now between him and Katya. His emotions swung from anger to despair. Anger at the Germans for starting the war; despair that it was ending this way. He couldn't accept that fate would destine him to perish in this impossible situation. The voice inside echoed this belief. It told him that he and Katya would be together again, that everything occurred for a reason, and that it was all part of a universal plan to teach him a lesson he had yet to master.

He looked out over the wall at the bombed-out truck and the empty space beyond it. Anger bubbled again up to the surface, and Felix vowed that neither the Germans, nor the Soviets – nor fate itself – was going to stop him from getting back to Katya. This wasn't a game, and there would be no mercy for anyone who tried to stop him. He'd do whatever he had to do. German soldiers were no longer fellow humans to him, but obstacles that had to be obliterated. When he aimed his gun at enemy soldiers, he no longer saw a father, a brother, or a son. He saw uniforms that needed to stop moving, uniforms that kept him from all that he loved.

Felix glanced over at Dima, who was still pensive and distant. He sat against the wall, chain-smoking cigarettes, gazing into the cloudless sky. Felix tried to engage him in conversation several times but never received a reply. Dima stood up and scanned the area north of them with his binoculars. A minute later, he sat down again.

"I'm out of tobacco," he said to Felix. "Do you have any?"

Felix was surprised by the question. Dima knew that Felix didn't smoke and never had. "I don't smoke, Comrade Lieutenant."

"Oh," Dima said, his voice flat and hoarse. He put his knees together and leaned forward until his head rested on them.

"Comrade Lieutenant," Felix said, "are you feeling all right?"

Dima didn't reply.

Felix looked at the horizon once again for signs of the approaching Germans. Seeing none, he walked over to Dima and sat down beside him. A light breeze picked up and it felt good against his sweaty skin.

After a minute, Dima lifted his head up. "Do you remember Vera?" he asked.

"Vera," Felix repeated the name hoping it would spur his memory. "No, I don't remember any Vera."

"Sure you do," Dima said. "She was in our class. Short, with brown curly hair. Shy."

"Vera Nadakov? Is that who you're talking about?"

Dima nodded.

"What about her?" Felix asked.

"I can't stop thinking about her," Dima said. "It's driving me crazy."

Felix was puzzled. Why Dima would be thinking about Vera? He remembered her as a nice girl who was pretty enough, but much too timid to be popular with the boys.

"You know she had a crush on me in seventh grade?" Dima said.

"Really? Vera? I had no idea. You two were such opposites."

"She used to write me love letters and apologize for being so shy around me. They were the nicest letters anyone's ever written me," Dima said. "I remember I even cried once reading one."

"So what happened?" Felix asked.

"Nothing really," Dima said. "She was so quiet and thoughtful and courteous and praised me so much that I felt uncomfortable around her. It's so strange. She was so *good*, and she told me that I was good too. That made me so anxious I couldn't stand it. If she'd cheated on a test or called me an idiot once in a while, I would have been relieved. But all she ever did was tell me what a good person I was."

"Didn't you hit her with your slingshot once?"

Dima nodded. "Yes, I hit her with a little stone. I did it on purpose. I wanted to make her mad at me. I wanted to hear her curse and call me names, so I flung a little stone at her with my slingshot and it hit her in the side of the head. She started bleeding and they took her to the nurse to bandage the wound. I was suspended from school for three days."

"You'd always told me that was an accident," Felix said, "that you didn't mean to hit her."

"Yes, that's what I told everyone," Dima said, "but it wasn't true. I did it on purpose. When I came back to school, she wrote me a letter saying she still loved me. Can you believe it?"

"Wow," Felix said. "You never told me any of this before."

"The next year she moved away and I've never seen her since. I've never really *thought* about her since. And now, for some reason, I can't *stop* thinking about her," Dima said, putting his head down again.

Felix took a drink from his canteen. He didn't feel a need to say anything. Dima didn't need anything resolved. He only needed someone to listen. Felix patted him on the shoulder a few times and offered him his canteen.

Dima took a drink. "Too bad I don't have that slingshot anymore," he joked, "we could use it now."

Felix laughed and looked at the bombed-out truck again. He thought it strange how one of the tires still held air while the other three were in tatters. Then it hit him. "Dima," he said excitedly, "you see that truck?"

"Yes, what about it?"

"We *can* make a slingshot," Felix said. "A *giant* one that could launch the Molotov Cocktails at the German tanks. We can use the rubber inner tube of the truck tire for the elastic band!"

Dima was skeptical. "I don't know," he said, "we'd need a winch to draw it back, and a massive fork to hold the inner tube. I'm not sure how far it could launch anything, and aiming it would be rather tricky. It's a neat idea, but I really don't think it'll work."

"It *will* work," Felix said. "Didn't you tell me you *made* that slingshot with your dad? And you were a hell of an aim if I recall. We'll put it on the roof to increase its firing distance, and the Germans won't be able to see it as they approach."

"But we don't even know which direction the Germans will be coming from. They could attack from the front of the building or behind us. Who knows?"

Felix wasn't deterred. "We can make it mobile," he said. "We'll make it so we can aim it in any direction and move it backwards or forwards if we need to."

Dima put his chin on his hand and looked at the sky for a second. "Well, it's worth a shot at least," he said. "Let's give it a try."

They set to work immediately. The mobility part turned out to be the most difficult. After considering several options, they decided to use some large steel rods they found in the scrap metal heap and attach them to the roof facing out from each side of the building. They mounted the steel rods in such a way that they could slide either one slightly forward or backward to adjust their aim. But their mobility was limited to manually taking the inner tube and winch to whatever side the Germans were approaching from.

Once they finished constructing the slingshot, they filled some of the tin cans the Germans left behind with dirt until they weighed the same as the Molotov Cocktails. They test fired several in the slingshot. Their preliminary tests went better than expected, and they were able to launch projectiles nearly ninety yards. But hitting a target ninety yards away was a different story. For that, they'd have to rely on Dima's expertise.

All the men had gathered around to observe the test firing. "You gonna be able to hit 'em, Comrade Lieutenant?" one of them asked.

"Of course he will," Felix answered. "When we were kids, he could hit a bird in a tree from thirty yards away."

"I'll hit 'em," Dima said confidently. "You men do exactly what I tell you and I'll hit those bastards."

"Maybe the giant slingshot will be our next secret weapon," someone joked.

Everyone but Felix laughed. He was thinking how ninety yards wasn't much when it came to combating tanks, whose firing range was much greater. But ninety yards was about sixty yards farther, he knew, than anyone could throw a cocktail by hand.

Ivanovich ran across the roof to Felix and Dima. "Comrade Lieutenant," he said, "we've spotted something on the north side."

Dima used his arm to twist his neck to the side until a loud pop could be heard, then stood up and stretched. "Tanks?" he asked.

"No, Comrade Lieutenant, so far we've only seen one man approaching."

"One man?" Felix repeated, unsure that he'd heard correctly.

Ivanovich nodded his head.

They went to the north side of the roof to have a look. Dima used the binoculars and Felix the scope on his rifle.

"He's over there now," Ivanovich said, pointing to a cluster of small bushes.

When Felix leveled his scope on the area, a German soldier leapt out and started toward the warehouse at a full run.

"It's a German soldier," Felix said. He focused in on the man, preparing to shoot, but then, strangely enough, recognized him. "No, it's not a German soldier, it's . . ."

"Fedushkin!" Dima shouted. "Shoot that bastard!"

Felix removed his finger from the trigger. He was relieved that his earlier premonition about Fedushkin dying hadn't come true. Felix certainly wasn't going to shoot him. But why was he coming back? And where were the others?

"I said shoot him!" Dima repeated. "He's probably joined the Germans, that traitor."

Felix put his rifle down. Fedushkin was close enough now that he didn't need the scope. Dima put his binoculars down and took his rifle from his shoulder.

"He might be able to tell us something," Felix said.

Fedushkin was rapidly nearing the warehouse, and Dima took aim at him.

Felix thought about Dima's threat to send him to the firing squad for any further insubordination, but he couldn't just stand idly by. As long as he could still breathe, he had to uphold his values. He had to do what he knew was right. He laid his hand on the barrel of Dima's rifle, forcing it down toward the roof.

"Damn you," Dima cursed under his breath. It was too late to shoot. Fedushkin was only a few yards from the front door now. Felix started running across the roof to go down to meet him. Dima's voice trailed behind. "I warned you, Varilensky," he shouted. "God dammit, I warned you!"

Felix found Fedushkin gulping water from a canteen one of the men gathered around had given to him.

"Where's everyone else?" the men asked him.

"Dead," said Fedushkin.

Silence.

"We'd run out of ammo," he continued, "and decided to make a run for the Soviet lines. We'd made it about halfway when the Nazis spotted us and started firing." He paused to take another drink of water. "We kept running, but then our own comrades started firing at us!"

"They thought you were Germans?" someone asked.

"I don't know," Fedushkin said. "We dropped our guns and held up our hands as we ran, but they still kept shooting at us! They hit Volkov in the chest and killed him. We had no choice but to turn back. We would've all been killed if we kept going. But damn, we were so close!" He shook his head and sighed.

Felix heard footsteps coming from the other end of the warehouse and wondered if it was Dima.

"We ran back to the same spot we'd started from – a shallow, muddy trench," Fedushkin continued. "We were bombarded with mortars and machine gun fire by the Nazis. With no weapons, we decided we had to surrender. I took my white t-shirt off and we wrapped it around a stick and waved it. When they stopped firing at us, we put our hands up and started walking. They directed us to walk to their trench, but when we got closer, they started shooting us! I was the only one to get away alive."

"What did you do? Where did you go?" the men asked Fedushkin.

"I ran to a building, but I didn't know what to do once I got there. Then I saw a dead Nazi and got the idea to put his uniform on and try to make my way back here."

"Nobody stopped you?" Felix asked.

"Once," he said. "But I got out of it by pretending I was wounded in the throat, and of course there was lots of blood on the Nazi uniform to prove it." He finished off the last of the water from the canteen, and Felix handed him his.

"So what was the fighting like there? Who's winning?" Felix asked.

"I couldn't tell at first," Fedushkin said. "Neither side seemed to be going anywhere. But as I made my way back here, I could see the Nazis starting to fall back."

"They're retreating?"

Fedushkin nodded.

Some of the men grinned and slapped each other on the back. "Very good. Very good," Ivanovich said. "Felix, you were right," someone shouted.

"That's the good news," Fedushkin interrupted.

Everyone grew quiet. Felix heard the footsteps close behind him and glanced over his shoulder. He saw Dima, pistol in hand. "And the bad news?" Dima asked.

"They're headed right for us, Comrade Lieutenant," he said. His hands started to tremble.

"How many?"

"I don't know," he answered, "Ten . . . a hundred . . . a thousand . . . ."

Felix wasn't sure if Dima's pistol was pointing at him or at Fedushkin.

"How much time do we have?" Dima asked.

"They might be here in a few minutes, or maybe another hour. Who knows?"

All eyes were on Dima and his pistol. He opened his mouth once, but no sound came out. Then he put the pistol back in his holster. "I will deal with you later," he said. Felix wondered who he was referring to.

"All right," Dima continued, taking a big breath and addressing all the men. "Tell everyone manning a firing point on the south side to come here to the north side. We'll need to reposition the slingshot as well. Let's get ready!"

Only a few minutes after they moved the slingshot and readied the Molotov Cocktails, Felix spotted the Germans with his scope. There were three tanks, a car, and two motorcycles. Half a dozen troops sat on the top of each tank. After another minute, Felix, with his excellent vision, could make out the various vehicles without the help of the scope.

"I'm surprised they don't fire on our warehouse," one of the men said.

"They're probably hoping to check back into their hotel and get some sleep," Felix joked.

The sun was low in the sky and cast long shadows on the approaching convoy.

"If they want to sleep, they're coming to the right place," Ivanovich said. "We'll make sure they get *permanent slumber*, right Comrade Lieutenant?"

The men laughed nervously. Felix caught Dima with a brief grin on his face, but it was gone as quickly as it had appeared.

One of the tanks was driving with its hatch open. Felix could plainly see the upper half of a German soldier casually smoking a cigarette. He mentioned this to Dima, who then surveyed the tank with his binoculars.

"I'll be damned," Dima said, and put the binoculars down. He furled his eyebrows and then put the binoculars back up to his eyes. "Damn," he said again.

"What?" Felix asked. "What is it?"

"Well, I'm not sure," Dima started, then paused again. "But I don't think they know we're here." He looked with the binoculars one last time. "The way they're approaching . . . it's like they think this whole area has already been cleared."

"Boy, are they in for a surprise!" Ivanovich said.

When the tanks were about two hundred yards away, Dima addressed the men on the roof. "Remember," he said, "as I told you all earlier, we have to let them come in like there's no one here. Our best hope is to fight them in close where we can use our nail bombs and cocktails. Don't do anything until I give the word."

As the convoy neared their range of fire, the men became still and quiet. A few crossed themselves when Dima wasn't looking. The tanks began to slow, and one of the tank drivers looked through a pair of binoculars at the warehouse. Felix and the others held their breath and sunk low behind the wall around the roof.

Dima whispered aloud, "Come on, come on, keep going, just a few more yards."

Felix and the others had made several holes in the wall earlier so they could see, and Felix looked through one now at the convoy. The tank driver with the binoculars made a hand motion to the other vehicles, and they all came to a stop. They were about twenty yards out of reach of the slingshot, and Felix felt his heart racing. What was going on? Had they been spotted? He took a long, slow breath, using his inner voice to help him focus his mind.

The car – gray with a black iron cross on the side – pulled ahead of the others. The driver yelled and gesticulated wildly with his hands, and it seemed to Felix that he was ordering them to hurry, to get moving. Felix saw a man laying down on the back seat of the car, and wondered if he might be a wounded officer.

"That looks like a general's car," Ivanovich commented.

Felix had his doubts but kept them to himself. "Yes," he said, "I think it is, and he's lying in the back seat. That explains why three tanks and two motorcycles are escorting the car."

The news spread quickly around the rooftop. "It's a Nazi general!" they whispered to one another.

The rest of the convoy started moving again. The first tank pulled in front of the car, the second rode on the right flank, and the third on the left. The two motorcycles sped past all of them and would reach the warehouse in a matter of seconds. As the tanks rolled forward, Dima signaled for Ivanovich to pull the winch back, and Felix placed a cocktail in the pouch of the inner tube.

"That's it," Dima whispered, "keep coming. Keep coming."

A shot rang out unexpectedly and Felix saw one of the motorcyclists fall to the ground. One of the men from below must have fired.

Another shot rang out and the second motorcyclist fell to the ground. The convoy came to a stop again. "Damn it," Dima cursed as he tightened the tension on the slingshot. "All right, let's give 'em hell," he said. Felix lit the cocktail, and Dima gave the signal to launch. Ivanovich disengaged the clasp and the Molotov Cocktail took off like a rocket – streaking high into the sky.

The German convoy never saw it coming. The cocktail landed with a vengeance right on top of the first tank – its fire quickly covering the entire topside, including the six men riding there. They jumped off and ran and rolled on the ground trying to extinguish the flames. A few seconds later, the tank's crew tumbled out, screaming and on fire as well.

The men riding on the top of the other two tanks climbed down and dove to the ground. One tank came to an abrupt halt and began firing on the warehouse, while the other turned sharply to the left. With the building being rocked by tank-fire, Ivanovich had trouble resetting the slingshot. His hands were trembling so badly that he dropped one of the cocktails. Luckily it didn't break. Felix took over and quickly reloaded and adjusted the slingshot. They launched it, and though the aim was good, the distance was off and the flaming bottle sailed well over the tank firing at them. The tank started driving in reverse while continuing to fire its shells and bullets at the warehouse. Dima yelled for Ivanovich to hurry and pull the winch back to the same exact place. The building trembled in its foundations, and it seemed like an eternity before Dima finally gave the signal to launch.

But the wait was worth it – another hit! The left side of the retreating tank was engulfed in flames, and the tank crew quickly scrambled out. One of them grabbed a fire extinguisher and began dousing the flames, but Felix took aim at the uniform and stopped it from any further movement.

There was still one more tank, and the car, and the infantry on the ground. "Let's get the car!" the men yelled.

"No, that car can't hurt us. We've got to get that other tank!" Dima shouted.

They loaded another cocktail, but Felix feared the tank was already out of range. Felix watched the cocktail fly through the air and land right next to the car, startling its driver who veered sharply to the right and smashed into the side of the retreating tank. The front of the car was mangled and undriveable, but the crash didn't slow the tank at all.

Dima had them pull the winch back as far as it would go. He adjusted the aim, then released the clasp. Ivanovich crossed his trembling fingers as the cocktail streaked toward its target. The tank was already out of the range they'd practiced for, and soon enough it would realize it could stop and fire on the warehouse with no fear of being hit by return fire.

The cocktail smashed into the ground, just to the right of the tank, spreading fire in an oblong circle. The distance had been good enough, but not the aim.

"Load another one!" Dima ordered.

"The tank's out of range," Ivanovich protested.

"Load it, damn it!" Dima said. "We'll hit the car."

The driver had helped the wounded man out of the back and they were hiding behind the vehicle. Dima and Ivanovich launched two cocktails that just missed the car, but convinced the Germans that they couldn't stay there. They made it no more than a few steps from the vehicle before being struck by bullets.

Felix and the others had begun firing on the German infantry on the ground, and Dima and Ivanovich started launching nail bombs as fast as they could. The tank that had escaped now began its retribution, shelling the front of the warehouse and the rooftop mercilessly. A large section of the wall in front of Felix was obliterated, and chunks of concrete rained down on top of him. He quickly rolled to another position and resumed firing – picking off German uniforms meticulously one by one.

The nail bombs proved to be extremely lethal, and the German troops decided to make a desperate run for the west side of the warehouse. But there was really nowhere for them to go, and they were methodically cut down.

After a while, the gunfire became more sporadic, and the tank that was ravaging the warehouse eventually stopped firing and began to retreat. Nobody was sure why, though Felix guessed it might have run out of ammo.

The men were exultant. They'd done it! They'd finally won a battle decisively. And they'd done it with their own ingenuity. "You did it, Felix!" they yelled. Felix corrected them. "*We* did it," he said.

"Let's see if they're stupid enough to come back for another thrashing!" the men boasted, slapping one another on the back. "Hell, a few more battles like that, and we'll be the ones encircling Berlin!"

Felix used his scope to check on the bloody uniforms splayed on the ground. None of them moved, not even in the slightest. Except one. Felix watched as the wounded man who'd been riding in the back of the car staggered to his feet and raised his arms over his head. His age and the epaulets on his uniform confirmed his higher status. They now had a German officer prisoner of war. Even Dima smiled this time.

The man started toward the warehouse, stumbling every few steps, but managing to stay on his feet. Dark red blood covered the side of his wrinkled, leathery face. Felix couldn't tell what rank he was, but the invasion of grey on his otherwise black head of hair told him that he likely wasn't a mere lieutenant. As they rushed down from the roof, Felix was filled with anticipation. No matter his rank, he could be a valuable source of information. And if he was a colonel or a general, they might be able to use him as ransom should the Germans attempt another attack.

Felix and Dima were walking toward the man when a shot rang out and he collapsed to the ground. Felix turned and saw Fedushkin still aiming his rifle. Dima charged him and knocked him to the ground. "You idiot!" he screamed.

"That's what the Nazis did to *us* when *we* tried to surrender!" Fedushkin yelled.

"*We* are not Nazis!" Felix shouted back. He ran to the German officer, but it was clear he was already dead. A large chunk of the right side of his forehead was missing.

Dima removed his pistol once more, aimed it at Fedushkin and pulled the trigger. Another shot, another man with part of his head missing.

This wasn't war, Felix thought. War implied some kind of organized means of two enemies fighting one another. This was chaos. Madness. He wasn't sure he believed in Heaven, but he did believe in Hell. They were creating it for themselves. Right here, right now, they were building the walls and stoking the fires that would burn them and all those not yet born. And who was to blame? Who exactly was the enemy?

He looked to the sky, and the sun burned his face.

After they took the guns and grenades from the dead German soldiers, they retired to the warehouse to tend to their wounded and decide on the next move. Three more men had been killed in the fighting. Another four had minor wounds.

The sun would be setting soon, and under a thinly-veiled threat of mutiny, Dima relented to the men's wish to get back to their side of the line. They would rest for half an hour, then set off toward Leningrad.

Felix and Dima went to a corner of the warehouse and laid down on the floor. Felix used his pack for a pillow and prepared for some long overdue sleep. They were both too tired to make any kind of bed for themselves.

"Tell me," Felix asked Dima tiredly, "why did you choose me to go with you that time to take out the machine gun? Any other man you would have picked had more experience than me."

Dima took a drink from his canteen, then replied, "I selected you because I knew you'd hit him. We had very few bullets; you were a logical choice."

"But I'd never shot anyone or anything from that distance. I'd never even used a scope before," Felix said.

"Yes, I know. But I knew you'd hit him. I remember you were a good shot when we trained together."

Felix yawned and stretched his arms. For the first time since the war started, he felt cautiously optimistic about his side's chances. They'd only won one small battle, but he'd seen in that battle a fury and a determination that had surprised him. The men hadn't prepared and fought so hard because they'd been ordered to. They did it because they wanted to. They wanted to win. They wanted to beat the Germans in their own way, to show them their resourcefulness and fierceness. Perhaps they were tired of being beaten time and again. Or perhaps it was sheer vengeance. Whatever the reason, Felix started to think their situation wasn't so hopeless after all. As Dima pointed out, they didn't necessarily need to turn the tide on the Germans. All they needed to do for now was stop them from advancing on Leningrad. *That* was their goal. *That* would be a victory.

Just before Felix fell asleep, he realized that his premonition about Fedushkin dying before the end of the day had come true. But he convinced himself that it was just coincidence – nothing more, nothing less. It was a chance event. That was all.

Shortly before the sun went down, the deep buzz of approaching planes could be heard, but no one paid it any attention. Not until the ground around them erupted like a volcano, and the warehouse burst into flames, did anyone think of the possibility of a German airstrike.

The warehouse became a flaming inferno in a matter of seconds. Those who weren't killed by exploding shrapnel were quickly consumed by smoke and flames. Felix and Dima struggled together toward the outside, but only Felix made it. When he realized Dima wasn't with him, he ran back into the warehouse. The last thing he remembered was tripping over Dima's motionless body and the suffocating smell of the thick, acrid smoke.

~

Глава Шестая — Chapter Six

Rats in a Whirlpool

Hate drips from my ego,
    that vertigo,
    that somehow eludes me.
That which cannot be destroyed,
    that which cannot be enjoyed.
This affliction,
    this condition,
    that confounds me,
    surrounds me,
    until early dawn
Of each and every day.
The harder I try,
    the farther I fall.
The louder I scream,
    the softer you call.
I see your lips move,
    but hear nothing at all.

The End Of Sorrow

Katya turned in her chair to better see her coworker behind her. He was pacing back and forth once again, treading over the same well-worn area on the red and tan rug. She was fairly sure she'd heard him correctly but was so stunned by what he'd said that she wanted to be absolutely positive. "I'm sorry, Lev. What did you just say?" she asked.

"I called you an idiot," Lev repeated, his eyes looking like little black sunflower seeds behind his thick glasses. "You're stupid."

Katya tried to figure out why he would say something like that to her. She'd merely made a suggestion that they sweep out the warehouses and railroad cars to try to reclaim the flour left in the cracks and corners and such.

Lev stopped pacing and glared at her. "We can't waste our time on stupid ideas that lead nowhere."

Katya opened her mouth to say back to him that he was an asshole and that she wasn't going to take his verbal abuse. She didn't say that though because she'd recently learned a very useful trick from Petya. She'd noticed he often took a second before answering someone and had asked him about that peculiar trait. He'd told her that he developed the 'one-breath rule,' as he called it, when he lived in the orphanage. Before saying anything, he would make himself take one complete breath. He found that quite often after he took that breath, what he had planned on saying would change.

Katya took a long, slow breath in, closed her eyes, then exhaled. It was one thing to her to not be able to love her enemies (the Germans), it was quite another to have no compassion for her fellow countrymen. She pictured Jesus in her mind and tried to respond as she thought he might if he were in this situation.

"Lev, it's important to me that we treat one another with respect," she started. Her heart was beating rapidly. "If you don't like one of my ideas, then I would prefer you criticize the idea, and not me personally. I feel . . . annoyed when you do that." She hated confrontations.

"I don't care how you *feel*," he said. "I don't give a damn about your emotions. My job is to keep Leningrad from starvation, not pamper a spoiled little girl."

"I see," Katya said. She was hungry and tired but had already decided how she was going to react. She stubbornly refused to hear Lev's analysis of her. To respond with compassion, her grandmother had told her, you need to take *yourself* out of the equation. "Are you frustrated with the difficulties of your job and the demands on you and your time?" she guessed.

"Yes. This job is impossible. How do you feed a city when you have no food?" He gesticulated wildly with his hands. "What does the director expect from me? To wave a magic wand and create a million loaves of bread out of thin air?"

Katya breathed a little easier. She had guessed correctly what was bothering him. "Lev, you work very hard. I know, because I see you every day," she said. "You've been putting in long hours, and like everyone else, you're probably not getting enough to eat. You haven't seen your son since he left for the front and you're under an immense amount of stress every day. You're trying to do, as you said, the impossible – keep the people of Leningrad from starving. I imagine you're feeling overwhelmed." Lev sat down, and Katya could see his face soften. "Why don't we call it a day?" she said.

Lev took his glasses off and pressed the palms of his hands to his eyes. Then he yawned and squinted at the clock on the wall. "Where on earth does the time go?" he muttered under his breath. He put his glasses back on and peered at Katya over the top of them. "No, let's finish up," he said, a slight frown forming at the corners of his mouth. "I'm sorry about those comments I made. Please accept my apologies. You're right. I have been on edge lately, and it's not right for me to take it out on you. You work just as hard as I do, and I shouldn't attack you like that. You deserve to be treated better."

Katya felt pleased about how things had turned out. Despite what she had originally wanted to say, she'd been able to respond to Lev with compassion and empathy. She pictured Jesus in her mind once again and saw he was smiling.

"Apology accepted," she said. "I imagine you're embarrassed because you'd like to have talked to me more courteously."

"Yes. It's ridiculous the way I treat people these days," Lev said. "I hate it. But I have no patience. My anger erupts at the drop of a hat. I'm always hungry and the weather's turning colder . . . .. But it's no excuse! I have to get control of myself!" He stood up and resumed his pacing, leaning forward and holding his hands behind his back. He mumbled something inaudible, then stopped abruptly and stood up straight. "All right, that's it," he said, looking at Katya. "I'm finished feeling sorry for myself. Leningrad needs me. She needs all of us to be strong. Now, let's get back to work. We'll implement your idea to sweep out the warehouses and railroad cars and hopefully reclaim some more flour. I doubt it will be very much, but every little bit helps." He grabbed his pencil from the table. "Let me add that to the list now before I forget."

Lev jotted down the idea in his notebook and Katya excused herself to refill her glass with water. That was the only way she made it through each day, by drinking cup after cup of water to trick her stomach into thinking it was full. Her hunger, and everyone else's, was only going to get worse though, and she was in a position to know it.

When she returned, she asked Lev if they were on track for the new rules and ration cards that were to take effect October 1st.

"Yes. We'll be ready," Lev answered. He went to the window and opened the drapes. It was pitch black outside. All the street lights had been turned off – anything at all that would indicate there were still people living and working in the vast city had been concealed, lest the German bombers see something to aim for. "I can't believe next week will be October already," he said. "Before you know it, winter will be here."

Katya thought of Igor and wondered how he'd coped today. She was concerned about him because he was still a growing boy. For him to go with so little food was even more difficult than for an adult. "So nonworkers and children will be reduced to one-third of a loaf of bread a day, and a pound of meat for the month," she said. "Is that right?"

Lev sighed. "Yes, I'm afraid so," he said, still looking out the window. "The rules are draconian, but as the director says, we have to do it to even give the city a chance of survival. There'll be some cereals, macaroni, pastries, and butter for them too, but not much – hardly enough for an adolescent boy, that's for sure. How old did you say Igor is?"

"He's going on thirteen."

"Do you have any extra food on hand?"

"Yes, I do," Katya said. "My father made sure of that early on. But it's going rather quickly. Igor eats like a horse. I'm afraid I'll have to start locking the food up while I'm gone." Katya waited for Lev to turn away from the window. "Lev," she said, looking him in the eyes, "the director is a wonderful, energetic man, and he's doing a tremendous job."

"But?" Lev said.

"But I wish he'd realize that a twelve-year-old boy needs twice as much food as a five-year-old boy. He puts them on the same ration and it just doesn't make any sense to me. Could you have a talk with him? He respects your opinion. He'll listen to you."

Lev went to his notebook and started writing while he answered her, "I've already talked to him about it," he said. "He stresses that the food must go first to those making a direct contribution to the war effort. I can't see him changing his mind on any of the regulations." He tapped his pencil on the table and looked up at the ceiling. "Why don't you find Igor a job?" he asked. "Then his ration will be increased."

"I've tried," Katya said. "Every day I've been looking." She ran her fingers through her hair and stretched her neck to each side and then down toward her chest. "I guess I'll just have to keep trying." She looked up at the portrait of Lenin that hung next to the door and noticed what dark shadows the kerosene lamp was casting upon it.

"I just jotted down another idea," Lev said. "We should check the breweries. They've all been closed down and they might still have some grain left in storage."

"Good idea," Katya said. She took a drink of water and contemplated the dismal numbers she'd written down earlier. Leningrad had 2.9 million citizens and an additional 500,000 troops defending the city, so they needed to feed a total of 3.4 million people. They only had enough food on hand to adequately feed half that number. "Is there absolutely no way at all to get supplies from the outside?" Katya asked.

"For now, no," Lev answered. "The only open route to the mainland is across Lake Ladoga, and there's no ships, piers, highways, or warehouses that can handle the amount of food we need. If any ships make it across the lake without being sunk by the Germans, then that's a bonus. But we shouldn't count on much from this route." He started tapping his pencil on the table once more. "No," he said firmly, "we must make all calculations based only on what we currently have."

Katya suppressed a yawn and pinched herself to try to wake up. So many people's lives depended on the job she and Lev and the director did. It was a tremendous weight – oppressive at times – but Katya was determined like she'd never been before. She loved Leningrad with all her heart and soul and vowed to see to it that it survived. She couldn't allow it to perish from earth.

She and Lev worked late into the evening and Katya was beyond exhausted by the time she left. She wrapped a scarf tightly around her head and neck to combat the chilly wind that had started blowing from the north and set off on the long walk home. The sun was now setting before 8:00 p.m. each night, and the days would only get shorter and the weather only colder from here on out.

As she walked, she continued to think of strategies for finding more food and for making their existing supplies go further. She thought about the food situation both day and night. It haunted her dreams – people as thin and brittle as corn stalks in autumn, people dying by the hundreds each day in the bitter cold of winter. She couldn't let it happen, not here, not in Leningrad.

She said another prayer for the siege to be lifted, for the winter to be mild, and for Felix and her father to return home safe and sound. She didn't know if her prayers would ever be answered, but that wasn't the point. Prayer wasn't a means to an end for her. The point of praying was simply to reaffirm her own faith in the universe.

The wind picked up, blowing right through her light jacket, and she shivered with cold. She'd have to start wearing her fur coat soon if this kept up. The streets were all deserted, and she made the trip with nothing but the immense leafless trees and the howling autumn wind to keep her company. There was no shelling now, and the quiet felt strange. But she knew the Germans would begin again with Germanic precision at 7:00 a.m. the next morning. They always did. Katya hoped that would be their downfall – that the Germans' obsession with order and precision and rationality would doom them in this chaos that had become her home.

She thought of her friends at the hospital and considered stopping by, if not to help out, at least to say hi, but it was late and she still needed to make dinner and wash some clothes once she got home.

The End Of Sorrow

It was all very peculiar to her – how and why she'd been reassigned from her work at the hospital to assisting the city's food supply official. She was convinced that her father had something to do with it, despite the fact that she hadn't heard from him since he left for Moscow nearly a month ago. He had never liked her working at the hospital, even more so since the Germans starting targeting them.

At first, Katya was upset about the switch, but it didn't take her long to realize how important her new job was. She still went to the hospital almost every night, but it was on a volunteer basis now. She liked to keep busy, liked the fact that it kept her from thinking about things she had no control over – like where her father and Felix were and what had happened to them.

She walked past a massive streetcar lying on its side, a victim of one of the Luftwaffe's never-ending bombing runs. On the other side of the street, a mangy white horse pulled an overloaded wooden cart as two soldiers marched alongside lugging machine guns over their shoulders. The younger soldier reminded Katya of Felix, and she longed once again to feel the touch of his hand caressing her cheek. She closed her eyes, imagining him walking next to her, and smiled at the image.

As difficult as life was, she was not *entirely* unhappy. She surprised even herself with her disposition. There was death and destruction all around her; she had little to eat each day; she worked ten hours with Lev, then another three at the hospital; she came home every night to a cold apartment and her roommates' endless grievances. And yet through it all, she managed to find moments when she was grateful to be alive, thankful she had two legs to walk on, two arms to work with, and a pounding heart that kept fighting to remain open.

She very nearly passed her block because they'd recently whitewashed all the street signs. If the Nazis broke into the city, it was hoped they would get lost in a maze of nameless streets and avenues. Even the number of her apartment building had been whitewashed.

Inside her building, the stairwell was dark and she climbed up with extreme caution, testing each step before she shifted her weight to it. Under the conditions Leningrad survived in, she knew that the slightest injury could easily lead to one's demise. To break a leg or catch the flu these days meant almost certain death.

She heard a man pounding on a door above her and yelling, "Guzman! Guzman!" When she reached her floor, he called out to her, "Is that you, Guzman?" Katya recognized Shostakovich's voice.

"No," she said, "it's me. Katya." She knocked on her door and called out Igor's name.

"Oh, thank goodness you're here, Katya," Shostakovich said. "Where's Guzman? Have you seen him? He's not in his apartment. I don't know where he could be..."

When Igor opened the door, light streamed into the hallway and Shostakovich's round face came into focus. "Calm down, Dmitry," Katya said. She could smell alcohol on his breath. "I'm sure he's fine. Igor, have you seen Guzman today? Do you know where he is?"

"I saw him a couple hours ago," Igor said. "He told me he was going to the market."

"The market? So late in the day? Why would he be going to the market?" Shostakovich peered at Igor over his black-rimmed glasses.

"Dmitry, would you like to come in and have a cup of tea?" Katya asked. "You seem rather agitated."

"Yes, actually, I wouldn't mind that." He walked in and sat down on a chair and began rubbing his glasses on his shirt. Katya put a kettle of water on the stove.

"Guzman said he was going to sell his fur cap," Igor said.

Shostakovich stood up. "What? His fur cap? He's going to need that for the winter. Has he lost his mind?"

"He said he had two of them," Igor said.

"Oh, he said that? He has two of them?" Shostakovich sat back down again. His eyes looked down at his lap and his facial expression softened, shifting rapidly from fervor to thoughtfulness.

Katya laid her hands on top of his. "What's wrong, Dmitry? Why are you so upset?"

Shostakovich fidgeted with the bottom button of his shirt. "It's just that winter is coming on," he said. "And who's going to look after an old Jew? He's such a dear old man. He doesn't realize the degree of anti-Semitism out there."

"Yes, he's just like Felix," Katya said. "Both of them choose *not* to see it."

"It would be good if Jews could live peacefully and happily in Russia, where they were born," Shostakovich said, slurring a few of the words. He took a deep breath, sat up straighter, and added, "We need to remind everyone that the dangers of anti-Semitism are real. The infection is still very much alive."

Katya took three tea cups from the cupboard and set them on the table. "Guzman and Felix are both very passionate people," she said. "I don't think either one of them would ever leave Leningrad voluntarily." She set three small spoons next to each tea cup. "We still have a little sugar left. Would you like some in your tea, Dmitry?"

"Yes, please," he answered. He crossed his legs, only to uncross them again three seconds later. "I've found that most all Jews are passionate," he said. "Everything is concentrated in them: the love, the fear, the tenderness, the fight, the yearning . . . . That's why I love Jewish folk music. It's happy and tragic at the same time – laughing through the tears."

Igor had left the kitchen and hadn't returned, so Katya only poured

The End Of Sorrow

tea for herself and Shostakovich. "Felix told me once he heard a Jewish influence in your music," Katya said.

Shostakovich nodded. "Yes, that's true," he said.

She sat down next to him. "I always hear such wonderful things in your music, Dmitry," she said. "I wish more people heard your beautiful ideas so they could talk about them and discuss them."

"Art destroys silence," Shostakovich said and took a sip of tea. "Some think art is all about beauty and the such, but I don't buy it. Art to me is the pursuit of truth." He set his tea cup down and his trembling hands spilled half of the tea.

"I'm so sorry," he said, rising quickly from his chair. "Let me wipe this up."

Katya stood and took his trembling hands in hers. "Dmitry," she said, holding his gaze, "don't worry, Guzman is going to be fine. You and I will see to it. We'll take care of him."

"No, no, no. I'm afraid not," Shostakovich said.

"Why not?"

"Because they're making me leave the city," he confessed. "I've held them off as long as I could. They're evacuating me to Moscow, and then who knows where."

"Evacuating you? But I thought all the rail lines had been severed," Katya said.

"No, not by rail, by plane over Lake Ladoga. They're making Akhmatova go too."

"Anna's leaving too?" Katya nearly choked on her own words. She took a sip of tea to soothe her throat, but it hurt to swallow it. "I heard her reading poetry over the radio just the other day. She's such an inspiration to everyone. I can't believe you're *both* going."

"I think it's absolute cowardice to leave the city, but they're forcing us out," Shostakovich said. He tried to drink more of his tea without spilling it. "I don't want to talk about it anymore though. What's done is done." He crossed his legs in front of him again. "How's Felix getting along?"

Katya couldn't answer right away. She was still shaken by the news about Shostakovich and Akhmatova leaving the city. She wanted to cry. It seemed like *everyone* was leaving her. "I don't know," she finally answered, her voice trailing off. "I haven't heard from him."

"Yes, well the communication system has really broken down. I wouldn't worry too much if I were you. Mail to and from the front is tenuous at best. What about your father? Is he back from Moscow yet?"

"No," Katya said, and sighed. "I haven't heard from him either." She poured more tea into Shostakovich's cup. "Perhaps you could make some calls for me?" she said. "See what you can find out?"

"Me?" Shostakovich said, eyebrows arching over the thin black frames of his glasses. "Why do you think *I* could be of any help? I'm just a simple composer, and one who's an 'enemy of the people' at that."

"You're no *simple* composer, Dmitry," Katya said. "You're famous. Everyone knows Shostakovich – not only here, but in the West too. Besides, you told me once that Comrade Stalin himself has called you before."

"Well, that's true. That's true. But it's not as though he called to tell me how much he liked my music."

"I remember you told me you talked about the process of composing music, about inspiration," Katya said. She leaned forward to hear him better. The alcohol on his breath invaded her nostrils.

"I only spoke of inspiration because I couldn't get him to understand what I was talking about. It was the only time I've ever spoke of inspiration. If you ask me, it's nothing more than . . ."

"Dmitry, please," Katya interrupted. "Just do what you can to find out what happened to my father. This not knowing is maddening."

"All right. All right," he said. "I'll see what I can do, but I make no promises." He stood up, finished his tea, then went to the door. Katya followed him.

Shostakovich gave her a quick, but tight embrace. "Thank you for listening and thank you for the tea. I feel much better now," he said. He opened the door and stepped out into the dark hallway. "If I don't see you again before I leave, take care of yourself, Katya. Remember, we *will* win this fight. I'll finish my Seventh Symphony and we'll perform it here in Leningrad – whether the Germans are still sitting outside or not. You'll see."

"But what will the cost of victory be?" Katya asked. "How many people must die? How many loved ones must we lose? How much destruction must our beloved city suffer?"

Shostakovich was already making his way down the stairwell. He responded by reciting one of the recent popular sayings. "Leningrad is not afraid of death," he sang, his voice echoing throughout the empty stairwell, "death is afraid of Leningrad."

Katya closed the door to her apartment, leaned against the wall, and wrapped her arms around herself. It was getting colder, and she was finding it harder and harder to keep warm. She heard a solitary explosion in the distance, but it was just noise to her anymore. She went back to the kitchen and looked out the window for the stars, but could only find a few faint ones. A tear slid down her cheek. It seemed that the stars too were abandoning her to fend for herself.

The aroma of the fried potatoes filled the entire apartment and brought Igor into the kitchen. He slouched in his chair at the table as Katya spooned some of the potatoes from the frying pan onto his plate. It wasn't much.

Katya planned each meal in advance and this was all she had allocated for tonight's dinner.

"You're awfully quiet tonight," Katya said. "Is everything okay?"

He didn't answer.

Katya had noticed a subtle shift in Igor and was worried about him. He moved less and less each day, preferring instead to lay curled up on his bed under several blankets. It also seemed to be an effort for him to speak. She started thinking again about how to increase his ration when there was a knock at the door. She answered it and returned with Petya, who stopped at the kitchen doorway and leaned against the side. He had lost a fair number of pounds recently, but was still overweight. "Sorry," he said, "I didn't know you were eating." He stared at the food on their plates.

Katya sat down at the table. "Did you make it out to the countryside today?" she asked him. "Any luck?"

"I went," Petya said, "but it was a waste of time. Those damn peasants are so edacious. They've got all these beets and potatoes and cabbage in their cellars, but they won't trade any of it. They have closets full of fur coats and expensive jewelry now. The only thing they'll trade for anymore is vodka."

"Sorry it didn't work out," Katya said. "You really need to find a job that's directly involved in the war effort, then your ration would be increased."

"Don't you think I know that?" Petya said irritably. "You've told me that ten times already. Every day I look, and there's nothing available for a cripple like me. Everyone's biased against someone with a disability."

Katya suppressed a weary sigh. Everyone seemed to be on the edge of quarrel these days. "Petya, I'm really tired. It's been a long day," she said. "I was only trying to help. I understand it's been difficult for you to find a job, and I imagine you're more than a little angry about it."

"I'm sick of it," he said. "I don't get enough to eat, so I have very little energy and I have to hobble all over the city begging people for a job, and they take one look at my leg and then make up some bullshit excuse why they can't take me." He sat down beside Katya at the table. "Those damn Germans make me so furious. They should either take the city or leave. What do they plan to do? Sit in their trenches outside the city and starve us all to death?"

"That's what I heard," Igor said.

Petya looked at him. "What did you hear?"

"I heard the Nazis were digging in, that they'd given up on taking the city."

"That's a bunch of lies," Petya said. "They're not going to sit out there in the Leningrad winter and wait for us to wave a white flag. They'll freeze to death the same as us."

"Well, that's what I heard," Igor said, his mouth full of food. "They're going to blockade the city so no food or supplies get in and bomb us every day until we surrender."

"Who told you this?" Petya asked.

"Guzman," Igor answered.

Petya put his elbows on the table and propped his head up. "I've had it with the Germans," he said. "They said they were coming to 'cleanse the world of communism.' I hardly see how blockading Leningrad is going to accomplish that."

Katya started eating and Petya watched her as she did so. "Petya," she said, putting her fork down, "I feel uncomfortable eating in front of you like this when I know you must be terribly hungry."

"If you gave me some you wouldn't be uncomfortable anymore," Petya said. He laughed awkwardly, and Katya could tell that it was forced.

Katya thought highly of him. He took care of Igor when she wasn't around and was always available to help her with anything she needed. She considered him a good friend, making what she was about to do all the more difficult.

"I think it would be best if you left, Petya," she said. "I need to ensure that Igor and I have enough food to survive and I'm not sure that we do."

Petya's forehead wrinkled in astonishment and his jaw dropped. He stood up, bowed dramatically, and said, "I am sorry to have disturbed you this evening. That was not my intention. Please forgive me." He didn't wait for a reply before limping down the hallway.

Katya felt scared for what she'd just done. It was necessary, but still hurt like hell. "Petya," she cried out, "wait." She got up from the table and went to him.

He stopped and turned to face her. "No," he said, "you're right. I can't be asking for you to share your food with me. I understand the situation. We all need to fend for ourselves now."

Katya looked at him and recalled how he'd told her that after they'd shot his parents, he'd clung to his dead mother's side for two days before someone found him. She reached her long, slender arm out and squeezed the fingers of his right hand. She felt so sorry for him. He'd been 'fending for himself' for his entire life.

Petya faked a quick smile. "I'm going to go back to those peasants tomorrow to trade my bottle of vodka. And I'm going to find a position that will increase my ration," he said. "You don't have to worry about me."

She watched him walk down the hallway and out the apartment. "I will anyway," she said.

When she returned to the kitchen, Igor was already eating his last bite of food. She sat down and recited a short prayer. She asked God to watch over Felix and to also give her the strength to uphold her values, because it was getting more difficult with each passing day. One of her biggest fears was that her compassion and humanity for those around her would crumble under the weight of the daily deprivation of Leningrad under siege.

* * *

"But why didn't you just shoot them?" Franz asked, the big blue vein on the side of his forehead protruding slightly. He craned his neck to look at the six prisoners lining up to his right.

"Because they were already dead," the German soldier replied. He frowned thoughtfully and flicked his cigarette butt to the ground. "Well obviously they weren't, but there were bodies all over the place: Russian, German, and of course Falkenhorst himself. These two," he said, pointing at the prisoners on the far right of the line, "were laying just outside the warehouse – which was still burning – and they weren't moving so we assumed they were dead too."

"You should always put an extra bullet or two in their heads just to be sure," Franz said. "They're tricky bastards. They'll pretend to be dead, then get up and shoot you in the back after you walk by. I'm telling you this because you're new to this front, and you don't want to learn the hard way."

"Well now I know," the German soldier said. "I'll be more careful next time."

Franz was looking at the two men again when the wind picked up. He held his hand over his eyes to prevent dust getting blown in them again. He was sure the prisoner with the dark, curly hair and grey eyes was a Jew. He'd recognize that nose anywhere. "So these are the only two to have survived?"

The German soldier nodded his head, then walked inside the building and closed the door behind him.

They certainly didn't look like much, Franz thought. Sure they were both bigger than he, but then most everyone was. It was difficult for him to believe that these two pitiful looking Russians were in any way responsible for taking out Major Falkenhorst and all his men.

Franz would be helping transport these two and the four others to a camp farther behind their lines and was bitter about it. He hated that the German army expended its food, time, and effort on these sub-humans. It would be better just to gas them and bury them in shallow graves.

The prisoners stood in a row against the wall. Franz saw a couple of them shivering uncontrollably in the cold autumn wind. They had no coats, and Franz smiled at their discomfort. They deserved what they got.

It amazed him that Leningrad had held out as long as it had. Didn't they know that they'd already been beaten? He just hated people who didn't give in when it was obvious they had lost. But maybe it was for the best, let the Jews and communists die of hunger, cold, and artillery shells. It was better that way than having to fight them in combat. They seemed to be getting progressively more deceptive and stubborn every day that the war dragged on. The slaughter of Falkenhorst and his men testified to that.

Franz was steadfast in his faith in the Fuhrer and his directives. He had led them to unimaginable victory so far, and it was preposterous to question his judgment. The decision to move the entire 41st Panzer Corps and several Motorized Divisions to the Moscow front had taken him by surprise at first since Leningrad had yet to fall, but then, he thought, it was only a matter of time until the city began begging to surrender. They were bombing Leningrad daily and their spies reported that the food situation grew more desperate each day. Already, they'd received accounts of citizens dying of hunger.

Yet another officer came up to Franz and asked him to point out the two men responsible for taking out Falkenhorst. Everyone wanted to see the two Russians who had managed to kill the formerly invincible warrior. Major Falkenhorst, or Old Leather Face as most of the men called him when out of earshot, had been famous for his ruthlessness, not only with the enemy, but with his own men, for never losing a battle, and for always escaping unscathed from seemingly inescapable situations. Franz had idolized him for his toughness and uncompromising nature with enemy forces. If he were still alive, all these Russian prisoners would have been shot by now. Falkenhorst was a man who knew what it took to win a war. He'd been experienced – unlike the choirboy in charge of Franz's platoon, who'd somehow been duped into believing that the Russians were actual human beings. They weren't. They were animals, and the choirboy would learn that soon enough.

A truck lumbered into the courtyard and came to a stop in front of the prisoners. Franz and another soldier, Otto, herded the prisoners into the back and then joined them. A third soldier hopped in the front to drive.

On the way to their destination, Otto rested his rifle on his lap while Franz kept his pointed at the prisoners at all times. Franz hated the Russians. They were sneaky sons-of-bitches, and you couldn't let your guard down for one second. What truly amazed him though was that no matter how many they killed, they just kept coming. They wouldn't give up. It reminded Franz of when he was on vacation as a kid and had caught rats in traps just so he could throw them in a whirlpool he'd found and watch them drown. That's what the Russians were like – rats caught in a whirlpool. It was inevitable that they would drown, yet still they fought, refusing to accept their fate.

The truck bounced and squeaked and shifted its occupants relentlessly from side to side. Clouds of dust made the air nearly unbreathable, and the wooden benches they sat on were hard and cold.

"Are we even on the damn road?" Franz asked. He didn't expect an answer from Otto, who kept to himself most of the time. Otto reminded Franz of that lunatic, Alfred Liskof, who had tied him to a tree and left him for dead. They both thought too much and didn't dislike the Russians enough in Franz's opinion. But Otto was no Alfred. For starters, he was about thirteen years younger.

"What do you think, Otto?" Franz said. "Did the Jews make this road?"

Otto ignored him, but Franz was used to it. They'd made this long, boring trip several times before and it was the same every time. Franz would try to amuse himself by provoking Otto. Sometimes it worked. Sometimes it didn't.

"Hey Otto, what do you call one Jew drowning in the sea?"

Otto stared at him, then looked away.

"Pollution. Ha-ha! But wait, it gets better. What do you call ten million Jews drowning in the sea?"

Franz paused for the punch line, then said, "the solution!" He then proceeded to laugh at his own joke as if it was the funniest thing he'd ever heard. He had a high, nasal laugh that sounded like a squeal.

"You get it?" he asked between laughs, slapping Otto on the knee.

The prisoner with the dark, curly hair and grey eyes said something while looking at Franz.

Otto spoke some Russian, and Franz asked him what the man had said.

When Otto didn't answer right away, Franz shook his shoulder. "Hey, what did that fucker say?"

"He said you laugh like a pig being slaughtered," Otto said.

"Is that so?" Franz said, pointing his rifle at the man. "Well, you tell him he *is* going to be slaughtered like a pig."

Before Otto could translate, the man said something else, and Otto translated that. "He says for us to go back to Germany. He says we'll never win because they'll never give up, that we're doomed to repeat Napoleon's fate."

Franz was reminded of the stupid stories Alfred used to tell him about Napoleon suffering a humiliating defeat just when victory seemed to be within his grasp. "You tell him we are not the French. We're German, and nobody has beat us and nobody will. The Aryan race will rule the world, and you animals will be put in your place." Franz looked at the prisoners and was filled with hate. "You tell them that," he said to Otto. "You tell these stupid rats what I said."

Otto spoke to the men in Russian, but when he finished they all started laughing. Otto even grinned a little himself.

"Why are they laughing?" Franz demanded. "You son-of-a-bitch. What did you say to them?" The thick blue vein on the side of his forehead started to bulge.

"Just what you told me to tell them," Otto said.

Franz squinted and pushed his lower lip up as he eyed the Russians. "There was absolutely nothing," he said, "nothing whatsoever funny in what I said."

"Certainly not," Otto replied. "They should be paralyzed with fear. I have no idea why they would find it funny." He then said something else to the Russians, and they all laughed again. "Oh, sorry," he said to Franz, "I was just trying to clarify what I said to them earlier."

Franz saw Otto trying to suppress a grin and figured out Otto was having fun with the Russians at his expense. Franz decided to get even the only way he knew how.

He waited a few minutes until the time was right, then said, as casually as he could, that he'd been talking to Major Halder a short time ago.

Franz watched Otto's grin vanish in a heartbeat. He knew that would get his attention. "The major wanted to know how the men were doing," Franz continued. "What the morale was like."

Otto straightened his posture and gripped his rifle firmly. "Yes, well, he's a brilliant commander. Of course, he'd want to know about those things. He's the best there is." Otto took out a pack of cigarettes. He didn't take one for himself, but he did offer one to Franz.

Franz had plenty of cigarettes, but took one anyway and tucked it in his pocket. The tide had turned, and now it was his turn to suppress a grin. "He asked specifically about you," Franz added.

Otto stiffened even more.

"I told him you were doing well," Franz said, "but that you seemed to have a certain *fondness* for Jews." Franz waited a second to see Otto's reaction, then added, "He seemed rather displeased about that."

Otto's voice was suddenly very flat and serious. "I'm no lover of Jews," he said. "I understand just as much as the next German the problems they create for society." The lines sounded rehearsed, and perhaps being aware of it, Otto added with conviction, "In fact, I think we could solve a lot of the world's problems by getting rid of the Jews."

Franz smiled openly, showing his sharp, tiny teeth. "Well, there's Jews right here in this truck," he said, pointing to each one of the prisoners. "What should we do about it?"

"You don't know that."

"I'm positive that one there with the big nose is a Jew," Franz said. "I can tell."

"Your evaluation of the size of a man's nose isn't very scientific."

"Ok," Franz said. "I have a surefire way to tell a Jew from a Russian. If they fail the test, then we'll 'get rid of' them, as you say we should."

Franz felt pleased with himself as he noticed Otto starting to blink uncontrollably, as he always did when he got really nervous.

"We were instructed to take these prisoners to a specific destination," Otto said. "If we don't deliver them, then . . ."

"If anybody asks any questions, we'll just say they tried to escape," Franz interrupted. Then he yelled to the driver to stop the truck.

"This is ridiculous," Otto said. "They're all Russians. We're wasting time."

"We'll know for sure in just two minutes," Franz said.

They forced all the prisoner's out and over to the side of the road. It was a big open area, surrounded by black fields that had been burned a few weeks prior. The road was straight and flat, and one could see a half mile in either direction.

"Let's make it interesting," Franz said to Otto. "Since you're so sure there are no Jews in this bunch, I'll bet you my meat ration for the next week that at least one of them fails the test. And if I win, you give me that bottle of schnapps your father sent you. Deal?"

Otto sighed heavily but nodded his head anyway.

"Ok, first of all, we have to blindfold them so they can't cheat," Franz said. "You know these bastards will cheat every chance you give them."

"What exactly is this surefire test that you've got?" Otto asked. "I'd like to hear it first."

"You'll see soon enough," Franz said.

Otto and the driver forced the prisoners to their knees and blindfolded them while Franz stood guard with his rifle. When they were done, Franz started looking through his German-Russian dictionary. He didn't trust Otto to translate the right thing.

Once Franz had found the phrase he wanted to say, he had Otto and the driver untie the prisoners' hands. Then, starting at the beginning of the line, he said in broken Russian, "Make cross." Franz waited a few seconds, then nudged the man with the butt of his rifle and repeated his demand for him to make the sign of the cross.

"I don't think he understands what you're trying to say," Otto said.

"He understands well enough," Franz said. "He just doesn't know how to do it. Here's your first Jew, Otto." Franz raised his rifle to the man's head and was just about to squeeze the trigger when Otto repeated the command to make the sign of the cross in correct Russian. "Da," Franz said. He'd been close, but had put the stress on the wrong syllable and had mangled the ending a little bit. Franz repeated the phrase exactly as he'd heard Otto say it and poked the man with his rifle once again.

The man slowly moved his hand to his face and touched his index finger to the bridge of his nose and then to his right shoulder. He'd done it wrong already. The order was top then bottom, not top then right. And he should have done it faster, not touched his nose like that, and should have had his thumb and his first two fingers touching together, not spread apart. Franz looked at Otto and smirked. When the man had finished, Franz yelled "Nyet!" and shot him above the left eye. The shot echoed through the dull autumn sky, and a flock of birds fled from their perch in a nearby tree.

The man's body had barely hit the ground when Franz started poking the next man in line and repeating the phrase for him to make the sign of the cross. The man sat back on his knees and said something in Russian in response.

Otto partially stifled a short, "Ha."

"What did he say?" Franz asked.

"He said ... hmmm, how shall I put it politely ... for you to go have sex with yourself," Otto said.

The man then made the sign of the cross perfectly, moving his right hand in an exaggerated fashion from his forehead to his stomach, and then to his right and left shoulder. But Franz again yelled "Nyet," stuck the barrel of his rifle to the man's temple and pulled the trigger.

"You idiot!" Otto yelled. "What are you doing? He did it correctly."

"No, he didn't," Franz said. "He went from right to left. I saw him."

"You imbecile. You're a Catholic. Of course you do it from left to right," Otto said. "Russians aren't Catholic. They're Orthodox, like the Greeks. Orthodox Christians go from right to left."

"What are you talking about?" Franz said and looked at the driver.

"I think he's right," the driver said meekly.

Franz looked beyond Otto and the driver and saw some refugees coming down the road. There were two of them, an old woman pushing an overladen cart, and an old man with a cane hobbling alongside her. Franz would usually drive on the return trip, and he liked to veer at the refugees and force them off the road or even clip their wooden carts so that all their belongings came tumbling out. But he didn't have time to taunt them now. He was eager to get through the next two men, because the two he really hoped to shoot – the ones who had ambushed Falkenhorst and his men – were at the end of the line. He made an agreement with Otto that he would consult him first before deciding if the sign of the cross had been made correctly, then quickly moved on to the next prisoner.

The man unfortunately did it right, although Franz argued with Otto that he seemed fairly unsure of himself and didn't actually have his thumb and first two fingers touching together. The next man didn't even attempt to make the cross. Instead, he raised his head and spit blindly in front of him, striking Franz on the chin. Then he tried to get to his feet and charge, but Franz shot him before he could do so.

"You see?" Franz exclaimed. "They're animals. Complete animals." The dead man lay sprawled on the road, his left arm awkwardly tucked underneath his torso, a small puddle of red blood forming in the dark dirt of the road. Otto had a look of disgust on his face, and for a moment, Franz thought he was going to vomit.

Franz stepped in front of the next man, the one with the curly, dark hair and grey eyes. He pointed his rifle at him, but then turned to Otto and the driver. "You know, there's only three left. Let's just shoot them and be done with it – three less communists in the world." He looked at the driver to see his reaction. "If we do it now," Franz added, "we can be back in time for dinner."

"No, the deal was only for Jews," Otto said. "You've already won your bet. Let's just put these three back on the truck and get going."

He's just like Alfred, Franz thought. A coward. "You know as well as I do that if we go all the way there and back that we'll miss dinner and will be lucky to get some beans and bread. There certainly won't be any meat left. Who wants to be on that miserable bumpy, dusty road for another two and a half hours?"

"Yeah, I'm hungry," the driver said. "We'll just say they all tried to escape."

The two refugees on the road were getting nearer, and Franz saw Otto looking at them. "Don't worry about them," Franz said. "They don't have anyone to tell."

"Come on, Otto," the driver said. "No one's going to care about a bunch of prisoners anyway."

The wheels of the cart the old woman was pushing made a high-pitched squeak that annoyed Franz and hurt his ears. He thought it odd that they kept approaching. Most refugees steered clear of any situations where there was shooting going on. "Tell them to move on," Franz said to Otto, "or else they'll be shot too."

Franz didn't care about Otto's objection anymore. Otto couldn't very well report on him without implicating himself, and besides Franz had the driver on his side. He wanted to kill these last two whether they were able to make the sign of the cross or not. They'd killed at least two dozen German soldiers, including Falkenhorst, and deserved to die themselves. There would be no trickery about it though. There was no honor in that. Franz wanted them to see exactly what was coming. That was the German way. Germans didn't need to be sneaky, because they were Aryan. They were superior.

Franz yelled for the driver to take the prisoners' blindfolds off. Otto was still conversing with the refugees, who, instead of passing by, were actually crossing the road toward them. "I told you to get rid of them," Franz yelled to Otto.

"They want to trade us something for some food," Otto said.

"Tell them we're not interested," Franz said.

"I did," Otto said. "They're very persistent."

Stupid Russians, Franz thought. He'd shoot them if he had to. He turned toward them and waved his rifle as a warning, but they kept approaching. The old woman was thick, like a tank. She pushed the rickety cart right toward Franz, all the while saying the same thing over and over. The old man with the cane stopped and talked with Otto. He was covered in blankets from head to toe and it was hard to see his face.

Franz knew the Russian phrase for "go away," and said it to the old woman. In response, she grinned, and the sun glinted off her gold tooth. She grabbed the blanket that covered the contents of her cart and pulled it off in one big, swooping motion. Under the blanket was a man with a submachine gun pointed right at Franz.

The man pulled the trigger and the gun let out a rat-tat-tat. All three bullets struck Franz in the chest and he fell to the ground. He heard a pistol fire and Otto scream. Then he saw the driver attempt to run away but get cut down in a hail of fire from the submachine gun.

Franz was in extreme pain. The old woman was looking down on him, smirking. He was finding it difficult to breath, and even more difficult to believe that his life was ending this way. "You sons-of-bitches," he muttered. "You tricky sons-of-bitches. There's no honor in that. No honor at all . . .."

* * *

Dima stretched his arms out close to the smoldering fire. He was hoping to warm up his cold hands, but the fire had ceased giving off any heat twenty minutes ago. Endless, thick gray clouds filled the sky and a fine mist that continually switched to light rain and back permeated the air. Felix had gone off with three of the partisans to gather more firewood. Dima didn't know where the rest of them had gone, nor did he care.

For three hours, he'd been sitting there thinking. Thinking about so many unpleasant things. He wished he could flip a switch and turn off all the thoughts in his head. But he couldn't, and he felt completely at their mercy. He let his head fall back so he could feel the mist on his face. It only made him colder, but he didn't care.

The others had finished eating their meal of stale black bread and slightly rancid grilled horse meat a half hour ago. Dima had been working up the courage to take his last bite ever since. He pinched his nose with his fingers, put the food in his mouth, chewed it quickly, and swallowed. He was amazed he'd been able to keep everything down so far. The Germans hadn't fed them much of anything for the two weeks Felix and he were in their POW camp. His stomach was weak, and he'd lost a lot of weight for such a short time span. He'd lost a lot of things in such a short amount of time: his pride, his dignity, his confidence, and with the exception of Felix, every man under his command.

His teeth chattered with cold as a shiver ran up his spine, and he wondered, how could you be a commander if you had no one to command? You couldn't, he decided. That was the depressing answer.

His career was dead. He wouldn't be surprised if he faced a court martial for getting every one of his men killed. And for what? What had he accomplished? Two weeks ago, he would have been able to answer that question without hesitation. But now . . . now he just didn't know anymore.

The Nazis had beaten him badly. Nearly every day, they'd interrogated him in a small room with an extremely bright light. If they didn't like his answers, they let him know it with a swift whack from a club or by burning a hole in his skin with a cigar. Dima had never experienced so much pain in his life. Each time he took a deep breath now, he felt a sharp, stabbing pain just above his stomach and wondered if they'd broken one of his ribs.

It was during their ninth *talk* that Dima had broken down, when he just couldn't take it anymore, when the lack of food and sleep and warmth became too overwhelming. They'd promised not only to end the physical punishment but to also give him a bowl of hot stew with bread and coffee. They'd brought it in and set it on the desk so he could see it and smell it. Then they continued shining the bright light in his eyes, badgering him with questions, and whacking him with their hard little stick. They said to just tell them one little thing that might be of use to them, just one little thing, and then they'd give him the food and let him sleep.

And Dima had given in. He'd told them about the poor distribution and shortage of ammunition. They said that was common knowledge, so he told them something else until they were finally satisfied. Then he ate the food, drank the coffee, and slept for twelve hours. When he woke up, he hated himself thoroughly. He despised his body for betraying him. Even now, as his hands and feet went numb from the cold and from not moving in so long, Dima wasn't going to do anything about it. He wanted them to suffer.

Felix and the others returned with armloads of firewood and stacked them under a large pine tree where it was still fairly dry. Dima only knew the names of two of the partisans so far. The tall, skinny one who had been hiding under the blanket in the cart and was now helping Felix stack the wood, was Misha. The stout woman with the gold tooth who'd been pushing the cart was Olga, who was apparently in charge of the rag-tag group. Everyone seemed to fear her, and Dima didn't understand why, though he had heard her threaten Felix with bodily harm twice already, and they'd only been in the camp four hours now.

Dima had learned that the members of the group had been involved in the battle for Mga, and, having been thoroughly routed by the Germans, had fled to the woods where they'd remained ever since. They fought behind the lines now as partisans – destroying German ammo dumps, attacking supply convoys, blowing up roads and bridges, and severing telephone and telegraph wires. There were ten of them (eight men and two women), but their numbers kept growing as more and more ordinary citizens became disgusted with the brutality of the German occupation.

According to Olga, Felix and Dima were now a part of this group. Dima didn't care. He had nothing to go back to, but Felix didn't like it. He protested that he wanted to return to the Leningrad front, but Olga claimed authority vested in her by the Party to keep him here.

He heard Olga's voice now. She was threatening Felix yet again. "Don't cross me, kike," Dima heard. "You do what you're told or I'll have you shot. I'm in command here, and the sooner you get that through your thick kike skull, the better."

Felix started to say something in response, but Olga cut him off and walked away. The mist turned into light rain as Dima watched her go to her tent and disappear inside. Then he got up and followed her. Outside her tent, he pulled the canvas door to the side and saw her leaning over a map, a kerosene lamp hanging from the ceiling.

"Comrade, might I have a word with you?" he asked at the doorway.

"No, I'm busy," she said, not even looking up. The map was crudely drawn and showed the locations of forests, streams, nearby villages, and roads and trails. German positions were indicated with swastikas.

Dima came in anyway. "I've noticed," he said, "that you seem to have some problems with Comrade Varilensky."

Olga wrinkled her short, fat nose and snorted. Dima could tell she was surprised at his insolence. He was a little surprised himself. Misha had already warned him to be wary of her, and yet here he was. "That's none of your business," she said. "Now get out, before I throw you out."

Dima grabbed a stool from near the entrance and sat down. "I'm making it my business," he said. He expected her to get more angry, but instead, he thought she looked intrigued by his challenge.

"I'm in charge around here," she said, "in case you didn't know. I suggest you don't get on my bad side, because I can be very *unpleasant*."

"Oh, I understand that you're in charge," Dima said. "I don't question your authority." He crossed his legs in front of him and wrapped his hands around his top knee. "As for getting on your bad side, I don't really care."

Olga raised her eyebrows. "I don't have a problem with you," she said. "You're a Russian. I only have a problem with your Jewish friend."

"Well, good," Dima said, "I'm glad we're clear on that. I came here to tell you that if you've got a problem with Varilensky, then you've got a problem with me too. If anything *unfortunate* happens to him, you'll have to answer to me. Are we clear on that as well?"

Olga took a step toward him. "Are you threatening me?" she asked.

"Absolutely," Dima replied.

"I could give the word and have you killed right now," she said.

"You could," Dima agreed. "But I want you to know that I can put a bullet through your head faster than you can utter another obscenity-laden order."

Olga retreated a step, and Dima knew he'd gotten to her. "Either you're really crazy or really stupid," she said.

"That's for you to decide," he said, "but you lay off Felix and do your best to keep him out of harm's way, and you don't have to worry about me plunging a knife into your throat while you sleep."

Dima got up and went to the door of the tent.

"I already regret we rescued the two of you," Olga said.

Dima said nothing. He opened the tent door and saw that the rain had turned back into a fine mist.

"Don't think for a minute that you've won," Olga said, just before he slipped through to the outside.

Dima turned and looked at her. "Oh, I don't think that at all," he said. "I know I've already lost. That's why I came to speak to you in the first place."

He went back to the campfire, but Misha had taken his seat. Felix was stoking the fire on the other side, and Dima sat down on a log behind him. Misha pulled a flask out of his coat, took a swig, then offered it to Dima. He accepted it and took a drink. It burned his throat, and he gasped as it went down. Misha grinned and laughed. "Good stuff, huh?" he said. "An old farmer from the village sells it. He makes it himself." Dima handed it back to him and Misha took another drink. "It's the only thing that keeps me going out here. Not only does it keep the bears away, it gives you some really interesting dreams at night." He laughed and passed the flask to Felix who took a drink and gasped just as Dima had done.

Dima studied Misha's face and clothes for few seconds. He had gray worker's pants on and a shabby brown coat. Most of the other partisans were dressed similarly. None of them wore uniforms.

Misha saw Dima looking his way and ran his arm down the sleeve of his coat. "Pretty stylish, huh?" he said in jest.

"It looks warm at least," Dima said.

"Don't worry," Misha said. "We'll get you guys some warmer clothes. We'll head into the village tomorrow evening and see what we can find."

Felix had set up a tarp to keep the rain off the fire, and he made one last adjustment to it before sitting down.

"So what did you think of our little rescue earlier today?" Misha asked. "Those Nazis guarding you didn't know what hit 'em when Olga pulled that blanket off. Rat-tat-tat, and just like that, three less Nazis. That was the second time we've tried that stunt. It worked like a charm the first time too."

Felix and Dima stared at the fire, neither responding.

"It was certainly a lot more fun than what we've been doing lately," Misha said. "For the past few days, we've been hauling farm machinery out here to the woods to hide it from the Germans. Talk about boring."

Dima felt his body becoming warm once again as the fire came back to life and the alcohol spread out from his stomach.

"Where are you from?" Misha asked. "Me, I'm from Moscow. Don't know if I'd want to be back there now though. I hear the Nazis are closing in and that it's complete chaos there. Not like here. Ha-ha!"

Misha handed Dima the flask once again and he took another sip. "We're both from Leningrad," he answered.

"I knew it," Misha said. "I can tell immediately if someone's from the country or the city, and when I saw you guys, I just knew you were from the city." He pulled out a pouch of tobacco and a piece of newspaper and offered to roll a cigarette for Felix and Dima.

"He doesn't smoke," Dima said, referring to Felix, "but I'll take one."

"Doesn't smoke?" Misha said. "How on earth do you make it from day to day?"

Felix continued poking a stick at the logs and coals, situating them so that the fire burned brighter and hotter. "You're pretty damn good with fires," Misha said and handed the flask to Felix again. "Tell me, what was it like to be a German prisoner?"

Felix took the flask but didn't answer Misha's question. Dima had an idea the Germans had beaten Felix just as badly as they had him. He'd seen the burn marks on Felix's hands and neck, but every time Dima had asked him about it, Felix would only reply that it was over and he didn't want to revisit it – that nothing positive could come from dwelling on what they'd done to him. Dima wondered if he, too, had broken down and told the Germans some important piece of information. Since Felix used to do clerical work for the army, he probably knew quite a few secrets that the Germans would find interesting.

But somehow Dima just knew that Felix hadn't broken down. He'd noticed a change in Felix since those days long ago at the beginning of the war. He was no longer hesitant. With each passing day, he seemed more determined about things, less unsure of himself.

"I understand," Misha said. "You guys are probably exhausted. It's been a long day. I think I'll turn in myself." He stood up, handed Dima the cigarette he'd rolled, and stretched his arms over his head. Dima currently had the flask and held it out for Misha to take with him as he left, but Misha waved it off. "No, you guys can keep it. You need it. I've got more anyway."

The camp was deep in the woods and Dima found the quiet difficult to deal with. There was only the crackle of the fire and an owl hooting in the distance. His thoughts drifted back to that day two weeks ago when the German bombers set the warehouse afire. He thought about that a lot now – how Felix had risked his life to go back into the inferno to rescue him. Felix claimed that they'd made it out together – each helping the other find the way outside. But Dima knew better. He remembered struggling toward the exit, the thick smoke blinding and choking him. He remembered seeing Felix a few steps in front of him, his broad back pointing the way for him to follow. Then he remembered falling to the ground, unable to take the smoke anymore. He crawled on his hands and knees for a few seconds, then collapsed completely. A long list of regrets began screaming at him, and he knew the end of his life was near. Before he lost consciousness, he heard Felix calling out his name. He'd wanted to answer but had blacked out as he tried.

And then the next thing he remembered was the dusty boot of a Nazi kicking him in the side. He'd opened his eyes and saw he was twenty yards from the burned-out shell of the warehouse. Felix, still unconscious, was lying next to him.

In spite of everything Dima had said and done to Felix (even threatening him with the firing squad!), Felix had risked his life to go back into the burning warehouse to save him. Dima couldn't get over it, couldn't comprehend it. And he was so full of raw hate for Felix that he detested him now even more than the Nazis. Felix was an idiot – a bloody fool to do what he did. Didn't he understand anything in this world? Anything at all?

He looked at Felix now, sitting across from him, staring at the fire, deep in thought. Dima guessed he was probably thinking about Katya, probably worried about her well being – even though he himself was in such a precarious situation. How could Dima have been friends with him? They were nothing alike.

Dima took another big drink from the flask and afterwards Felix blurred and then split into two. Dima refocused his eyes and put him back together. "I know what you did," he said, slurring a few words.

Felix looked up. "You do?"

"Da," – yes – Dima replied.

"They told you?"

"Who?"

"The Germans, of course."

Dima was really feeling the effects of the alcohol. He thought Felix was trying to trick him out of the conversation he wanted to have. "Don't play games with me," he said. "I know you ran back into the warehouse to save me."

Felix motioned for the flask and then took a swig. "Oh," he said.

"Why did you lie to me about it?" Dima asked. "Why did you say we made it out together? That without me, we wouldn't have made it?"

Felix shrugged his shoulders. "Partly because I don't remember everything," he said. "The last thing I remember is the two of us still inside the warehouse."

Dima wasn't sure if he believed him. Even if Felix didn't specifically remember pulling his unconscious body to safety, he must have figured it out later. He watched Felix empty the last of the liquor from the flask. "It was a stupid thing you did," Dima said.

Felix fixed his eyes on him. "No, it wasn't," he said. "It wasn't stupid at all."

Dima felt his emotions starting to get the best of him, but he didn't care anymore. He was tired of holding them in check. "Bullshit!" he yelled. "You could have been killed."

"You would've done the same thing if our positions had been reversed," Felix said.

Dima shook his head. "You're a bigger fool than I thought if you believe that," he said.

"No, I'm not," Felix said. "If you were in my shoes, you would have done the same thing. I know you."

"You don't know me at all," Dima said, his voice rising. "You knew me when we were kids, but that was a long time ago. We're very different now. You're a . . ."

"You're still that same kid I grew up with," Felix interrupted.

The mist grew more and more dense until it turned into light rain once again. "I wish," Dima answered, shaking his head again. "I wish I was, but I'm not. Life was simple back then. Not like now. Now, everything's so fucking complicated."

"It doesn't matter if you see it or not," Felix persisted. "I do. You're still that same kid who wants to change the world. The same kid who cried for days after your pet mouse died. The same kid who wants to save everyone and everything."

"That kid," Dima said, dropping his head and staring into the fire, "died a long time ago." He closed his eyes and felt a strange pain near his heart, like someone had stabbed him with a tiny knife. He'd never felt anything like that before. It was like a wound had suddenly been opened and all of the pain and misery it had been holding inside was now gushing out. He opened his eyes to try to stop it, but it kept coming.

"Tell me the truth," he said to Felix. "If you have any respect at all for me, then tell me the truth now, because I really want to understand. I want to know why you risked your life to drag me out of that warehouse."

"All right," Felix said, "I'll tell you the truth. I did it because I'm selfish."

Dima breathed a sigh of relief and his emotions died down. He understood selfishness. That was what he was accustomed to seeing in those around him. He nodded his head at Felix.

"I did it," Felix continued, "because I wanted you to continue living. I wanted you to survive to see the end of this war, and to fall in love and get married and have children and grow old, fat, and happy. I risked my life for you because I consider you my friend. Despite all that's happened between us, when I look at you I see that same person I grew up with – the same person I had so much fun with, the same person I admired and . . ."

Dima took a deep breath to calm the rage that was rising within him. The other negative emotions he kept in check – anger, jealousy, hate – could come out, but not rage. He could never let that one out. Closing his eyes, he concentrated on his breathing and counted down from twenty. But when he reached zero, he still felt only marginally in control.

Rage was always there for Dima, just beneath the surface. It had accumulated through years and years of denying himself, of always trying to do what everyone else expected of him, of trying to live up to what his father – the great engineer and decorated Civil War hero – had done in his life. This endless drive to please others, to receive their accolades and to avoid their criticism, had built a mountain of resentment within Dima. And unbeknownst to those around him, this seemingly harmless mountain was filled with molten rage, and it took a tremendous amount of effort to keep it in, to prevent it from erupting and burning everyone and everything around him.

Dima was desperate to know why he was feeling so much rage right now, though he wasn't sure he'd like the answer. He decided to refocus his energy on containing it, but it was too late for that. "Shut up!" he yelled, jumping from his seat. "Just shut the hell up!" His eyes were glossy and his throat hurt. He inhaled quickly to try to keep the glossiness from trickling down the edge of his nose.

"I did it," Felix added, "in short, because you're worth saving."

"Shut up you son-of-a-bitch!" Dima charged at him and knocked him from his seat to the ground. "Damn you," he said under his breath, "you don't understand fucking anything in this world – nothing." But Dima's voice betrayed him and he could no longer keep the salty water in his eyes from streaming down his face. He turned and started for the woods, kicking a small log and breaking a low-hanging branch that was in his way.

"You asked for the truth," Felix said as Dima walked away. "You asked for the truth and you got it!"

Dima started to run. He had to get away. "And I'd do it again if I had to," he heard Felix's voice call out after him. He ran and ran until he tripped and fell and didn't get back up. He stayed there and cried in shame and the light rain soon turned into a downpour, mixing with his tears and washing them into the earth, where they were accepted unconditionally.

~

Глава Седъмая — Chapter Seven

Forever Hungry Ghosts

Senses alight,
    walking at night;
I feel what God had in mind,
    when he was bored,
    on that dreary day long ago.
But he was at his peak.
And in his own image,
    to a fault,
    to today,
    am I.
God's creation,
    from his imagination ...
I see him,
    from time to time,
    in glimpses,
    when I'm not thinking,
    when I'm at my peak,
I am He.
And He is me.

"It's coming your way!" Petya shouted. The sound of claws struggling to get a grip on a polished wood floor and the plodding footsteps of Petya chasing behind filled the apartment.

A second later, the black cat came racing around the corner, slipped and rolled on its side, then regained its footing and charged toward Igor. Igor spread his feet wide and sunk low to the ground to block the hallway. The cat made a quick decision to try to squeeze by his right side. Petya made it around the corner just in time to see the cat jump over Igor's outstretched leg and down the hallway. Igor lunged after it and caught it by its hind legs before it got away, but the cat screeched, then bit and clawed Igor's hands viciously until he let go.

"Damn it," Petya said. "You had it."

Igor slowly got to his feet and inspected the blood from the scratches on his hands. "Where did it go?" he asked.

"In my room," Petya said. "I'll go get it. You stay out here and keep a lookout for Oksana. She shouldn't be back for another three hours, but you never know with her."

Igor nodded while he licked the blood off his hands.

Petya went into his room, closed the door behind him, and sat down on his bed to rest for a minute. It took so much effort to move his body, and he was so damn hungry. They'd been chasing the cat for the last fifteen minutes.

He bent down and saw the skinny creature hiding under his bed. It hissed when it saw him and wedged itself further into the corner of the wall. It was probably the last pet left in their building. Petya used to see and hear cats and dogs wherever he went, but not anymore. As hunger became more dire, all the cats, dogs, and birds in the city had started to disappear.

He retrieved a pair of thick leather gloves from a drawer and put them on. It was a terrible thing he was about to do, but he'd convinced himself and Igor that it was the lesser of two evils.

He crawled under the bed until he could reach the cat and then grabbed it by the tail and pulled it toward him. It made its terrible high-pitched screeching sound again and sunk its claws into the hand that wouldn't let go of its tail. But Petya's gloves were too tough and thick for the cat's claws to reach his skin.

Once he got the cat out, he put it on the bed and wrapped his gloves around its neck and squeezed. It thrashed its body from side to side and bared its fangs and claws, but it was all in vain. Petya would not release his grip.

After a short time, the cat stopped moving and Petya let go of its neck and stared into its lifeless eyes. It was the first thing he'd ever killed in his life, and he felt a strange mix of immense power and overwhelming guilt.

So many times in his life he'd wanted to kill that cat for waking him up at night, for stinking up the apartment, for pissing in his shoes. And now he'd finally done it and he didn't know whether to jump for joy or pray for forgiveness.

Igor came in and saw the motionless cat lying on the bed. "Do you know how to skin it?" he asked.

Petya shook his head no. He was trying to convince himself that it had been an act of mercy. After all, the cat was old – already half blind – and had been slowly starving to death. "I'm sure I can figure it out though," he said to Igor.

"My pa made me skin a squirrel once," Igor said. "It was really hard. I hated it."

As poorly as Petya was handling the sudden decrease in food, Igor was in even worse shape. He moped around the apartment all day and rarely went outside anymore. Petya hated that the boy had to live through something like this at his age. Igor was on the verge of adolescence, and Petya knew from his own life how difficult that time was.

Petya took his gloves off and laid his hands on the cat. "I'll skin it," he said. It seemed so strange to him that the cat was dead when its body was still warm. "I put that little stove up on the roof. You go make sure the fire is going good. We'll need some hot coals so we can roast the meat."

Igor left the apartment and Petya carried the cat into the kitchen and set it on the counter. He opened a drawer and grabbed the sharpest knife they had. He decided to cut the cat's head off first since its eyes were still open and looking at him. As he did so, a strange voice whispered loudly, "You snake. You're going to burn in hell."

Petya spun around quickly, his eyes searching frantically for the voice's owner. He gripped the knife in his hand and held it out in front of him. "Who's there?" he called out. He looked down the hallway and under the kitchen table. No one answered, and he wondered if the voices from long ago were coming back to play tricks on his mind again.

So many times Petya felt like an imposter, a fraud who only looked like everyone else. *They* didn't hear voices without owners. *They* took sanity for granted. Petya didn't. He couldn't. Sanity to him was the ice of a frozen lake. Most of the time, the ice was thick and Petya stood firmly on top and only had to deal with the fear. But that he pushed as far back in his mind as he could.

The fear was with him because the ice wasn't always so thick. There were times – sometimes hours, sometimes days – when the ice was thin and as he walked across, it would splinter and crack. This was his advanced notice that the faces he saw and the voices he heard may no longer be real. A few times the thin ice had given way under his feet and he'd fallen in. Those had always been the most terrifying times of his life: not being able to tell right from wrong, dreams from reality, real voices from those only in his head. It was like being caught between two worlds – unable to be in one or the other. Looking in from the outside, and looking out from the inside.

Those instances when the thin ice of sanity had given way, Petya had been able to pull himself out fairly quickly. His greatest fear was that one day he would fall so far through the ice that he wouldn't be able to pull himself out, and instead be caught underneath looking up through the ice where he had once been. Longing to be as he was. Unable to get back on the right side of that ice. Forever trapped beneath its surface.

He returned to skinning the cat, deciding the voice hadn't been real. If the voices were indeed coming back, it was vitally important that he maintain his composure. It seemed that his life was always one misstep away from spinning out of control.

Today was October 8th and Petya still hadn't been able to find a position that would increase his rations. He was completely out of food except for a small bag of sunflower seeds he'd stolen from Oksana. He had lost twenty-eight pounds in the last six weeks, going from 206 pounds down to 178. If he hadn't been so overweight before the war started, he thought he might have already starved to death.

Igor arrived with some wooden skewers and Petya sliced the meat into square chunks and put it on them. They went up to the roof and roasted the meat over the orange coals in the small stove. It was a gray, cloudy day, but at least there was no wind so the temperature was bearable.

When the meat was done, they sprinkled it with salt and the only seasoning they had left – dried parsley. Petya chewed each bite thoroughly, and tried to imagine that it was chicken and not cat. Igor sat as far away as he could be, curled up in the corner like a desperate animal, ready to lash out at anything that came close to him or his food.

Petya took out his bread ration for that day and ate it along with the meat. The bread was hard and heavy and tasted terrible. It was filled with barely edible ingredients that gave Petya a stomachache every time. He heard another voice and wondered whether or not it was real, whether or not he should ignore it. "Did you say something?" he asked Igor.

"Yeah," Igor said, "you didn't hear me? I asked you why God hates us."

"Why does God hate us?" Petya thought it an odd question, coming from Igor.

"Yeah, if he didn't hate us, he'd rescue us, right?"

The thought occurred to Petya that perhaps God was a lonely child, like Igor. A lonely child with a child's mentality of good and evil, love and vengeance, judgment and eternity.

"Since when did you develop an interest in religion?" Petya asked. It felt strange to him to talk about God and religion so much these days. Before the war, the subject was taboo. But now everywhere he turned he saw old ladies making the sign of the cross, children saying prayers, and now Igor opening a discussion with him on God.

It all reminded Petya very uncomfortably of that part of his childhood spent with his aunt. A terrible memory flashed through his mind of him as a six-year-old boy being whipped by her for using the Lord's name in vain. The part that hurt the worst was that Petya hadn't actually said it. She'd misheard him.

"Katya talks about it all the time," Igor said. "She says there's nothing to be afraid of as long as we keep our faith in God." He took his last bite of food, then licked his fingers. "But I don't believe her," he added.

"Well, maybe God hates us because we haven't praised him enough," Petya said.

"Why do we have to praise him?"

At first, Petya thought Igor's innocent question was just childish ignorance, but then he wondered the same thing himself. Does an omnipotent God have low self-esteem? Does he need his creation to stoke his ego like a parent to a child? And if he doesn't get his way, he throws a temper tantrum and floods the earth – destroying all who don't appease him?

"I honestly don't know, Igor," Petya said. "I don't know why we have to praise him, and I don't know why he doesn't rescue us. Maybe it's because he's dead – like the philosopher Nietzsche says."

"He's not dead," Igor said. "He's just not coming back."

"What?" Petya exclaimed, surprised to hear such a shrewd notion coming from Igor's lips.

"I said I don't think he's coming back. He's seen what's happened here." Igor moved closer to the stove and held his hands over the top. "Maybe he can't face it."

Petya couldn't believe his ears. Did Igor just say what he thought he did, or were the voices conspiring against him again? Either way, he felt lost. He was accustomed to looking at Igor as a witless juvenile, but found it difficult to think of him in those terms after what he just said.

Petya leaned his head back, looking up at the endless gray sky. He had so much hate for religion. It had poisoned so many people, and they, in turn, had passed that poison on to their children. The whole world was infected. Even here in the Soviet Union, where religion had been banished as a relic from the past, people still worshiped and believed. If he could, Petya would burn every holy book, every church, every synagogue and mosque in the world. People needed to be educated. They needed to understand how cruel and detrimental religion really was.

The air raid sirens began their unearthly wailing again, echoing through the cavernous streets and lifeless ruins of collapsed buildings. Petya heard them, but kept walking. He wouldn't go to a shelter unless they forced him to. There was a time when he would have ran to the nearest shelter, a time when he valued safety above all else. But he was beyond that now.

He was dying. Little by little, day by day, cell by cell. Not an hour passed when he didn't think about that. Let the German planes come and drop a bomb on him. That wouldn't be such a bad way to die – quick and painless.

And symbolic too. What more could a writer ask for?

He was coming back from another failed attempt to get a position that would increase his rations. He wasn't bitter about it not working out though. He'd learned to lower his expectations so that he wouldn't be stung by rejection.

There were a lot of lessons he'd learned about protecting himself, like not getting too close to anyone because they would eventually leave or be taken away. His parents were taken from him. His uncle would leave almost as soon as he got back from some trip, and his aunt, for all the beatings and abuse she directed at Petya, was also his sole friend and confidante, and she was arrested by the communists and shipped to a gulag in Siberia for her religious beliefs.

Petya was sent to live in an orphanage after that, where the other kids mercilessly picked on him because of his disfigured leg. His only saving grace had been his intelligence, and he'd learned to wear it like a coat of armor.

He stopped now and looked at the sky above him, then laughed, though he didn't know why. Every day seemed to bring something new and unexplainable into his world. Like now, everywhere he turned, he saw everything saturated in a strange, purplish tint – the dark, bombed-out buildings, the wet pavement, the streetcars that passed slowly and quietly down their tracks. He felt like a ghost walking up the stark streets of a deserted city. Even when others passed by, they seemed surreal, like they were a backdrop to a dream he was having.

Petya began to wonder if he really did exist. Perhaps he had already died and was a lost spirit condemned to haunt the streets of the city that he loved, but never really appreciated when he was alive.

The more he thought about it, the more he terrified himself. What proof did he have that any of this was real? How could he prove that it wasn't all just a dream?

The only way he was able to calm himself was to accept the fact that he couldn't prove it. He didn't know that it wasn't all just a dream, but he did know that – whatever it was – it was beautiful. It was mayhem and despair and destruction, and it was also beautiful beyond words.

He shivered and wondered if ghosts could feel cold. And why shouldn't they? They were probably forever cold, he thought.

He came to his favorite statue in all of Leningrad – one of the few that wasn't surrounded these days by planks and sandbags. Pushkin, the greatest Russian writer ever to live, towered over him, a pigeon perched on his left shoulder.

Petya continued on, thinking again how it was October 8th, 1941 already. It occurred to him that time was constantly being burned, that his past was being deconstructed, dissolved by the simple passing of day to day, week to week, month to month, year to year.

He had spent three years of his life in Odessa, on the Black Sea. Three wonderful years. And yet he could barely recall anything he had done there – the people he knew, the music he listened to, the major events that took place. What had happened to that time? Was it lost forever?

It seemed sometimes that it wasn't really he who had lived there. He tried to picture himself in his apartment doing something – anything! What did he sit on? What did he think? What did he look at?

He couldn't recall anything. Nothing at all, besides that the apartment had high ceilings that he was quite fond of. In general, they had been good years. He remembered that much. But the life he'd lived was slipping away, slipping through his grasp like a handful of sand. He needed something to hold onto, something to think back on and look forward to again. How could one live life without that? What was life except a collection of memories and accomplishments?

He climbed over the rubble of a bombed-out building and felt so very weary. It was more than just physical exhaustion. He was tired of the anger and hatred and fear that ran his life. He wanted to feel more often like he felt now. He wanted the freedom that this spaciousness gave him. The freedom to take a step back from the habitual thoughts and reactions that dictated every minute of his life. Why must he be doomed to live his life trapped by what other people said or did to him? Why did he give this power to others to make him angry or jealous or irritable? Why couldn't he let go of his hatred of religion?

If he could live his life over, he'd do it differently. He'd laugh more at himself, rather than others. He'd take more walks with no destination or goal in mind. He'd be more vulnerable and less guarded. He'd sleep in on Saturdays and not feel guilty about it. He'd read more poetry and less news. He'd listen to more music and less gossip. He'd notice more often when people smiled, and less when they frowned. If he could live his life over again, he'd notice more often how wonderful the smell of the ocean was, and the sheer perfection and simplicity of a wave crashing to shore and dissolving into nothingness.

* * *

Felix peeked his head above the rocks and watched Misha walking toward him over the narrow, winding road. After he saw Misha wave his right arm high in the air, Felix prepared to light the match. But then Misha unexpectedly fell to the ground. Felix stopped and listened intently, but could hear no gunfire or anything else out of the ordinary. There was a squirrel chattering in the large oak tree next to him, but nothing else.

He glanced at the dynamite he'd wedged into a crack in the rock, and deliberated whether to light the fuse and run or go check on Misha first. Misha was lying face down in the road, and Felix wondered if he'd merely passed out. He knew Misha had been drinking heavily that day, even more than usual. As Felix looked down the slope, he saw Misha begin to move his right arm, then his left, then shake his head and climb back to his feet. Felix struck the match, lit the dynamite, and scrambled down the side of the massive rock, jumping the last six feet to the road below.

Misha was still brushing himself off when Felix reached him. "What happened?" Felix asked.

"I don't know," Misha said. "It was weird. Everything just blacked out all of a sudden."

"You and Dima need to stop drinking that poison all day long," Felix said.

"No, it wasn't from the alcohol," Misha said. "It was something else."

Felix waited to hear what else it was, but Misha didn't elaborate. They hurried over to the cluster of trees where Dima and another partisan, Yuri, were waiting. Yuri, a large man with wide shoulders and forearms as thick as tree limbs, was the first to meet them.

"What took you so long?" he asked. "I could have done that in half the time."

Felix ignored him and searched for Dima. He found him still sitting on the same fallen tree as when he'd left. He was smoking another cigarette and had no reaction when the dynamite exploded and filled the air with its deafening boom. Dima hardly had a reaction to anything anymore, and Felix was troubled by the apathy, and sometimes downright animosity, that seemed to rule his life these days. Dima had fallen under Misha's influence, and the two of them got drunk together nearly every day now.

Yuri left the thicket of trees to go inspect the road, and Felix followed him. He could see right away that they'd been successful. The dynamite had smashed the humongous rock and caused a mini avalanche that now blocked the road and made it impossible for German trucks, tanks, or cars to pass by.

The four of them picked up their things and began marching to the little village of Lestovo, where they were to meet up with the rest of the partisans. Several inches of snow covered the ground, and when they stepped, their boots would make either a sucking sound as they sank into the mud or else a crunching sound as they stomped over dead leaves. The sun was hidden behind thick clouds once again and it was cold, but at least they were all dressed for it. They wore thick, heavy coats, wool scarves, hats, and insulated leather mittens.

Felix walked in front with Yuri, who carried his rifle at his side with his left hand. Yuri was quiet for a change, and Felix used the time to reflect on how Dima hadn't been the same since the fire at the warehouse. Dima seemed to be lost in his own world these days, constantly pondering things and muttering unintelligible thoughts and ideas that only he could hear. Felix tried to engage him, but Dima never talked. He kept it all inside.

Felix glanced over his shoulder and saw that Misha and Dima were dragging behind once again. He tugged on Yuri's coat and the two of them stopped to allow their comrades to catch up.

"I'm getting sick of those two drunkards," Yuri said while he lit a cigarette.

Yuri had spent the last eight years of his life in a gulag in Siberia and not a day went by when he didn't remind others of it.

"For eight whole years I suffered injustices that you can't even imagine," Yuri said. "But not once, I tell you, did I ever lose faith in my country. I knew there would come a day when I would be called upon to serve her." He spat on the ground as he watched Misha and Dima walk gingerly around a muddy area. Dima seemed to be the more drunk of the two now and looked like he was focusing all his concentration on putting one foot in front of the other. "Not like those idiots," Yuri continued. "They have no honor. They have no shame!" He shouted the last sentence in their direction, but neither of them acknowledged him.

Felix thought of his own time spent as a prisoner of the Germans and wondered how similar his experience had been to Yuri's. His interrogators had beat him every day – sometimes two or three times a day. But Felix had told them nothing. He simply went within himself, blocked out the pain, and instead thought of Katya. When they'd finally got to him was when they sat him outside the room where Dima was being interrogated. They made him sit there for two hours and listen to his friend scream and plead for an end to the punishment. Then they told Felix they'd stop torturing Dima and even let his comrade sleep and eat, on one condition – that Felix tell them some piece of information they might find useful.

"Perhaps you should walk a mile or two in their shoes before you judge them so harshly," Felix said to Yuri. "You know Dima was captured by the Nazis and they . . ."

"What could be worse than *eight* years in Siberia?" Yuri interrupted. "Nothing – that's what. Did I tell you how in the winter the frost would be three inches thick on the *inside* of the windows? It was so cold in those barns they kept us in that you could see your breath. And we had to work outside all day long where it was twenty degrees below zero. You *never* got warm. A quarter of the men froze to death every winter. You don't know how good you have it here. You get hot food and fresh bread . . ."

"And booze too," Misha added as he and Dima finally caught up. "Don't forget about that."

Yuri finished his cigarette and flicked the butt at Misha and Dima. It bounced off Dima's coat, but he didn't even notice. A few steps later, Dima tripped and fell to the ground.

"Leave him there," Yuri said. "Serves him right."

Dima made it to his knees, but it looked doubtful that he would make it up to his feet.

"Alcohol is the biggest poison man ever invented," Yuri said. "And you two fools are living proof."

Misha went over to Dima, but then saw Felix was coming to help, so he continued walking. "What on earth possessed them to ever let you out of Siberia?" he said to Yuri.

Felix rolled his eyes. He'd already heard this story a half dozen times.

"They set me free to defend my country from the enemy," Yuri said and launched into his long explanation of how he'd ended up here with the partisans. Misha winked at Felix as they passed one another and Felix knew that Misha was patronizing Yuri. He did it for entertainment.

Felix pulled Dima to his feet, then put his arm around him and helped him walk. They were quiet for a time until Felix turned his head toward Dima and said, "You can't go on like this, you know. You're killing yourself. You're going to go blind drinking that concoction the old man makes."

"So what if I'm killing myself," Dima said, slurring the words. "What's it to you?"

"You're my friend, and I want to help you in some way," Felix said, then paused. "But I don't know what to do."

"You can leave me the hell alone," Dima said. "That's what you can do."

"No," Felix said, "that's the one thing I can't do. I can't just stand by and watch you drown yourself. We're too young for that. You may have given up on yourself, but I haven't."

"Who said I gave up?" Dima said. "Just because Misha and I drink a little bit to keep warm, you think I've given up?"

Felix was pleased that Dima was even talking to him. His previous attempts at conversation had been complete failures. He tried provoking him into continuing. "Hell yes, you've given up," he said. "Look at you. You're a drunk. You can't even walk by yourself."

Dima pulled away from Felix and began walking on his own, staggering from side to side, but managing to stay on his feet.

"You think you're so fucking perfect, don't you?" Dima said.

Felix didn't want the conversation to switch to him. "I'm not perfect," he said, "but at least I'm not a drunk. At least I don't deny what's bothering me. I face it head on, rather than trying to drown it with liquor."

"I don't do that," Dima said. "I'm just trying to . . . . I mean I just want to . . . . Oh just leave me alone, will you!" He marched out in front of everyone, stumbling as he did so, just barely managing to maintain his balance.

Felix tripped on something beneath the snow and stumbled a few steps himself, until he caught hold of a tree that prevented him from falling. Felix patted the tree's trunk and said thank you. He was impressed with how *solid* the tree was and wished for some of that solidity himself to guide him through these difficult days.

He caught up to Yuri and Misha in time to hear Yuri talking about the Panzers breaking through their lines. Felix knew that the part about the Panzers meant he was approaching the end of his story.

"We simply weren't prepared to fight against tanks," Yuri said. "Our entire regiment was in complete chaos only thirty minutes into battle . . . if you can call it a battle that is. I don't think we inflicted a single casualty on them. Anyway, after we were encircled, all the men wanted to surrender, but I wouldn't do it. I said they could be cowards if they wanted to, but I wasn't going to. I told them I was an honest man and took an oath to protect my country. I was going to make sure I lived to fight another day! I left them and made it past the German lines by going through a minefield and wading through a swamp."

Felix knew there was still another ten minutes to the story – painfully boring details about how he made it through the minefield and swamp – so he tried to cut the story short. "So that's how you ended up as a partisan?" he said.

"Yep, that's how it happened," Yuri said, puffing his chest out like he always did at the end of the story. "Been fighting those bastards behind the lines ever since."

They came to the now familiar village of Lestovo with its two dozen small clay houses and stone church that had been turned into a horse stable by the communists. Felix had already learned about the precarious life of those in small villages like Lestovo, and how difficult it was for the partisans to know who to trust. When the partisans weren't there asking for something, then the Nazis were there plundering the villagers' meager possessions and threatening their lives over information on the partisans.

"Weren't there some goats there when we came this way last week?" Misha asked, pointing at a small, empty pen.

"Yes, I remember them too," Felix said. "The Germans probably took them."

The village used to full of cows, pigs, chickens, and goats, but every time a group of Germans came through, they helped themselves to some livestock. Fortunately, the villagers had enough potatoes, cabbage, beets, and canned raspberries and tomatoes stored away in various hiding places to get them through the winter. They even had enough food to sometimes give to the partisans.

"The Nazis are such fools to treat the villagers so badly," Misha said.

"I agree," Felix said. "For all their sophistication and organization and Blitzkrieg, they're clueless about how to make friends out of former enemies. It's like their invasion plans covered every single detail, except what to do once they won."

"They haven't won yet," Yuri said.

"I know," Felix replied. "And they're not going to either."

They all stopped and looked at a crude wooden cross marking a new grave. A bouquet of dried flowers rested on top of the freshly dug dirt.

"The worse they treat the villagers, the more our numbers grow," Yuri said, looking at Felix. "I'm glad they're so brutal with them. People are getting a glimpse into what life under their rule would be like."

Felix studied Yuri's face for signs of 'the look,' as he now called it. Felix had seen it three more times since he first saw it on Fedushkin's face. And each time, the man had died before the sun rose the next day. One time the man died a few minutes after Felix saw it on his face – he had tried, unsuccessfully, to defuse a landmine. The other two times, the men had died much later after Felix saw it, but without exception each man died before the sun of the new day.

Why he, and he alone, saw these things made no sense to Felix. When he least expected it – as he was casually talking to someone or happened to glance at them as they passed by – he would see an unmistakable look on their face that told him that person was going to die soon. It had become as clear to him now as if the word "death" was scrawled onto their forehead.

Seeing nothing on Yuri's face, Felix breathed a sigh of relief and looked away. The villagers were gathering in front of one of the houses up ahead, and when they got closer, Felix could see that Olga had ordered one of the villagers to be taken into custody. The man's wife, who wore a thin, white apron and had been peeling potatoes on their porch watched as two partisans held her husband by the arms.

The crowd grew larger by the minute. Men in tattered old coats like the partisans wore, women with scarves wrapped around their heads, and half a dozen children with frightened faces listened in as Olga preached her sermon to them. "The Nazis have started a war of extermination!" she shouted. "They want to destroy Russia – to annihilate us from the face of the planet. The only way to survive is if we all fight them to the death. And here," she said, pointing to the man in custody, "is a traitor, who, instead of fighting the Nazis, has chosen to help them destroy us."

"Vladimir, what did you do?" one of the men in the crowd asked.

"I'll tell you what he did," Olga responded. "He told the Germans where the farm machinery was hidden."

Felix and the others were now standing a few yards away from Olga. They watched as Vladimir, a bony man with long arms that hung nearly to his knees, hung his head, indicating that the accusation to be true.

"We have no choice but to win this war against the fascist aggressors," Olga said. She signaled to Yuri, and he stepped forward and aimed his rifle at the man. "And this is what happens to German collaborators. Let this be a lesson to everyone."

Olga nodded to Yuri, but Felix laid his hand on the barrel of Yuri's rifle and he did not shoot.

Felix didn't want to speak up. Unbeknownst to the people who knew him, he actually hated confrontations. They tied his stomach in knots and set his heart racing. But he didn't let that stop him. It was more important to him how he felt after the event, than during. And if he wasn't honest, if he didn't speak up about something when he had the opportunity, then he would feel terrible afterwards. His neck and shoulders would be tight and he'd be filled with regret. No, he couldn't stand by and watch this. "Give him a chance to redeem himself," he shouted.

The villagers all turned to look at him.

"There's no room for compromise," Olga said, her face contorted with barely concealed rage. "The only way we'll smash the Nazis is with an iron fist."

Felix felt the familiar tension come over his body. He felt slightly nauseous and noticed his jaw was clenched tightly. He took a deep breath and continued. "Give him a second chance," he said, addressing the villagers. "He's made a mistake – as we all do. Give him an opportunity to make up for it. We could use him as a double agent and set a trap for the Germans."

"There are no second chances in this war," Olga shouted. She looked squarely at Yuri and said, "I order you to shoot."

"There are always second chances," Felix said. He put his hand on Yuri's shoulder. "This man was in a Soviet prison not long ago for crimes against the state. He was given a second chance, and here he is – defending his country, fighting the Nazis behind the lines every day."

A few of the villagers nodded their heads. "And if he betrays us again?" one of the them said. "What then?"

Another villager answered him. "If he betrays us again," he said, "we'll carry out justice ourselves – the old fashioned way, with a rope and a tree."

"Yes, he's not going anywhere," Vladimir's wife said. "Give him a second chance."

The crowd looked to Vladimir. "The Germans offered me money to tell them," he said, raising his weathered face to look back at the crowd. "But I wouldn't do it. Then they threatened to burn down our house, and I didn't know what to do. Where would we live? How would we make it through the winter without a house?" He looked expectantly at the faces of his neighbors. "If you give me another chance, I will make up for it."

The partisans and villagers all turned toward Olga now. She pulled her hat from her head, spat on the ground, then wiped her mouth with the back of her hand. "Of course, we'll give you another chance, comrade," she said. Then she motioned for the two men holding his arms to let go. "And if the Germans burn your village down because of this traitor," she said, addressing the crowd, "you will have Comrade Varilensky here to thank." She smiled sarcastically at Felix, and the rapidly fading sunlight glinted off her gold tooth.

Felix felt relieved that the confrontation was over. No doubt Olga hated him, but he couldn't let that stop him from being who he was. He answered to no one but his own guiding conscience – that voice inside him that saw everything clearly.

"Let's move out!" Olga hollered, and the motley group of partisans started heading back to camp. Olga waited for Felix, then pulled him aside and whispered in his ear, "You think you're pretty smart, don't you kike?"

"What I *think*," Felix said, ripping his arm away from her, "is that we're all in this together – you, me, the villagers . . . everyone. And we're not going to win this war until we start acting like it."

"I've brought down many a man smarter than you," she continued. "Be happy with your little victory here today, because it was your first and your last."

The partisans trudged the mile and a half to their camp in silence. The clouds had dispersed and Felix could see the thin moon low in the sky. He remembered reading that where the sun did not strike the moon's surface, the temperature would fall to -261 degrees fahrenheit. That made the 31 degrees he had to endure on earth a little easier.

Yuri told him that in the village he grew up in, they called it a Blood Moon during the month of October. Felix thought it appropriate given the number of lives being lost across Russia recently. He'd heard earlier that day that Kiev had fallen. It was rumored that as many as 600,000 Red Army troops had been taken prisoner there. Kiev, in Felix's native Ukraine, was the mother of all Russian cities and Felix could hardly believe the news that they'd surrendered.

The whole world was watching Leningrad now. If the city couldn't hold out, then Hitler would move all the troops stationed there on to Moscow. And with Moscow barely holding on as it was, a couple hundred thousand extra German troops would surely tip the balance. And if Moscow fell, then all of Russia would likely fall. Hitler could then focus on Great Britain, and how long could they hold out? At best, the war would end in stalemate, except now all of Europe and Russia would be under Nazi rule.

Felix contemplated the moon once again. Only a small sliver of it could be seen, as though it had shrunk and would soon be extinguished. But the entire moon was still there, Felix knew. Even when one couldn't see any trace of it, it was still there. It was a matter of faith.

* * *

"Guzman!" Petya shouted and banged on the door again. "Open up. It's me, Petya. Are you there?"

Petya waited a few seconds, then kicked the bottom of the door. He was cold and hungry and didn't like having to stand in the hallway any longer than he had to. "Guzman, we're all moving into Katya's apartment today. I've come to help you. Open the door."

Katya had invited everyone on the floor – Petya, Oksana, and Guzman – to move into her apartment so they could conserve their scarce firewood. Katya's apartment was also the only one on the floor that still had windows. All the rest had sheets of plywood and were as dark as night no matter if the sun was shining or not.

No one would be expected to share their food, but they would at least be available to help one another out. Katya was particularly worried about Guzman, who seemed to move slower and speak less each day. Oksana and Petya's roommate, Boris, hadn't been heard from in a month, and Oksana speculated he was either dead or had found a way out of the city to rejoin his wife and daughter. Petya had already searched Boris' room for food, tea, vodka, or cigarettes, and had come up empty.

"Guzman! I'm going to leave if you don't open up," Petya said and kicked the bottom of the door one last time. He knew Guzman was there. The old man was too weak to go anywhere. Petya was starting to wonder if he might be dead when he heard some shuffling and a few weak coughs that told him the old painter was finally coming to let him in.

"I've been knocking on your door for five minutes," Petya said as Guzman opened the door.

Guzman was covered from head to toe in dark blankets. He said nothing in response. His face was pale and ghostly.

Petya felt awkward being so close to someone who was so near death. "How are you feeling?" he asked.

"Like a sprinn chiign," Guzman mumbled.

"Like a what?" Petya said and turned his ear toward him.

"Like a spring chicken," Guzman repeated.

It took Petya a second, but he realized the old man was making a joke. He laughed, then added, "Yeah, like a spring chicken in a wolf's den."

Guzman managed a weak smile.

"What do you need to take to Katya's?" Petya asked, looking around his cluttered apartment. It was obvious Shostakovich hadn't been there in a while to play the piano. It was covered with newspapers and dirty clothes and the bench was lying on its side.

"My pillow and sheets and blankets," Guzman said. His breathing was heavy and labored and he leaned against the wall for support. The hair from his long arching nose had started to blend into his newly grown beard. His lips couldn't even be seen behind the curly black and gray hair that now covered his face.

"And my hat and coat," Guzman added.

Petya thought to argue with him about that. The next time Guzman went outside would be when they took his body to the cemetery. There was no way he was going to make it down those stairs and then back up again in his condition. His health had gone far downhill in the past two weeks.

The apartment smelled like urine and Petya traced it to a bedpan in the bedroom. He emptied the bowl out the window, as everyone did these days, then collected the items Guzman wanted and took them over to Katya's apartment. When he returned, Guzman was still standing in the same place. He was staring at an oil-on-canvas painting hanging on the wall opposite him. "I painted that when I was twenty-seven," he said.

Petya looked at the painting, but wasn't sure what to say about it. It was the Winter Palace, though all the colors were very dark – the sky was almost black, and the palace itself wasn't much brighter.

"Isn't it the ugliest thing you ever saw?" Guzman said.

Petya looked at Guzman, saw the slight smirk on his face, then laughed himself. "Actually, it *is* the ugliest painting I've ever seen."

"Good. Good. There's hope for you yet, my boy," Guzman said and patted Petya on the shoulder.

"Do you want to take it over to Katya's?" Petya asked.

"No. It's better left here – where it's always been."

"What else do you want me to take over?"

Guzman scratched his chin and looked around the apartment. "My boots," he said. "I'll need those."

"What about food?" Petya asked. "Do you want me to bring that? Or do you want to get it yourself?"

"Food?" Guzman said. "What's that?"

Petya laughed again, but he wasn't sure whether or not to believe him. "Okay then," Petya said, "why don't you make your way over there, and I'll get your boots and gather up your firewood."

Guzman shuffled his way slowly down the hallway of his apartment, keeping close to the wall and coughing every few feet. When he reached the door, he turned and shouted, "Vanya!"

Petya was puzzled. "What did you say, Guzman?"

"Vanya, please don't forget to feed my parakeet while I'm gone. Promise me you won't forget."

Petya thought he might be joking again, but Guzman's hollow stare said otherwise. The old man was losing his mind. That was something Petya could sympathize with. "I won't forget," Petya said. "I promise."

"Thank you, Vanya. Thank you. I know I can count on you," Guzman said and continued on his way to Katya's apartment.

Petya collected Guzman's boots and another blanket he found in the closet and took them over to Katya's apartment. Guzman was laying on the couch there, still mumbling incoherently. "We'll meet again one day, Marfusha. I promise," he said. "Life is so very long and we're so very young. Vanya! Let's not be late this time. Have them get the sleigh ready."

Igor was curled up in a thick, cushioned chair on the other side of the room. "Who's he talking to?" he asked Petya.

"Ghosts," Petya said, and went back to Guzman's apartment to gather the firewood. Before he did that though, he went into Guzman's kitchen to see if he had any food he'd overlooked or forgotten about. Nearly every drawer and cupboard Petya opened was completely empty, and he wondered where all of Guzman's plates and bowls and silverware had gone. Perhaps he'd sold them at the market, Petya thought.

In the last cupboard he checked, Petya found a little glass container with something black in it. He pulled it out, took the lid off, and was surprised to see that it was black tea. There wasn't much – perhaps enough for three or four cups – but it was a godsend nonetheless. Petya hadn't had tea in a month and missed that almost more than food.

After he took the firewood over to Katya's, he decided to take advantage of the peace and quiet of Guzman's apartment and the still hot fire in his ceramic stove to try to write. He boiled some water to make tea with, then cleared a space on Guzman's piano, turned the bench upright, and sat down with pen and paper.

Despite the slow, daily starvation, Petya continued to attempt to write. He was convinced that great works of art were often created when the artist was suffering. The more the suffering, the greater the work of art would be. Nothing else mattered to him besides his novel. If only he could complete his masterpiece, then he'd show them. Then everyone would know how great he was. They'd be sorry they ever doubted him.

He picked out one of Guzman's books and tossed it in the fire, then held his frigid hands over the top of the stove. Transporting Guzman's things to Katya's apartment had been exhausting. He had so little energy these days and was always, always cold and hungry.

After a few minutes, he sat back down, hoping inspiration would strike. His mind was dull from the lack of food, but he had no shortage of thoughts. Hundreds of them came and went every minute. Unfortunately, he didn't find any of them interesting enough to expend his precious ink and paper on.

Petya believed he was destined to write something very profound – a novel that had an impact on society, that made people question their closely-held beliefs, values, and ingrained habits. This was his destiny, and all the suffering he'd accumulated in his life, including the immensity he was now enduring, was but preparation for this work of genius. All the pain and sorrow in his life was for educational purposes only, so that he might know that aspect of life that so tortured humanity. He needed to have a full comprehension of it if he was to have a chance at educating anyone. His suffering was the compost from which a new understanding would bloom for him. And then he could let others in on that profound understanding.

He had faith that the particular path he was on would eventually get him to that place. As long, of course, as he stayed on the right side of the ice of sanity, as long as he could differentiate real voices from the imaginary ones from his head.

He stared at an orange pot on the windowsill as he tried to think of what to write. The pot had been home to a plant that had long since died, and he noticed the corner of a piece of paper sticking out from underneath it. Petya slid the pot over, picked up the piece of paper, and saw that it was Guzman's ration card.

There was a knock at one of the doors on the floor, and Petya tucked the card in his pocket and went to see which door it was. In the dim light of the hallway, he saw a young man standing in front of Katya's apartment.

"Can I help you?" Petya asked, sticking his head into the hallway. He saw the man was holding a package in his right arm.

"I'm looking for Katerina Selenaya," the man said. "Do you know if she's home?"

Petya walked over and unlocked the door, then held his finger in front of his lips. "Shhh, the boy is sleeping," he said. He didn't know if Igor, or Guzman for that matter, were actually sleeping, but he didn't want them to overhear. "You have a package for Katya?" Petya asked. "I can give it to her for you."

The man pursed his thin lips and shifted the package to his other arm. "I have special instructions to give it only to Katerina Selenaya," he said. "I ask you again, comrade, is she home?"

"No," Petya said, "she won't be home until late this evening. I am her brother. Can't you just give it to me and I'll give it to her when she returns?"

The man licked his chapped lips as he studied Petya for a moment.

"Surely you don't want to have to come back here again this evening," Petya said.

"You're her brother?" he asked.

Petya nodded. "You see," he said, pointing at the number on the apartment door, "we even live in the same apartment."

"Then why did you just come from that other apartment?"

"I was over there helping our neighbor," Petya said. "He's ill and not doing so well." He tried to get a look at the writing on the top of the box. "Who is the package from? Is it from our father?"

"No, it's from a . . .." The man tilted the package toward the light coming from the apartment. "It's from a Comrade Shostakovich."

"Ahh, it's from Dmitry," Petya exclaimed. "We've been expecting it for quite some time now. We'd nearly given up on it." Petya held out his hands and the man reluctantly handed it over. "Don't worry, comrade," Petya assured him. "I'll make sure my sister gets it."

The man looked like he was about to say something and Petya quickly closed the door before he could do so. He listened for the man's footsteps to turn and walk down the hallway. But instead, the man knocked on the door again.

Petya gripped the package tightly with both arms and remained quiet. After a few seconds, he heard the man mutter, "Ah, to hell with it," and walk down the hall.

When Petya could no longer hear any footsteps, he opened the door again and went back to Guzman's apartment. His hands were shaking as he tore open the box and read the letter lying on top:

Dear Katya,

I made some calls as you requested and found out what happened to your father. I'm so sorry to have to be the one to tell you this. I was informed that he died of a heart attack while in Moscow.

Such is life that all our best men are taken from us when we need them most. He will be sorely missed.

I've pulled a few strings to send you this little package, because I worry terribly about you and Guzman getting enough to eat. Please don't give it all to Guzman. I know you, Katya. You'll need your strength too, so make sure you get enough to eat as well.

I hope this finds you in good health and spirits. I'm sure Guzman has been telling you how things were better "in the old days." But don't listen to him. The times are rough now. There's no arguing that. But the more Russia suffers, the more her soul shines bright. It does no good to reminisce about the good old days, because there were none. Times were rough before the Germans invaded, and times were rough before the revolution. The tsar was a butcher, and the people of Russia were poor and hungry. Russia was in constant turmoil and the vast majority of people were miserable while the fat bourgeois pissed on the backs of the workers and peasants. How conveniently the great Western humanists forget this!

They'll never understand the people of Russia. They don't want to understand, because we're different than they. Our skin may be the same color, but we're nothing like them and they can't accept that. But I'm through thinking about them. Devil take them and their smug lives contemplating how they're always right!

Sorry I've rambled on so. I've been a nervous wreck lately. I hope this letter and package get to you. It has been no small feat. I am in Kuibyshev now, and I was able to buy three cans of caviar, a bottle of vodka, and some cigarettes here. The vodka is the real thing, not that lethal stuff the peasants make and then pour into empty vodka bottles. I've included the vodka and cigarettes because I know they're in high demand there and you should be able to trade for something you really need, be it food or whatever. The caviar I leave at your discretion. You can probably trade it for more food, but if it's not worth it, then eat it yourself. These items are meant for you and Guzman equally (though I beg of you not to show him the vodka or cigarettes, for I know he'll want them. Please trade for them first). I don't know if I'll be able to get any more packages to you (assuming this one even made it), but I'll try.

I miss my dear Leningrad. I hope she's holding up well. Take care of her for me.
- Dmitry

PS I've finished putting the final touches on my Seventh Symphony. I hope to have it performed soon – in honor of you brave Leningraders.

Petya set the letter aside and dug through the wadded up newspaper in the box until he found the treasure. It was a beautiful sight: that brand new bottle of vodka, those cigarettes, and those cans of caviar. He nearly wept at the sight of them.

* * *

"Look at them," Yuri sneered, nodding with his head to someplace behind Felix. Felix turned and saw Dima and Misha sitting around the campfire passing a flask back and forth.

"It's not even noon yet, and they're already drunk," Yuri said. He scowled and ran his fingers along his upper lip. "I think it's past time our *leader* stop tending to her rats and put an end to this." He started for Olga's tent, leaving Felix standing alone.

The 'rats' Yuri referred to were actually five baby mice Olga had found in the woods and had taken in as pets. She spent lots of time lately feeding and caring for them.

Felix sighed and looked up at the sky, wondering if the sun would succeed that day in its struggle to break through the thick clouds. He walked through the muddy snow toward the fire to warm his hands up. "Hey there Varilensky," Misha said, slurring a few words.

Dima had his eyes closed and was holding his head in his hands.

"I told you that stuff would make you go blind," Felix said to him.

"Go to the devil," Dima replied.

Felix poured some hot water into a tin can to make tea. "No, I think I'd rather just sit here," he said and sat down in between Dima and Misha.

"Yes, yes, stay," Misha said, patting Felix on the shoulder. He offered Felix the flask, but Felix waved it away. Misha passed it over to Dima, who took a swig, passed it back, and then held his head in his hands once more.

"You're just in time," Misha said to Felix. "I had an epiphany about God and was about to enlighten Dima. Now, you get to hear too." Misha paused to hiccup, then continued. "I say before you that God was, without a doubt, drunk when he created man."

"That's not an epiphany," Felix said. "That's lunacy."

"No, wait," Misha said. "Let me explain it to you. He'd been drinking a lot of his most recent creation – wine – and was feeling all this love and peace and joy. He was overflowing with it, and that's when he created man, in that state. He was ecstatic about it. He thought man was the best thing he'd ever created. But he sobered up later on and realized what a mistake he'd made. Man could only *glimpse* the state of bliss that he – God – had been in. It could never last for them. He realized how much pain and suffering they would create for themselves, and how desperate they would be to know that love, peace, and joy again, no matter how briefly."

"So what's your point?" Felix asked.

"My point, dear comrade, is that the only way one can know God is by attaining the same inebriated state he was in when he created us."

"So that's why you're always getting drunk," Felix said. "So you can be one with God?"

"You got it," Misha said, and took another sip from the flask. "I see things very clearly when I'm drunk."

"No," Dima spoke up, "you're wrong." He took his hands away from his unshaven face and interlaced them in front of him. "God was completely sober when he created man."

Felix was surprised to hear Dima speak on the subject of God. He usually avoided those conversations or else would try to convince others that evolution had already proved that God did not exist.

"He knew what he was doing," Dima continued. "He knew that the odds of figuring out the path to him would be extremely difficult. He did it to make it interesting, because his previous attempts had all been too easy. He decided to triple the amount of greed and jealousy and vengeance and anger. 'Now let them find their way!' he laughed. That's how he is."

Misha raised his eyebrows, looking puzzled. "How is he?" he asked.

"Spiteful," Dima said.

Nobody spoke after that. Felix poured some more hot water into his tin cup, and Misha rolled a cigarette. Dima leaned in toward the fire with his arms on his knees. He held the flask in front of him and seemed to study it. Then he took another sip and stood up. He stumbled slightly, then swayed in place for several seconds and Felix was afraid he'd fall into the fire. He started muttering to himself again, then shook his fist in the air and looked up at the sky. "Damn you, God!" he yelled.

Misha grinned and pulled a twig out of the fire and used it to light his cigarette. Felix wanted to shake Dima by the shoulders until he snapped out of this funk he was in. But he knew that wouldn't work. He'd learned that he couldn't 'educate' people out of their doldrums. He took a sip of tea and caught a glimpse of Dima's face as Dima turned and walked toward the woods.

Felix didn't want to believe what he'd just seen on his friend's face. He was horrified. It was 'the look.'

He wanted to run after Dima and look in his eyes again, hoping he was wrong. But he knew he wasn't wrong. He'd just seen the same look of impending death that he'd seen on Fedushkin's and the other's faces. The thought of Dima dying before the sun of the new day was too much for him to bear. He didn't know what to do. He'd tried subtly warning people before, but that hadn't helped. He couldn't let it happen to Dima, though. He couldn't, and he *wouldn't* let it happen. Felix decided he would personally make sure that nothing befell his friend for the rest of the day. He stood up and scanned the area now, but saw nothing out of the ordinary.

Yuri came storming out of Olga's tent alone. He marched over to Misha and Felix and picked the flask up from the ground. "The party's over, you miserable drunkards," he said.

Misha watched Yuri empty the flask's contents onto the muddy ground around the campfire. He didn't seem to care, but Dima, who had finished urinating and was coming back, looked angry. "What the hell are you doing?" he said, as he drew nearer.

"Something that should have been done a long time ago," Yuri said. "I'm through standing around watching you two contaminate this group."

Dima clenched his hands into fists. "Then perhaps you'd like to sit," he said, and threw a punch at Yuri's face. It hit him squarely above the left eye, and Yuri retaliated with a kick to Dima's groin that sent him wincing to the ground in pain.

A small crowd of partisans gathered around to watch the fight, and Felix rushed in to try to put an end to it. "Stop it!" he shouted to them both, but Dima had gotten back on his feet and was already charging at Yuri. Felix used the skills he'd mastered studying the Russian martial art form, Sambo. He caught Dima as he went by and used his own force against him. Felix then slid off to the side and used his arms to push Dima down to the ground. No sooner had he done it, than he began regretting it. He needed to *protect* Dima from harm, not inflict it.

Dima got up quickly, mud and snow stuck to his coat. Yuri moved in and threw a punch at Dima's head, but Felix quickly moved inside and used his forehead to strike Yuri on the cheek. Not only did Yuri's punch strike empty air, Felix's retaliatory head-butt left him staggering from side to side trying to maintain his balance. There was now a small cut near Yuri's eyebrow and blood trickled down the side of his face.

"Just let it go, you two," Felix warned, but neither man seemed to listen. They charged at one another and Felix jumped in between them at the last second and was struck by two hard blows: one to the middle of the back, and another that landed on his jaw. He couldn't tell who had thrown which punch, but it didn't matter. He wrapped his right leg behind Yuri's legs, then in one swift push, sent him to the ground. Then he slipped around behind Dima and locked his arms up.

"Let me go!" Dima screamed.

Olga stormed through camp and pushed people to the side until she reached the melee. "What the hell is going on here?" she demanded.

Nobody answered.

She saw Yuri, with the trickle of blood running down the side of his face, and Dima struggling to free himself from Felix's hold. "You again, huh?" she said, looking squarely at Felix.

A young female partisan spoke up. "No, it wasn't him," she said. "He was trying to break up the fight."

"Silence!" Olga shouted.

Yuri left the scene, and Felix released his hold on Dima. Felix walked a few paces away and noticed there was blood in his mouth and that one of his teeth was now loose.

"Consider this your last warning," Olga said to Felix. "The next time you cause a ruckus, you get the shack."

'The shack' referred to a small, crude shed that had neither plumbing nor heat. The last man to serve the standard three day, three night sentence there had died of pneumonia a week after his release.

Olga looked at Felix, then Dima, then spat on the ground, and then looked at Felix once more. "Varilensky," she said, "you've earned yourself double-guard duty for the next week." She turned to Dima next, but only grunted and walked away.

As the crowd dispersed, Felix returned to the campfire and tried stretching his now aching back from side to side. The young woman who had spoken up in his defense came up to him and told him what bullshit it was that he was punished and not Yuri and Dima. "Why didn't you say anything?" she asked.

Felix had seen her for the first time only a few days ago. He didn't even know her name yet. "You wouldn't understand," he answered.

"Try me," she said, smiling.

Felix stopped trying to massage his back, and looked up at her. She was cute, with short brown hair that curled inward at the ends and green luminous eyes the color of emeralds. Felix liked how she scrunched up her nose when she smiled, the way a baby does.

"Comrade Leminskaya," Olga yelled from the door of her tent. "Come here, please."

It was strange for Felix to hear Olga say please. He couldn't recall her ever using that word before. The young woman put her hands on her hips and shifted her weight to her left leg. "If you want me to walk on your back later, let me know," she said. "I've been told I'm pretty good at walking over men." She winked at Felix, then added, "And after that, you can tell me all about this stubborn streak of yours." She turned and walked away, and despite the heavy clothes and long coat, Felix could tell she had a seductive way of moving.

When she reached Olga, Felix overheard Olga warn her "to stay away from that troublemaker."

Misha took a drag from his cigarette, then blew the smoke into the fire. "I think Natasha likes you," he said.

"Who?" Felix asked.

"Natasha. That little temptress you just talked to. She joined last week. Apparently her whole village was burned to the ground by the Nazis." Misha offered Felix his cigarette, but Felix waved it away. "Oh, that's right," he said. "I forgot you don't smoke. Anyway, Olga seems to have taken a liking to her."

"To who?"

"To *Natasha*. What's wrong with you?"

"Nothing," Felix said. "Just lost in thought, that's all." He couldn't get that look that he'd seen on Dima's face out of his mind. It had to have been a mistake. Perhaps he'd imagined it. Others might have the look and die, but not Dima. It couldn't happen to Dima.

"Well, a roll in the hay with her will clear your mind," Misha said. "She's sweet and innocent and trusting – not to mention a great body." He finished his cigarette and threw it into the fire. "Exactly the way I like 'em," he said. "Except every damn time I get her alone, she just asks me about you – where you're from, why you're so quiet. I think she's crazy about you. You should let her give you that backrub sometime. If you're lucky, she might stick around afterwards and give you something else too."

"I don't think a backrub is going to do any good," Felix said. "Something feels out of place in my spine."

"Damn it all, man. That's not the point," Misha said. "It doesn't matter if your back is really hurt or not. The point is getting her in bed, and a nice arousing backrub is a great way to start. Boy, I've got so much to teach you."

"I already have a girl," Felix said.

"So?" Misha said. "What's that got to do with anything?"

Felix took a sip of tea from his tin cup.

"Oh wait," Misha said, "you're not talking about Anna, I hope. Listen to me, you don't want anything to do with her. I learned that the hard way."

"No, not Anna."

"Well, who then?"

"She's in Leningrad still."

"Your girl's in Leningrad?" Misha said incredulously. "Well you've got to move on then. This is war. Who knows if you'll even be alive tomorrow? You might as well have some fun while you can. That's what booze and women are for – to make life bearable, to have a little fun. Tell me, when's the last time you saw her?"

"Right before dawn on September 9th."

"Are you serious? It's the middle of October now. You've got to move on with your life. I'm sure *she's* moved on by now. If there's one thing I know, it's women."

"No," Felix said. "You definitely don't know her, and you've never met anyone like her."

"I know women," Misha said, using his index finger to tap the side of his head. "When the rooster's away, the hens will play."

The fire crackled and popped, and Felix finished the last of his tea. "I'm going back to Leningrad as soon as I can," he said. "I can't stand being without her for so long. It's killing me."

"You want to get *in* to Leningrad? Are you crazy? The whole city is starving. The Germans have it blockaded and nothing gets in or out. You're much better off here. We've got food and liquor, and even women like Natasha to keep you warm at night. What more could you ask for?"

Felix stood up and turned to go.

"Let me introduce you to Natasha later," Misha said. "A night with her will lift your spirits and make you forget all about this girl from Leningrad."

"No, you don't understand," Felix said. "I don't want anyone else."

He walked to his tent and found Dima fast asleep and snoring loudly. Felix took off his muddy boots and laid down on his own bunk. He noticed a sense of hopelessness in the back of his mind, a deep concern that things were stuck and were never going to get any better.

After several minutes, he closed his eyes, and in that space where you're no longer awake yet have not fallen asleep, he saw Katya. It was a gray winter day and she was dressed in a white fur coat and hat. She was walking contentedly in the park, as beautiful as he'd ever seen her. It began to snow – big fluffy flakes gliding lazily down to earth. She stopped and lifted her head toward the sky and caught a snowflake on her tongue.

There was a strange, dark figure approaching from behind her. It was neither man nor beast, and it kept getting bigger as it drew nearer. Felix called out to warn Katya, but she didn't hear him. It was as though Felix didn't exist for her.

When the figure was almost upon her, Felix tried to scream, but instead woke up. He stared at the ceiling of the tent for a second, then closed his eyes again to try to return to that place where he was with Katya. He longed to feel the touch of her skin, hear her childlike laugh, taste her lips on his. But try as he might, he couldn't return to that place. There was an unbearable tightness in his chest and back. The pain consumed him and he felt powerless to struggle against it. But neither could he accept the pain. He dwelled in that place in between and hated every second of it.

He had to get away. He had to get back to Leningrad to be with Katya. Her birthday was tomorrow and it was going to be a long day knowing he had to spend it without her. If only he could know that she was getting along all right, he'd feel better. At first, they told him to wait because they said the Germans were going to overtake the city any day. Now that that hadn't happened, they told him to wait because the Red Army inside the city would be breaking out soon. Felix had his doubts about that happening, but saw little choice except to stay where he was at for now.

He heard some movement and turned his head just in time to see Dima taking his pocket watch from his hiding place under his bunk. Felix pretended to be asleep while Dima looked around suspiciously before slipping out the door. Then Felix put his boots back on and decided to see just where Dima was going with his most precious possession.

He saw Dima walk hurriedly into the woods, obviously not so drunk anymore as he nimbly ducked under and then around the branches of a cluster of evergreens. Felix followed him from a safe distance, wondering where Dima could be headed without his rifle.

Felix followed him all the way to Lestovo, and watched as he disappeared into the house of the old farmer who sold the homemade booze. When he came back out, he was smoking a cigarette and had a large glass bottle in his right hand.

* * *

Dima never saw the fallen branch which was to have such a grave impact on his life. He stepped on it awkwardly on his way back to camp and fell hard to the ground. His ankle throbbed with pain and he had to bite the edge of his coat sleeve to keep from screaming.

After the pain subsided somewhat, he checked the bottle of booze he'd gotten to see if it had broken. It hadn't. He then elevated his ankle as he deliberated what to do next. He was a half mile from Lestovo and one mile from camp. He doubted he could manage to walk to either.

A pine cone was poking him in the back, so he moved over a few inches to get more comfortable. The forest floor was covered with snow, but just an inch or two underneath it was a layer of brown leaves, pine needles, and acorns. A woodpecker battered a tree in the distance. Other than that, all was quiet.

After a minute or two, Dima heard someone walking his way and wondered if they were friend or foe. When the person drew nearer, he could see that they were both friend *and* foe. It was Felix, and Dima thought it appropriate that Felix should be the one to enter his life at this particular moment.

"What happened?" Felix asked as he approached.

"I twisted my ankle on that branch," Dima said and pointed at it. The branch laid there innocently, unaware of its role in the game of fate being played out.

"It's going to be dark soon," Felix said. "If it's going to take longer than usual, we'd better get a start now. Let me help you up."

"No," Dima said, refusing Felix's outstretched hand. "I think I broke something. It's never hurt this bad before."

"Then, let me see if I can carry you," Felix said. He tried to lift Dima over his shoulder, but groaned in agony and nearly collapsed to the ground himself. "I can't carry you," he said. "That blow to my back earlier today threw something out of alignment."

"How ironic," Dima said.

The sun was low on the far horizon.

"What time is it?" Felix asked.

"I don't know," Dima said.

"You don't have your pocket watch, huh?"

"No."

"Yeah, I didn't think so."

Dima noticed Felix looking at the full bottle of liquor lying next to him. "You want some?" he asked sarcastically.

"I'm surprised you haven't opened it yet and started drinking again," Felix said.

"I'm through drinking," Dima said.

"Ha," Felix scoffed.

Dima didn't say anything in response, but instead made his way to his feet and carefully began shifting his weight to his hurt ankle. When he got to about thirty percent, he shrank back to the ground, cursing and whimpering all the while. "Damn it, that hurts!" he said. "I can't put any weight at all on it." He held his ankle in the air again. "This is the story of my whole pathetic life. Just when I decide to try – to really give it my all – the world conspires against me."

"Damn you!" Felix said, glaring at him. "What the hell is wrong with you? You think this is some kind of game? You'll freeze to death if you have to spend the night out here."

Dima shrugged his shoulders. "Probably," he said. "But what is to be done? I guess what is meant to be is meant to be."

Felix crossed his arms across his chest and kicked at the ground with his boots – a sure sign that he wanted to say something, but wouldn't allow himself to for one reason or another. "What is it?" Dima asked.

"Nothing," Felix said.

"Come on, what is it?" Dima persisted.

"It's *you*," Felix said. "What's happened to you? Where's the Dima I once knew? The one who refused to give up? The one who laughed and danced and told jokes? The one with those big ideas and big ambitions?"

It was a fair question, Dima thought. Felix had a right to know. "I'll tell you what happened," Dima said as he pulled out a cigarette and stuck it in his mouth. "All my life I've been waiting for that time when I would have everything together – when all the pieces of my life would fall into place." He struck a match and lit the cigarette. "And they did. Everything came together when the war started. I felt comfortable, confident. I knew my place in the world."

"And so?" Felix said.

"*So*," Dima said. "Then everything fell apart again." The wind picked up snow from the ground and blew it in circles. "It's not supposed to happen like that," he said. "I always thought that once you got everything together, it was supposed to stay together."

Felix squatted down next to Dima. "You know what my dad always used to say to me when I was feeling like you are now? He'd say, 'The dog who always feels sorry for itself will try like hell, but never catch a fox.'"

"What the hell does that mean?" Dima asked.

"He'd never tell me," Felix said and laughed. "He'd just say, 'Don't you forget that.' And I haven't!"

Dima laughed, a brief, exhaled "ha."

"But I've thought about it for years now," Felix continued, "and I think it means that having sympathy for yourself, instead of empathy, will bring you nothing but sorrow. That you'll never get what you really want – no matter how hard you try – unless you first learn to be a true friend to yourself."

Dima inhaled deeply on his cigarette and then blew the smoke over his head. "I wish my father had given *me* that advice. You know what he told me when he gave me the pocket watch on my sixteenth birthday?"

Felix shook his head. "No, what?"

"He told me, 'You're a man now. Go make a name for yourself.'"

Felix took a drink of water from his canteen and looked at the setting sun once again. "That was all your father knew," he said. "There's no rule that says we have to repeat the mistakes of our parents."

"Too late for that," Dima said. He finished his cigarette and shoved the butt into the snow. "I think you should go."

"Where?"

"Anywhere," Dima said. "You should just leave."

"Why?" Felix asked. "Why do you think I should leave you?"

"Because I'm already dead, that's why."

The sun set another inch on the horizon, and the wind picked up and blew snow flurries around the forest. Felix stood up and sighed. He folded his arms across his chest and kicked at the ground with his boots for a minute, then walked away without another word. Dima watched him leave, the sound of his departing footsteps burning his ears.

Furry, brown squirrels dove from branch to branch, tree to tree. A nearby owl watched them intently, but didn't move from its perch. Dima checked his ankle again, surprised at how swollen it had become. He'd sprained his ankle before, but it had never gotten *this* big. It no longer hurt, but it didn't hurt because both of his legs were now numb from the cold.

He leaned back against the tree, propped his injured leg up on a nearby rock, and watched the snowflakes do their exotic dance as they floated down from a single, large gray cloud above his head. He hadn't paid so much attention to falling snow since he was a kid. Ever since he'd come to the understanding that what was important in life was what other people thought of you, he'd forgotten how neat snowflakes were. He caught a few with his gloves and was mesmerized by their intricate design – so mathematical and yet so beautifully simple.

The cloud moved on and he saw the stars. All those hundreds of thousands of stars. He'd forgotten about them too. The vastness of the sky astounded him. He could see straight above himself for miles and miles. No, he corrected himself, for millions – even billions – of miles. The sky was full of little bright dots and Dima didn't think he'd ever seen so many stars in his life. His grandmother had told him once that each and every star was a guardian angel for someone, and he tried now to pick out which one was his. Was it that bright one in the Ursula Major constellation? No, he decided, it had to be that faint one in the thick fog of the Milky Way – the star whose light appeared to still be shining, even though it had probably burned out a thousand years ago.

It seemed to Dima that reality was always playing catch-up to history, not the other way around. He heard the unmistakable sound of twigs being snapped and dead leaves being crunched under the snow and was relieved that Felix had come back for him. "Over here," he shouted.

There was no reply. The twigs stopped being snapped and the dead leaves stopped being crunched. Dima peered through the snow-covered forest, but couldn't make out anything in the dim light of the moon. "Felix," he called out, "is that you?"

Again there was no response, but the sounds of movement did begin again. As they drew nearer, Dima could hear not one, but *two* sets of footsteps. Then he heard whispering, but it wasn't the barely-above-a-whisper, strangely poetic way that only Russians could speak. It was gruff and stilted. It didn't flow. Then he distinctly heard the German word, "slowly." Dima knew that word well from his days spent as a German prisoner of war. His interrogator always said *slowly* when commanding a subordinate to burn Dima's skin with a cigar.

Dima felt his neck and shoulders tighten. He strained to hear every noise the forest made. *Snap*, came a sound from his right. *Crunch*, came a sound from his left. The Germans were converging on him from opposite directions. He could make out one of them – a quarter of his body stuck out from the trunk of a tree. Then he heard the one on his right side sprint from out of the dark to within twenty-five yards.

So it was time to die, Dima thought. He never imagined it would be like this – so lacking in glory, so all alone . . ..

He was breathing very quickly now, trying to think what he should do before dying. When he was a small boy, his grandmother had made him memorize the Lord's Prayer. Should he recite it? No, he didn't want to do that. He didn't believe in heaven. If he was going to die, he was going to that place where one was neither dreaming nor awake, the place where nothing existed – not even himself.

Dima heard the encroaching shadow on his left speak clearly in German to the other shadow, and it destroyed Dima's last, tiny bit of hope that the strangers might still be Russian. He expected to hear any second the sound of a grenade rolling through the leaves and snow. But that sound never came. They were being quite discreet, and Dima guessed that they didn't want to make any noise that might draw attention to themselves. Perhaps they were afraid of the partisans, whom they had to know operated in this area.

Whatever the case was, they kept moving from tree to tree, getting closer and closer, until they were no more than ten yards away. Dima could see them quite clearly, but he had neither gun nor grenade and so couldn't defend himself. He tried to remember some words of German he'd picked up, but none of them made sense together.

The German on the left spoke again, saying in badly broken Russian, "Soviet soldier, surrender."

Deciding he had little choice, Dima raised his hands above his head and said in Russian, "I surrender. I surrender."

* * *

"Coming, coming," Petya sang as he hurried down the hallway to answer the door. "Who is it?" he asked cheerfully. He expected Katya to answer. Today was her birthday and he'd invited her over for a celebratory dinner. He'd decided to host it in his room in his old apartment so they would have some privacy.

"It's Igor," came the response. Petya's good mood, enhanced by a shot of vodka and the anticipation of spending time with Katya, was immediately in peril.

He opened the door and looked down at Igor's grimy face. He was sure the boy hadn't taken a bath in at least a month and a half now. "She's not coming over, is she?" Petya asked with an air of resignation.

Igor furled his eyebrows and stuck his bottom lip out. "*Who's* not coming over?"

"Katya."

"How should I know if she's coming over?" Igor said. "She ain't home yet."

"What do you mean she's not home yet? She told me she'd be home by now. She explicitly said she'd be home by 7:30." Petya heard a squeaky drawer open and close and looked down the hallway at Katya's apartment. "You little devil," he said to Igor. "She's there. You're just playing games with me."

"No, that's Oksana," Igor said.

Petya scratched the back of his neck, then held his hand to his cheek in thought. "Well, then what do you want?" he asked irritably.

"Oksana says she knows we killed her cat, and . . ."

"Shh!" Petya pulled Igor inside his apartment. "Not so loud," he said. He listened for more noises coming from Katya's apartment. "You never mind what that crazy old bitch says," he whispered to Igor. "She can't prove anything."

Petya had pulled Igor close to him, and Igor bent his neck back to look Petya in the face. "But she . . .," he started to say before he was cut off.

"*I said*," Petya reminded him, "to keep your voice down."

"She says she knows ways of getting even," Igor said, still a notch or two above a whisper, "and that I'm not going to like it. She said if I tell her what I know that I won't get in trouble – that only you will."

Petya wrapped his fists around Igor's blankets and pulled him to within a few inches of his face. "You rat on me," he said, "and you'll be sorry. You better just keep your mouth shut." He heard someone coming up the stairs and let go of Igor.

Petya tried to recognize who was coming by their footsteps, but he couldn't do it. Everyone went up and down the stairs so slowly and carefully now that he couldn't differentiate them from one another. When the person got to the third floor, Petya leaned out his doorway and saw by the dim light that it was Katya. "Good evening, Katya," he called out. "Are you ready for your birthday surprise?"

"Hi Petya," she said. "Yes, I'm very excited. I was thinking about it the whole trip home." She walked to her apartment door, then squinted down the hallway at Petya. "Oh my, you look so nice. I can't come over wearing this. Let me change my clothes," she said as she walked into her apartment, "then I'll be right over."

Petya patted Igor on the head and pushed him out into the hall. "Don't worry, we'll be fine," he said. "We just need to stick together. Okay?" He winked at the boy, closed the door and went back to his room.

He combed his hair again and rehearsed the evening in his head one last time. He knew this was his best chance of getting to Katya and had spent the entire day planning everything. Rubbing the last few drops of his cologne onto his face and neck, he double checked that everything was ready and in place. As he was smoothing out the wrinkles in his bedspread, he heard Katya's knock at the apartment door.

He went to the mirror and plucked a stray hair from his right eyebrow, then brushed some lint off his sweater. He whistled as he walked on air to the front door. After he invited Katya in, he bowed, took her hand, pressed his lips to it and said, "Bon jour, mademoiselle."

She smiled. "Oh, you Frenchmen are so debonair," she said and laughed. She was wearing a black sweater with knitted red and yellow flowers on the front and tiny blue ones on the sleeves. She'd been letting her hair grow longer of late, and it now reached the middle of her neck. Two earrings with hanging red and blue stones dangled from her ears. But more than anything, Petya's attention was drawn to her long black eyelashes and chestnut-brown eyes. He could look into those eyes forever and never get bored.

He showed her to his room, then closed the door behind them.

"Oh my, it's warm in here," Katya said. "That's nice. I'd almost forgotten what heat feels like."

Petya had taken the stove from Guzman's apartment and had also chopped up several picture frames to use as firewood. "Yes, well that's the first of many pleasant surprises," he said. He invited her to take a seat on the edge of his bed (since he had no chairs, it was the only place one *could* sit in his room), then Petya unveiled a bottle and two small glasses. He poured two shots of vodka, then handed one to Katya.

Katya sniffed the contents of the glass. "Wow. Real vodka?" she said, her eyes open wide. "I could probably get drunk just from smelling it. I haven't had anything to eat since breakfast."

Petya held his glass up. "Happy birthday," he said. "May you live a long and healthy life, and may all your wishes come true."

"To good friends," Katya said and clinked his glass.

Petya grimaced slightly at the word *friend*. He knew that's how Katya thought of him, but he was out to change that tonight.

They downed the shot in Russian fashion in one gulp, and each gasped a little at the end.

"You are definitely full of surprises," Katya said. "If there's one thing

I appreciate in people, it's unpredictability. It's boring to always know what's going to happen. I like not knowing. It's more fun that way."

"Well then, on that note, close your eyes and get ready for your next surprise."

Petya had prepared a tray beforehand. On a small silver platter he'd found in Guzman's apartment, he had arranged two teacups with loose tea leaves (courtesy of Guzman), a can of caviar (courtesy of Shostakovich), and four slices of bread (courtesy of Guzman's ration card). The tray was lying on his bed covered with one of his old shirts, which he now removed.

"Okay," he said. "You can open your eyes now."

Katya looked down at the tray and gasped. "Oh my goodness," she exclaimed, "where did you get all this?" Petya had never seen her eyes as big as they were in that moment and he felt proud of his accomplishment.

"That," Petya said, "is a secret. Suffice it to say, I'm a lot poorer now." He pulled the tray closer to them. "Let's eat one slice of bread with caviar now," he said. "Then we'll have the second one a little later. And for dessert, we'll have some tea."

"Sounds good to me," Katya said. "I think I lost two pounds just today. You can't imagine how hungry I am." She paused, then added, "I take that back. I'm sure you *can* imagine how I hungry I am."

He laughed.

Katya stared at the caviar. "Wow, I still can't believe it," she said. "Pinch me."

Petya pinched her lightly on the arm.

"I'm must be drunk already," she said. "I didn't even feel that."

He pinched her again, but harder. "Ow," she said, slapping his hand but laughing all the while. She tried to pinch him back, but he grabbed her arm and wouldn't let her. "That's all right," she said, grinning. "I'll get you later."

They caught each other's eye for a moment and neither looked away until Katya broke the silence. "You look quite handsome tonight," she said.

"Mercí," he replied in French and spread the large orange caviar on two slices of bread. When he finished, he noticed that Katya was still staring at him and smiling.

"You know it feels strange to say this," she said, "but you look so *different* since you've lost so much weight." She studied him with her eyes. "You look . . . healthier."

"Ha-ha. Yes, it's this new *starvation* diet I'm on," Petya said. "It does wonders, huh? It's the best diet I've ever been on. My skin has completely cleared up – no acne at all – and my double chin has been reduced to one."

They both laughed for a long time.

"It feels so good to laugh again," Katya said, placing her hand on his and squeezing lightly. "It's something you take for granted when things are going your way."

Petya handed her a slice of bread with caviar. "All right," he said. "Enough talk. Let's do something else we used to take for granted – eat." He closed his eyes and sunk his teeth into the caviar, moaning as the tiny little eggs popped in his mouth. After he swallowed, he opened his eyes and saw that Katya hadn't taken a bite yet. She was praying.

Petya usually got angry when he saw people praying or making the sign of the cross. Praying especially irked him. It reminded him of his aunt shaming him into praying for forgiveness for whatever 'terrible' thing he'd done that day – use a curse word, not do what she had told him to, not memorize a Bible verse correctly . . . . He wasn't angry now though – not with Katya. He was only curious. "What did you pray for?" he asked after she'd finished.

"Oh, it was just a short, simple one," Katya said. "I prayed that every man, woman, and child might find peace within themselves. I believe that's the only way we'll ever have peace in the world."

Petya watched Katya take a bite of food, but as she chewed it and moaned with pleasure, he looked past her, at the bluish-gray wall and the drawing he'd placed there of a witch about to be burned at the stake. He'd put that drawing there to remind himself of the true nature of his fellow man. "Humanity scares me," he said.

"How so?" Katya asked.

"Its capacity for cruelty," he answered. "Its bloodthirsty vengeance, its craving to see others trip and stumble."

She put her bread down. "You feel afraid when you see acts of coldheartedness, because you'd really like there to be more kindness in the world."

"Yes . . . I mean no. I'm not sure. You don't expect us to be nice to the damn Nazis, do you?"

"I struggle with that one," she said. "But I do believe kindness toward the devil still brings more kindness into the world."

Petya nearly laughed, but saw she was serious. "That's easy for you to say. Things like this," he said, pointing to the drawing of the witch about to be burned, "don't affect you."

"That's not true," Katya said. "I know exactly what you're talking about. Sometimes I get so afraid that I'm going to be crushed by the senselessness of this slaughter and destruction, this fire of madness that we keep feeding. This war is breaking my heart. I can feel it inside me. This tearing and squeezing and hardening. How can a heart survive day after day of that? I see these young children starving to death or being killed by bombs and I wonder why the world has to be like this. I even find myself questioning God sometimes, wondering how he could let this happen. I mean what does a four-year-old boy have to do with anything?"

There was an explosion in the distance, then a crackle of gunfire, then a wailing scream that quickly faded into the black of the night. "Katya, if there is a God," Petya said, "I hate him."

"Petya, don't say that! You can't hate God."

"No, it's true. I've never told anyone before, but I'm telling you now. What kind of a God would let his people suffer the way he does?"

Katya looked across the room pensively. The fire made a sudden hissing sound, and one of the candles flickered like it was caught in a draft. Petya leaned over and laid on his side, supporting his weight with his right elbow. "Katya," he said, "I just don't understand it. Does God want to stop evil, but isn't able? Then he's impotent. Is he able to stop evil, but not willing? Then he's malevolent. If he's both willing and able to stop evil, then why is there evil?"

Katya looked at him. "Voltaire's argument."

"Right."

"But what if evil didn't exist?" Katya said. "That whole argument falls apart then."

"Yes, but who could deny that evil exists? This war and the Nazi atrocities are proof enough. Did you hear what they're doing in the villages now? They're..."

"I know what's happening," Katya interrupted. "But what if what people call evil is simply a result of men and women making bad decisions trying to get something they want?"

"For example?"

"For example, I heard the German newspapers said Germany needed security, and that's why they invaded our country – to prevent any future assaults to their peace and well being. But surely there were other, less violent, options."

"They were lying when they said that," Petya said. "They never viewed us as a threat to their security. What they've wanted all along is to kill us and take our land. If that's not evil, then what is?"

"But to me, if you look underneath the strategy they took, you see that what they're really needing is peace, and safety, and probably also respect," Katya said. "They want to be strong enough so that no one else will ever be able to do to them what was done after The Great War. There's nothing evil about wanting to be safe. The problem is with the strategy they chose to meet their needs – pre-emptive war. You know it's so easy for us humans to sink into that primal urge, that might makes right, that violence is an acceptable way to get what you want."

"I didn't know you thought that way," Petya said.

"Neither did I," she said, laughing. "It just came to me. I've been struggling with this ever since the war started."

The End Of Sorrow

Petya poured them each another shot of vodka. "I have no idea how we got onto this subject," he said.

"I remember," Katya said and hiccupped. "We were talking about God. Speaking of whom, you know it was his son, Jesus Christ, who taught that peace and understanding is the best route – not the easiest – but the best. It's unfortunate that so many of the people in this world who profess to follow his teachings don't adhere to it."

Petya handed Katya her glass of vodka, then picked his up in preparation to make a toast. "To hypocrites," he said, holding his glass up high in the air.

"To hypocrites," Katya repeated and laughed. "Ourselves included."

"Here, here!" Petya said. They clinked glasses and downed another shot.

Katya ate more of her bread with caviar, and Petya tried to stare at her without being noticed. He was so happy just to be with her. She had such wonderful thoughts. He wanted to sit there and listen to her forever. Listen to her talk about God and philosophy and art and poetry. "I've never met anyone quite like you," he said. "You're so open to new ideas and so unattached to your existing ones."

"I enjoy talking to you too," Katya said. "My conversations only go so far with Igor." She giggled infectiously and Petya couldn't help but join her.

"So," Petya asked as she took another bite of food, "how is it?"

"Mmm, without exaggeration, it's the best thing I've ever had in my life. Talk about a surprise!" She pulled her sweater off over her head, reducing her to only two more layers of clothes. "It's so warm in here," she said, then grabbed Petya by the arm and added, "Not that I'm complaining. It feels wonderful not to have to wear so many clothes. You don't mind do you?"

"By all means," Petya said, grinning, "feel free to take off as many clothes as you like."

Katya didn't laugh, and Petya knew he'd blundered. He busied himself spreading the last two slices of bread with caviar, all the while chastising himself for what he'd said.

After another minute or two, the tea kettle boiled and Petya got up and took it out of the stove. When he turned back around, he saw Katya sprawled out on the bed and feared she might have passed out. But then she spoke. "Your ceiling is spinning around in circles," she said.

"Yes, I'm glad you noticed," he said. "That was your next surprise. It took me forever to set that up."

Katya laughed uncontrollably, covering her mouth with her hands and rolling from side to side. Petya laid down beside her and she playfully punched him in the arm.

"You're so funny," she said. "I never would have guessed it. I remember when my father and I first moved into this building, I thought you were this dark and mysterious figure. You always seemed to be deep in thought and tormented by something."

"You got the tormented part right," he joked.

"Seriously," Katya said, "what's it like to be Petya Soyonovich?"

"Well, before you moved in, my life was very simple," Petya said. "I was all by myself. I was bitter, depressed, and without hope. It was great fun."

"And now?" Katya asked. "After I moved in?"

"Now," he said and sighed. "Now, I suffer even more, because I have hope. I have hope that I might one day find someone like you to share my life with."

"I've never heard of someone suffering *more* because they had hope," she said.

"You've never met anyone like me either."

"That's certainly true," she said, twisting a strand of hair around her finger.

Petya stretched his neck behind him and then down toward his chest until it cracked. He heard a voice say, "You miserable snake. Nothing but lies come out of your mouth."

"Katya, did you just say something?" he asked.

She shook her head no. Petya took a deep breath. *Not now,* he pleaded. Please don't let the voices come back now.

"But I was just about to ask you something," Katya said. "I want to hear more about the tormented part."

Petya was desperate to tell somebody about the strange things going on in his head, but decided he couldn't come right out and tell Katya about the voices. That would scare her away for sure. But he could talk about it in a roundabout way. "Well, I'm confused a lot," he said. "Some days I don't know what to think. Lots of ridiculous memories flood my mind and I have no control over them. I wonder sometimes if that's a sign of delirium – when you lose control over the thoughts that come into your mind."

"What kind of thoughts?" Katya asked.

"For instance," Petya said, "I'll be walking down the street and, for no discernable reason whatsoever, remember when I was a child in a school play and forgot my line in front of everyone. Or I'll be preparing dinner and suddenly recall the time I told an inappropriate joke to some people I didn't know that well." He moved the tray from the bed and slid closer to Katya. "I don't know what's worse, this chronic remorse or losing control of when and what I want to recall. Isn't that exactly what happens to someone who's a lunatic? They have completely random thoughts – things they would just as soon forget, like drowning a puppy because it wouldn't shut up, or being molested as a child. These thoughts and memories force their way to the front of the line, and one grows weary of fighting them and gives up. Then these random thoughts have the run of the house. I'm so afraid of ending up like that – of letting them win."

Katya slid her hand into Petya's. It was something so simple, so basic, and yet Petya was overcome with gratitude. He'd let himself be vulnerable and felt supported and understood, and not judged, as he feared he might be.

The candles cast dark shadows on the wall, and Petya was mesmerized by the edge, where the darkness disappeared so suddenly, so completely. He shifted farther up the bed so his head was beyond Katya's and he could feel her hair touch his face. It was all so wonderful, but at the same time he noticed this sense of sadness he couldn't explain. "Why do we Russians suffer so?" he asked.

Katya pulled back until their faces were in front of one another. "Because we understand that there's this incredible connection between ourselves and all other living beings and the earth and the trees and the sunshine, and . . ."

"And," Petya interrupted, "we mourn that life isn't lived that way – with that comprehension. Right?"

Katya nodded and brushed her bangs away from her eyes.

"You know, I've had that same thought," Petya said. "There's this sense I get when I read Pushkin or hear Tchaikovsky's music. It's so sad sometimes that I want to cry, but I love it and don't want it to ever stop. It's like joy and sorrow are indistinguishable in that moment."

"Yes, I know what you mean," Katya said. "I've always believed that joy and sorrow come from the same fountain." She was starting to slur her words.

"What about all those poor souls who *don't* understand that?" Petya asked.

"They're doomed," Katya said. She giggled and repeated the word, "Do-o-o-omed."

"Doomed to what?" Petya asked. "Doomed to live in Siberia harvesting icicles?"

Katya laughed and tried to make scary shadows on the wall with her hands. "Doomed to live their lives over and over as forever hungry ghosts," she said in her best attempt at a scary voice. "Do-o-o-omed because they can never consume enough of anything to end their misery."

Petya laughed as he watched the figures she was making on the wall. "Is that a dog?" he asked.

"No, you dummy," she said. "It's a hungry ghost. See how it's eating and eating."

"That's not a hungry ghost," Petya joked. "That's a dog who's really old and has only one ear for some reason."

Katya fell into a fit of laughter, and Petya wanted time to stop so he could stay in that moment forever. If there was a heaven, he was sure it was something like this.

"Next, you tell me," Petya said, "what it's like to be Katerina Selenaya."

"What do you want to know? My favorite color?"

"No, how about who's been the biggest influence on your life?"

"That's easy," she said. "My grandmother. She was my hero growing up. She was the one who taught me what love was. She did it not by telling me, but by *showing* me in her day to day actions. She was the greatest person I ever knew."

"I've often thought about what your family life must have been like as you grew up," Petya said. "You always sparkle when you talk about your grandmother. It makes me bitter to think that I might have been born into a family like yours. Instead, I was surrounded by ignorance and dogmatism."

"I'm sure your aunt did her best, Petya. At the very least, she loved you," Katya said.

"Yes, probably. But that didn't matter to me. That I was loved meant nothing." He took a deep breath and exhaled slowly like he was smoking a cigarette. "I know that my aunt and uncle loved me. They loved me as family members always love one another – distantly, thoughtfully, and all too often, reluctantly. But to be loved means nothing to the unhappy. But to love! To love means to live! It means there's something in the world for you and gives you a reason to get out of bed in the morning." He ran his fingers through Katya's hair, then held her head close. He so wanted to kiss her on the lips. "I want to both love and be loved," he added.

"Speaking of love," Katya said, pulling away from him. "Isn't it time for our third toast?" By tradition, the third toast was always to love.

"Yes, of course," Petya said. "Forgive me my bad manners." He got up and poured them each another shot, then handed Katya her glass. "To love," they said in unison and toasted.

After Katya finished drinking, she tried to set her glass back on the tray, but missed and it fell onto the floor and rolled under the bed.

"Whoops," she said, "sorry about that."

"Don't worry about it," Petya said absently. He was contemplating how love had always been the villain in his life, never the hero. He laid down and listened to the fire crack and pop. "Do you think you could ever love me?" he asked.

"I'm not sure how to answer that," she said and paused. "I always feel constrained with the number of words we have to express this thing called love. We have one word, but it refers to so many different things – from the way you feel about a pet, to the way you feel about your parents, to the way you feel about your boyfriend. On the one hand, I think it's deep never-ending love that makes the world go round. But on the other

The End Of Sorrow

hand, I don't think of love as something that's static, something that never changes. I can love someone one minute, but not the next. And then of course . . ."

She's evading the question, Petya thought. "Of course she is," he heard a voice answer. "She doesn't want to answer you. She hates you."

Petya hoped if he ignored the voice, it would go away. "What about this minute?" he asked after Katya finished speaking.

"In this minute . . .," Katya said, pausing again.

Petya held his breath. "She'll never love you," he heard the voice say. "Why should she? You're a snake." Petya saw things starting to spiral downward. The voice was so convincing.

"What are you grinning about?" Katya asked.

"Oh, nothing," Petya said. "Nothing I can't handle."

"Is it something painful?"

"You could say that." He closed his eyes briefly and begged the voice to leave him alone. "But you're evading my question," Petya said.

"What question?" she asked, hiccupping again. "Oh wait, I remember. In this minute . . . I am in love with the whole world. So yes," she said, nodding her head gingerly, "I do love you."

"She's lying!" the voice screamed.

"No!" Petya yelled. "Shut up!"

Katya pulled back, her face pale and frightened.

"Oh no, not you, Katya," he said, stroking the side of her face. "I didn't mean you."

"Then who were you talking to?" she asked. "As far as I know," she said, looking guardedly about the room, "I'm the only one here."

"I heard someone outside," Petya lied. "You didn't hear them?"

"No," she said. She sat up on the bed and grabbed her sweater. There was no sign on her face of the gaiety they had shared just a few moments ago. "I'm tired," she said. "Tired and drunk. I should probably get going."

"No, no," Petya said. "Please stay. We'll have tea next. I just have really good hearing, that's all. I'm sorry about that. Really, I am." He picked up one of the candles and excused himself to go to the bathroom. "I'll be right back and we'll have tea," he said. "Wait for me."

He seethed with rage. Here he was so close to getting what he dreamt about every night, and now after what just happened, it was probably out of reach. How he despised those voices in his head!

In the bathroom, he banged his head against the wall, hoping to punish the voices with some pain. After a few minutes, he calmed down and decided he didn't want to give up just yet. He might still be able to salvage the evening. He reviewed all that had gone well so far. Katya was drunk. They had been feeling very connected. She'd already helped him along by taking off some of her clothes. And most importantly, there hadn't been a single mention of Felix. Then Petya remembered that Katya had said she loved him! How could he have forgotten that? As he returned down the hallway, he felt much better than when he'd left.

He opened the door to his room and saw Katya curled up on his bed crying.

"What's wrong?" he asked, rushing over to her side. "It's not because of what I said earlier, is it? I told you I wasn't talking to you. I was . . ."

"No, it's not that," she said. "It's probably because I've drank way too much. The room keeps spinning . . .."

"What happened?"

"I just suddenly felt so lonely after you left," she said. "Why does everyone always have to leave me? My mother left me when I was a child. My grandmother left me when I was a teenager. My father left a few months ago, and I haven't heard from him since. Felix left me. Shostakovich left me. Where are they all?" she asked through her tears.

He put his arms around her to comfort her.

"Everyone's left me," Katya cried. "Everyone!"

Petya pulled her close. "My dear sweet Katya," he said. "Not everyone has left you. I'm still here. I'm still here for you and I'm not going anywhere."

She buried her face in his chest and sobbed. Petya felt an incredible space open up within him. He felt whole, like an unknown part of him that had been missing had now been found and put back into place. He kissed the top of her head, then she pulled away slightly and he tried to pull her back in and kiss her on the lips.

"No, no," she said. "Friends don't do that."

"But we can be so much more than friends," Petya said.

"I don't want to," Katya said. "I like our relationship as it is. Felix is my lover."

Petya cringed at the mention of Felix's name. He moved in and kissed the side of her neck. She pushed him away, more forcefully this time.

"Stop it," she said and got up from the bed.

Petya stood up, wrapped his arms around her, and she collapsed into him. "It's okay," he said. "Felix is gone. It's been six weeks now. He's not coming back." He picked her up and laid her on the bed. She did not resist.

One of the candles he'd lit started flickering wildly, and Petya went over and blew it out. He pulled his sweater off over his head, then smoothed down his hair. Katya remained in the same position he'd left her in. When he went back, he kissed her arms from the wrist to the elbow and then climbed on top of her. She didn't say anything and didn't move. "Katya?" he asked and ran his hand along her cheek.

She didn't answer. She'd passed out.

So many times Petya had fantasized about an opportunity like this.

Now it was finally here. He could do whatever he wanted and she wouldn't resist. He leaned over her and kissed her once more on the top of the head. He ran his fingers through her hair and behind her ears. Everything about her was so beautiful to him.

He knew he could have his way with her, and though the thought intrigued him, he wouldn't do it. He didn't want it to be like this. Maybe it was love, maybe it was respect, maybe it was cowardice, he didn't know.

He lifted her head up, stuck a pillow underneath, and spread a blanket over top of her. Then he lit a cigarette and poured himself another shot of vodka. He wanted to get even more drunk – to have his thoughts get muddled and sparse, to shut up those damn voices. He liked to feel numb when all else failed. What he would have liked more than anything was for Katya to be madly in love with him and be his and his alone. But reality had never cared much about what he liked or disliked.

* * *

The two Germans sat on a fallen tree across from Dima. The tree had been dead a long time, its bark rotting and its once solid trunk spongy to the touch. The Germans were eating smoked meat and drinking water and looking at Dima with eyes of antipathy. Dima, with his hands and feet tied together, wondered why they hadn't killed him yet. There was something going on, he knew. These two Germans weren't alone out here in the woods.

The three of them had been sitting there for twenty minutes, and the shorter German came over now and tried asking Dima something in Russian. Dima, not understanding the man's badly broken Russian, answered in the form of a riddle: "Twelve pears hanging high. Twelve men passing by. Each took a pear and left eleven hanging there. How can that be?"

Dima maintained a somber look on his face all the while, and the German scowled and walked away.

Faint sounds in the distance announced more arrivals, and the shorter German went and hid in the woods, while the other one sat up close to Dima and held his knife tight against Dima's throat.

Unlike last time, the newcomers walked quickly and boldly. Dima could see them approaching – two figures walking side by side in the pale moonlight. They were speaking in Russian, and Dima wanted to warn them to watch out, but the knife was too tight against his throat. He was afraid to swallow for fear that the movement of his Adam's apple would alarm the German soldier into cutting him. The German had his face right up next to Dima's, and Dima could smell the sweet and peppery scent of the smoked meat he'd eaten. He wasn't much older than Dima, and still had yet to outgrow his chubby cheeks of boyhood. His eyes were small, and darted back and forth from the figures in the distance to the spot where his partner was hidden.

The newcomers were much closer now, and Dima recognized the broad chest and determined gait of the one on the left. It was Felix. He was carrying a pair of crutches.

The unsuspecting duo walked right past the German soldier hiding behind the big bush. He stepped out – behind them now – and spoke in his horrible Russian for them to surrender. Felix and the other man stopped and raised their hands slowly. Dima swallowed, and the blade of the knife pressed harder into his skin until a trickle of blood ran down the shiny metal and onto the German's tightly-clenched hand.

The three prisoners sat next to one another, each with their hands and feet tied together. The two Germans stood several yards away discussing something, but always keeping a close eye on their prisoners. An owl sat on a branch and hooted softly from time to time as Felix whispered to Dima the story of what had happened. The man Felix had arrived with was Vladimir – the same Vladimir that Olga had wanted to shoot earlier that day.

At first Felix was going to go to camp to get someone to help him carry Dima, but Lestovo was much closer, so he decided to go to there instead. He went door to door looking for someone willing to help him get Dima back to camp, but no one wanted to help. They were all afraid. Some wouldn't even open their doors to him.

The tenth door he'd knocked on was Vladimir's. He wasn't home, but his thin, frail wife was, and she answered the door. She'd been crying, and wrung her hands nonstop as she explained to Felix how the Germans had just been there and had taken her husband against his will. Her husband was known for his intimate knowledge of the woods, and they took him so he could show them firsthand where the partisan camp was. Felix thanked her for the information and ran to the next door. Again, no one would help, but they did offer him a pair of old crutches. He accepted them and started running back to Dima.

On his way, he ran into Vladimir, who had managed to slip away from the Germans and was running ahead of them to go warn the partisans of the impending attack. Felix had been trying to get as much information from him as he could, such as how many troops were involved and which direction they were coming from, when the two of them had been caught.

The shorter German came over now, pointing his rifle and shushing the three of them to be quiet. Then he went back and stood with the other one, who had his arms folded across his chest and was shaking his head from side to side. They were waiting for the rest of their platoon to catch up before they did anything with their prisoners, Dima speculated.

It was also clear that they recognized Vladimir, but since they couldn't communicate with him, they would have to wait for the translator in their platoon to explain why Vladimir was caught walking through the woods with a Russian, and especially a Russian who was armed and appeared to be a partisan.

Once the rest of their platoon arrived, Dima figured the end would come fairly quickly for the three of them. It would only take a minute for it to become clear that Vladimir had slipped away to warn the partisans.

Vladimir whispered softly that he'd seen two groups of German soldiers, with forty to fifty men in each group. One group was coming from the north and the other from the south.

"Our comrades are as good as dead," Dima whispered to Felix. "There's no way they can fight off two full platoons."

"Why do you think these two," Felix said, pointing with his head toward the Germans, "aren't with the rest of their platoon?"

"I'm not sure," Dima said. "Maybe they were sent ahead to make sure they weren't walking into a trap."

The shorter German soldier came over again and shushed them, this time raising his chin and crossing his right index finger under it, in imitation of slicing someone's throat.

After the German walked away again, Vladimir whispered to Dima, "I think we better stop talking."

"Or else what?" Dima said.

"Or else they'll kill us," Vladimir responded.

"They're going to kill us anyway," Dima said. "They're just not going to do it until the rest of their platoon arrives. All they're going to do for now is make threats." He was sitting on something hard – an acorn, he guessed. He tried moving an inch or two to his left, but the ropes made it difficult. "Might as well get comfortable," he said. "Enjoy the last few minutes of our lives."

"Yes, I agree," Felix added, "but it's impossible to get comfortable like this. You'd think they'd at least give us a blanket to sit on so our asses don't get so cold."

Dima laughed quietly. His own lack of fear surprised him – that Felix could poke fun at their current predicament amazed him. He never imagined the last few minutes of his life would be spent joking lightheartedly.

"Maybe if we ask them nicely, they'll tie us up to a tree instead so we'd at least have something to lean back on," Dima jested.

"Yeah, is that too much to ask?" Felix said. "This position is killing my back."

Dima laughed again. He felt grateful to be spending this time with Felix. "Listen," he said, "I'm sorry about that earlier incident – hitting you in the back. It was a cheap shot and I regret it."

"Oh, that was you? I couldn't tell which one of you did it," Felix said.

One of the German soldiers again got out a piece of smoked meat and started eating it.

"He's making me hungry," Dima said. "He took my bottle of booze. The least he could do is give me a bite of that sausage."

Felix laughed. "Perhaps you'd like a cricket instead?" he said.

"A cricket?"

"Yeah, you don't remember? When we were eleven, I bet that you couldn't eat a live cricket every day for a week," Felix said. "I thought there was no way you could do it. You were so easily grossed out back then. If my mom made us eggs for breakfast, the yolks of your eggs had to be completely cooked through. If they were the least bit runny, you wouldn't eat them."

"Huh," Dima said. "I'd forgotten all about that."

"You had this magnifying glass that I just loved, and I got you to bet it," Felix said. "I remember counting the days until it would be mine."

Dima gave Felix a sidelong glance and grinned.

"So the very first day," Felix continued, "I nearly won. You almost spit the cricket up three times before you got it down."

"Those things tasted so nasty," Dima said.

"But then you seemed to get the hang of it, and for the next four days you ate them in one gulp. I started to get nervous and made all these plans to keep you occupied for the entire last day and evening so that you would forget about our bet. Then I would wake you up at one minute past midnight to tell you you'd lost."

"You had your dad take us to a soccer game," Dima said. "And in the evening you served us bowl after bowl of ice cream. Then you told ghost stories for two hours and I fell asleep. I remember I had a strange dream about being chased by giant crickets and I woke up fifteen minutes before midnight, ran outside, found a cricket under a rock, and gulped it down just before your grandfather clock started chiming."

"I was so mad," Felix said.

"You bet your brand new soccer ball that you got for your birthday," Dima said.

"Yeah, and you never let me forget it. Every time we would play soccer, you'd say, 'Guess how I got this great ball!'"

Dima laughed. "I still have it," he said.

"After I was done being mad," Felix said, "I remember being so impressed that you were able to do it."

"I did it because you and everyone else told me that I couldn't and I was going to prove you all wrong."

"That's the Dima I admired," Felix said. "You loved to prove people wrong about you."

"Yeah, but I never stopped," Dima said.

"What do you mean?"

"I mean all my life I've been trying to 'prove myself' once and for all and be done with it."

"Prove yourself to who?" Felix asked.

"To *everyone*," Dima said. He took in a deep breath and sighed. "But I've never been able to. I've had to keep proving myself over and over and over. I've never found a point where I could stop."

"You could stop now," Vladimir said, "and figure out how to save us."

"You know," Felix said to Dima, "I think we played out this situation about a hundred times when we were kids. How did we get out of it then?"

Dima thought a minute. "I remember what we did," he said. "They'd have you tied up, and I'd jump out of that old willow tree and wrestle them to the ground."

"Yeah, but you always died when you did that," Felix said. "You'd rescue me, but get shot while doing it and have this big, dramatic death. For ten minutes, you'd flop all over the place, grunting and groaning and telling me to go on without you. Your last words would always be in this strained whisper, saying, 'Felix, promise me you'll never give up. Promise me.'"

"Yeah, I remember that," Dima said, laughing.

There was a sound in the distance and both of the Germans stood up to look. It was the first time they both looked away, and Dima used the opportunity to pull his pantleg out of his boot, undo a few laces, and get a small folding knife out.

"You still have your knife?" Felix said. "I know you somehow kept your pocket watch when the Germans had us – though I have no idea how you managed that – but I didn't know you were able to keep your knife as well."

"They found my knife," Dima said. "This is a different one I just got from the old farmer that sells the booze."

"He gave it to you?"

"No, I traded my pocket watch for it."

"Oh," Felix said, sounding surprised. "I owe you an apology then. I thought you'd traded your watch for the booze."

"No," Dima said, "I told you I was through with drinking. I thought about some of the stuff you'd said and decided you were right. I *am* too young to give up. The old man liked the watch so much, he just gave me the booze. I took it to give to Misha."

Dima was sawing his way through the ropes.

"Hurry," Vladimir whispered.

"I didn't think you'd ever get rid of that watch," Felix said. "I thought it meant more to you than anything."

"Yeah, it used to," Dima said. He was three-fourths of the way through the rope tying his hands together. "But not anymore," he said, grinning. He strained to pull his hands away from one another, and the last bit of rope snapped in two.

Both of the Germans were still looking off in the distance, but they lowered their rifles and seemed to relax. The taller one began walking in the direction the sounds were coming from.

"It must be the rest of their platoon from the north," Vladimir said.

Dima was sawing furiously on the rope that tied his feet together.

"Give me the knife when you're done, then make a run for it," Felix said. "We've only got a few more seconds."

"That ain't gonna work and you know it," Dima said. "We've got one chance of getting out of this and one chance only." He cut through the last few threads of rope that bound his feet.

"Dima wait," Felix said breathlessly.

Dima turned to him.

"I saw 'the look' on your face earlier today," Felix said.

"You mean the look that tells you that man is going to die that day?"

Felix nodded his head. "Yes," he said, "*that* look."

Dima closed his eyes for a second. "Well then," he said, "give my best to Katya. You've been a good friend, Felix." He leaned onto his feet and prepared to stand. "I promise," he added, "no big, dramatic death this time." He smiled at Felix, looking just like that kid who'd won the bet.

He jumped to his feet and the two Germans immediately turned and saw him. Dima threw his knife at the closest one and it struck him in the shoulder. Then he charged at the man, letting out a furious scream – like all the rage he'd ever held inside was being unleashed.

The German was stunned from the knife wound and Dima's ungodly scream, but the other German, who was about fifteen yards away, took aim and shot Dima twice in the torso.

"No!!" Felix yelled.

But the bullets didn't slow Dima down. He kept coming. He kept charging until he tackled the German to the ground. Then he pulled his knife out of the man's shoulder and plunged it into his throat, killing him instantly. Dima grabbed the man's rifle to shoot the other German, but as he did so, he was shot three more times himself – once in the leg, once in the arm, and again in his torso. And yet again the bullets didn't stop him. He returned fire and his second shot struck the man in the center of the chest, sending him sprawling to the ground.

"Hurry!" Vladimir yelled, "before the rest of their platoon gets here."

Dima pulled his knife out and staggered over to Felix. Blood was running down his arm and he felt like he was going to faint. He managed to cut the rope that bound Felix's hands together, then he handed the knife to Felix to finish the job.

While Felix cut the rope around his feet, Dima fired a few rounds at the approaching Germans. He could see at least thirty, maybe more, in the distance. "Felix," he called out. Black splotches started cascading in front of his eyes. "Felix, you have to get back to camp and warn the others."

Dima looked back and saw Felix cutting the ropes around Vladimir's wrists, and then everything went completely black. He could feel himself lying on the ground and wanted to get back up, but couldn't do it. He'd command his arms and legs to move, but they wouldn't respond. It was as though the signal his brain sent got lost somewhere along the way. He opened his eyes and saw a blurry figure over top of him. The person was screaming and yelling at him. Dima recognized Felix's voice, and couldn't resist using the last bit of energy he had to say, "Felix, promise me you'll never give up. Promise me." He wanted to laugh again, but didn't have the strength. His eyelids were closed again and wouldn't heed his instructions to open. The Germans were shouting and shooting, and over top of it was Felix's voice, arguing with Vladimir.

"He's dead!" Vladimir said. "Let's go, before we are too."

"No!" Felix screamed. "I can't leave him. Oh God, no. Dima! Dima!!"

Dima wanted to tell Felix not to worry, that everything had already been decided, that it was useless to struggle against fate. His death was meant to be that day.

He felt his body being lifted into the air and knew Felix must be picking him up to carry him. Always the hero. Fighting through the pain, blocking out all doubt. That was Felix.

As he was being carried, Dima noticed that a hollow sensation had sunk into his stomach and his chest felt tighter than it ever had before. Then he couldn't feel anything. His mind started racing – searching for something to think about, something to distract him. But there was no running away this time.

Everything slowed down. Thoughts and images moved through his mind as if it were a lazy river on a warm, summer day. He saw himself as a young teenager helping a man in a wheelchair cross a busy street. Then he saw himself as a young boy, laying under an apple tree with Felix on a beautiful fall day. He didn't know what they were talking about, but he felt a tremendous sense of gratitude and connection flowing through the two of them.

Dima thought it strange that these particular images were coming to him. Where was that big fight he'd had with his father when he was fifteen? Where was that time he'd won the school math contest? Or the time he'd received perfect marks on his report card?

Then Dima saw his mother and father and sister sitting around the tiny table in the apartment he'd grown up in. They were all so young. Dima was seated at the table too, and everyone was looking at him, telling him to do something. But he couldn't understand what they wanted.

Then the image became more focused, and Dima was no longer a young man being carried through a forest, but a small boy sitting at a table with his family surrounding him. He looked down at his hands and saw that they were tiny. They were the hands of an infant.

His family continued to encourage him to do something. His sister, with her short blonde hair and pink dress. His father, with his favorite brown sweater. And his mother, with her bright blue eyes and her long hair exquisitely wrapped on top of her head. What did they want of him?

He looked down at the table and saw some kind of food there. He didn't know what it was, but it smelled good and he saw that everyone else had a similar piece of food on a similar yellow plate in front of them. The food was rectangular and mostly dark, but the top of it was covered with some creamy white stuff. He grabbed it with his right hand and held a piece up to his face so he could get a closer look at it. His family started talking at him even louder now. They were all smiling and laughing and looking at him. His father was holding up the first finger of his right hand and pointing at Dima with his left hand. His mother and sister were pretending to chew and pointing at the food on his plate.

Dima tried to put the food in his mouth, but was only partially successful – most of it ended up smeared across his cheek. As he chewed this wonderful new food, he looked around the table once again and saw his family now clapping and cheering for him. He thought it was the most wonderful feeling in the whole world and hoped his entire life would be like this.

And then the light slowly faded to dark. He wanted to yell – to plead with his family not to leave him – but there was nothing. Not even the breath in his chest.

~

ТРИ – Part III

What anger wants it buys at the price of the soul. **– Heraclitus**

A lie told often enough becomes the truth. **– Lenin**

Глава Восьмая — Chapter Eight

The Lake, the Moon, and the Lies

I live in despair,
    feeding off your fear.
I am the darkness
    that will never disappear.
I am that, which you know not,
    and always will I stay
    in the back of your mind
    til your dying day.
The politics of success,
    breed an emptiness so true.
And the suffering remains
    as the truth escapes you.
In circles goes the mind
    whose eyes cannot see
    that the meaning of life
    is the mystery of me.

The End Of Sorrow

When darkness settled over the sea between Peterhof and Leningrad, it came completely, and a million stars were visible high in the night sky. They were tiny points of light that never moved and never changed. They were there before the city existed, when it was flat and cold and populated only with bears and birds and squirrels. They were there on May 16, 1703, when Peter the Great paraded in and proclaimed a new city, a Venice of the North, for the Russian empire. They were there when a hundred thousand serfs died constructing the city out of the rock and woods and marsh. They were there in 1917 when the last Tsar, Nicholas II, was arrested and imprisoned, and a few months later as well when a little man gave a big speech that shook the world. The man, fresh from exile, spoke from a balcony to the crowd below. He proclaimed the freedom of the Russian people and a new dawn for humanity. He was Vladimir Ilyich Lenin, and the city was named in his honor.

Adolf Hitler despised Lenin's ideas and despised the city where they were brought to life. Though never publicly announced to the German citizenry, Hitler had decided that Leningrad would not be allowed to surrender. The city's populace was to die along with the doomed city, which would be razed to the ground once it was captured. Random shelling of civilian objectives was authorized, and any inhabitants attempting to flee the city were to be shot down.

In early November, 1941, Leningrad was on the edge of catastrophe. Hundreds of people were dying of starvation or starvation-related causes every day, and winter had barely begun. The only meager supplies of food making it into the city were over Lake Ladoga, but the lake was stormy and ice-laden now. Very few boats could make the trip and those that did still had to dodge death from above, for the German fighter planes and dive bombers never ceased in their attacks. When German forces captured the city of Tikhvin, the last remaining supply route was severed and Leningrad teetered even closer to the abyss. The city had enough flour for seven days, cereals for eight, fats for fourteen, sugar for twenty-two. There was no meat.

After the fall of Tikhvin, Hitler spoke of the besieged city at Munich, stating, "No one can free it. No one can break the ring. Leningrad is doomed to die of famine." Indeed, if the city was to avoid a quick descent into oblivion, it would need help. But from where? The battle for Moscow was in full swing as the German's Army Group Centre under Fedor von Bock advanced closer and closer to Russia's capital. South of Leningrad, the great city of Kiev surrendered to the German's Army Group South. France had long since fallen, and the Soviet Union's sole ally, Great Britain, was fighting for its life from a relentless Luftwaffe bombing campaign. The United States remained isolationist – unable to keep completely out of the war, but unwilling to explicitly enter it either. Japan, Germany's ally in the Pacific, continued to overtake China and the rest of Asia as the Soviet government kept a wary eye on its far east borders.

So the stars looked curiously on as the Russians and Germans played their deadly game and the people of Leningrad slowly starved. They watched hopes for love and peace recede, taking their place in line behind hopes for food and warmth. The stars wanted to know – as did the rest of the world – what drama would the City of Dramas play out now?

On the eastern horizon, a small sun peeked cautiously over the edge of the earth and the stars gave way to another new day. Large clouds as white as the freshly fallen snow moved quickly over the still sleepy city. One behind the other, in perfect military order they flew across the sky – over the canals, over the frozen Summer Gardens, over the Winter Palace, and then out to sea.

And when they were gone, the shelling began, and then the screaming.

Always the screaming.

* * *

Katya awoke to the steady ticking sound playing over the apartment loudspeaker. She rubbed the sleep from her eyes and was disappointed to recognize where she was. She'd had horrifying dreams of a dark, cryptic figure stalking her, and of her beautiful Leningrad being methodically destroyed by an unseen enemy. She had convinced herself it was just a dream, nothing to be upset about. But now she knew it wasn't a dream. The loudspeaker confirmed it. It plugged into a special outlet in the wall and gave warnings and instructions during air raids. Other times it merely ticked, signifying that the Germans hadn't taken over the city. Yet.

A shell exploded in the distance, as if to confirm that the ugliness was all too real. Katya got out of bed and went to the kitchen for a glass of water. She was the first one up in the morning and was often out the door while the others were still asleep. Oksana was the next to get up, and lastly Petya. One never knew whether Guzman or Igor would make it out of bed that day.

Katya took great pleasure in this short time she had to herself. She always enjoyed the stillness of mornings: the tender light breaking around the low-lying clouds on the horizon, the quietness and clarity of those first few breaths of the new day. If evenings were when the wave of the day finally broke and crashed to shore, then mornings were when that wave was just becoming a wave – tiny, little ripples on a clear, calm lake.

She sat by the window reading a book of poems by Akhmatova. She did that every morning for inspiration and reassurance. The sun was shining through the window and she slowly turned the ring Felix gave her, watching the sunlight dance off the two small diamonds surrounding the ruby. She missed Felix more than words could say, and knew this as a fact because she'd tried writing several poems to express the depth of her longing and none of them were able to do it. Each night she went to bed, she was sure the next day would be the one where Felix finally came back. Despite everything, she hadn't lost her faith. She knew they'd be together again.

Her breakfast consisted of water and a slice of bread, and she liked to close her eyes and pretend it was summer and she was having a picnic at Tsarkoye Selo. Located in lush countryside just outside the city, Tsarkoye Selo was the summer home of the former Tsars and Tsarinas. Katya had visited there often as a little girl and fondly remembered how the whole area would come alive in June. Lilacs, birch trees, and flowering bushes of every sort would burst forth with blooms and everywhere one went, a fragrance, as sweet as the most expensive perfume, would follow.

She heard Igor stir and looked over at the bed he shared with Guzman. Neither of them were doing very well, but Guzman was definitely the worse of the two. The funny, self-effacing man she knew was long gone, replaced by an incoherent moaner who slept nearly all day and night. He was lying in the same position he was always in – on his back, head turned to the right, arms folded across his chest. Igor used to complain about Guzman's snoring and so they now slept head to toe next to one another. Though the two of them were over half a century apart in age, they both reacted similarly to the lack of food. Neither had been up in the past two days except to go to the toilet. Katya was gradually accepting the fact that Guzman was going to die, but she'd grown far too attached to Igor to let him go so easily. She needed to find a way to get him more food.

"Ahhh!"

Katya startled at Igor's bloody scream. He had pushed himself against the wall – as far away from Guzman as possible. "What is it?" she asked. "Did you have a nightmare?"

Igor kept screaming, holding his folded hands in front of his mouth, as if to protect himself from the air. "Ahh! Ahh!"

Petya and Oksana sat up in their beds, though Guzman didn't stir in the least.

"Igor, what's wrong?" Katya asked as she made her way toward him.

"He's cold," Igor said, looking at Guzman.

"We're all cold, sweetheart," Katya said. "We'll need to get the fire going again."

"No, it's not that," Igor said. "He asked me to wake him when I got up, so I tapped him on the leg, but he didn't wake up. Then I grabbed his foot and it was cold."

Katya shook Guzman and called his name but understood that he wasn't going to answer. He'd died in his sleep.

She was surprised that the first feeling to come over her was one of relief. Ever since Guzman had lost his ration card and couldn't get a replacement, Katya had been sharing her meager rations with him. She was only a few days away from using the last of the food her father had stockpiled before he left for Moscow, and then she would have nothing left except for whatever she received from her ration card.

"It's all right, sweetheart," Katya said to Igor and held the frightened boy in her arms. "It's nothing to be afraid of."

He buried his face between her neck and shoulder and cried. Katya was sure he was reliving memories of his parents dying and wondered if he'd ever really grieved for that loss. She kissed him lightly on the temple and noticed he was hot. "I think you might be running a fever," she said. She got up to get a thermometer, terrified to think that he might have the flu. In these days and times, that meant near certain death. And not only that, but with their weak immune systems and in their cramped quarters, everyone else would probably catch it too.

With trepidation, she watched the red line in the thermometer slowly rise to 98, then 99, then 100. It didn't stop until it reached 103.

She gave him some aspirin and considered staying home from work to look after him, but knew that she couldn't. Igor saw her look at the clock. "I know you need to leave," he said, squirming out of her arms. "You don't have to stay here with me."

"No, you're wrong," Katya said. "I do have to stay here with you." She put her arms around him again. "That's the only way we're going to make it through this."

She stayed with him for another twenty minutes until he fell back asleep, then finished getting ready herself. Oksana had already left, and so Petya was the only one available to look after Igor and take care of Guzman's body.

Katya was hesitant to ask him for favors. Her relationship with him had changed dramatically after the birthday dinner he'd given her last month. She didn't remember anything from that night, but knew that when she'd woken up she was lying on Petya's bed and her sweater was on the floor. She'd asked Petya what had happened, and he'd replied, "Nothing," but had said it with a peculiar grin on his face. Ever since then, Katya had decided to distance herself from him. She'd made a vow to be faithful to Felix and felt ashamed for what she might have done or allowed to happen.

"Petya," she said, "would you be willing to take care of Guzman's body today? I need to leave for work."

He didn't answer, but that didn't mean much. He often didn't answer her questions.

"Also," Katya continued, "Igor's running a fever. Could you keep an eye on him? Make sure he drinks some water and give him some more aspirin at noon."

Again, Petya didn't answer, but at least he didn't say no.

Katya felt a twinge of envy as she hurried out the door for work. A part of her wanted to stay in bed half the day like Petya, but her conscience wouldn't let her do that. Not while the threat of mass starvation still loomed so large.

She hoped it wouldn't be too windy today. She could handle the cold, but the wind always went right through her many layers of clothing and chilled her emaciated body to the core.

"You're late," Lev said, as Katya walked into the office.

"Yes, I know. I'm sorry. Igor is running a fever and one of my roommates died during the night."

Lev tilted his head forward and looked over his glasses. "Who was it?"

"Guzman."

He took off his glasses and pinched the bridge of his nose. "Everywhere one goes these days, you see people dying. I had to step over a corpse at the foot of my building's stairwell last night. And I cursed at it – the corpse. Can you believe it? The poor man had died and I was angry at him for dying where I might trip over his body and hurt myself. These are such strange times we live in."

Katya took her coat off and sat down at the table.

"So Igor's not doing so well?" Lev asked.

"He gets worse every day. He just lies in bed all the time or in a chair by the stove. He complains he's always cold and he chews on those horrid oil cakes. They're so coarse you can't even bite into them. They used to only be fed to cattle."

Lev got up and wandered over to the window.

"He hardly talks anymore," Katya continued. "He has these deep blue circles under his eyes and has no interest in anything. It was only two months ago that he was still putting on this act to try to impress me – pretending he was older and more mature than he is. But now, he doesn't say anything. He doesn't even throw his temper tantrums anymore. He's just dead to the world and I'm at my wit's end with him. He's still a kid, with his entire future ahead of him. It's just so unfair."

"And now he has a fever?" Lev asked.

"Yes," Katya said. "And it's quite high."

Lev looked out the window. "I hope it's not the flu."

"It's not," Katya said.

"How do you know?"

"I just know," she said. "It isn't the flu. It can't be."

Lev turned to face her. "You're quite fond of him, aren't you?"

She nodded, staring at the top of the table.

Air raid sirens started wailing, but neither Lev nor Katya had any reaction. They were a daily occurrence. They both looked at one another as they always did to see if the other wanted to go to the shelter. Since it was nearly impossible to get any work done there, they both hated to go down there.

They reached a nonverbal agreement with a look that they would stay where they were. Wanting to change the subject, Katya asked Lev what he thought they should do about the rumors going around the marketplaces.

"You're going to have to be more specific than that," Lev replied, speaking loudly so he could be heard over the sirens. "There's more rumors going around than I can count these days."

"The rumors about the sausage being sold at the markets," Katya said, "that it's not entirely from *animal* sources."

"Ahh yes, *that* rumor," Lev said. "What do we do about it? Nothing. It's none of our concern. Let the police handle it. Personally, I think there's probably some truth to the rumors. That's what this proud city has been reduced to – cannibalism. You should keep an eye on Igor. I've heard that children are the ones to *disappear* first."

"Yes, I've heard."

Lev started pacing back and forth in front of the window and Katya knew that some bad news was forthcoming. "The director has ordered another ration reduction," he announced.

Katya felt a lump settle in her throat. "Oh no. Not again," she said. Every ration reduction meant the deaths of thousands more people. "How much?"

"Workers will be reduced from 400 grams of bread a day to 300. Everyone else will get 150 grams," Lev said over the sirens.

So many people were already dying. Katya shuddered to think of the effect this latest reduction would have. A working adult needed 2,000 calories a day, and the current ration of 400 grams of bread supplied only twenty-five percent of that – a measly 500 calories. She didn't even want to think about how many calories 300 grams would be.

She thought back to the prophecy Igor had told her when he saw all the mushrooms under the tree: 'Many mushrooms – many deaths.' It was clear that the prophecy was coming true. The only question was how many deaths.

"Must we?" Katya said.

Lev held his hand to his ear. "What?"

Katya raised her voice. "I said, must we?"

"We have no choice," Lev said. "Lake Ladoga is beginning to freeze and we won't be able to count on the supply boats making it across for very much longer. And now that Tikhvin has fallen, the supply port won't even have any supplies to deliver soon. We need to tighten our belts to buy some time."

Katya wondered how much further people could tighten their belts. They were already punching new holes in them to keep their trousers from falling down. "What are we going to do once the lake freezes?" she asked. "We don't have enough food in the city to last for more than a week or so."

"Once the lake freezes, we'll be able to drive trucks over the ice. We just need to know when it will be cold enough – when we'll have thick enough ice for the trucks. I don't think I need to tell you we have no margin of error left in calculating the situation. If we can expect the lake to freeze early enough, then we won't have to cut the rations any further."

"You said 'we.' You mean the director wants *you and I* to figure this out?"

"Yes."

"Why us? How on earth are we to do it?"

"He didn't say."

Katya thought she heard the sound of planes approaching, but she wasn't sure and tried not to let it distract her. "How long do we have?" she asked.

"He wants it by six o'clock this evening."

"What? With all their power and connections, they can't figure it out, and they expect the two of us to come up with the answer by tonight?"

"I know. I know," Lev said. "I had the same reaction when he told me, but he was in no mood to hear any argument. The situation is quite desperate. Every hour counts."

Katya was positive that she heard planes now. She wondered if they bothered Lev like they did her. It was excruciating to know that the enemy could kill you from so far away – without ever seeing your face, without ever knowing that you existed.

Lev was pacing in front of the window once again, leaning slightly forward, hands behind his back. Katya called out his name to ask him a question, but he didn't seem to hear her.

"Lev," she called out a little louder, "what if we can't retake Tikhvin?"

He stopped, took a deep breath, and held his chin up as he addressed her. "We need to be strong in the face of fear and diligent in the defense of the motherland," he said. Katya hated that answer. That was what he always said when he didn't want to respond to a question because the answer was too painful.

She understood now that if they couldn't retake Tikhvin – and soon – then it was the end. The entire city, all 2.5 million people, would die of mass starvation within a matter of weeks.

One problem at a time, she told herself. *One problem at a time.*

The room was cold and she grasped her arms with her hands in front of her. She noticed her arms had become so thin now that she could wrap her hands around her elbows and touch her pinky finger to her thumb.

"So how do we figure out this data for the lake freezing?" she asked. "Where do we begin?" She looked over at the portrait of Lenin, as if he could tell her.

Lev looked out the window and began to answer, but was cut short by a thunderous boom. The window exploded into a thousand shards of glass that crisscrossed the office. The floor shook, dust filled the air, and Katya crawled underneath the table in a state of panic and confusion.

Then all was eerily quiet. For a minute or two, Katya had no idea who she was, where she was, or what was happening. As the dust settled, she started to come to her senses and could see through the newly created hole in their wall that the building across the street had been leveled by a bomb.

She heard footsteps in the hallway, and then the door opened and a voice asked if anyone was there. Katya managed to let out a weak "yes," and two men ran into the room, looking around for the voice's owner. Katya recognized them. They were Civil Defense Corps workers from next door. They saw Lev laying by the window and went over to him.

Katya was uninjured – fortunate to have been looking away from the window at the portrait of Lenin next the door. Lev, on the other hand, had been struck by the flying glass and knocked to the floor by the force of the explosion. He wasn't moving and his eyes were closed. Katya feared he was dead. She climbed out from under the table to go to him. Her feet crunched the glass shards all over the floor. She saw bright red blood streaming down the side of his face from a dozen or so scratches. He was still breathing, though, and one of the men looked over his shoulder at her and said Lev had only superficial wounds and probably a minor concussion. He would be all right in a few days.

Katya held her hands out in front of her to see if she had any cuts. Finding none, she felt her face and was relieved to find it too had no scratches or blood. As they loaded Lev onto a stretcher, she shook her head to get some of the glass shards out of her hair. Then she helped them take Lev outside by holding doors open. They rushed him off to a hospital, and Katya turned her attention to the wreckage surrounding her. Pink dust covered everything and sunlight bounced off the millions of tiny shards of glass in the street. She could hear the cries for help of people trapped in the rubble and the shouts of the Civil Defense Corps workers as they tried to rescue them. Katya felt helpless. She was so weak from starvation she knew she couldn't help dig the survivors out. She watched two workers pull a man up from underneath a big slab of concrete. His arm was bloody and looked broken, and she realized she could help out by putting her nursing training to work tending to the wounded.

She had just finished dressing a hand wound and putting a woman's leg in a splint when her director appeared and pulled her aside. He wasted no time making it clear that he still wanted the ice data by six o'clock that evening. Katya tried to explain that Lev was incapacitated and that she didn't have the expertise to figure out something like that, but he cut her off. "I have every confidence that you will get the information to me," he said. "And if not, your commissar and I will have a little chat."

Katya appreciated that he was so open with his threat. At least she didn't have to guess what the consequences of failing to carry out the order would be. She went back to the office, where the workers were already cleaning up the glass and preparing to install plywood over the broken windows.

Whatever course of action she decided on, she knew she couldn't stay there. The demand weighing on her was bad enough, but now they were blocking out the sunlight and the outdoors. She needed the sun and the earth and the sky more than ever now. She needed to trust that God had not abandoned her, that an answer – if one existed – would be provided. *Faith*, she reminded herself. *Faith.*

She left the office and walked toward the library, hoping to find a chemistry textbook there with information on how ice forms. She had strong doubts that the idea would result in the data she needed, but it seemed like her best, if not only, option.

There was a loud explosion in the distance that startled her. She'd grown accustomed to hearing explosions, but was still on edge after having one strike so close. She said a short prayer for Lev, then sighed. Sometimes she just couldn't comprehend what was going on around her, how drastically things had changed since June. So often she thought she must be trapped in a nightmare – hers or someone else's. What had happened to the joy in life? The laughter? Where had they gone?

She tried to clear her mind. As she walked, she tried to simply breathe the air and notice the sights and sounds around her. It was easy enough to notice the cold. That was something that never left you. It was only November 12th, but it felt like mid-December. Winter had come early.

She'd seen the first snowflakes of the day early that morning. They had been scattered and casual and had drifted through the air aimlessly. But now they were no longer sparse and indifferent. Now, they fell with a purpose. Heavily. Hastily. They piled up on whatever they found – tanks, barricades, trees, steps, bushes.

Katya usually loved it when it snowed – things both big and small, wide and narrow getting covered in a soft, silvery blanket. Everything slowing down from its usual hectic pace. It seemed like a betrayal of Mother Nature to be in a hurry when she was so diligently painting the most exquisite art right before your eyes.

She didn't feel that way about snow now. More snow meant more death. For many people, it took all their energy merely to walk. To have to wade through snow drifts was too much for them – it was on the other side of that ever shrinking line between what was doable and what wasn't.

She walked past another newly constructed street barricade – a barbarous thing made of ferroconcrete and railroad iron. Even the pretty white snow piling up on top of it couldn't mask how hideous it was. Stretching from one sidewalk to the other, it was built to withstand not only tanks, but air bombardment as well. Past it, a sentry at the bridge shouted, "Halt! Who goes there?"

"It's me. Katya. How are you today, Nikolai?"

"Cold," Nikolai said. He looked at her papers as a formality.

"You seem rather down," Katya said.

He handed her papers back to her. "Tikhvin has fallen," he said.

"Yes, I heard."

"We're dead," he said, motioning with his hands all around him. "We're all going to die here."

"No, we're not," Katya said. "We'll get Tikhvin back."

"Before or after we all starve to death?" he said sarcastically.

"The lake will freeze soon," Katya said, "then we'll be able to evacuate people if the food supply gets any worse." She knew it wasn't really feasible to evacuate many people (and where would they go?), but she kept that part to herself.

"Yes, that's true," he said, sounding cautiously optimistic. "You've got a point there. When will it freeze?"

"That's what I need to figure out."

"If my grandfather were still alive, he'd know," Nikolai said. "He loved to play hockey and was the one who decided when the ice was thick enough for us to make our rink. I remember he used to . . ."

Nikolai's story reminded Katya of Felix telling her about his ice fishing trips with his father, how they drilled holes through the ice, then dropped their line through and waited for a fish to bite. It sounded rather boring to her, but Felix said he enjoyed it because he got to spend time with his otherwise extremely busy father.

Katya stopped with a sudden realization. That was it! That was the solution to her problem.

She bid a quick farewell to Nikolai and hopped on a streetcar heading toward the university. She wondered why she hadn't thought of it earlier. Felix's father could help her. He was a brilliant scientist, and one of the very few who had refused to be evacuated from the city. She was sure he could help. She just didn't know if he was still alive.

The hallways of the university building where Felix's father worked were cold, unlit, and smelled of ammonia and dog feces. Katya could hear the dogs yelping and scratching at the walls of their cages. She was surprised that lab animals still existed. Except for one small pack of stray mutts that she saw or heard in the distance from time to time, it was a rare thing to see cats or dogs in the city anymore. Many of them had already starved to death or been eaten by their owners.

Katya last saw Felix's father three weeks ago at his apartment. She went there once a week to check on him and his wife and help them out with little things. The last time she went, she noticed how pale his face had become and that he had puffy eyes – the first sign of dystrophy. She'd stopped going after that. She didn't have the strength, either physically or emotionally, to continue it. It was too far to walk. It was too cold. She didn't have the time. She couldn't bear seeing him and his wife wither away. But more than all of that, his dimming iron-grey eyes reminded her too much of his son.

She knocked on his office door warily, equally afraid that he wouldn't answer and that he would. He was doing research for the army now, she knew, and members of the armed forces (in particular the front line troops) received much better rations than civilians. But even then it wasn't always enough. Felix's father was proof of that.

A voice finally answered from the other side of the door. "Yes?" it said. "What is it?"

Katya wasn't sure if it was Felix's father or not. The man's voice sounded so nasal and strained. And she thought it strange that he didn't open the door, but given how paranoid most people were these days, it wasn't all that out of place.

She took a chance that it was him. "Hello," she called out. "It's me. Katya."

"Katya?" the man repeated. "Katya who?"

She imagined he was being spiteful because she'd stopped visiting them. "Katerina Selenaya," she said.

He still hesitated.

"Felix's girlfriend," she added.

"Oh, *Katya*," he said, suddenly sounding like the man she knew. He opened the door and held out his arms for a hug. "You'll have to forgive me my dear. Lately, my brain has been a bit . . . umm . . . foggy."

He looked even worse than when she'd last seen him. His whole body was rigid and his arms and legs shook visibly when he moved. His eyes had sunk so far into his head as to be nearly unseeable.

"Come in. Come in," he said. "It's not much warmer in here, but a little at least." His office consisted of a desk crammed into the corner of a small laboratory. In the middle of the room were counters filled with microscopes and beakers and vials. The windows had been broken, and – like Katya's office now – were covered over with plywood. Two *koptilkas* (smoky lighting devices) provided the sole lighting for the room.

There was an uncomfortable silence between them that Katya let linger because it was even more uncomfortable to ask the usual questions. She didn't want to look at him and tried her best not to without him noticing. After another long minute, she gave in and asked how his wife was getting along.

She waited with a sense of dread as he cleared some papers off a chair.

He motioned for her to sit down. "She passed away last week," he said.

That was the answer she was afraid of, but strangely enough she didn't feel much of anything for him. She had no urge to hug him, take his hand, or even to say she was sorry to hear of the news. It was as if he'd just told her he'd bought a frying pan. That she felt so little disturbed her more than the news itself. "Did she suffer much?" she asked.

"Yes, she was in terrible pain," he said.

"Well, it's a good thing it's over then," Katya said, surprised to hear the words coming out of her mouth.

He looked at her strangely and she berated herself for her insensitivity. She knew how much he loved his wife, and that he must be terribly heartbroken now. *Was that the best she could do now? Was that as much compassion as she had to offer?*

As difficult as that had been, the next question would be even worse. Every time they saw one another, they stumbled along in their conversation until one of them got up the courage to inquire about Felix. Each time, they hoped that the other had the answer.

Conscious of the time constraints of her mission, Katya broached the subject first. "Have you heard anything of Felix?"

He hung his head. "No, nothing," he answered.

"Well, I'm sure he's okay," she said, hoping to move away from the subject as quickly as possible. "I think we'll hear something soon. I hear that communication with front-line troops is getting better."

"Yes," he agreed. "I'm sure we'll hear from him soon."

Katya ventured a look at his face, saw how sallow his cheeks were, and quickly looked away. He was almost completely unrecognizable from the man she knew before the blockade started.

"I need to get straight to the point," she said, "because I don't have much time. Leningrad itself doesn't have much time. I'm here because I'm hoping you can help me with some calculations on ice formation."

"I see," he said.

Katya thought he sounded disappointed, but realized his feelings were less important to her than the city's survival.

He listened patiently as she explained the situation to him, and when she finished, he asked only one question. "How much weight would the ice need to hold?"

Katya didn't know the answer. Lev hadn't told her anything about that. "I don't know," she said. "I guess however much a truck with supplies weighs."

"A truck?" He raised his eyebrows. "You're going to have to wait quite a while before the ice is thick enough to hold a truck. You might better start out with something smaller."

"Like what?"

"You could start out with horses pulling sledges until the ice can support a truck."

"All right," Katya said. "Perhaps you could make estimates for both, for sledges and trucks?"

"Certainly. I can do that," he said. "But I'm a bit busy right now. They've got me training dogs to run under tanks."

"Why would they want to do that?"

"They're going to strap explosives around the dogs, then detonate them when they're under the tank."

"Oh my," Katya said and gave a little gasp. She hated the way animals were treated these days, was repulsed by it. She had one dark secret in her life, one violent fantasy, and that was to go back in time and burn the teachings of the French philosopher Renee Descartes before the sickening lies spread to the rest of humanity. It was Katya's belief that he had set mankind back at least a thousand years with his misguided writings on separateness – that the human body and mind were two distinct things, and that animals were very different from humans because animals had no souls. It was all because of his teachings that animals were considered 'machines,' and scientists could torture and kill them in experiments and still maintain a clear conscience.

"So now we're forcing animals to fight in our war?" she said aloud. "What next?"

"We've got to win somehow," he replied.

His statement sounded so obvious, but Katya couldn't help but think "at what cost?" Did being at war mean you could throw away your values and ethics? So long as you won, nothing else mattered?

She allowed herself to drift away for a second to the world she thought might have evolved without Descartes' teachings. In that world, everyone understood how they were interconnected with everyone and everything else, and they acted accordingly. It was a peaceful world, and she felt cheated that things hadn't turned out that way. So many opportunities man had been given over the centuries to put an end to war, but here they were in the 20th century engaged in the biggest and bloodiest war mankind had ever known.

She opened her mouth to argue with Felix's father about his statement, but decided against it. "I need to give the information to my director by six o'clock this evening," she said.

He took a pocket watch out and checked the time. "I'll do what I can," he replied.

"Please do," Katya said. "Thousands of people's lives are depending on it."

"I understand."

Katya got up to go. She didn't want to disturb him while he worked. "I'll be back in an hour," she said.

He didn't respond. He was already digging through a thick stack of books piled in the far corner.

Katya opened her eyes, jolted awake by someone grabbing and lifting her legs off the bench she was laying on. "What are you doing?" she cried.

The man immediately put her legs back down. "Oh! Forgive me, comrade," he exclaimed.

There was another man standing near her head. He took a step back as Katya sat up. "We thought you were . . ." he started to say. She saw a cart in front of her with two corpses on it and finished his sentence for him, "dead."

"We're so sorry, comrade," the man who'd grabbed her legs said. He was tall and lanky, with a long nose and a gray fur hat pulled down tight over his ears.

They didn't need to explain anything to her. She'd put the pieces together herself. The two men were gathering corpses from the university grounds. They saw her laying motionless on a bench in the hallway and assumed she must be dead.

"It's all right," she said. She looked at the bluish corpses and shuddered. One of them was a young female about her age. Her eyes were still open and Katya turned away. "Be on your way, please," she said to the men.

"Yes, of course," they said, apologizing once more and then trudging down the hallway with their grim cart of death, its wheels squeaking like a rabbit caught in a vicious trap.

When they were out of sight, Katya checked the time and saw that an hour had passed. She had meant to do some work while she waited for Felix's father, but she'd fallen asleep. It's all she wanted to do lately: sleep, sleep, sleep. She was constantly tired and had so little energy because of malnutrition. She packed up her notebook and went back down the hallway to check on Felix's father.

Opening the door a few inches, she stuck her head in and called out.

"Just a little longer," he answered. "I'll come get you when I'm done."

She closed the door and went back to her bench. Taking her notebook out again, she hoped she could do some work, but found she couldn't focus. She thought of so many things, but no matter what her mind started out on, it ended on Igor. She could think of little else lately, and made a vow not to let him leave her like the others had. She'd do everything she could to make sure he made it through this wretched affair alive. He was so precious to her.

After another hour passed, she started to wonder if Felix's father might have forgotten about her. She knocked on the door and slowly opened it. She saw him sitting at his cluttered desk staring straight ahead at the wall.

"Is everything all right?" she asked.

"Katya?"

"Yes, it's me."

"Oh good. I was waiting for you to come back. I'm afraid I'll need your help."

"Sure," she said. "What can I do?" She walked over to him and looked down at the sheet of paper on his desk. It was covered with his handwriting, but she couldn't make out a single word or number.

"I've worked out the basic formula," he said, and pointed with his pencil at some scribbles on the paper. "Here, let me show you." He put his pencil to the paper and wrote something, but his hand shook so badly that the result was just more scribbles. "Actually, this is where I need your help," he said. "It's difficult for me to . . . umm . . . write . . . lately."

Katya took the pencil from his hand. He looked like a ghost, and she mentally added him to the list of people who had left her. "I'll write," she said. "You just tell me what to write."

He coughed loudly then spent a minute clearing his throat. "To support a man on a horse," he began, "the ice will need to be four feet thick. And if..."

"Wait a minute," Katya interrupted. "The ice needs to be *four feet* thick to support a man on a horse?"

The End Of Sorrow

He squinted at his scribbles on the paper. "Oh no. I'm sorry. That should be inches. Four *inches*."

Katya felt a flash of fear. Perhaps this had all been in vain. His numbers might be complete nonsense and if they used them, all the trucks would fall through the ice. "I'm feeling a little concerned about the accuracy of these numbers," she said.

"As well you should be, dear," he said. "My brain doesn't work as well as it once did. But I can assure you that these numbers are correct. I've double checked them, and they agree with my own experience when I used to go ice fishing."

Realizing she had little choice, she asked him to continue.

"Now, according to my calculations," he said, "at twenty-three degrees above zero, four inches of ice will form in sixty-four hours. At fourteen above, it will take thirty-four hours to form four inches. At five degrees above, it will take twenty-three hours. Obviously we need more than four inches of ice since we want to haul supplies over the lake. A horse pulling a sledge with a ton of supplies requires seven inches of ice. A truck carrying a ton of freight needs a minimum eight inches of ice. I'm afraid I don't know how much a tank weighs, so I can't calculate that, but I do know that once the lake freezes – I mean *really* freezes – you'll have ice three to five feet thick. Enough to hold pretty much anything. If you . . ."

Katya wrote furiously, afraid she might miss some important detail.

When he finished, she looked at the clock and saw it was already 5:10 p.m.. The trip back to her office took her very close to her apartment and she wanted to stop by and check on Igor. If his fever got any worse, she'd go to the hospital later and beg one of the doctors to come see him that night.

She gathered her things and rushed to the door, so preoccupied with Igor and her deadline that she almost forgot to thank Felix's father. She knew this was the last time she'd ever see him, but she didn't know what to say. "Goodbye" seemed too shallow, but what more was there to say? It really was goodbye. She was surprised at how unemotional she was. *What was happening to her?*

She said thank you, gave him a hug, and recited her current favorite Akhmatova poem. He bowed his head as he listened.

> *Give me bitter years of sickness,*
> *Suffocation, insomnia, fever,*
> *Take my child and my lover,*
> *And my mysterious gift of song –*
> *This I pray at your liturgy*
> *After so many tormented days,*
> *So that the stormcloud over darkened Russia*
> *Might become a cloud of glorious rays.*

***

Petya awoke from his nightmare with a gasp. His hands gripped the blankets so tightly that his knuckles turned white, and his whole body was drenched with cold sweat. It was nothing new to him though. It was that same dream, that same image of his parents being shot while he looked on as a four-year-old boy. His mother's blood-stained face was so vivid, like time hadn't passed at all.

He tried again to recall those two days he'd spent clinging to her side after she was killed. What did he do? What did he think? Feel? Did he cry? He didn't know any of the answers. He'd never been able to recall those two days.

He laid in his bed now staring at the cracks in the ceiling. He was still tired, but the prospect of returning to that dream kept him from falling back asleep. It used to be when he was tired and couldn't sleep, he'd toss and turn relentlessly trying to get comfortable. But he didn't have the energy for that anymore. He didn't even have the energy to get up and put more wood in the stove, even though he was quite cold and knew the fire must be nearly out by now.

He kept a knife under his mattress and deliberated whether or not to get it out. One of the voices had returned to speak to him and was even more persistent than the last time. "You feel how weak you are?" it said. "That's because Igor is stealing your strength. You can't let him do this to you. You can't let him win. Kill him now while you have the chance."

Petya reached under his mattress, felt the cold knife in his hand, and decided the voice was right. Oksana and Katya were both at work, and now *was* the perfect time to kill him. All day long, the boy had been delirious and talking nonsense from his fever. It would be no surprise if he died. He was sound asleep in Katya's bed and it would be easy to do – probably easier than strangling Oksana's cat.

"Don't use the knife, you fool," the voice hissed. "Suffocate him with a pillow!"

Petya picked up one of his pillows and looked around the room suspiciously. He saw Guzman's corpse laying in the same position as it had been that morning and cursed himself for not taking care of it earlier in the day. That's where the voice was coming from, he decided. It was Guzman seeking his revenge.

"What are you waiting for?" the voice demanded. "Kill him now and stop him from stealing your strength!"

"Shut up!" Petya shouted. "Just leave me be!"

Igor opened his eyes and turned his head toward Petya. "What?" he asked weakly.

Petya put the pillow back down and saw the clock out of the corner of his eye. It was going on six p.m. already. Oksana would be home from work soon. "I said, help me get rid of Guzman before Katya and Oksana get home."

Igor groaned and pulled the covers over his head.

"Stop your whining," Petya said. "I can't get him down the stairs alone."

Igor protested again, but eventually got out of bed and helped. Together they dragged Guzman's body down the stairs and outside. It was snowing and the sun had long since set. Petya sent Igor back upstairs for the sled so they could load Guzman's corpse on it and pull it to the morgue.

Petya leaned against the building and lit a cigarette as he waited for Igor to return. He didn't dare sit down because it was too much of a struggle to get back up. Just hauling Guzman's body down the stairs felt like a marathon. Nothing was easy these days. Even getting out of bed was a chore.

He heard crunching snow and thought someone might be approaching, but when he squinted into the darkness he couldn't see anything. Then the sounds stopped. He tried to focus on his cigarette and enjoy every second of it, because he only had a couple left. He inhaled deeply and looked at Guzman's body lying on the icy sidewalk, his blue legs protruding from the blanket they'd wrapped him in. Petya didn't like being alone with the corpse and hoped Igor would be back soon.

"You should have killed Igor when you had the chance," a voice said to Petya.

Petya kicked Guzman's body. "Shut up," he said. "I'm not falling for any of your tricks. I didn't kill you."

"Whose ration card is that in your pocket?" the voice asked.

"It wouldn't have made a bit of difference if I hadn't taken your ration card," Petya said. "You were going to die anyway and you know it."

Petya heard the snow crunch again and then Oksana rounded the corner of the building and walked toward him. She had a smug little grin on her face, and Petya wondered how much she'd overheard. She glanced at Guzman's corpse, then at Petya, then went in the building without saying a word.

"She knows! Oksana knows. You've got to get rid of her!" the voice screamed to Petya.

"Damn you," Petya said and kicked Guzman's corpse even harder. "Just shut the hell up and leave me alone!"

Someone else was approaching and called out Petya's name. He recognized Katya's voice and watched the small chin and high cheekbones of her face come into view from out of the darkness.

"Who are you talking to?" she asked.

"The Nazis of course," he replied. "Who else would I be talking to?"

Before Katya could say anything more, Igor emerged from the stairwell with the sled. Her eyes opened wide. "What on earth are you doing up?" she asked.

"Petya made me help him."

"Petya!" she said, glaring at him. "He's sick. He needs to be in bed." She took her mittens off and felt Igor's forehead with the back of her hand. "You're burning up," she said.

Petya watched her take Igor by the arm and lead him back upstairs. Every week she seemed to grow more affectionate toward the boy.

After they left, Petya loaded the body on the sled, but decided he didn't have the energy to haul it to the morgue. Instead, he pulled it to the courtyard and buried it under a few feet of snow. It was no big deal, he told himself. There were corpses everywhere these days. At least he'd buried the body, unlike those lazy bastards who just left them lying on the street or sidewalk.

When he made it back to the apartment, he saw Katya and Oksana conversing quietly around Igor's bed. Katya put her hat and mittens back on and prepared to head out. If Oksana had said anything to her, she didn't reveal it. Katya only asked Petya one thing – how he'd made the trip to the morgue so quickly.

"I ran," he said straight-faced.

Katya gave him a little look of disgust, but pursued the point no further. "Igor has a fever of 104," she said.

Petya felt a twinge of guilt for forcing the poor boy out of bed. He didn't know his fever was *that* high.

"Are you going straight to the hospital now?" Oksana asked Katya.

"No, I need to go to the office first," she answered. "I have to deliver some information to my director."

"Whatever it is, it can wait," Oksana said as she put the tea kettle on the stove. "The boy needs to see a doctor. He's been sweating terribly. You see how his sheets are soaked?"

Igor sat up and let loose with a dry, hacking cough.

"You hear that?" Oksana said.

"I know," Katya said, "but what can I do. My director has threatened to call in my commissar if I don't deliver the information by six p.m.. I already took a big risk is coming here. I don't have much time left now." She buttoned her coat up and pulled her scarf tight. "It's only an extra forty minutes," she said. "That's not going to make a difference."

Petya climbed back into bed and pulled the covers up tight to his neck. Katya hurried out the door and Oksana shook her head as she watched her go.

The apartment loudspeaker was broadcasting inspiring words from a poet who was in the infantry: "Comrades, we fight for our freedom! We fight for our honor. We fight on behalf of every man, woman, and child who has been crushed by the fist of tyranny throughout history. Our cause is just. This battle must not be lost . . ."

After the water boiled, Oksana made two cups of herbal tea. She set a blue cup down, presumably for herself, on the small table where the lamp was and gave the orange cup to Igor. The soldier-poet ended his patriotic exhortation and an announcer reminded listeners that Stalin would be making an address the next evening at ten o'clock. One of the numerous marches Shostakovich had written then began playing. Oksana hummed along to it.

Igor took a few small sips from his tea, decided it was cool enough, then gulped down the rest of the cup. He fell asleep a few minutes after that.

The voice in Petya's head had started up again, telling him all sorts of things about Oksana. "That bitch is planning something for you," it said. "She knows you killed her cat and now she knows you stole Guzman's ration card. She'll probably tell Katya as soon as she gets the chance."

Petya decided he needed to act pre-emptively. Before Oksana said anything to Katya, he had to discredit her testimony – make Katya believe the woman had lost her senses and was talking nonsense.

He opened his eyes part way and saw Oksana walk to the kitchen. He got out of bed quietly and poured the tea from Oksana's blue cup into Igor's orange cup. Then he put the orange cup back in the same exact place she'd set the blue cup on the table.

He pretended to be asleep when Oksana came back in the room. He peeked at her from under his blankets, watching the puzzled expression on her face as she picked up the orange tea cup and examined it. She looked at Igor's empty blue cup, shook her head, mumbled a few curse words, then went back to the kitchen.

Petya fell asleep after that and didn't wake up until Katya returned home a couple hours later. The music from the loudspeaker was gone. It had been replaced by the metronome-like ticking that played when no program was being broadcast.

He overheard Katya and Oksana having a heated conversation near the front door.

"They gave me some more aspirin and a can of condensed milk," Katya said. "They said it's probably just a cold, that he'll be all right if he gets some rest."

"You don't get a fever of 104 from a cold," Oksana said, obviously struggling to keep her voice down. "He needs to see a doctor."

"Oksana, I tried," Katya said defensively. "All the doctors were busy or resting."

"You should have *insisted*," Oksana said. "You've done enough for them with all your volunteer work that they could certainly do this one little favor for you. You let people walk all over you."

"Oksana, you don't understand. They work so hard and get so little time to rest."

"And what about you?"

"Me?"

"Yes, you," Oksana said. "Don't you work hard? Don't you help others all the time? Why is it you don't deserve some help once in a while?"

Petya waited to hear what Katya's answer would be, but there wasn't one – only the never-ending ticking from the loudspeaker.

***

The wind was ice-cold and whipped over the top of the snow, stinging Felix's cheeks and stabbing into his lungs. He ducked down and tried to settle into his foxhole to better protect himself, but it was pointless – as was his being there on the side of the road in the first place.

Olga had ordered him to watch for German activity along the road and then report back at the end of the day. It was a stupid assignment. Felix knew it. Olga knew it. Everyone in camp knew it. There *was no* German activity on the road, and there wasn't going to be. All their tanks and trucks and cars were frozen solid. When the Germans launched their invasion, they'd expected victory before winter set in. As a result, neither their armies nor their vehicles were prepared for cold weather, especially weather *this* cold.

Five hours had crawled by and Felix was now almost completely indistinguishable from the snowdrifts around him. Even his recently grown beard was covered white with snow. It was the sixth day in a row that he'd been assigned this ridiculous order, and in all that time, he hadn't seen a single thing come down the road – unless you counted squirrels.

Perhaps he should start reporting them back to Olga, as Misha had suggested: *Three brown furry rodents were seen traveling south in loose formation. Looked nervous and seemed to be searching for something. Unable to ascertain if they were advanced scouts, Nazi Sympathizers, or lost troops.*

Felix stretched his head out and looked up the road to the north. The wind had been building a snowdrift there since he left yesterday, and it now stretched completely across the road – six feet high and at least twelve feet in width. Felix remembered when he was a kid how excited he would be seeing snowdrifts like that. He and Dima would tunnel into them and make snow forts and pretend to battle Napoleon's armies. It was always great fun and they'd stay out there for hours, until Dima's mother called them in for hot cocoa.

The memory made him bitter. He couldn't think about Dima anymore without a pain in his heart. Why did he have to die? Why was Felix allowed to live when his friend's life was cut short? None of it made any sense, and Felix was sick of the way things were. He couldn't accept that the world could be so ugly and unfair.

He looked at the giant snow drift once again. The road was completely impassable to anything but a snowplow. He was supposed to stay until sundown – still another hour away – but he didn't care. He was numb with cold and he'd had enough. He got up and went back to camp.

Life as a partisan under Olga's command had become more about fighting boredom than the enemy. They rarely ventured out, and when they did, it was to do what Olga referred to as "intelligence gathering missions." Felix mockingly referred to these trips to the neighboring areas as "gossip crusades," and joked that no other military outfit in all of Russia had more rumors in their arsenal than they did. "We've got enough rumors to kill a dozen old widows in one shot," he liked to say. Misha loved that one and always laughed.

The partisans had fled their former camp a few weeks back after Felix had run in shouting that two German platoons were approaching. At first, Olga had accused him of lying and threatened to have him shot on the spot, but it wasn't long before it became clear that he was telling the truth.

Everyone knew that Olga didn't want to leave that camp. She'd made herself a nice, cozy shelter and wanted to stay there through the winter.

They'd set up camp again ten miles farther north, and Olga had quickly seized materials from a nearby village and conscripted several partisans to build her a new shelter against the bitter winter cold. When they finished erecting it, she snuggled into it like a bear and rarely came out. It had a little stove that provided lots of heat and, in short, was a comfortable place to wait out the winter.

Felix hated it. He hated all the comfortableness they had. He hated sitting around the campfire all day long listening to people gossip and trade rumors.

He, Misha, and Yuri shared a hut together now. It was made out of mud, straw, and ice, and a little stove kept it nice and warm on the inside. When they'd first lit the stove, Felix had expected the structure to melt and collapse after a few hours, but he came to understand what the Eskimoes had known for so long – a little melted snow will freeze again and act as cement between the blocks of ice. The inside of the hut might melt a little, but the frost on the outside would counteract it.

The entrance to the hut was waist-high and Felix struggled to crawl through it now with his bulky clothing and frigid muscles. Misha was sitting on his homemade bed smoking a cigarette. "Welcome home, sweetheart," he said, and blew him a mock kiss.

Misha had long since run out of booze and was in general quite miserable. Olga had repeatedly denied his requests to venture to Lestovo (now considerably farther away) – no matter what fantastical reasons he came up with. The worst of his withdrawal symptoms had passed, but he wasn't quite so easy going as he used to be, and his tongue had grown considerably more caustic.

Felix took his coat off and Yuri helped him hang it by the stove to dry. Misha offered him a puff from his cigarette and Felix accepted it. He'd started smoking, for the first time in his life, shortly after Dima had been killed.

The tobacco was harsh and Felix struggled to keep from coughing. He sat down on his own homemade bed, which consisted of several inches of bark and a foot of straw. The bark covered the frozen ground, and the straw served as a mattress. Felix found it annoyingly comfortable and considered getting rid of it.

"Misha picked up an extra week of guard duty today," Yuri announced.

"How the hell did you know?" Misha said. "It just happened an hour ago."

Felix wasn't surprised that Yuri had found out already. "An hour is an eternity around here," he said. "It's ridiculous how fast gossip spreads through this camp." He held out the cigarette for Misha to take back, but he waved it away. "What did you do this time?"

"What does it matter?" Misha said irritably. "She just makes shit up if she really wants to get you." He wrapped his arms around his knees and pulled them close to his chest. "I think it's about time someone challenged that bitch's authority."

Yuri's long bushy eyebrows arched in surprise across his forehead, then he frowned and nodded his head in agreement.

"How about it, Yuri?" Misha said. "You used to be a captain in the army. How about we stage a coup and make you the leader?"

Felix wasn't sure if Misha was serious or if he was just trying to entertain himself again.

"It's not that I wouldn't mind," Yuri said, "I'm tired of sitting around here doing nothing. But leaders can only be leaders if others will follow them. I've been around long enough to know that people won't follow me."

"People won't follow you?" Misha said in mock amazement. "But why? You're such an honest man. And you're certainly no coward. Don't people know that?"

Now Felix knew for sure that Misha was trying to amuse himself.

"They *should* know that by now," Yuri said, leaning forward and studying the dirt floor.

"Certainly they should," Misha agreed. "Perhaps you should tell them outright so they know for sure. Stop beating around the bush."

"Yes, you may have something there," Yuri said. "Perhaps I've been too subtle." He crossed his massive arms in front of his chest and held his hand to his chin.

The wind picked up outside and blew some snow flurries through the entrance of their hut. Felix adjusted the blanket that served as a door in a vain attempt to keep them out.

"What about you, Felix?" Misha said.

"What about me?"

"How about you lead our coup."

"Why me?"

"Because you have everyone's respect," Yuri said, cracking the knuckles of his enormous hands. "Olga has only their fear."

Felix didn't have a chance to reply because Olga's voice shouted his name from outside their hut. "Varilensky! Come out here!"

"What does that witch want now?" Misha said.

Felix shrugged his shoulders as he got his coat on. "I don't know," he said, "but I'm sick of it."

Over the past several weeks, Olga had taken every opportunity she could find to punish Felix for something – trivial infractions of rules she often made up on the spot. Felix learned not to argue with her, to just perform whatever ridiculous task it was that she ordered. He knew she had it out for him and didn't want to give her anything she could use to accuse him of insubordination.

"I heard her complaining earlier that the stew we had for lunch had too much salt," Yuri said.

Misha got up and grabbed his coat. "It'll be interesting to see how she blames that one on him since he wasn't even here," he said.

Felix crawled through the small opening of the hut to the outside and saw Olga standing there with pistol drawn. Two recently joined partisans flanked her and they grabbed Felix by the arms.

"Why aren't you at your post, comrade?" Olga asked, grinning as though someone had just given her a birthday present.

Felix saw her gold tooth gleam briefly in the pale winter light and wanted to knock it out of her mouth.

"I gave you direct orders to stand watch on the road a mile west of here until sundown," Olga continued. She looked at the faint sun on the horizon. "Clearly, you have disobeyed my order."

Yuri and Misha made their way out of the hut, and a few other partisans came over to see what was going on.

"That order was bullshit and you know it," Felix said. "Everyone in camp knows it. There hasn't been a vehicle down that road in a week, and the road is completely impassable now."

Olga raised her voice a notch. "This group will not survive if orders are not carried out as specified," she said. "Infractions must be dealt with swiftly and severely." A couple more partisans had gathered around, and Olga seemed to say this more for their benefit than Felix's. "This is not your first infraction," she said and took out a piece of paper. She began listing every instance – some real, some made up. "You were involved in a fight against your fellow comrades on October 16th. You reported six minutes late for guard duty on November 9th. You were again late on November 12th . . ."

Felix listened to the charges with a rising sense of fury. When Olga finished, nearly the entire camp had gathered round to watch.

"I think everyone will agree that I've been more than patient with you," Olga said. "You've been given numerous opportunities to improve your behavior and you've chosen every time not to do so. In the best interest of this group and this war, you are to be executed."

"My death will be in the best interest of no one except the enemy," Felix said.

"Shut up! Enough of your lies and provocations! We're all quite tired of them," Olga said.

"If I'm to be shot, then I'll speak my mind," Felix shouted back. "All we do is sit around this damn camp while the Germans march on Moscow and starve Leningrad to death. What have we done to fight the enemy lately? We cut one of their telegraph wires. That's it! How are we going to win the war that way?"

"Shut him up!" Olga yelled to the partisans holding Felix's arms.

"We don't answer to *her*," Felix said to the other partisans. "We answer to the Russian people! And right now, I couldn't look a single one of them in the eye and say that I'm doing all I can to defeat the enemy."

"Spare us the lecture!" Olga yelled. "You're not in charge here. *I* am."

"Leaders need to lead," Felix said, "and you've done everything but! The only thing you're good at is cursing and making threats. Nobody joined the partisans to escape the war." Felix looked around him and saw Yuri and others nodding in agreement. "We all know Tikhvin has fallen to the enemy and that the people of Leningrad will perish unless it's retaken. Why aren't we joining the battle there? Why aren't we *fighting*?"

"Take him out to the woods!" Olga ordered the two men holding Felix's arms.

"No!" Felix shouted. "If I die, it'll be at the hands of the enemy, not you!" He kicked his right leg out in front of him as far as he could and knocked the pistol from Olga's hand. It landed at Natasha's feet and she picked it up. But when Olga held her hand out for it, Natasha wouldn't give it to her. Instead she pointed the pistol at the men holding Felix. "Let him go," she said.

All color drained from Olga's face, and as the two men stepped away, Natasha tossed the pistol to Felix. No one tried to intervene as he pointed it at Olga.

She lifted her chin and held her arms out to the side. "So?" she said. "What are you waiting for, kike? Shoot me."

Felix lowered the pistol. "No, I'm not going to shoot you," he said.

"You better," Olga replied. "Because I'm sure as hell going to shoot you as soon as I get the chance."

Felix tucked the pistol inside his coat. "I think it's past time we go our separate ways."

"I'm not going anywhere," Olga said.

"Yes, but I am. I'm going to join the fight at Tikhvin," Felix said. "I'll leave camp in half an hour."

"Good riddance," Olga said. She walked away from the crowd and disappeared behind the door to her hut.

Felix looked at all the expressionless faces staring back at him and had no idea what any of them were thinking. He felt sad to be leaving them. He'd been through a lot with some of them: the incident where Misha helped rescue him and Dima from the Germans, the time he and Dmitry and Natasha rescued the two little girls from the house fire started by Nazi flamethrowers, and, of course, the close call with the landmine with Yuri.

He lifted his head toward the flat winter sky and saw the sun was beginning to set. On the opposite horizon, through the leafless branches of a birch tree, was a full moon.

"Are you really going to Tikhvin?" a voice shouted from the crowd.

Felix recognized Natasha's voice. "Yes," he replied.

"What difference is one man going to make there?" someone else shouted.

"A lot more than one man makes here," Felix replied.

He went back into his hut and started packing. He didn't want to answer any more questions. All this explaining and pondering was useless. He knew what he had to do.

After a few minutes, Yuri came in and started packing his things as well.

"What are you doing?" Felix asked.

"Going with you of course."

"You don't have to do that," Felix said.

"I know," Yuri said. "I want to."

Felix stopped packing. "It's not going to be easy," he said. "Tikhvin's a long ways from here. It'll be cold as hell. And the Nazis will be well dug in."

"Doesn't matter," Yuri said. "I want to fight. And if you'll lead the way, I'll follow."

Misha came in and saw the two of them packing their things. He sat down on his bed for a moment, then stood up, then sat back down again. "To the devil with you both!" he blurted out and pulled the blankets off his bed . "You think I'm going to stay here by myself? I'd be bored out of my mind." He began packing his things. "Not that you two are much fun anyway, mind you."

Felix was pleased that he wouldn't be making the journey alone. "With the three of us going, we'll surely tip the balance and send the Nazis running out of Tikhvin," he joked.

Both Yuri and Misha laughed, though Felix thought it sounded a bit forced. There was no doubt some apprehension about the decision they'd just made.

Felix didn't have much to pack. He had three blankets, two wool undershirts, a sewing kit, a canteen, five packages of canned fish, half a pound of dark chocolate, a loaf of bread, and a razor. He kept his spoon (as all Soviet soldiers did) inside his boot. He stuffed the remaining items in his pack, careful not to damage his most important possession – a letter from Katya, given to him the night before he left for the front.

Felix and Yuri took the stove apart and packed it away. Then they were done, and as is the Russian custom before leaving a place, they sat down and were quiet for a moment. Felix wanted to take out the letter from Katya and read it again, but the thought of her was too painful right now. He stood up and grabbed his pack. "Ready?" he asked.

"Da, davai," – yes, let's – Yuri said, and got down on his hands and knees to make his way out of the hut.

Felix went next, and as soon as he got outside and stood up, Yuri pushed him to the ground and fell on top of him as a gunshot sounded. There was a lot of commotion and shouting, and then four other loud cracks that echoed through the camp.

It had all happened very quickly and Felix saw none of it. When Yuri rolled off of him, Felix began piecing the events together. He saw Olga near the door of her hut sprawled out in the snow, breathing heavily and wheezing with each inhalation. She was still holding onto a rifle with her right hand. Behind him, gathered around the campfire, was a large group of partisans – perhaps the entire camp – and half of them had their weapons pointed in Olga's direction.

Felix figured out that Olga must have tried to shoot him, missed because Yuri had thrown him to the ground, and then the other partisans shot Olga before she could take aim again.

He was puzzled why so many of his comrades were gathered around the campfire. He saw they all had their bags packed and their rifles around their shoulders.

Yuri was standing next to Felix and grinning. "Word travels fast around here, huh?" he said.

Olga was wheezing louder and it was darker and colder than it had been just a few minutes ago. Everyone was looking to Felix and it took a while for it all to sink in for him. The moon was full. The wind had died. He was the new leader of the partisans.

"Let's move out!" he shouted, and led the way.

"What about Olga?" someone asked.

Felix kept walking. He didn't look at their former leader nor did he hesitate in his answer. "Leave her there," he said.

* * *

It was late morning when Petya woke up and he was surprised to see that Katya hadn't left for work yet. He was even more surprised when she moved into the soft light of the sun shining through the window and he saw how attractive she still was. Despite her sunken cheeks and ever-expanding forehead, she retained that distinctive beauty Petya had always found so irresistible.

He watched her remove a pot of boiling water from the stove and strain it into another pot. When she finished that, she strained it a second time into its final container. Petya counted the containers and saw she'd finished three, but still had five more to go. It was a long, arduous process, but necessary to make the polluted river water drinkable.

All those things one took for granted before the blockade – food, running water, heat, electricity – were gone. Life was very simple now. You had only one goal when you got out of bed in the morning – to get enough to eat to make it to the next day. You didn't have to worry about deciding between tea or coffee, mashed potatoes or fried, or whether to buy chocolates or cake for your friend's birthday. Petya's biggest decision each day was how much of his bread ration to eat for breakfast and how much to save for dinner.

Katya went over to Igor, sat on the edge of his bed, and took his temperature. After that, Igor coughed long and hard, then blew a tremendous amount of phlegm into a handkerchief.

Petya had no sympathy for the boy. He got what he deserved. The familiar voice in Petya's head had convinced him that Igor was poisoning him somehow. Petya just couldn't figure out how. How was Igor able to poison Petya's food when he'd become so careful with it? He kept his bread ration in a special pocket he'd sown on the inside of his shirt and he ate it only in seclusion.

Katya took out three tea cups and poured some of the water she'd finished making drinkable into them. She gave one cup to herself, one to Igor, and one to Petya. Petya looked into the cup at the brown water. It smelled awful – like tea made with acorns and rotten eggs. He didn't want to drink it and pushed the cup away.

"Petya," Katya said, pushing the cup back toward him, "you need to drink water. The doctors say that if you bathe twice a week and drink three glasses of water each day that you can survive for a long time."

"That's how you're being poisoned!" a voice hissed in Petya's ear. "It's the water."

Petya shuddered at the realization. It wasn't *Igor* that was trying to kill him. It was Katya. She was poisoning both of them. That's why Igor was so sick.

She was standing over another pot of water she'd put on the stove, glancing impatiently at the front door every few minutes. Petya wondered if he'd vastly underestimated just how cunning and devious she was. Could it be that she was putting on an elaborate charade? Always *pretending* to be so kind and considerate? What a terrific way that was to hide the fact that you were trying to kill somebody.

"I told you she hates you and wants you dead," the voice whispered in Petya's head.

Petya watched Igor to see if he drank his water. He did. The fool.

Then he saw Katya drink her water and was surprised, but decided she must have somehow managed to just put the poison in his and Igor's water.

Katya got up and went to the kitchen and Petya used the opportunity to pour the water from her cup back into the pot of water on the stove, and then pour the water from his cup into Katya's. When she came back, he pretended to drink from his now empty cup.

"Good," Katya said. She came over and poured some more water into his cup.

Petya smiled to himself. He'd foiled her little plan. And wouldn't she be surprised when she was the one who got sick instead of him?

He heard footsteps coming from the hallway outside and watched Katya rush to the front door and wait. A few seconds later, someone knocked and Katya quickly opened the door.

"Comrade Doctor," he heard her say, "thank you so much for coming. I know you're terribly busy and I really appreciate you stopping by."

"Yes, well, I don't have much time," a gruff voice answered. "Where's the boy?"

A doctor. That was smart, Petya thought. A good way to make Igor's eventual death look like it was from natural causes. And to think, Petya used to believe Katya was such an admirable and innocent soul.

The doctor came in and started examining Igor. He took out an old-fashioned listening tube from his pocket and pressed it to Igor's chest. Then he pressed his fingers into Igor's belly, felt his pulse, looked at his tongue, and concluded authoritatively that the boy had bronchitis. "Make sure he drinks plenty of fluids and gets some rest," he said as he wrapped his scarf around his neck and buttoned up his coat to go back outside.

Katya thanked him profusely, then got bundled up herself and accompanied him out.

Petya listened to them make their way down the stairs, then crawled out of bed and went to the mirror to comb his hair. He hardly recognized the stranger staring back at him – the long narrow face, the scruffy neck and cheeks, the clear but hideously pale skin. He hadn't weighed this much – 146 pounds – since he was a teenager. He'd unwillingly dropped sixty pounds since the start of the blockade.

The comb wouldn't go through his hair, which was long and greasy and full of snarls. His last bath had been in September and his last haircut had been in August. He put the comb down and pulled a hat down tight over his head. Then he got his coat and boots on and went to get his daily rations.

The first line he waited in took him two hours. That was to get the allotted bread from his own ration card. Then he waited in the bitter cold again at a different distribution point to get the bread from Guzman's ration card.

As he neared the front of the line, he noticed that the normally ill-tempered lady was giving out rations with scarcely a rude word. She probably no longer had the energy to be explicitly offensive anymore, Petya guessed. It was difficult to muster the energy for a lot of things these days. Things one used to do with ease, without a second thought, were now a tremendous struggle. Lifting one's arm was done only as a last resort. One opened doors only far enough to squeeze through. Carrying things was out of the question, unless it was an absolute necessity. Going up stairs was the most arduous part of one's day, and something that had to undertaken with patience and concentration.

The middle-aged woman waiting in front of Petya was the opposite of those who grew deathly thin – she was puffy. Her arms and legs were like balloons, and her hands were so fat that she had trouble grabbing her bread ration. Her neck barely fit through the collar of her thick wool sweater and she was constantly sticking two fingers inside the collar to pull it away from her throat. If Petya didn't know better, he'd think she was obese. But it was all an illusion. She was just as deprived and ill as everyone else.

When Petya got his ration, he stepped away from the others and put it in the pocket on the inside of his shirt. He wouldn't eat it until he got home and could lock himself in the bathroom. He put Guzman's ration card in the pocket as well (he kept his own ration card in his boot so he didn't confuse the two).

To get home, Petya had to walk halfway, then he could climb aboard one of the remaining streetcars still running and it would take him the rest of the way. The first street he walked down was wide and covered over with snow drifts. Petya seemed to be the only one on the street, but he knew better. There were muggers hiding in the alleys, ready to jump you for your ration and your ration card. He tried to keep a close eye on each alley he came to, but his attention was mostly on his ration. He couldn't wait to get home and eat it, no matter how coarse and bitter the bread was.

He thought back to two months ago when he was just beginning to feel the effects of the blockade. He vividly remembered the first time he went two days without food. The first twenty- four hours had been relatively easy, and he actually felt rather refreshed at one point – like he was somehow being renewed. But from twenty-four to thirty-six hours, his legs hurt and he got a terrible headache that wouldn't go away. It burned when he urinated, and he noticed in the mirror that his tongue was coated in a strange white film. He had terribly bad breath, as well as a nasty taste in his mouth, and that had puzzled him most of all. It had been his understanding that food caused bad breath. How could he have a terrible taste in his mouth and bad breath if he hadn't eaten in so long?

Once all the discomfort had passed, he'd just felt unbearably weak. If he got up too quickly from lying down, he'd get light headed. His hands and feet had tingled a lot. He was, of course, used to those sensations now.

He recalled the foods he used to have on a daily basis – buckwheat with butter, borscht soup, fried eggs. They were ordinary and mundane, but he recalled them with such sweet fondness now that one would think he'd eaten stuffed sturgeon with a thick slice of Napoleon cake for dessert.

Petya approached another alley and peered around the corner cautiously. Seeing nothing except an abandoned, snow-covered car, he started to walk by it when a dark figure jumped out from behind the car and start running at him. Petya tried to get away, but with his disfigured leg, he knew he wouldn't be able to outrun the man. Just before he was tackled to the ground, Petya saw someone walking on the other side of the street and tried to get their attention, "Pomogee mnye!" – help me – he shouted.

Petya's attacker – thin and bony with a black scarf wrapped around his mouth – flashed a knife with a long blade in front of Petya's eyes. "Give me your bread and your ration card or I'll kill you," he threatened. He had a crooked nose and spoke with a hoarse voice.

Petya was so frightened, he could barely speak. "It's in my . . . my . . . umm," he stuttered.

The man situated his knee so that it pushed on Petya's stomach. "Give it to me!" he growled through the scarf and pressed the blade to Petya's cheek.

Petya reached in his pocket and retrieved Guzman's ration card and handed it over to the man.

"And the bread too!" the man said.

"I . . . I . . . don't have any bread."

The man reached into Petya's pocket himself and found the bread. "You liar," he hissed. "I said I'd kill you."

Petya watched the man raise the knife over his head and thought only that it was a strange way to die, not what he expected. Then something struck the man's arm and the knife went flying into a snowbank.

"Beat it, you coward!" a voice shouted.

Petya's attacker scrambled to his feet amidst sharp strikes from a wooden cane, then ran away down the alley. He looked over his shoulder halfway down, saw no one was following him, and slowed to a walk.

Petya sat up and started cursing.

"Are you all right?" the man asked and offered Petya his hand. He had dark eyebrows and a thick white beard that covered his face and neck.

Petya took the man's hand and got to his feet. "He stole my bread ration."

"Oh no, what a terrible thing," the man said and shook his head. "In all my fifty-six years I've never seen such a terrible time as now. People have been turned into animals fighting for their survival. Do you still have your ration card?"

Petya knew that if he lost that he was as good as dead within a week. Luckily the thief had only gotten Guzman's card, Petya's was still tucked safely inside his boot. "Yes, I've still got my card," Petya said, brushing the snow off himself. "He didn't get that."

"Good," the man said, "then give it to me."

The wind was strong and Petya was uncertain of what was said, but when he saw a pistol in the man's hand, he knew he'd heard correctly.

"Give me the card now or I'll put a hole in your stomach," the man said.

Petya could hardly believe it. "Is this a joke?" he asked.

"I've already killed three people," the man said. "You don't want to be the fourth. Just give me your card and you won't get hurt."

"If I give you my card, I'll die anyway," Petya said.

"Maybe," the man said. "But if you don't, you'll die for certain right here and now."

Petya could find no flaws in the man's logic and pulled the card out of his boot and handed it over.

The man glanced at the card, then made Petya lay back down on the ground. "Count to thirty," he said, "and then you can get back up. You get up before that and I'll shoot you."

Petya did as he was told.

"Animals," the man muttered as he walked away. "That's what people have become – complete animals fighting for their survival."

Petya laid there and stared up at the gray winter sky, wondering if God was laughing at him like the other kids at the orphanage always had. The ground beneath him was hard and cold and a frozen clump of ice was sticking painfully into his spleen. The wind blew snow off the top of the nearby snow drifts and into Petya's face. He could hear bombs falling in another sector of the city – the high-pitched whistle followed by the earth-shaking boom.

He had stopped counting at twelve. Perhaps he wouldn't get up at all. He was tired of trying. Tired of doing what the voices in his head demanded. His entire life had been nothing but hurt and shame. His eyes were welling up with tears, and he tried to stop all that pain inside from getting out. He squeezed his eyes, gritted his teeth, tried to focus on his outrage, but nothing was going to stop it this time. One tear rolled down his cheek, then another, and then the flood gates gave way and the tears flowed like a raging river.

The stove was still warm when Petya got home and he wrapped his hands around it to thaw them out. Igor was still in his bed, but he wasn't moving or making any sounds, and Petya wondered if he might have died from the poisoned water Katya gave him. He snuck up closer to see if the boy was still breathing. He saw his chest rising and falling ever so slightly, and decided he must just be sleeping very deeply.

Petya added some more wood to the fire and noticed Oksana had rearranged her blankets and pillow so that her head would now be near the stove, instead of her feet. Petya went over to her neatly-made bed and put it back the way it used to be, taking extra care to make sure there were no wrinkles and the pillow was only half-tucked under the blankets – the way she always made her bed.

He laid down on his own bed and fell asleep quickly. Forty-five minutes later he woke up, and for once it wasn't because of his empty stomach or cold bed. In his head, a new voice had emerged, and this one claimed that it was God himself. It was a man's voice – deep and full – and it spoke to him calmly, patiently.

Petya thought it would disappear when he woke up, but it didn't. The voice kept up its continuous stream of monologue and Petya was mesmerized by it. The voice was particularly convincing because it was more rational than the other voices. When it explained that it was speaking only to him and that was why no one else could hear it, that made sense to Petya. When God had spoken to Moses or Joan of Arc, no one else had been able to hear his voice either.

The new voice was different from the other ones in his head, and even argued with them. When they told Petya he was corrupt and despicable, the voice of God told them they were wrong, that Petya was one of his children and therefore worthy and good. And when Petya thought he heard Guzman's voice again, the voice of God reassured him that the dead man wasn't speaking to him. The voice belonged to a disciple of the devil, and Petya needed to ignore it and never do its bidding.

The voice of God also told Petya that he had a very important mission for him and that it was "of the utmost importance" that Petya be prepared for it. It wouldn't tell Petya what exactly the mission was, but it said the clues would be provided when the time was right.

Petya heard sounds coming from the hallway, then the door opened and Oksana and Katya walked in carrying firewood.

"They delivered a pile of firewood to the courtyard," Katya said. "Could you help us bring it up before it's all gone?"

It was bad enough she was trying to kill him. For her to then ask for his help was galling. He was about to tell her to go to the devil when the voice of God spoke to him again. "Help them," it commanded.

Petya found that he couldn't ignore it like he could sometimes with the other voices. He heard the wind howling outside and wanted more than anything to snuggle further into his bed, but instead he got up and joined in on the grueling operation.

It was difficult to know how much firewood one should try to carry each time. The more you carried, the fewer trips you had to make, but on the other hand, the heavier the load, the quicker you tired. Fortunately and unfortunately, the decision was made for them because after only a few trips, the pile of wood was gone. Everyone living within a block of the delivery had come to take some.

Petya collapsed back into bed, feeling weaker than he ever had since the blockade started. The voice of God started speaking to him again, telling him it was important to sustain himself physically. Petya explained to the voice that he'd lost his ration card and there was no bread for him to eat. "I could try to steal Oksana's ration card though," Petya offered.

"No, thou shalt not steal," the voice responded.

"I understand," Petya said sheepishly. "Perhaps you could make me some bread, like that story in the bible?" he suggested.

"No, that would endanger the mission," the voice answered. "If you have no bread, then eat meat instead."

Oksana and Katya were in the kitchen, and Katya called out to him. "Are you talking to us, Petya?"

He sat up in bed, ignoring Katya's question and explaining to the voice that he had no meat, nor anything to trade so he could buy meat at the market. Out of the corner of his eye, Petya saw the faint outline of a figure standing in the hallway. He was startled and turned to look at it, but there was no one there. He studied the area for a minute, looking closely at the pair of boots on the dingy floor, the crooked frame of a painting of a birch tree forest, and a tiny, long abandoned cobweb near the ceiling. Just when he was about to look away, he found the faint bluish outline once more. It was like a hollow person was standing there. They had an edge around them, but nothing inside that edge.

"Oh," the voice said, "but you *do* have access to meat."

* * *

"One of you drank it!" Oksana screamed. "And don't try to deny it!"

Katya hurried into the room from the kitchen to see what the commotion was about. She'd just been in there a moment ago. Oksana had been getting ready for work, and both Petya and Igor had been in bed still asleep.

"What's going on, Oksana?" Katya asked. Petya and Igor were sitting up in their beds, staring blankly at Oksana. Igor was wiping the sleep from his eyes, and Petya was yawning and stretching his arms.

"I poured myself a cup of water," Oksana said, "then I left for a moment. And when I came back it was gone."

"Your cup was gone?" Katya asked.

"No, my cup is still there. Someone just drank the water. And I know it was one of these two scoundrels," she said. She had her hands on her hips and her bottom lip pressed tightly over the top one. Her hair, which always used to be black and curly, was now the same dingy shade of white as last week's snow. She'd given up trying to style it and it hung like a wet mop over her head.

"Igor," Katya said, "did you drink Oksana's water?"

"No," Igor answered. "Why would I drink her water? I have my own." He pointed to a chipped white tea cup by his bed, and it was indeed half full of water.

"Then *you* must have drank it," Oksana said, scowling at Petya.

"I was sleeping," Petya said. "Besides, why would I drink your water. I could just as easily get my own."

Poor Oksana, Katya thought. She really was losing it, just as Petya had been telling her. "Maybe you already drank it and just forgot," Katya suggested.

"No," Oksana said adamantly. "I didn't drink it yet. I distinctly remember pouring it, then setting it down, then going to get my coat."

"Just like you *distinctly* remembered rearranging your bed," Petya said.

"I *did* rearrange my bed," she said, then put her hands to her ears and shook her head back and forth like a mad dog. "You're all making me crazy!" she shouted then grabbed her coat and stormed out of the apartment.

Petya tapped the side of his head with his index finger. "You see?" he said to Katya.

She nodded her head and briefly had the thought of asking Petya and Oksana to move back to their old apartment. They were *both* losing their sanity, and she was caught in the middle. But, like it or not, they were stuck with one another. Among other things, Katya knew there simply wasn't enough firewood for them to live in two separate apartments.

Igor wrapped his arms around his chest and coughed. It was a thick, horrible sound that didn't reflect the fact that he was getting better. He hadn't had a fever in the past week and had much more energy now.

Katya sat down on the edge of his bed and put her arm around him. "The doctor said the cough might take a few weeks to go away," she said. "Just try to bear with it."

When he finished his coughing spell, he blew his nose then asked Katya whether or not Oksana was going crazy.

Katya was uncomfortable using the term 'crazy' in the presence of Petya, even though he insisted he wasn't sick in any way. "She's just under a lot of stress," she answered. "Just like the rest of us."

"She's starting to act like Guzman," he said. "Is she going to die too?"

Katya handed him his breakfast bread ration, and he took it but didn't eat right away. "We're all going to die," she said. "It's just a matter of when."

Igor looked across the room at Petya, then back at Katya. "Do you think the end of the world is coming?" he asked.

She felt very sad realizing Igor had never known their grandmother and her wonderful teachings. Katya wished the *whole* world could have received her teachings. Maybe then this war never would have happened. "I think we're living in very dark times," Katya said. "Times not unlike when Jesus lived. People are scared and clinging very tightly to their beliefs. This was what happened in Jesus' time. The Romans ruled the world with their military might and culture, and the Jews had become complacent and dogmatic. Jesus shook all that up. He challenged the establishment – not just the Jewish rabbis, but the Romans as well. He taught that there was to be no allegiance to any country, ruler, or even rabbi. One's allegiance should be only to God, he said. And one should love thy enemies because peace and love was the only way to everlasting life. It's . . ."

"What a pack of lies," Petya said from the other side of the room. He sat up in his bed and threw the covers off. "Don't listen to her, Igor. That's not what Christianity teaches you at all. It says you get one chance in this world and that's it. You get it right and you go to heaven. You screw up and you go to hell. It's that simple. You don't get into heaven by practicing peace and love, you have to sing God's praises, sacrifice animals to him, convert the heathens, and build stone temples in his honor. Thank you, Lord, for our suffering. Praise be thy name."

It wasn't easy for Katya to hear Petya's venomous words on God and religion, but she wanted to practice what her grandmother had taught her. More than that, she wanted Igor to see firsthand that one didn't have to be afraid of other people's ideas and opinions – that you could hold onto your own beliefs no matter what everyone else thought.

"I'm not going to let you poison this young boy's mind with that garbage," Petya continued. His face was flushed and his eyes were narrow slits beneath his eyebrows. "Religion has been a plague on mankind from the moment someone invented it."

Katya knew that the subject of religion triggered painful memories in Petya. He'd told her horror stories about how his Baptist aunt had raised him. She felt angry that there were people like that out there – desecrating Jesus' wonderful teachings. She took a deep breath and tried to cultivate gentleness in her words and tone so that she might calm the storm inside of Petya. "I'm curious to hear more about why you think this," she said, turning to face him.

"No other concept has caused more harm and suffering than the idea that there is a God," Petya said. "Hundreds of millions of people have been slaughtered throughout history – all 'in the name of God.'"

She opened her mouth to argue with him, but then caught herself and tried to hear past his thoughts and find that place in him that was so full of pain. "You feel outraged when you think of how many people have died in battles and pogroms and inquisitions because of religion," she said. "You value peace and harmony among people and you feel furious when people resort to violence to spread their beliefs."

"Yes," Petya answered quickly. "But it's not only that. Religions tell people what to do, how to think, what to believe. And it's all a bunch of lies!"

Katya looked at Igor and saw him taking it all in. "If I hear you right, Petya," she said, "you feel desperate because you value freedom and autonomy. It's important for you to have freedom of thought, freedom of action."

"Of course," Petya said. "And these damn religions don't give anyone any freedom. Instead, they tell you that you should suffer – that you're flawed and evil by nature. They tell you that you're a horrible person 'unfit in the eyes of the Lord.' To them, man *deserves* to suffer. He has to *pay* for his sins. And the first sin he commits is to be born."

"You'd like people to know they're okay just as they are," Katya said. "You feel outraged when you see religions telling people they're inherently flawed and sinful by nature. Is that right?"

For the first time since Petya started talking, Katya saw him pause to take a breath.

"I'd like you to know that I *do* think man is inherently good by nature," Katya said.

"But that's not what Christianity or Judaism or Islam teach," Petya said, throwing his hands out in front of him. "All they do is teach people to judge themselves and judge others. Does that make the world a better place? Does people hating themselves and hating others make the world a better place?"

"I feel very sad to know that that's how religion was taught to you," Katya said. "I think the true message of Jesus' teachings have been mostly lost over the centuries. I'm certain it was never God's intention to confuse and constrict man with layers of rules and commandments. It was men who did this – men who had their own motives for adding to and arranging his word. To me, it makes no sense to blame God for the pitfalls of religion or the things that have been done in his name. It's not God's fault."

"And what of heaven and hell?" Petya said, leaning forward as he spoke. "Don't you think these silly concepts of heaven and hell are just extreme examples of reward and punishment? Do as the preacher tells you and you go to heaven. Disobey him and you go to hell. It's all just a tool to reinforce authority and control. That's what religions are for – to keep people in line, to keep them doing what those in authority want them to do."

"You'd like people to be able to make their own decisions without concepts of right and wrong, good and bad," Katya said. She was fascinated that she could not only hear his passionately held point of view, but even see how they both wanted the same thing in many instances.

"Exactly! That's what the world needs. We don't need a new god. We need to get rid of all our existing ones and start recognizing man as holding the key to the future. Humanity is all we need. We don't need Jesus Christ and never have."

Katya felt a shift in the conversation. Petya looked less tense and wasn't in such a rush to speak. "It's important to you for people to have faith in themselves and each other," Katya said. "You'd like people to believe in themselves, believe in humanity. Right?"

Katya watched as his shoulders slowly inched down from his ears. He nodded his head and leaned back onto his arms. He looked calm and at ease. Katya felt no fear, only sympathy for him. He seemed to be so scarred by something she held so dear to her heart.

"I think the most difficult part of religion is learning how to sift through all the debris that the Truth has been buried under," Katya said. "For example, did you know that for the first two hundred years after Jesus' death, his followers stuck close to his teachings and abstained from military service at all costs? They believed in Jesus' teachings that you couldn't destroy evil by destroying your enemies. Jesus taught that only love could overcome hate. It wasn't until rulers co-opted Christianity that certain wars became not only 'just,' but even ordained by the Lord Almighty."

Igor wrinkled up his pug nose as if in deep thought. "Does God judge you when you die?" he asked.

Katya ran her fingers through his ratty hair and pulled him closer to her. She was proud of the way she'd handled herself. "I don't believe in the Christian idea that God is anything like man," she said. "To me, God is all-embracing. He is in everyone and everything. He's pure love and light. He's not vengeful, judgmental, or proud. Those are qualities of man, not of God."

Petya shifted his position and sat up straighter. "Has God ever spoken to you?" he asked. "What does he sound like? What does he say?"

"I can't say I've ever literally heard his voice," Katya replied. "But I suppose if I did, it would be a calm, patient voice that reassured me when things weren't going well, complimented me when no one else would, and told me I was okay just as I am."

Petya leaned forward and seemed to contemplate Katya's answer. He propped his head up with his left hand and looked down at the floor.

There was a knock at the front door and Katya went to answer it. She was surprised to see a Red Army soldier standing in the hallway holding two heads of cabbage in his arms. He was dressed in an officer's uniform with a heavy wool greatcoat, fur collar and fur hat. "Hello, Katya," he said and took his hat off.

It took her a few seconds before she recognized him. He was Felix's commanding officer when he was doing clerical work for the army.

"How is Felix?" he asked cautiously.

"I haven't heard from him since he left for the front in early September," she said.

He was silent a moment and pursed his lips. Katya was surprised at how little he'd changed since she last saw him. Many of the people you hadn't seen in a few months were barely recognizable to you. Their skin would be dry and scaly and tight around the bones. They would speak slowly and easily lose their train of thought. Their gums would be swollen and bleeding, and their teeth would be in decay.

But this man wasn't one of the walking skeletons of the city. He was a military man and an officer, and though he was still probably hungry all the time, he was far from starving.

"Oh, here," he said, holding out the two cabbages. "These are for you."

Katya took them and was immediately worried that Petya might see or overhear. She didn't want to share them. These life preservers were for her and Igor only.

The man then reached into his pocket and pulled out four chocolate bars and handed them to Katya. "And these too," he said.

Katya was speechless. The gifts were literally gifts of life. "I . . . I don't know what to say."

"You don't have to say anything," he said. "I only wish I could do more."

She put the chocolate bars in her pocket and wrapped the cabbages in the blanket hanging around her shoulders. As wonderful as the gifts of food were, Katya couldn't help but think that they would only delay the inevitable for Igor. "You know," she said, "there is something else you could do. You could find a position for my cousin, Igor, to increase his rations."

"I'm afraid I can't help you there," he said.

Katya dropped her head and stared at the buttons on his coat. "I understand," she said.

He cleared his throat and said, "I wish I could stay longer but I've got to get to . . ."

"Wait," she blurted out and grabbed him by the arm.

He looked slightly alarmed at her hand that gripped his sleeve.

"I . . .," she stuttered, "I really need your help." She couldn't believe how difficult that was to say. "I need you to get Igor a position."

"I just told you," he said, "we don't have any open positions." He put his hat back on. "Now if you'll excuse me, I need to . . ."

"Don't deny me this," Katya said, maintaining her grip on his sleeve. "This isn't just a favor. It's a matter of life and death. He's going to die unless he gets more food."

He looked her in the face and she didn't turn away. "Hmm," he said and paused. "I guess I could look around for you. See if anything comes up. What is he doing now?"

"He's not doing anything now. He's just a boy."

"A boy? How old is he?"

"Twelve," Katya said, then quickly added, "but he's very capable."

"I don't think so," he started to say.

"He can do anything you ask of him," Katya said. "You must have a need for *something* around there," she persisted, "*anything* at all."

"No, we're well staffed right now," he said. He tried to gently pull his arm out of her grip, but she wouldn't let go.

"Please," Katya said. "Surely you can find some small tasks for him to do. I'm begging you."

He looked past her, into the apartment, as he scratched behind his ear with his free hand. "I guess it wouldn't hurt us to have a courier to deliver stuff once in a while. Can he walk alright?"

"Oh yes, he can walk – even run – if you give him enough food."

"I don't know," he said. "Let me get a look at him first."

Katya let go of his sleeve and hurried back into the apartment. "I'll get him right now," she called out over her shoulder. She went into the kitchen first to stash the chocolate and cabbage in the cupboard. Her hands trembled as she tried to get the key in the heavy padlock that safeguarded her food from Petya and Oksana.

The cupboard was bare except for a couple cubes of sugar, some small potatoes, and a container of dirty, coarse salt. The potatoes – five in all – were all that remained from when she traded her fur coat at the market last month. She set the cabbage and chocolate bars on the second shelf, locked the cupboard, then rushed in to Igor to try to comb his hair.

Katya was grateful that Igor was the only one who didn't look dramatically different from what he used to. He'd certainly lost weight like the rest of them, but he didn't look like a completely different person like Petya or Oksana. He just looked like a skinny kid.

"Listen to me, sweetheart," she said to him. "There's a man at the door who could save your life. I'm trying to convince him to give you a job so your rations will be increased. He wants to see you, so you need to look as healthy as possible and be very nice to him. Do you understand?"

Igor nodded his head.

Katya picked up a needle from her sewing materials, poked her middle finger, then squeezed a few drops of blood out. She rubbed them on Igor's cheeks until his pale, sickly skin looked rosy.

"Okay, let's go," she said. "Smile a little and try to look lively."

As they walked to the front door, Katya felt her heart sink because she no longer saw the man in the doorway. She was about to chase after him when he reappeared.

"This is Igor," Katya said, turning toward the boy.

"Zdrastvooyte!" – hello – Igor said and saluted.

The man smiled and saluted back. "How well do you know the city, young man?" he asked.

"Not too well," Igor answered. "I've only been here since August."

"Oh, he's being modest," Katya said. "He used to go out wandering around the city all the time before they implemented the curfew. I even sent him out on errands myself to buy things for me. He's very reliable."

Igor let loose with another one of his long, awful coughs, and Katya saw the man frown. "Don't worry about that, comrade," she said quickly. "He's just getting over a cold. It sounds much worse than it is."

"I don't know," he said. "He doesn't seem . . ."

"Oh please," Katya interrupted. "*Please, please* take him. He's not going to make it if you don't."

The man hesitated yet again, then unexpectedly cleared all expression from his face. "All right then," he said. "Maybe next week you could send him over and . . ."

"How about right now?" Katya said. "He has nothing to do, and there's no time like the present, right?"

"Well . . . I guess. Are you ready, son?"

"He just needs to get his coat and boots on," Katya said. She then threw her arms around the man. "Thank you," she said, nearly crying, "thank you so much. You won't regret it."

The hard snow crunched loudly under Katya's boots as she walked to work. The temperature had dropped fifteen degrees from the day before, but she was so cold all the time now that she barely noticed the change. The unexpected gifts of food and a job for Igor had renewed her spirit and given her hope that things were starting to change for the better. When she got to the office and saw Lev sitting at the table, she was convinced things were indeed improving.

"Good morning Lev," she said. "How are you feeling?" Besides some scratches on his face, he actually looked healthier than before.

"Katya!" he said and looked up. "Oh, it's nice to see your friendly face again. I'm feeling much better, thank you. They feed you quite well in the hospital, and I needed the rest even more than I knew. As soon as this ringing stops in my ears, I'll be as good as new."

She sat down next to him and cleared some space on the cluttered table.

"Congratulations on getting the ice formation data to the director that day," Lev said. "It couldn't have been easy."

"No," Katya said. "It wasn't. I made it back to the office ten minutes after six and our kind, sweet director still called in my commissar to tell her of my 'failure to perform to the best of my abilities.'"

"And?" Lev asked.

"That's it," Katya said, understanding he was asking if she'd received any punishment. She'd been let off with a strict warning: do exactly as you're told from now on or you'll be relieved of duty. The significance of the threat was not lost on her. She understood that to lose a job meant you also lost its commensurate ration.

"He's not an easy man to work for," Lev said. "Short on appreciation; long on criticism. And he expects you to carry out every order unquestionably." He emphasized the last word, then got up and started pacing in front of the plywood where the window once was.

The pacing meant more bad news, Katya knew, and she wondered what it was this time. When it came to the food supply or the war, there was never any *good* news. Military victories were as rare as a full stomach. Had the Germans broken through the lines somewhere? Had another warehouse been hit by a bomb?

"All right, Lev," she said after watching him pace for a few minutes. "Out with it."

"What?"

"Give me the bad news," she said.

"How did you know?"

"We've been working together a while now and there's been enough bad news that I know when it's coming," she said. "So what is it?"

"Okay, but you're not going to like it." He took a deep breath in. "The director has ordered a fifth ration reduction."

Her mouth fell open and she covered it with her right hand. "For the troops?" she asked cautiously.

"No," Lev said. "It's for the civilian population."

She placed her hands over her eyes. "No!" she practically screamed. "He can't cut rations *again*. People are already dying by the thousands. He might as well just hand out death certificates."

Lev sat down and arranged some stacks of paper on the table.

"He can't do it," Katya continued. "He has to cut the troops' rations. Those on the front-line already get *twice* as much bread as we do. Plus they get meat!"

"I knew you wouldn't like it," Lev said. "I don't like it either, but those are our orders. We need to get started on the preparations. There's a lot to do. He wants it implemented on the twentieth. That only gives us the rest of today and tomorrow to get ready."

"Is he in?" Katya asked.

"Why?" Lev replied.

Katya knew he would've said 'no' instead of 'why' if their director wasn't in. She left the room and walked down the hallway toward his office.

"Katya, don't be a fool," Lev shouted after her.

She stopped in front of his door, closed her eyes, and saw her grandmother. She was sitting in her rocking chair, knitting, and telling Katya about Jesus' Sermon on the Mount. Of the eight beatitudes, Katya had always liked number eight the best: "Blessed are they who are persecuted for the sake of righteousness, for theirs is the kingdom of heaven." It had given her great comfort as a child to know that no matter what happened to her dissident grandmother here in the Soviet Union, she was assured of a place in heaven in the hereafter. Katya silently recited the saying now, realizing it was the first time she was doing it not for her grandmother, but for herself.

She knocked on the director's door but didn't wait for him to answer before walking in. She found him sitting in a chair, a short, barrel-chested officer standing next to him. They were leaning over a table looking at a large map. Katya didn't know who the officer was and didn't care.

"Comrade Selenaya," her director said, "What is it? Can't you see I'm busy?" He had a long, thin nose, and by the way his nostrils flared, she knew he was annoyed.

"Sorry for the intrusion," she said. She regretted her choice of words as soon as they came out of her mouth. She wasn't sorry in the least. "I'd like to speak with you about your orders for the latest ration reduction," she continued.

"There's nothing to discuss," he said. "Please continue with the preparations."

She felt her hands shaking, but stepped closer to the two men anyway. She saw the map was of Leningrad and the surrounding area. Russian positions were marked in red, German in black. "I'd like you to reconsider the order," she said, "because I cannot carry it out in good conscience. You've ordered the deaths of tens of thousands of people."

Two kerosene lanterns provided the light for the room, and Katya wondered how he'd managed that when the rest of the city had long since run out of kerosene. The officer – bald headed and bespectacled – arched his eyebrows and folded his arms in front of his chest.

"It's a temporary reduction," Katya's director responded. "As soon as the situation improves, civilian rations will be returned to their current levels."

"But you can't make the civilian population shoulder the entire burden of the cut," she said. "You've got to cut the troops' levels."

He glanced at the officer. "Cut our troops' rations? You should be ashamed of yourself, Comrade Selenaya. They're putting their lives on the line every day for you, and this is how you want to repay them?"

"I know the situation," Katya said. "They can absorb a cut. Leningraders can't."

Her director raised his voice a notch. "We have a job to do," he said, motioning to the officer next to him, "and that is to see to it that we win this war."

"I thought your job was to see to it that Leningrad didn't starve to death," Katya said.

He stood up quickly, nearly knocking over one of the lanterns. "Leave this office now and carry out the order you've been given," he said.

"No."

The officer grunted and let his arms drop to his sides. "Then you can consider yourself relieved of duty," her director said. "I won't have anyone on my staff who disobeys direct orders."

"When orders are unjust, we have a moral obligation to disobey them," Katya said.

"Get out of this office now!" he shouted.

Katya walked to the door but stopped and turned back before going through it. "So that's it?" she asked. "The decision to cut rations has already been made?"

Her director paused, just slightly, before saying yes, and this gave Katya the answer she was hoping for. She knew he'd hesitated because he hadn't yet presented his recommendation to Comrade Zhdanov and the Leningrad Defense Council. No decision concerning Leningrad was ever final until they said so.

If the cut was to take place in two days, then the Defense Council had to formally approve the decision that night to give them one day to issue and implement the order. Katya had delivered some last-minute documents at one of their previous meetings, so she knew where and when they met. She also knew that her director's recommendations were often accepted as a matter of course.

She had to ensure that didn't happen this time.

Clouds had moved in and blotted out the moon and the stars by the time Katya arrived at the bunker. The guards at the entrance shined a light in her face and asked why she was there. She told them she needed to deliver some last-minute documents again. They remembered her from the last time and checked her papers, searched her for weapons, then let her pass to the inside.

The bunker was buried deep in the ground and fortified with thick layers of concrete. Katya opened the door and walked down a narrow corridor, wondering how she was going to get the guards on the inside to let her into the meeting. When she'd delivered the documents last time, she'd had to give them to one of the guards to take in. Hardly anyone was allowed into these all-important meetings where the fate of Leningrad was decided.

Four guards were stationed outside the meeting room and Katya walked up to the one seated at the table and explained that she once again had important documents her director needed right away.

"Give them to me," the senior guard – a lieutenant – responded and held out his hand. "I'll take them to him."

"No, I can't this time," Katya said. "I have specific instructions to deliver them myself."

The man eyed her warily, then disappeared into the room and came back out a minute later. "He said he's not expecting any documents," he said to Katya.

"Well he must have forgotten," Katya said. "Why would I come all the way here if he didn't really need them?"

"I suggest you leave now," the guard said to her. "This is a secure area. Unauthorized personnel are not allowed to be here."

"He's going to be very angry when he realizes he needed these documents," Katya said.

"You may leave the documents if you wish," he replied, "but you need to go or else I'll be forced to put you under arrest."

"Very well," she said. "Will you give me a moment to retie my scarf? It's terribly cold out there tonight." Before he could respond, she undid her long scarf from her head and neck. She didn't really need to retie it. She just needed to buy some time to think of another way into the meeting.

The guard tapped his foot impatiently as she slowly wrapped the scarf around herself. When she was only halfway finished after two minutes, he stood up and ordered one of the other guards to escort her out. Before he reached her, the door to the meeting room burst open and a pasty-faced, middle-aged man smoking a cigarette emerged. He looked worn down, but he wasn't a walking corpse like most of the people Katya saw these days. He still had some meat on his bones.

The guards quickly came to attention, and Katya knew it was he – Zhdanov – the boss of Leningrad. "Is there any paper in the toilets?" he asked in a hoarse voice.

One of the guards had been reading Leningradskaya Pravda and he handed the newspaper over to Zhdanov.

Katya went up to him before he got very far. "Forgive me, comrade," she said. "I know your time is precious, but this is very important. I'm wondering if you're completely aware of the all the implications of the latest ration reduction."

He seemed surprised and pulled the cigarette out of his mouth. "I'm quite familiar with the facts," he said. "We don't want to cut rations again, but we have little choice."

Katya spoke quickly, afraid she'd be thrown out before she could argue her point. "To cut civilian rations to the levels proposed is murder," she said. "I beg of you to revise it and have the troops shoulder some of the burden."

"We already reduced the troops' rations a week and half ago," Zhdanov said. "I don't remember the exact amount, but their levels need to be maintained for . . ."

"Yes, I know they were cut," Katya interrupted. "But they're currently receiving 600 grams of bread plus 125 grams of meat. Rear-unit troops are getting 400 grams of bread and 50 grams of meat. It's not much, I agree, but it's no comparison to civilians: right now factory workers only get 300 grams of bread and everyone else gets a miserable 150 grams. No civilians get any meat."

"How do you know this information?" he asked.

At that moment Katya's director emerged from the meeting room and saw her. "What are you doing here?" he said and promptly moved in on Zhdanov. "Guards, remove her immediately."

They grabbed her by the arms and started taking her to the exit.

"My apologies, comrade," Katya heard her director say. "I was unaware . . ."

"Does she work for you?" Zhdanov interrupted.

"She used to," he replied. "She was let go this morning for insubordination."

"She looks familiar," Zhdanov said. "I swear I've seen her before."

"She's Grigori Selenii's daughter."

"Katya?" Zhdanov said.

"Yes, that's her name."

"Oh my, she's all grown up. I remember when she was just a little girl. Comrade Selenaya," he called out. "Come back here."

The guards let go of her arms and she walked back to him.

"You probably don't even remember me," Zhdanov said. "I used to bounce you on my knee when you were just a little girl. My goodness how you've grown."

Katya didn't remember him, but believed his story. Her father knew many people and was constantly inviting them over to their apartment.

"I'm sorry about your father," Zhdanov said. "He was a good man."

Katya covered her mouth with her hands. "He's dead?"

Zhdanov nodded. "Forgive me," he said. "I assumed you knew. He suffered a heart attack in Moscow."

Katya wasn't completely surprised by the news, but it still shook her. She thought of Igor and how he was her only living relative left now. She wanted to cry, but had to hold it back. She had to be strong right now.

Zhdanov turned to Katya's director. "She was just telling me that front-line troops are still getting 600 grams of bread and 125 grams of meat," he said. "Is this true?"

"Yes, comrade, that's correct."

"For some reason, I was under the impression they were getting much less than that," Zhdanov said. "Your proposal to cut civilians' rations by so much without cutting the troops' by a single gram makes little sense to me."

"You've said before, comrade, that our number one priority in food distribution was to make sure that the troops were able to sustain their energy so they could protect the city."

"What point is there in protecting a city if all its people are dead?" Zhdanov said.

Katya's director opened his mouth to say something, but then seemed to think better of it.

"I think we need to reconsider this latest reduction," Zhdanov said. "Don't you agree?"

"Yes, comrade," came the reply.

Zhdanov took another drag from his cigarette then dropped it to the ground and snuffed it out with his boot. "If you can't make recommendations that are in the best interest of Leningrad, then perhaps I should get someone else." He looked at Katya. "Like Comrade Selenaya here," he added.

"That won't be necessary," Katya's director said. He cast a malicious glare in her direction. "I'll be more careful with my recommendations from now on."

* * *

Felix cursed under his breath at whichever partisan behind him had allowed himself to be spotted. It had complicated things but he couldn't worry about it now. He needed to get his rifle into position before the light of the moon returned. He sprawled out more in the thick snow so his arms were better supported, then took aim at the machine gun nest ninety feet away from him. The moon crept over the edge of the monstrous black cloud and Felix found his target – a dim figure with binoculars looking out from behind the sandbags.

Felix had found that many German positions along the Tikhvin front were vulnerable to attacks at night, especially when the wind howled or the snow fell like a midsummer's downpour. The Germans didn't seem to expect it

– attacking at three in the morning in the bitter cold apparently wasn't in their 'rules of engagement' book. In fact, Felix found the more uncommon were the tactics he used, the more successful the attack was.

He clenched his jaw and felt his own sour blood fill his mouth. Whenever he tasted blood, he thought of Dima – poor, confused Dima who'd wanted to change the world and himself for the better. But the Nazis hadn't given him that chance. Now Felix was going to see to it that they got no more chances. He was going to do everything he could to eliminate the Nazi infestation of his homeland. That's what the Germans were to him now – pests. Pests that needed to be exterminated, just like the cockroaches that had invaded Katya's apartment one summer.

Felix squeezed the trigger and the bullet from his rifle went through the man's hand to his cheek, and first the binoculars, and then the man fell from sight.

One less cockroach.

The other German soldier quickly engaged the machine gun and bullets flew frantically in every direction. They struck all around Felix, but he remained still. Even when one of the bullets burned a hole straight through his left arm, he did not move.

As the tat-tat-tat of the machine gun wound down and more German soldiers arrived, Felix closed his eyes and thought of Katya. Was she still alive? Or had the lack of food or a German bomb taken her to the next world? Felix wanted nothing more than to marry her and live a quiet life. He wanted to make passionate love to her in the evening and wake each morning to see her lying next to him. He wanted to have children – a little boy who looked like him, and a little girl who looked like her. He wanted to take trips to the country to pick mushrooms and teach his son how to swim in the river. He wanted a normal, uneventful life with friends and family and pets and poetry.

His anger began to boil. Those fucking cockroaches wouldn't let him have that life. They were killing his friends and his family and everything inside of him that *believed*.

He felt blood rushing to his face and a warming sensation flowing through his freezing body. He opened his eyes and saw the snow by his arm turning red. Then he set his sights on the machine gun nest once more and found in his sights two cockroaches yelling and gesticulating to one another in their annoying, systematic insect way. Felix took aim at the head of the first one, but then adjusted downward for its throat. If he hit it just right, the bullet would go straight through its throat and strike the cockroach standing on the other side of it. Felix took in a breath and let it out slowly as he squeezed the trigger once more.

His shot hit the mark perfectly and two more cockroaches fell from sight.

The moon disappeared, and the Germans fired a flare into the sky. The machine gun barked to life once more and the soldiers outside the machine gun nest quickly ducked inside it. Felix stole a look behind him, saw no trace of the rest of his partisans, and wondered what the cockroaches were shooting at. He looked for more targets inside the nest, but they were all hidden now. He saw something that could be an arm, but he wasn't sure.

One thing he did know was that there would be more cockroaches coming. Where you saw one, you knew there were at least ten more.

He pushed on his loose tooth and tasted blood in his mouth once again. He pictured Dima in his mind – from the shy smile of his boyhood to the bloody, broken body he carried in his arms last month. Felix jumped to his feet and began charging at the machine gun nest. "Ahhh!" he screamed as he ran. Bullets whizzed by him, one grazing his cheek just below his right eye, but death was the only thing that was going to stop him now.

He gripped a grenade in his right hand and when he was close enough, threw it through one of the tiny openings in the nest. It exploded with a muffled thud and then the gunfire stopped and all was eerily quiet.

Felix quickly peeked his head around the sandbags of the entrance and saw six cockroaches lying on the floor. None of them seemed to be moving, so he stepped inside and began collecting their guns and grenades.

An officer in a Death's Head helmet suddenly stirred. The left side of the cockroach's body was bloody and mangled, but it was alive, and it looked Felix in the eyes and extended its right arm to him.

Felix didn't like seeing its face, didn't like the fact that it had two eyes, two ears, a mouth, and a nose. What bothered Felix most of all was the absence of emotion within himself. Even as he heard one of the few German words that he knew – *help* – Felix felt nothing.

He pointed his gun at the grotesque creature. "Back to the devil," he said, firing three shots into its exoskeleton.

He resumed gathering weapons from the corpses. Outside, a dozen and a half German troops approached the miniature front in the Tikhvin lines that had opened up. Felix took up a position behind some of the sandbags and started shooting. He saw a couple of cockroaches go down but couldn't tell if he'd hit them or if they'd dove for cover.

A great roar of yells and shouts built behind him. When Felix turned, he saw them springing from the snow like wolves from a dense thicket. His partisans charged forward, their battle cry rising like a wave. And for a change it wasn't the Russians who were in panic and falling back in disarray.

Felix savored the thick, salty taste of blood in his mouth as he took aim and shot two cockroaches in the back as they retreated. He wanted to shoot more, but they weren't in his line of fire. He leapt from the machine gun nest and sprinted to a different spot. Bullets whizzed by him again as he ran and another one grazed him on the arm.

He'd lost all fear of combat. The more cockroaches he encountered, the better.

He wanted to kill them all.

***

It had been a tremendous struggle for Petya to sever the arm at the elbow and he was now thoroughly exhausted. He rested as the fire in the stove came back to life, and when the coals were bright orange, he roasted the meat until it was well-done.

It had been snowing all day and he opened the window and gathered some of it into a large pot, then set it on the stove. When the snow had melted, he poured the water into a tea cup and sat down on his bed to eat. The meat was tough and hard to chew, but tasted good nonetheless. He thought it tasted a lot like chicken and was reminded of the time he had grilled snake a few summers back.

The voice of God in Petya's head had assured him it was not a sin to eat the flesh of another. In fact, the only thing that mattered to the voice was that Petya maintain his strength for his upcoming *mission*. When Petya questioned the voice about the mission, it answered only that it would be revealed in a way that Petya alone could figure out.

The lock on the front door made a clacking sound as someone opened it from the outside. The door creaked and groaned on its hinges and then Katya walked into the dimly lit apartment. Before she even took her coat off, she smelled the meat and asked Petya where he got it.

"From the market," he lied, and ate the last bite.

Katya scanned the room. "Where's Igor?"

Petya shrugged his shoulders. He was hesitant to say too much, because he knew the trees were eavesdropping.

"You don't know where he is?" Katya asked.

Petya shook his head.

"Have you seen him today?"

He nodded yes.

"Why can't you speak?"

Petya wanted to tell her that the trees recorded every word they overheard, but wasn't sure if he should. He thought about it some more, then pointed at the leafless trees that stood like petrified demons outside their window. "They're listening," he whispered to her.

Katya looked out the window. "Who's listening?"

Petya stood up and moved closer to the window. "*They*," he whispered, pointing his finger directly at the nearest tree.

Instead of coming closer to the window for a look, Katya took a step back.

"Don't be afraid, Katya. They can't hurt us as long as we have this." Petya showed her the *shield* he'd made with the tin can and piece of string.

"I haven't figured out how to stop them from eavesdropping," he said, "but they definitely can't hurt us."

"She doesn't believe you," a voice hissed in his head. "You're a fraud! A ridiculous, disfigured fool! That contraption you made is ludicrous. It doesn't do anything."

"Silence!" the voice of God thundered in response. "Pay no attention to him," it advised Petya. "He is an apostle of the devil and that is why he says these shameful things. Listen only to me. I am the only one who cares for you, the only one who loves you. You have scared Katya and endangered the mission by telling her about the trees. Now apologize to her."

Petya walked toward Katya, but for every step closer he took, she took an equal step away from him. "Katya," he said, "I'm sorry. I shouldn't have told you that. Just forget what I said. Okay?"

She nodded her head but continued stepping backwards. "Sure, Petya," she said. "I'll just forget it."

"You are such an idiot," a voice said to Petya. "She thinks you've gone completely mad."

"Katya," Petya said, "I'm not crazy. I know this looks strange and you don't understand it, but I can explain."

Katya had backed up to the wall and could go no further.

"You remember we talked about religion and God a while back?"

Katya nodded.

"Do you remember I asked you if God ever spoke to you directly? If he ever answered your prayers?"

"Yes, I remember." She held her arms up tight to her chest, hands clenched tightly just below her chin.

"Well, I hear him," Petya said excitedly. "He speaks to me."

Her lower jaw dropped an inch and she didn't respond at first. "What?" she finally said. "*Who* speaks to you?"

"God," Petya answered. "God speaks to me. He told me no one else can hear him. Only me."

"You . . . hear . . . God," she repeated slowly.

"Yes, and he's coming back."

"Who's coming back? Jesus?"

Petya nodded. "Look," he said, and pulled out the piece of paper he'd found in his old apartment's mailbox two days ago.

Katya took it and read the crude handwriting aloud: "Only God can save Leningrad. Pray to Heaven. The Time of the Apocalypse has come. Christ is now in the peaks of the Caucasus."

"You see?" Petya said. "I'm not crazy."

"Petya, this is from the Old Believers and Molokans that were pushed into the city by the war. Everyone has been getting these notes. It's not just you. I got one myself."

Petya felt relieved that he wasn't the only one God was communicating with. "You got one too?" he said. "Let me see."

"I can't show it to you," she said. "I already used it to light a fire."

He could see she was lying, but he couldn't figure out why. She was a good Christian. He expected her to be excited and to support him.

"Well, regardless of that," Petya said, "I realize now I've been living a life of sin, and it's important we repent before it's too late." He wanted to tell her about his dishonesty, about his stealing the package meant for her and Guzman, but it was even more difficult than he thought. The words didn't want to come out. He felt dull and had trouble breathing. Admitting his deception meant admitting what a fraud – what a pariah to society – he really was.

"Katya, I . . .," he began.

"Shut up you fool!" a voice hissed in his ear. "You don't have to tell her a damn thing. She can't prove anything!"

Footsteps echoed in the hallway outside the apartment, then the door unlocked and Oksana walked in. Katya rushed over to her. "Hello, Oksana. How are you doing? How was work today? Here, let me help you with that bag."

Oksana seemed perplexed by the unusual attention and held fast to her bag.

"Would you like me to make you some of that herbal tea?" Katya asked, continuing her string of questions. "It was terribly cold out today, wasn't it? Did it affect your arthritis?"

Petya watched them both, feeling relieved that his confession had been postponed.

Oksana started taking her coat off. "The cold was awful today," she said to Katya, "just awful. My hip can barely move anymore. It feels like it's frozen."

"Oh, I can just imagine," Katya said, helping her with her coat. "It must be absolute torture for you to go up and down those stairs. Have you seen Igor today?"

"To be honest," Oksana said, "I don't know how much longer I can do it. I'm not a spring chicken anymore. I've asked to be evacuated but I don't think those bastards give a damn about an old woman like me."

Katya hung Oksana's coat up for her. "You're angry because you want them to care about you and value your contributions," she said, then asked again, "Have you seen Igor lately?"

Oksana held her nose up and sniffed. "What's that smell?" she asked. "Is that meat?"

"Yes," Katya said. "Petya had some."

"Where the hell did he get it? He has no money."

"That you know of," Petya said from the other side of the room.

"Oksana!" Katya said forcefully and put her face directly in front of hers. "I asked if you've seen Igor?"

"I . . . ," Oksana stuttered, "I saw him this morning . . . before I left for work. Why?"

Petya was looking out the window at the trees again when Katya went over to him and demanded to know where Igor was.

"How should I know?" he said.

"Damn you!" Katya screamed, her fear finally rising beyond her control. She pounded on his chest with her tiny fists. "What have you done with him?"

Petya didn't try to stop her in any way. He knew he had a lot of penance coming. "He's probably just working late," he offered.

Katya grabbed her hat and coat and fled the apartment.

"Where are you going?" Oksana called after her.

"To look for Igor," she hollered from the hallway.

Petya sat down on the edge of his bed and began putting his boots on.

"You're leaving too?" Oksana said. "Where are *you* going?"

"To help her look for Igor," he said.

* * *

The room kept shrinking – getting smaller and smaller as the weather outside got colder and colder. Every day, beds would be moved another centimeter closer to the small stove in the middle of the room. It was so crowded now that two people could only get by one another if one of them sat down.

The stove – with its flue stretching over to the edge of the room and out the window – was called a 'burzhuika.' Nearly every apartment in Leningrad had one. Katya woke up and stretched her hand out to see if the stove was still warm. She was always cold lately, no matter how many layers of clothes or blankets she had on. Resting her hand on the side of the stove, she was disappointed to feel it wasn't even lukewarm.

She had woken from a wonderful dream. She and Felix were in the Kazansky Cathedral getting married. All their friends and family were gathered around and he had just lifted her veil and kissed her. The dream had been even better than her constant daydreams of him, and she closed her eyes now and tried to feel again his lips pressing against hers, his warm breath on her cheek, the smell of his skin as she inhaled.

Folding her hands in front of her, she asked God once more to ensure Felix's safe return. Then she got out of bed, pulling one of the blankets with her, wrapping it tightly around her shoulders.

They had a small pile of kindling in the hallway that she could use to start a fire, but she could find neither paper nor matches to light it with. Careful not to wake her sleeping roommates, she went over to Guzman's apartment. She'd seen some matches there a while back and hoped no one had taken them yet.

The matches were right where she'd last seen them – on top of the now legless piano. She also found a piece of wadded-up paper and brought them both back to light a fire.

Petya snored loudly as she stuffed the paper in the stove and stacked a few twigs on top of it. It had been a fitful night of rest for her and she was glad it was over. Still half-asleep, she lit the paper and she watched it burn as if in a trance. One of the paper's edges turned bright orange, then quickly faded to black and crumbled. There was handwriting on the paper and Katya saw Shostakovich's name scrawled on the bottom. She felt disappointed that Dmitry had written Guzman and not her. And then the paper shifted and uncrumpled and she was able to read a few fragments of the letter:

" . . . items are meant for you and Guzman equally . . ."

" . . . the vodka or cigarettes, for . . ."

She tried to get the letter out of the fire, but it was too late. The whole thing was engulfed in flames.

She stared into the fire, unable to comprehend what she'd just seen. She thought back to the birthday dinner Petya had surprised her with a few weeks ago. He had mysteriously acquired caviar and vodka, but wouldn't tell her where or how he'd gotten them. And of course he had suddenly started smoking cigarettes after complaining for a month that he didn't have any and couldn't afford any. Items like cigarettes that numbed the pain of the constant cold and hunger were in high demand. They were the second most sought after good at the markets, right behind the most coveted item: vodka.

Katya was fairly sure the items were meant for her and Guzman, and not Petya and Guzman, but she had no proof. She certainly didn't want to believe Petya capable of stealing something so precious – something that could determine whether one lived or died. If he'd done that, she didn't know if she could forgive him. Anger burned through her just thinking about the possibility.

She looked at the bed where Guzman used to sleep, where Igor now slept so restlessly and let out little, muffled screams from time to time. She thought how Guzman might still be around telling his wry jokes and meandering stories had he received more food.

A neighbor had found the poor old painter's mutilated body buried under a thin layer of snow in the courtyard. Katya hated to think that Petya was the one who'd hacked off the arms and legs, but where else could he have gotten the meat he'd been eating lately?

She turned her head slowly, cautiously, to the other side of the room, where Petya slept. He had his blankets wrapped around him and only the bridge of his nose and his thick black eyebrows were visible. It seemed like he was always in bed, as if he thought he could hibernate his way through the blockade.

Katya was afraid of him. With each pound that disappeared from his now lanky frame, so too did an ounce of his sanity. If these were normal times, he'd be in a mental institution. But these were anything but normal times. Millions of people the world over were trying to kill one another. Scientists and engineers worked day and night to devise more efficient ways of eradicating people en masse. Men operated mechanized killing machines that prowled the ground, the sky, even the sea. And those who were the best at it – who killed the most people – were given medals and honors.

The whole world had lost its sanity. Petya fit right in. Maybe it was Katya and her cockamamy notions of peace and understanding who was the misfit. Perhaps *she* was the real lunatic.

She started getting bundled up to go to the hospital, wondering all the while how she could prove that Petya had stolen a package meant for her and Guzman, and wondering, too, what she would do if she *could* find a way to prove it.

She was going to the hospital to get her old nurse position back. If she was going to survive the winter, she had to get the worker level of rations. The non-worker level she was on now – a measly two slices of bread a day – wasn't enough to sustain her.

It could be worse, she thought. If her former director had gotten his way and not cut any of the troops' levels, she and every other Leningrader might be dead by now. The two slices of bread had kept her alive at least.

The editorial in the newspaper announcing the recent reduction – the fifth – stated in very stark language its necessity:

> ". . . it is not possible to expect any improvement in the food situation. We must reduce the norms of rations in order to hold out as long as the enemy is not pushed back, as long as the circle of blockade is not broken. Difficult? Yes, difficult. But there is no choice . . . .."

Lake Ladoga had finally frozen and the 'Road of Life,' as it was now called, was busy with people hauling food and ammunition into the city. Tikhvin was still in German hands though. Unless the Red Army could retake that city and its all-important railroad junction, there would soon be no more supplies to deliver.

As she walked to the hospital, Katya dreamt about food. It had become her favorite pastime. She liked to imagine eating all those ordinary foods she used to take for granted. Like raw carrots. She pretended she held one in her hand. What a wonderful, vibrant shade of orange it was! How sweet it tasted! She took bites in unusual ways – from the sides, from the opposite end. What an amazing vegetable! It was like tasting the whole universe: the rain that watered it, the sun that shed light on it, the ground that nourished it. That it could grow in the ground and you could pull it out and eat it just like that was a wonder of the imagination.

She dreamt of radishes, tomatoes, fried onions. And mashed potatoes! Thick, creamy potatoes with milk and butter and garlic. Oh, what she wouldn't give for a bowl of that right now.

Katya realized how little she'd really appreciated food in her life. It had always been available. Even in times of short supply, it was never that serious and she'd never gone hungry for days on end. She felt such regret for having ever taken food for granted. It was such a precious gift, and she had so often ate it without even knowing that she was eating it. She ate simply because it was time to eat – breakfast, lunch, dinner. It hadn't mattered if she was actually hungry or not.

If she made it through the blockade, she vowed to eat every meal with appreciation. She would no longer stuff her face while she was working or thinking of something else. No, she would concentrate solely on the food – its taste, texture, and smell, and appreciate its presence in her life.

As she rounded the corner of the next block, the hospital came into view. Rumbling up the street toward it was one of the never-ending stream of camouflaged trucks that dumped the wounded off. It came to a stop at the front door, and Katya approached, waiting for the driver to emerge. She hoped for the off chance it was delivering supplies and not more wounded, but she heard the familiar moans coming from the back and knew what its cargo was. The driver hopped out, said he had six wounded soldiers, then went in to the hospital. When he opened the door, Katya could see that the beds crammed in the hospital's hallway were all full. That meant they'd run out of beds and the men would have to remain in the truck – possibly all day – until the nurses could free some beds for them.

A nurse came out and began processing the wounded men. Katya didn't recognize her and wondered if she'd replaced any of the nurses she knew or was simply a new hire.

Inside, she saw several patients making candles. The hospital had run out last week and one of the wounded men had suggested that those who were able could make them – that they'd be grateful for something to do. The idea had worked brilliantly so far.

The hospital administrator was also the lead doctor, and Katya had to wait for him to finish an operation before talking with him. When he finally came out of surgery, he took off his blood-covered apron, threw it in a hamper, then invited Katya into his office.

He was a well-organized man and his desk reflected it. On its surface were two orderly stacks of papers, an electric lamp (that he obviously hadn't been able to use in quite some time since there was no electricity), and a black bowl with a lid. He motioned for Katya to sit, then sat down himself. "How are you getting along, my dear?" he asked.

"I'm alive," Katya said, "which is more than a lot of people can say."

"True, true," he said, running his fingers along his grey mustache. "I wish I could convince some of my patients of that wisdom. I just had to amputate a leg. I was hoping I could save it, but the gangrene was too bad." He took the lid off the black bowl and the room filled with a delicious aroma. He poured some of the soup into a tea cup and handed it to Katya. "Here," he said, "have some of this. There's even some meat in there."

Katya opened her mouth, about to say that she couldn't accept such a generous offer, that his job was so important and that he needed it more than she. But before any words came out, she put the cup to her lips and drank.

He picked up a large spoon and began eating from the bowl. "So what is it you want to talk to me about?" he asked in between noisy slurps.

"I'd like my old position back," she said.

"You want to be a nurse again? I thought you had an administrative position overseeing the food supply."

Katya took another sip of the soup. She couldn't tell what meat they'd added, but she guessed it was probably horse. "I don't have that position anymore," she said.

"What happened?"

"I'd rather not talk about it."

"I'd really like to know," he said, wiping soup from his mustache.

"I was let go because I had a disagreement with the director."

"It must have been one hell of a *disagreement* for him to let you go."

Katya saw a little piece of carrot in her soup and smiled. "He's the type of person who demands people carry out his orders unquestioningly," she said. The soup tasted good and she was looking forward to eating food of this quality every day.

"I see." He ran his fingers thoughtfully along his mustache once again.

"But that's all over," Katya said and drank the last of her soup. "I'm actually excited to be a full-time nurse again. I missed it."

"I'm not sure how to tell you this," he said, "but we don't have any room for you."

Katya tried to hide her shock. She expected her request to be a mere formality – that he would welcome her back with open arms. "You're always understaffed," she said. "I know that. You know that. That's why I come and volunteer in the evenings."

"Well, there's no question we could always use a little more help, but we're constrained as to the number of personnel we can take on."

Katya thought it strange he wouldn't look her in the face. "When I left," she said, "you told me you were very sorry I was leaving, that I was the best nurse here. And now you won't take me back? Were those words just lies?"

"No, it was the truth," he said. "I'd love to take you back, but I can't." He wiped some dust off the corner of his desk. "I just can't."

She felt her eyes filling with water, but wouldn't allow herself to cry. "I overheard two nurses saying they were going to Tikhvin next week to serve on the front there," she said. "You're definitely going to need some help around here then."

He held his hands out for her tea cup and she passed it to him. "Katya," he said, finally looking her in the face. "I think you should look at some different places, perhaps a different hospital. We're not going to be able to take you on here."

"Why? I don't understand," she said. "Is there something you're not telling me?"

He got up and closed the door to his office. "Listen, Katya," he said in a low voice, "you've made some powerful enemies with whatever you did. I've been warned not to take you back. I'm sorry. I wish there was something I could do."

Katya suddenly felt dizzy and had to get some fresh air. She hurried out of his office, excusing herself briefly, then slamming the door behind her. She walked quickly down the hallway toward the exit, but felt lightheaded and short of breath and had to stop. There was no place to sit, so she leaned against the wall and hoped the sickly feeling would pass.

One of the wounded in the hallway began moaning. It started as a whimper, but within a minute or two developed into an outright scream. He was lying on one of the makeshift beds just outside the surgery room. Katya held her hands over her ears to block it out but couldn't. No matter how hard she pressed, she still heard him screaming.

No nurses were responding, so Katya went over to him and asked what was bothering him.

"My leg!" he cried as he thrashed his head from side to side. "My left leg is killing me!"

"Where does it hurt?" Katya asked as she grabbed the bottom of the blankets so she could pull them up and get a look.

"Where I was shot," he said, "just below the knee."

She started pulling the blanket up to the man's waist, but then stopped and hurriedly pulled it back down. He had no left leg. It had been amputated. They must not have told him yet.

Morphine was in short supply, but Katya got some and gave him a small dose anyway. She couldn't bear the screaming. He calmed almost immediately, and she watched the tension melt from his face. "You're an angel," he said and smiled slightly.

"Tell me, what was the pain like?" she asked. She'd heard about this type of thing before – ghost pains, they called it – but this was her first experience with it.

The man had sparkling blue eyes and light blonde hair that hung down to his eyebrows. "It was like it was on fire," he said, keeping the slight smile on his face. "Like someone was pouring boiling water on it."

"And is it gone now?"

"Yes, it's gone."

She debated whether or not to tell him that he had no left leg anymore. A high-pitched whistle screeched through the sky outside and then an explosion shook the ground a few seconds later. A thin mist of dust fell from the ceiling and Katya heard someone curse loudly in another room.

"I felt safer at the front," the man said.

"Why?"

"You hear an incoming shell like that there, you can just duck in your foxhole," he said. "Here, there's nowhere to hide."

"I guess I've gotten used to it," Katya said. "The Germans rarely let up. They're either firing on us with their artillery or setting the city on fire with those awful incendiary bombs they drop by the dozen. Or both."

She'd caught her breath but still felt lightheaded, like she was floating. Things moved in slow motion. Words echoed in her head: ". . . nowhere to hide . . . I've gotten used to it . . ."

She turned to go, but he grabbed her by the arm. "So what does my leg look like?" he asked. "It's not too bad is it?"

She tried to change the subject. "So what did you do before the war?"

"I taught at the university," he said.

Katya was surprised. He looked quite young, no more than twenty-six she guessed.

"I get that reaction all the time," he said. "I wasn't a professor. I taught dance – the foxtrot, waltz . . . . I hope my leg heals all right so I don't limp or anything. Do you know how to dance?"

Katya thought of Felix briefly and how he'd taught her to dance the waltz. "A little," she said. She felt something strange in her chest. It was like something punctured one of her organs and all of the organ's contents were draining out. She tried to change the subject again, asking what front he'd been on. She knew from experience that wounded soldiers generally liked to talk about two things in particular: how they got wounded, and what the fighting had been like.

He took her hand in his. "Thank you for staying to talk with me," he said. "It's been a long time since I've seen a beautiful woman. It feels good."

She tried to force a smile, but couldn't.

"We were sent to Tikhvin," he said. "It's a complete slaughterhouse there."

The air was stale. It smelled of body odor and chemicals and she couldn't bear it much longer. She had to get away.

"Do you know about the other guys from my unit?" he asked. "How are they doing?"

She arranged the blanket so it covered him better. "I don't know," she said. "You'll have to ask one of the other nurses."

"Well, could you check for me?" he asked. "I'm in the Volunteers. First Division."

A flush of adrenaline rushed to her stomach. "You're in the Volunteers?"

"Yeah, what's left of us anyway."

"What regiment?"

"The Second," he said.

The room wanted to spin and Katya had difficulty stopping it. "You wouldn't happen to know a Felix Varilensky, would you?"

He stared straight ahead at the ceiling for a few seconds. "No," he answered, "don't believe I knew anyone by that name. What platoon was he in?"

"I don't know," she said. "I know he joined in early September though, if that helps any."

"Hmm," he said. "There were only three platoons then and I knew everyone from the 1st and 3rd Platoons. He must have been in the 2nd . . . poor guy."

Katya felt nauseous. "What do you mean?"

"Well, last time I saw them was when we moved up together during the failed offensive of September 9th."

"September 9th," Katya repeated. "That was the day he went to the front."

"The 2nd Platoon was the one that didn't fall back," he said.

She pulled her hand out of his. "I don't understand," she said.

"We got orders to fall back to our previous lines because we were overextended and the Germans were counterattacking," he said. "But the 2nd Platoon didn't fall back. They stayed where they were at."

"And then what?"

"And then the Nazis reclaimed the territory," he said.

The room started spinning.

"I'm sorry," he added. "They fought heroically that day. They really did."

Katya held onto the bed to keep from falling. "What are you saying?! You don't know that they're dead? They could have escaped or the Germans could have taken them prisoner."

"There was nowhere to escape *to*," the man said. "And the Nazis stopped taking prisoners on that front long before that."

The nausea rose to her throat and she swallowed to keep it down.

The man winced and gritted his teeth. "My leg's starting to hurt again," he said.

Katya turned away and started walking down the hall toward the exit.

"Wait," he called after her.

She kept walking.

"Wait!" he shouted. "Can't you check my leg for me? It hurts again."

Katya looked back at him over her shoulder, but kept walking. He was struggling to sit up.

Just before she reached the door, she heard a scream like no other she'd ever heard. It echoed down the hallway and penetrated her like the bitter winter wind. "My God! My leg!! It's gone! They cut off my fucking leg!"

She ran the last few steps down the hall and flung the doors to the outside open. The cold air hit her like a pile of bricks and she stumbled backwards, grasping for something to hold onto. Her hands found a cold, uneven wall and it stopped her from falling. She leaned against this strange wall for a second, trying to catch her breath. Then she saw what the wall was made of – corpses. Dozens of them were stacked like firewood, one on top of the other.

She backed away, staring at the frozen blue bodies, then fell to her hands and knees and vomited in the snow.

When Katya got home, she collapsed into her bed without taking her boots or coat off. It was a little past noon and she could hear Petya in the kitchen talking to somebody. When he came into the room a minute later, she realized he was alone and had been talking to his 'voices' again.

"Do you have any of that vodka left?" she asked him.

"No," he said.

"Any cigarettes?"

"No, they're all gone too."

"Maybe you can tell me where you got them, so I can go buy some," she said.

He came closer and sat down across from her and she wondered what kind of lie he was going to come up with this time.

"Katya, I have committed a grave sin." He said the words slowly as if he was unfamiliar with them. "Shostakovich sent a package to you and Guzman and I stole it. The vodka, cigarettes, and caviar were all meant for the two of you." He took a deep breath. "I'm very sorry for what I've done. I know it was wrong and I'm asking for your forgiveness."

Katya felt the puncturing sensation in her chest again. It was the same as at the hospital, except this time it didn't feel like anything was draining out. It was empty.

"Katya? Did you just hear me?" he said.

Instead of being full of anger and fury like she expected if she found out she was right about him stealing the package, she felt hardly anything at all.

"If you need time to think about this, I understand," Petya said. "I know it must be quite a shock to you."

She tried to concentrate on her breath as it flowed up her nose, down past her heart, and filled her lungs. The air seemed dark and heavy and weighed her down. "No, I don't need any more time," she said.

Petya exhaled loudly. "Thank you," he said. "You don't know how hard that was for me to say. Bless you for having the heart to find forgiveness. If anyone's going to heaven for sure, it's you, Katya."

"I don't forgive you," she said.

His mouth fell open. He looked like a ghost. "What?" he said dumbly.

"I said I can't forgive you. You've written my tombstone."

"No I haven't!" he protested. "You're going to make it through this. God told me to make it up to you, and I will."

"And how will you do that?"

"I don't know," Petya said. "But *I will* do it. I'll make it up to you. Just say you'll forgive me."

"I can't," Katya said. "I can't forgive you. I can't feel anything."

He was quiet a moment, then said, "I never expected this from you."

Katya saw the color gradually come back to his face. It turned red and he curled his lips in and bared his teeth.

"You remember," he said, "how I told you nothing happened when you got drunk on your birthday?" He didn't wait for an answer. "I lied," he said. "Fact is you couldn't keep your hands off me. You begged me to make love to you." He stood up and started thrusting his hips back and forth in a rhythmic motion. "And we did it all night long."

The words sliced through her like a bayonet.

"Do you feel something now?" he said sarcastically.

Katya wished she felt the way the soldier at the hospital had when he discovered his left leg was gone. But she felt the opposite of that.

Without saying anything or looking at Petya, she left the apartment and went outside. There was a slippery spot on the sidewalk where someone from an apartment above had thrown their garbage, and she slipped on it but managed not to fall.

She walked slowly, aimlessly, through the devastated city. Nothing had any color. Everything was only a lighter or darker shade of grey. The sun was menacing. It glared off the snow and stabbed her in the eyes.

She walked past a cemetery with its dozens of bodies piled up outside the front gate. Many had no coffins and were wrapped only in rags. The dead were piling up faster than they could be buried. And yet the earth continued to spin. The world didn't stop.

It didn't even seem to care.

She heard her grandmother's voice in her head saying, "Don't be afraid, Katya. God is always with you." But was he? She was usually so sure, but now doubt filled her mind. It was all so hard to take in. She'd been denied her old job – and its life-saving ration card. Petya had betrayed her in the worst way she could imagine. She was cold, starving, and trapped in a city on the brink of absolute disaster. And she'd been told that Felix – the love of her life – was, in all likelihood, dead.

Inside of her, she had moved to that place beyond anger, beyond outrage. Faith and compassion were nowhere to be found, and her thoughts wandered without direction in that cold bitter place where neither love nor peace existed.

She found herself passing through a park that her parents used to bring her to in the summer to feed the ducks. She recalled how cute the ducks were as they waddled out of the Neva river and took the bread from her tiny outstretched hand. She looked at the bench where her parents used to wait for her and saw there now a corpse covered in snow. It was frozen in the sitting position, looking out at the river whose water did not flow. The Neva was silent and still. It, too, was a prisoner of Leningrad.

~

Глава Девятая — Chapter Nine
The Coldest Winter

My love is like a shadow
    forever following you.
There, behind you
    around you,
I always surround you.
Look for me when winter dances with your heart,
    And steals your warmth
    Because it's what you most need
    To visit that place where the ice stops you.
Do not fear the fall.
You'll find me there, but do not call
    My name
Is written everywhere.
I'm always there,
    a baby's breath away,
    the sun of May . . .
There, behind you.

The charred remains of the destroyed German equipment were like dead animals littering the side of the road. Felix and the partisans walked from one piece to the next looking for anything they might be able to salvage before they headed back behind enemy lines. It was unclear whether the vehicles and equipment had been destroyed by the Germans retreating from Tikhvin or by the rapidly advancing Soviet forces.

It was December 12th and it had been an eventful month thus far. With fresh troops from the far east, the Red Army had mounted a successful counter offensive on the Moscow front. Around the same time, the troops on the Leningrad front managed to retake Tikhvin and were hurriedly putting the Leningrad supply route back together.

Felix lit a cigarette and leaned against one of the burned-out vehicles. It was a grey day and the sun hadn't been able to completely melt the fog that had been as thick as a storm cloud earlier that morning. The fog had painted all the trees and bushes white, and if it wasn't the middle of a war, it would be beautiful.

He leaned his head back and exhaled cigarette smoke into the frigid air. As he put the cigarette back to his lips to inhale, he heard that haunting sound from the forest again. A tiny shiver went up his spine and he tensed his shoulders as he strained to block out the words. It had been happening more and more of late. He would hear something – that no one else seemed to – that sounded distinctly like someone (or something) calling his name. It was just as unsettling to Felix as looking into another person's eyes and knowing that they're going to die soon. Whatever it was, he didn't want to hear its call. He didn't want to hear it, because he knew somehow that if he did, he would have to answer it.

Misha wandered up the road, stopping when he got to Felix, and sitting down on the front tire jutting out from the vehicle.

Felix scanned the forest once more for a clue as to the strange sound. Finding nothing, he turned to Misha. "What time is it?" he asked.

Misha pulled out a pocket watch. "It's almost noon," he replied.

In mid-December in Leningrad, the sun set before four o'clock in the afternoon. Felix began calculating how much more ground they could cover in the few remaining hours of daylight.

Misha pulled out a cigarette and lit it. "Did you hear?"

"Hear what?" Felix asked.

"About the Americans?"

"What about them?"

"The Japanese bombed one of their ports in the Pacific – sunk just about their entire fleet."

Felix took a long drag on his cigarette. "Good," he said. "Now we shouldn't have to worry so much about our eastern border. The Japs will be busy fending off the Americans."

Misha nodded and blew smoke out his nose. "I guess they're our allies now – the Americans," he said. "Think they'll help us march on Berlin?"

Felix quoted a famous line from *War and Peace*, but substituted 'America' for 'Austria.' "Oh, don't speak to me of America. Russia alone must save Europe," he said.

Misha grunted. "That's what I think too," he said. "But there's all sorts of talk about them sending us troops and supplies."

"I'll believe that when I see it," Felix answered.

"You don't think they'll help us?" Misha said.

Felix flicked the butt of his cigarette into a snow drift. "We've been fighting a couple million Nazi troops for half a year now and they haven't lifted a finger to help us," he said. "Seems to me they're content just to sit over there in their protected kingdom and watch. You know how they love to be entertained."

A Soviet infantry patrol with dogs marched single file down the road in front of them. The men were dressed in white camouflage, and even the dogs had swatches of dirty white sheets wrapped around them.

"Find anything?" one of the men called out to Felix and Misha as he passed by.

Misha shook his head. "Nothing."

The dogs were exceedingly thin and had strange devices strapped to them. Felix guessed they must be the 'suicide dogs' he'd heard so much about – the ones who were trained to run under German tanks, detonating the explosives on their backs.

Felix loved dogs. Only a few weeks ago he would have been outraged to see them being used in such a way. Now he looked at them with a practiced dullness, deciding that ethics and morality were luxuries in times of war.

The unmistakable buzzing of a plane filled the sky, then the plane dropped below the thick clouds and began to approach. It was a rare sight these days as most German planes had been grounded because of the bitter cold. Men started to scatter – taking shelter behind the destroyed vehicles or lying flat on the snow-covered ground. Felix was the only one who didn't make any attempt to hide. He stayed where he was at, lighting another cigarette, and watching the plane draw nearer. It was small – a fighter plane – and it opened up with its machine guns when it was within range. The bullets struck all around Felix as it reached him, but he didn't flinch. Instead, he leaned back and blew smoke over his head at the plane.

The pilot didn't circle back for another strafing run and eventually everyone came out of their hiding places. Natasha was the first to come up to Felix. "Why do you do that?" she asked.

He shrugged his shoulders. How could she possibly understand?

"Don't you care if you live or die?" she asked.

Felix looked her in the face, admired her green luminous eyes the color of emeralds. He knew she was fond of him – not because he noticed it himself, but because Misha kept telling him so.

"No, it's not that at all," he said. "It's just that if I was meant to die today, then I'll die. No use fighting against it."

He was surprised at her response. She smiled mischievously, scrunching up her nose the way a baby does. "Maybe you just need a good reason to live," she said and winked at him.

For a quick second, it dawned on Felix how sexy she was. She had a thin seductive neck, and despite all that clothing, Felix could tell she had a great body. But he found the thought distractive and pushed it out of his mind. Anything that didn't have to do with defeating the Germans was superfluous to him.

Walking to the middle of the road, he motioned for the partisans to move out. He wanted to cover another four miles of the road before they called it a day.

The partisans gathered around and trudged forward, forming an oblong circle with Felix leading the way. If it weren't for the rifles, one wouldn't be able to tell them apart from the countless masses of fleeing refugees. Both groups moved across the wintry wasteland with a distinct weariness, a palpable numbness to the death and devastation around them. Stepping around bomb craters and frozen corpses in the road was not only an everyday occurrence, it was mundane.

Felix's partisans had earned a name for themselves in the battle to retake Tikhvin. They had performed exceptionally well under his leadership – providing crucial victories against the Germans' left flank and suffering a mere two casualties for their efforts. They had performed so well, in fact, that they weren't broken up as Felix expected they would be. The lightning fast victories the Germans had compiled in the early months of the war had thrown the organization of the Red Army into chaos, and it was often the case that Soviet field commanders siphoned off members of partisan units who weren't officially 'on the books.'

It was no secret that the Soviet leadership wanted to strengthen the partisan movement in order to wreak havoc behind German lines. As part of this initiative, Felix was made a lieutenant and his partisans were fully recognized. In addition, they were assigned a political commissar to provide 'guidance' and 'motivation.' Comrade Volkhov was a short, thin man who wore wire-rimmed glasses and was disarmingly sincere considering the work he did. His surname, Volkhov, meant *wolf* and didn't fit him at all.

The partisans came to a German cemetery next to the road and stopped to look at the rows and rows of wooden crosses marking the graves.

"It's nice to see the fruits of our efforts, huh?" Volkhov said to Felix.

Felix didn't feel pleased at all. He'd heard about the mass graves they were digging in Leningrad. They dumped bodies – one to two thousand per day – in them as a matter of routine. Yet these revolting cockroaches each got their own individual graves. If he could, Felix would dig them all up. They didn't deserve to be buried in sacred Russian soil.

Approaching from the opposite direction were three soldiers on skis pulling a machine gun on a sled. Behind them was a group of German prisoners. There were six rows of three – eighteen Germans in all – and six Soviet soldiers walked behind and around them with their rifles pointed. The prisoners hung their heads low and when they passed by, Yuri spat at them.

In the second to last row, one of the prisoners was having trouble walking. His face, chubby and childlike, was covered with black and blue bruises and dried blood. He had no gloves and only a thin jacket to protect him from the cold. He held his arms tightly around himself, tucking his hands under his armpits, but shivered intensely nonetheless.

Felix watched him stumble on a slippery patch of the road and realized why he was having so much trouble staying on his feet. He had no boots. His feet were wrapped with pieces of cloth, and not only did they offer no traction, but there were so many layers of cloth that they had no flat surface on the bottom.

A few steps past Felix, the young man fell to the ground and one of the guards rushed over to him. Felix thought he was going to help him back to his feet, but instead he kicked the man in the ribs.

"Get back in line you son-of-a-bitch!" the guard shouted as he struck him with the butt of his rifle.

Felix doubted the German understood a word the guard was saying. The man was trying to get back to his feet, but every time he was almost there, the guard would kick him or hit him so that he fell back down.

The scene transpired only a few yards from Felix, but he saw it as if from a great distance. Something inside of him felt hot and tight, and he was uncomfortable with what was going on, but he didn't try to intervene. Instead, he told himself that the German got what was coming to him. The man had come to Russia of his own accord to kill and destroy. Now he was reaping those seeds of hate that he'd helped cultivate.

After a few minutes of trying to get back to his feet and being beaten back down, the German prisoner quit trying. He laid on the hard snow of the road, curling into the fetal position to protect himself from the blows of the guard.

"You won't get back in line, huh?" the guard said sarcastically and drew a pistol from his belt. Felix looked away. He heard the forest again – that strange sound like someone calling his name. He pulled his hat down tighter over his ears, but it didn't help. The sound was getting louder.

Two shots rang out, then the guard hurried down the road to catch up with the others.

Felix could hear the strained breathing of the cockroach, but he refused to look at it. It got what it deserved, he kept repeating to himself.

He felt an itch just above his stomach, like something was biting him – gnawing at his skin from the inside out. At first, Felix used his tremendous powers of concentration to try to ignore it, but found that he couldn't. He then took his mittens off and reached his right hand under his clothing to scratch it. He scratched long and hard, but it didn't seem to make a difference. The itch wouldn't go away.

And the forest wouldn't shut up.

* * *

The air was so cold that it hurt to breathe it, and Petya wrapped his scarf tightly around his face, leaving only a thin gap for him to see through. There weren't many people on the streets this early in the morning, but he knew there would be a long line at the bakery. People began arriving there well before it opened. He walked slowly so as not to slip, and tried not to think about the winter weather that was the fiercest he'd ever known.

There was a red trolley frozen in place in the middle of the street, and Petya thought back to when the trolleys were still running and how much he'd taken them for granted. He had always been miserable when he rode them, complaining bitterly about how crowded they were. But after having to walk everywhere for so long, he vowed he'd never complain about them again – if only they'd get them running once more.

The streets were slippery in places, and Petya, with his disfigured leg and pronounced limp, had to be especially careful. There was no manpower to spare for cleaning the streets, and every alley and avenue was covered with three to four feet of compacted ice and snow. If the city survived until spring, there was going to be one hell of a mess to clean up.

When Petya made it to the still-locked bakery, there were twenty-three people in line. Of those twenty-three, nineteen were women and four were old men. Petya took his place at the end, arriving a few seconds before a sickly boy who looked to be a year or two younger than Igor was.

An hour later, Petya made it up to the counter. He had two ration cards with him – his own, and Katya's. He presented them both. The woman squinted her eyes at the cards then gave him two hunks of bread. Petya stepped away, with the intention to put each ration and each card in a different pocket. Before he was able to do it though, he became confused and forgot what he was going to do. This happened to him a lot, and he'd learned that if he didn't fret about it and just waited, that it would come back to him eventually.

He overheard the boy behind him who was now at the counter. "It *is not* expired," the boy said. "Give me my bread. I'm hungry!"

"I told you, I can't give you any," the woman said. "That card is no good anymore. Tell your mother she needs to get a new one."

"Give me my bread!" the boy screamed and started to cry.

Petya finally remembered what he had intended to do, put the bread and ration cards in separate pockets, then started to walk away, pretending he hadn't heard any of the conversation that just took place. He didn't get far before that damned voice in his head told him he couldn't just walk away. There was a right and there was a wrong, and it was Petya's duty as one of God's disciples to set things right. Not that he wanted to. The voice told him *he had to*.

The boy was kicking the front of the counter and refused to move away. There were a dozen people in line behind him, but none of them said a word nor attempted to intervene. Petya went up to the counter and addressed the woman. "Let me see the card," he said. The woman handed it to him, and he saw that it was indeed expired. All cards had to be renewed from time to time in an attempt to stop people from using stolen or forged cards, or cards that belonged to the dead. When Petya had his ration card stolen, he'd had to wait until the next renewal to get another one. Going without a ration card for eleven days had been beyond difficult – it had very nearly killed him.

"Can't you give him some for today and he'll get it renewed for tomorrow?" Petya asked the woman.

She stared at him blankly in response, her pale, gaunt face framed by a fur hat and dark scarf. Just when Petya didn't think she was going to answer, she replied in a weary, well-rehearsed voice, "Comrade, I am accountable for every slice of bread. If I give any to people without the proper authorization, then I could face the firing squad."

Petya knew it was useless to argue with her, not only because what she said was true, but because she couldn't very well bend the rules with so many people watching.

He took out his own bread ration, broke off a quarter of it, then handed it to the boy, who immediately started stuffing it in his mouth. Petya led him off to the side and announced to the rest of the people in line, "If anyone else would like to help by giving him a piece of your ration, we'll be waiting here."

After ten people had gone to the counter, five of them stopped by afterwards and donated some of their ration to the boy. Once he had eaten all he wanted, Petya took him by the hand to take him home.

"It's dangerous for a young child like yourself to be walking around alone," Petya said. He wondered where the boy's mother was and why she'd let the card expire.

After a few minutes, they came to an intersection thick with snowdrifts, and the boy led them down the street to the right. The block seemed to be deserted and Petya was surprised at how few footprints there were in the snow. "What's your name?" he asked. "I'm Petya."

"Kolya," the boy answered.

Petya had noticed that the boy – like many Leningraders – had swollen and bleeding gums. "How is your mother doing, Kolya?"

"She's tired," he answered after a few seconds. "She's sleeping right now."

Their conversation, with long pauses and few words, was typical for the times. It took too much energy to speak.

The sun glared off the ice and snow, and Petya had to squint to see. At the next intersection, the boy took his hand away. "Our building is down there," he said, pointing to the next block. "Thanks for the bread."

The boy crossed the intersection, glancing suspiciously over his shoulder at Petya every now and then. Petya pretended to keep walking in a different direction, and when the boy stopped turning around to check on him, he changed course and followed after him.

After a short distance down the block, the boy turned down an alley and disappeared from Petya's sight. At the alley's opening, there were three abandoned cars piled high with snow, and Petya took out the long kitchen knife he now carried with him at all times.

The boy's tracks curved around the first car and in between the second and third. Petya followed the footprints to a partly demolished building and a small hole in the wreckage. He was quite sure now that his previous suspicions were correct. The boy was an orphan and living on his own. His mother had probably died of hunger or else in one of the bombings, and his father was likely at the front. There were orphanages all over the city to care for the multitudes of children like him, but many wouldn't go there voluntarily because they were afraid they'd never see their parents or any other members of their family again.

Petya made his way through the rubble, down a set of snow-covered stairs, and to a warped red door that couldn't be closed completely. He pushed the door, but it only opened ten inches before it got stuck on something. Putting the knife in his coat pocket, he pushed hard on the door with both hands until it opened enough for him to squeeze through.

"Kolya?" he called out in the darkness. "It's me, Petya."

No answer.

"Kolya, I know you're here. Come out."

"What do you want?" Petya heard a voice say, though he couldn't tell where the boy was at.

"I want you to come over to me so we can talk," Petya said. He didn't understand how the boy could possibly live here. It was so dark and cold. A snowdrift five inches high angled in from the door.

"About what?"

Petya squinted his eyes to try to see where the boy might be hiding. "About something of considerable significance to you," he said.

"Huh?"

Petya rephrased it. "About something important," he said. When he still didn't hear the boy coming toward him, he added, "If you come out, I'll give you a piece of candy." He didn't really have any, but hoped the trick would work.

He heard some shuffling coming from the far corner, and a few seconds later the boy appeared in front of him. "Where's the candy?" he asked before moving any closer.

"It's here in my coat," Petya said. He stuck his hand inside his pocket and pretended to struggle to get something out. The boy walked up closer. When he was a few feet away, Petya lunged at him and caught him by the arm. The boy cried out and struggled to get away, but Petya was too big for him.

He dragged the boy, kicking and screaming, from the basement to the outside. "What do you want? Where are you taking me?" the boy yelled.

Petya kept a tight grip on the boy's arm as he led him to the nearest orphanage. His intention was to put him there for his own welfare. He wouldn't survive on his own.

The closer Petya got to the orphanage, the more memories came back of what he went through when *he* was in an orphanage, all the taunting and outright ridicule he'd received. He thought of the only friend he'd had there – the other smart kid, Alexander – and how one of Alexander's distant relatives from Kamchatka had come and taken him away one day, leaving Petya all alone to fend for himself once again. He'd cried for three straight days after Alexander left.

When they got to the orphanage, Petya took one look at the dismal brick building and knew that he couldn't do it. He couldn't leave him there. He didn't want the boy to have to go through what he'd went through.

Back in the apartment, Petya found Katya in her usual spot – sitting in her chair facing the front door. She rarely moved from there, no matter what convincing argument Petya or Oksana came up with. Her journal was in her lap and she was pensively tapping a pencil to a page. That meant she was writing poetry, Petya knew.

She looked up at the boy.

"Katya, this is Kolya," Petya said.

She looked confused for a second, but then smiled and said hello.

Kolya looked back at her. "Hi," he said meekly.

"I found him living by himself in the basement of a destroyed building. He's going to stay with us now," Petya said. He saw a brief look of surprise on her face as he led the boy past her down the short hallway. He thought she would ask him some questions, but she didn't.

Kolya came to a stop next to the coffee table, looked briefly around the room, then returned to staring at his feet.

Petya patted him on the head. "Don't worry," he said. "I'll take care of you. You'll like it here."

Kolya shrugged and sat down on one of the beds.

The apartment was dimly lit but it should have been completely dark, because Petya had barricaded the window last night in an attempt to keep the trees from messing with him. He went over to the window now and saw that his barricade had been tampered with. The blanket was pulled to the side and sunlight was streaming in.

He turned toward Katya. "Did you do this?" he asked.

She shook her head no without looking back at him.

Petya's thinking started to get jumbled again and he sat down to sort out the onslaught of thoughts. Once he regained his focus, he asked her who did it.

"You know who," Katya said.

Petya did indeed know who – the trees. *Damn it.* "Did you see them?"

She shook her head.

"Well, did you hear anything?"

Again, she shook her head.

Petya was amazed and frustrated. "How the hell do they do it?" he muttered under his breath. He'd spent two hours constructing that barricade, even adding a series of tin cans on a string that would rattle as an alert to any attempted tampering. How could they have done it and Katya not heard anything?

As he started fixing the barricade, a familiar voice resounded in his head. "This is not necessary," it said. "*I* will protect you. The only defense you need against these demons is faith in me." Petya knew there was no point in arguing with the voice of God. It always won. It had drowned out all the other voices and Petya felt powerless to challenge its decisions.

He obeyed the voice and took the barricade down, and the sun's hazy light filled the apartment once more. The walls, black and dingy from the smoke of the stove and koptilka, had been stripped clean of their wallpaper. It had been made known that the glue holding wallpaper up was partially edible, and Petya, Oksana, and Katya had torn down all the wallpaper in the apartment and made glue soup.

Petya poured himself a cup of water that emptied their last container. He still had difficulty accepting that the water wasn't poisoned, but the voice of God assured him it was all right to drink it. It assured him of many things: that Katya was not (indeed, never was) trying to kill him, that the war with the Germans was a pivotal part of the Apocalypse, and that Petya was a good person – a sinner no doubt – but still a good person at heart.

Holding his breath so he wouldn't smell, Petya took a sip of the brown water. It tasted awful, but getting enough fluids was an absolute necessity in these times. He took another drink, then divided the rest into two cups. He gave one to Kolya and took the other over to Katya.

As usual, she ignored him, so he set the cup down on the floor next to her chair. "You need to drink more," he said. "You're the one who was always telling me that."

Her skin, once so smooth and alluring to Petya, was now dry and scaly and stretched tight over her face. Her eyes, once so mesmerizing, were now fantastically large and unnatural. Her whole body was wasting away. In any other time one would guess she had some debilitating disease. But her only sickness was hunger, and its devastating consequence, malnutrition.

Two weeks ago, Petya had spied on her as she gave herself a sponge-bath. He remembered how her ribs stuck out and her breasts were shrunken to the point of non-existence. He'd experienced no lust whatsoever in watching her. But then he hadn't felt any sexual drive at all in at least two months. That, too, was a victim of hunger.

Petya retrieved her bread ration for the day and held it out to her. Setting her pencil down, she took the bread and immediately began scraping some crumbs off the edges of it into her hand. Then she picked up a small saucer from the floor, wiped the crumbs onto it, and set it back down next to a small hole in the wall. A skinny mouse lived inside the hole. Katya had nicknamed it Prince Myshkin. It would come out in the late afternoon to eat the crumbs, and Katya would talk to it. With Igor no longer around, it seemed to have become her closest friend and confidant.

Katya rarely acknowledged Petya's efforts, though he'd been getting her rations for her for the past week – ever since she tripped over a corpse in the stairwell and sprained her ankle badly enough that she couldn't walk. Petya felt tremendous pity for her. Her prospects for getting a job and regaining her health didn't look good. He knew she'd checked every hospital in the city. None of them would take her, no matter how understaffed they were.

Petya believed that some people deserved what they got, himself for instance. He was a horrible person. He was selfish. He lied. He judged people harshly. And he was paying for it now. But Katya? No, she was a *good* person and didn't deserve this.

"Are you sure you don't want to lie down for a while?" Petya suggested to her. "It's best if you keep your ankle elevated. Sitting in this chair all day long isn't helping."

She didn't respond right away, but Petya had learned to wait. Reaction times weren't what they used to be.

He knew why she was always waiting there, staring at the door. She expected Felix to walk through any minute, as though he'd just stepped out to go get a newspaper.

"Katya, he's not coming back. There's no point in waiting here for him," Petya said.

"You're wrong," she answered. "He *is* coming back."

"Don't you remember? The soldier at the hospital told you – the Germans killed everyone in his platoon."

"No, we'll be together again," she said. "I just know it."

Petya sighed deeply. It was no use arguing with her.

The room felt colder than usual and he went over to the stove to check the fire. Just as he feared, the fire was nearly out. He wanted to chastise Katya for it, but he knew that wouldn't be right. Kindness was not just a nice thing to do, the voice of God had told him it was a prerequisite for getting into heaven.

He went over to his old apartment and grabbed another stack of his writing, then went to Guzman's and gathered the last few pieces of wood from the piano. The firewood deliveries had stopped in early December. Now you had to get wood to burn from wherever you could. They'd have to start chopping up their chairs and coffee table soon.

Petya wadded up a page of his writing and put it in the stove. Then he arranged the wood on top of it, lit a match and held it to the paper. His writing always caught fire quickly, and he took a fiendish pleasure in seeing it subtracted from the universe forever.

He saw Kolya hadn't drank his water yet. "Drink that," he urged. The boy did as he was told.

There was a strange knock at the door. Strange, because it sounded like someone was kicking the bottom of the door with their boots. Katya dropped her pencil and paper and stood up. "Yes?" she called out.

"Open the door," a voice called out. "It's me."

Katya limped to the door and opened it. Petya watched a ghost walk into the apartment.

"What are you doing here?" Katya asked.

"I thought you could use some firewood," Igor said.

Petya stared in disbelief. He was sure he'd killed Igor two weeks ago.

"I told you to stay away," Katya said. She looked over her shoulder uneasily at Petya. "It's not safe here."

"I was worried about you," Igor said. "I wanted to make sure you were all right."

Katya held out her arms and Igor set the firewood down and they embraced.

Petya thought Igor looked quite healthy for a ghost, certainly better than when he'd last seen him. His cheeks had some color and his lips weren't quite so thin anymore. What Petya couldn't figure out was why (and how) a ghost would carry a load of firewood.

"Well, since you're here," Katya said, "come in and tell me how things are going."

She pulled the hat from his head and his ears stuck out, just the way Petya remembered the boy from their first meeting back in August. It was gradually sinking in that he must have dreamed he killed Igor. This boy in front of him was no apparition.

"How's your courier job going?" Katya asked as she led him toward one of the beds so they could sit. "Do you like living there?"

Igor started telling her about how it was hard to sleep at night because all the men snored so loudly, then he saw Kolya. "Who's that?" he asked.

"That's Kolya," Katya answered. "Kolya, this is Igor."

Kolya looked up and said hi.

"What's he doing here?" Igor asked.

"Petya is going to take care of him," she said. "But we'll talk about that later."

Igor glanced at Petya, then reached into his coat. "I brought some food," he said. He pulled out a can of condensed milk, a small piece of chocolate, and some loose tea. "I thought we might celebrate."

Petya's eyes grew wide at the sight of the tea.

"Celebrate what?" Katya asked. "Is the war over?"

Igor frowned. "No," he said, hanging his head. "It's New Year's Eve."

Katya looked surprised and glanced over at Petya. He nodded his head in return. He'd told her that morning that it was New Year's Eve, but her short-term memory seemed to be failing her lately.

"Oh," she said, looking unsure of what to say next. "Well, of course, we'll celebrate then. We'll celebrate that we're still one step ahead of death."

Igor smiled. "Do you have any food for our celebration?" he asked.

Like most Leningraders, Petya, Katya, and Oksana had stopped sharing their food with one another a while back, but New Year's Eve was an exception.

"Of course," Petya said. "We have lots of provisions. We have some bread...." He searched through his coat pockets until he found a small tin of sardines. "And fish too!" He held it up for Igor to see.

"Wow," Igor exclaimed. "How did you get that?"

"And I have two potatoes left," Katya said. "We'll eat those too."

Petya thought she'd lost her senses again. There was no way she still had any potatoes left. But then she went to the kitchen and proved him wrong, returning with two fist-sized white potatoes.

Igor gathered up all the food they'd produced and arranged it on the coffee table. Petya wasn't nearly as excited about the food as he was the tea. He wanted to make it right away, but they were out of water. He'd already gathered and melted all the snow from the roof and windowsills. He'd have to go to the river.

"Where are you going?" Igor asked as Petya buttoned up his coat.

"We're out of water," he said. "I'm going to get some more. Keep an eye on Kolya for me."

Igor looked surprised. Petya didn't blame him. Petya had never helped out with getting water when Igor was still living with them. But things were different now.

* * *

Katya watched Petya walk to the front door and leave the apartment. As soon as the door closed behind him, she called Kolya over. The boy got up and went slowly toward her, his head down, as if he'd done something wrong and was about to be punished.

She had Igor get her thermometer from the kitchen so she could take Kolya's temperature. She'd already seen his swollen, bleeding gums, and now, up close, she could see he had puffy eyes. That usually meant dystrophy.

"Stick your tongue out," she said.

His small pink tongue was covered with brown dots and a white film.

"How long have you been living on your own?" she asked.

"My mom never came home from work last week," he answered.

"Your father's at the front?"

He nodded his head. His lips were so narrow and white that it didn't look like he even had any. "He hasn't been back to visit us in three months," he said.

Katya sighed, a small whimpering sound like a hungry puppy. She'd seen so much of this, but her heart still ached each time.

The thermometer read 97.3, and she was relieved he didn't have a fever. She kissed him on the forehead, then pulled him close to her and gave him a hug. "You're going to be all right, Kolya," she said. He wrapped his small arms around her neck and buried his face in her shoulder.

She noticed his hair, though incredibly dirty, was very much like Felix's: dark and curly. She thought how Felix had probably looked a lot like this little boy when he was his age.

"Go sit next to the stove to warm up," she whispered in Kolya's ear. He kept his arms wrapped tightly around her neck, not letting go. Katya imagined the boy was her son, and Felix the father. She thought how they might never have that opportunity – to get married and have children. Tears welled in her eyes, then slipped down her gaunt cheeks.

When Kolya finally let go, Katya dried her tears with the blanket she had wrapped around her. Then she led Igor into the kitchen to speak to him in private. Her ankle hurt, and she felt weak, both physically and psychologically. But she knew what had to be done. She had to be strong.

"Sweetheart, do you know that orphanage a few blocks from here?" She spoke softly so Kolya wouldn't overhear. "The one across from the school?"

"Da," – yes – Igor answered.

"I want you to take Kolya there. He's sick and they'll be able to look after him."

"I thought you said Petya was going to take care of him."

"Petya means well," she said, "but he can't take care of him. He's sick himself."

"I understand," Igor said.

Katya ran her fingers through his hair. "I see they've given you a bath."

"Yeah, I didn't want to," he said. "But they made me. All soldiers have to take baths at least once a month."

"So you're a soldier now?"

He nodded his head proudly. "If I keep doing such a good job, my commander said I could be promoted to sergeant before the war is over."

Katya smiled. "Just don't you forget you're going to college one day," she said.

"Oh, I won't," he answered. "That's the only way you can become an engineer."

"You're going to be an engineer, now? I thought you'd decided on being a pilot?"

"No, pilots can't put the city back together," he said. "I'm going to be an engineer so I can help rebuild the bridges and buildings the Germans destroyed."

Katya thought again how Igor was her only living relative left. She felt such affection for him and prayed every night that all his dreams would come true one day. She put her arms around him and held him close. "I love you," she said, "no matter what you become."

"I love you too," he said.

She held him tight and rocked slightly from side to side, then let go. "Now don't tell Kolya where you're taking him," she said. "In fact, hold his hand so he can't run away when you get close. He probably won't want to go, but it's the best place for him."

They left the kitchen, and Katya hobbled over to Kolya and sat down beside him. Her ankle was throbbing from standing and it felt good to sit. She looked Kolya in the eyes. "I want you to go with Igor," she said. "You're sick, and he's going to take you to a place where they can help you."

"I hate hospitals," he said.

"Don't worry," she said. "He's not taking you to a hospital."

Igor came over and took Kolya by the hand. He was a head taller than Kolya and weighed at least ten pounds more. Kolya looked up at him and Igor smiled. "It'll be all right," Igor said.

Katya was pleased to see Igor's tenderness and confidence. He had changed so much since he first came to live with her.

Igor led him down the hallway toward the door, Kolya looking back at Katya as he walked. She managed a short smile and waved to him. She knew she'd probably never see him again.

"Pakah," – see you soon – Igor said to Katya as they left.

"Bye," Katya said.

She didn't like Igor going unescorted but felt comforted by the fact that he knew the city well and was young and could run. There were no muggers or cannibals in the city who were willing to expend energy on running after someone.

As soon as they had left, Katya sank down onto her bed, exhausted. She felt haggard and cold, but not hungry. Her appetite had left her a week ago. A bad sign, she knew. Her body was failing her and there wasn't much that could be done about it. She had trouble thinking and remembering. Her muscles didn't always do what they were asked, and when she looked in the mirror, she saw a bony stranger looking back who frightened her.

After she lost her job last month, she'd spent a week checking every hospital in the city. None of them would take her, forcing her to look for work elsewhere. Another two weeks went by before she finally managed to convince a sewing shop to take her on. There, she'd spent all day in a large unheated room that caused her face and legs to go numb with cold. But it gave her the ration level she needed to survive, and that was all that mattered to her.

Her supervisor, Katya came to find out, was a former classmate of Oksana's. She kept Katya on even after Katya sprained her ankle and could no longer make it into work. Then, last week, she'd stopped by Katya's apartment unexpectedly, giving Katya the bad news that they were being audited by the food czar and could no longer keep her on the payroll, reducing Katya once again to the non-worker ration level.

It was getting harder and harder to find the energy to keep fighting. After she grudgingly accepted she might not live to see the spring, her view of the world started shifting. She wrote letters to every person, whether they were alive or not, who she felt resentment toward. She asked for their forgiveness and also told them she forgave them their misdeeds. Her grandmother's words from long ago were her guiding light, "If you forgive others the wrongs they have done to you, God will also forgive you."

She had even forgiven Petya, even if she didn't act that way. His sanity had slipped too far, and she wanted as little interaction with him as possible.

She pulled the covers over herself and didn't want to ever get out of bed again. Closing her eyes, she pictured Felix doing those endless push-ups on their picnic the day before the war started. She felt the hot sun, smelled the scent of freshly-cut hay when the breeze blew, saw Felix's athletic V-shaped back, his muscular arms, the tiny beads of sweat around the short hairs on the back of his neck. He'd been so strong, so sure of himself, so sure the world was perfect just as it was. She wondered if he still felt that way. Raising her arm to her face, she gently brushed the back of her hand along her cheek, imagining it was Felix. "Where are you, my love?" she whispered. "I need you."

***

A trip to the river for water was never an easy, short, nor particularly safe journey. The most difficult – not to mention the most dangerous – part was getting down to and up from the river. The great granite stairs leading to the river were covered with thick ice. Several times Petya had seen women slip and fall. Some to never get back up.

He pulled his sled with its clanking pots and pans down the wide, empty street. Occasionally he'd see another person pulling a sled, loaded either with their own pots and pans, or with one of the ubiquitous blue corpses that seemed to outnumber the living these days.

When Petya got to the banks of the river, he saw the stairs were icier than ever. He wanted to just ride the sled down the bank, but that was more dangerous than taking the steps. The slope of the bank was steep and there was no way to stop. You could end up drowning in one of the bomb craters in the ice. Or you might die a slower death if you fell off the sled and hurt yourself. You couldn't count on any of the hospitals to help. They were already packed to capacity, and the doctors rarely performed operations on civilians anyway – Leningraders were so undernourished that their blood wouldn't clot.

Petya debated the pros and cons of each method of getting down to the river and decided the sled option wasn't much more dangerous than the icy stairs option. He went to the least steep section of the riverbank, slid the pots and pans down on their own, then sat down on the sled. He aimed for a pair of snow-covered corpses lying next to one of the nearby holes in the ice. He hoped to use them to stop.

He gave himself a little push, and the sled took off quickly. In a matter of seconds, he collided with the dead bodies and was thrown off the sled. Fortunately he wasn't hurt, and he made his way to his feet and gathered the pots and pans.

In the distance, he could see one of the Navy's battleships. Every ship in the Northern fleet (what remained of it anyway) was stuck in the ice, completely immobile. They were still manned, though only partially, and their big guns pounded at the enemy lines from time to time. German planes had tried repeatedly to sink the ships, but without success.

Petya wound his way around the numerous corpses until he found a hole in the ice that wasn't yet frozen over. He dipped his can into the hole until he heard a splash and felt the rope jerk slightly. After the rope got sufficiently heavy, he pulled the can up and dumped the brown water into one of the pots. He would have to repeat this procedure many times to fill all of the pots and pans he'd brought.

The second most difficult, and critical, part of his journey was yet to come. Once he finished filling all the pots and pans, he had to take them, one by one, up the icy steps, then situate them on the sled so that a little bump wouldn't overturn them and make the entire trip for naught.

Petya returned to the apartment two hours later. Igor helped him bring the pots and pans of water up the stairs, then Katya helped him boil and strain just enough for that night. Oksana arrived home as they were finishing and surprised them all with a bottle of Georgian wine. "They gave it out at work," she said. "We were hoping for food, but it's better than nothing."

There was a lump of blankets on Igor's bed, and Petya had assumed that Kolya was buried under them sleeping. It wasn't until he went to check on the boy that he realized he wasn't there.

"Where's Kolya?" he asked.

"Who?" Oksana said, looking from Petya to Katya to Igor.

A flash of fear streaked through Petya's mind. Had he imagined the whole thing? Did the boy not really exist?

He grabbed hold of Igor. "Where's Kolya?" he asked, his eyes frantic.

Igor tried to get free of his grasp and go to Katya. "I don't know," he said.

"Where is he?!" Petya shouted, gripping him tighter.

"Let him go," Katya said. "Kolya ran away."

Petya released his grip. "Why didn't you stop him?" he said, looking at Katya.

"We tried," she answered, "but he got away."

Petya felt sad and full of grief. He'd made up his mind he'd take care of the boy, and now, through his negligence, Kolya was gone. He put his ragged brown coat on to go outside. "I'm going to try to find him," he said. "I think I know where he ran to."

"No, don't go," Katya said.

She was wringing her hands, and Petya thought her reaction odd. "I have to," he said as he walked out the door. "He's just a boy. He won't survive on his own."

Petya went all the way back to the abandoned building to look for Kolya, but couldn't find him there. He searched other nearby buildings as well, but all to no avail. He returned to the apartment heartbroken.

Katya did her best to console him, saying Kolya was likely picked up by a policeman or a Civil Defense Corps worker. The boy would be fine, she told Petya. In fact, he was probably already celebrating New Year's. Petya didn't believe her, and it wasn't until the voice of God said he'd watch over the boy that Petya felt better.

Their New Year's festivities got underway just after 8:30, their 'feast' consisting of Petya's small tin of sardines, several thick slices of bread, a can of condensed milk, a small piece of chocolate, two potatoes, a bottle of wine, and some loose-leaf tea.

There had been rumors for a long time that extra rations – canned meat or fish, butter, sugar, chocolate, or maybe even vodka – would be given out in celebration of New Year's. But in the end it was all just wishful thinking. Bread rations had been increased slightly on December 29th, but the fact was that more people were dying of starvation now than ever before. New Year's Eve – one of the biggest holidays of the year – turned out to be only slightly less wretched than every other day.

Petya took four pages from one of his old stories and handed each person a sheet of paper to serve as a plate. They had stopped using real plates a long time ago, as water was much too valuable to be expended on washing dishes.

Katya got up from her chair and walked toward the stove, but when she got there, she stopped and looked perplexed. Petya had noticed this behavior become more pronounced the last few weeks. She'd started to keep pencil and paper with her at all times so she could write things down, then refer to it in case she forgot what she was about to do or say.

She took her paper out now, but Petya could see there was nothing written on it.

"What is it?" Igor asked.

"I forgot what I was going to do," she said.

"Probably get the potatoes," Petya suggested.

"Oh yes," she said. "That's it. Thank you." She pulled the black, cracked potatoes from the coals and set them on the coffee table with the rest of their food.

For a short time, the four of them forgot their grievances against one another and enjoyed the food and drink and conversation. It took only a few sips of wine to feel drunk and warm.

Igor had the idea to put the condensed milk on top of the stove and add the chocolate to it. After the chocolate melted, they added some water and stirred it all together so they had enough for each person to enjoy some weak hot chocolate.

Halfway through their meal, the building shook from nearby explosions. The Germans were shelling the city again.

"Can't they leave us alone for *one* minute?" Oksana cried. She had her head wrapped in a white kerchief, and in the dim light of the candles looked like a mummy.

When the shelling ended, the metronome-like ticking from the radio suddenly stopped and everyone quit talking. One by one, their heads turned to the faded black paper cone of the speaker. Nothing replaced the sound of the ticking. Was it the end? Had the Germans finally broken through? Would the street warfare begin now? Or would they wake in the morning and the Germans be in control? Petya felt both scared and relieved at the prospect. Then a voice spoke, "Govoreet Moskva," – Moscow speaking – it said. Then the sound of the Kremlin chimes played, and a few seconds later, the national anthem.

As the music played, Oksana raised her glass of wine in front of her. Her arms were as thin as the twigs they put on the fire and her hands trembled badly. If her glass had been full, the wine would have spilled over the edges. "God willing," she said, raising her hand another inch higher, "we will prevail."

They all touched their glasses together and had another drink of wine.

"Of course we'll prevail in the end," Petya said as he set his glass back down on the coffee table. "God is clearly on our side."

"Then why doesn't he snap his fingers and send all the Nazis to hell?" Igor asked.

"He doesn't work that way," Petya replied.

"Why not?" Igor persisted, looking to Katya for an answer.

"I don't think we should be asking if God is on *our* side," Katya said. "We should be asking if *we* are on God's side."

The building shook again amidst a loud salvo of artillery fire. The shells weren't incoming this time. The ships frozen in the Neva river were firing, letting the enemy know that the new year was going to be just as miserable for them. Hopefully more so.

The festivities wound down rapidly, and by eleven o'clock, everyone but Petya was in bed asleep. It was the shortest New Year's celebration he'd had since he was four years old, and he felt cheated.

He stayed up and gathered the used tea leaves from everyone's cup, spooning them into a small tin can. He added a cup of water and set it on the stove to boil. He hoped if he boiled the tiny black leaves long enough he'd be able to have one more cup of tea.

While he waited for the water to boil, he listened to the radio. Someone was giving a patriotic speech about never giving up, about fighting the enemy with your last breath. Petya heard the words, but didn't feel the effect. He expended most all of his energy just making it from day to day. There wasn't much left for emotions.

His cup of water still hadn't boiled after fifteen minutes, so Petya threw in some of the precious firewood Igor had brought. Sometimes it seemed like you could add all the wood in the world to that stove and it still wouldn't be enough.

After another fifteen minutes, he tapped his finger on the top of the stove, hoping it would be too hot to touch. But it wasn't. It wasn't hot at all, and probably wouldn't be until spring.

* * *

Misha had somehow managed to get enough liquor for the partisans to throw a party in celebration of New Year's Eve. The alcohol was another homemade concoction nearly twice as strong as vodka. It had a brownish color, like cognac, and if you drank it straight, your throat would burn then feel extremely raw like you had a bad cold.

But nobody cared about that. Their festivity was about the here and now. They celebrated because they were alive. No one took that for granted anymore.

A group of partisans were decorating a small evergreen tree in honor of the New Year. They had learned to be inventive in combat, and that skill had carried over to other aspects of life. They decorated the tree with whatever they could make or find: miniature snowmen carved out of ice, painted pine cones on strings, shiny stars cut from tin cans, captured German medals pinned directly to the branches. At the top of the tree there was a small version of the red flag of the Soviet Union.

It was close to midnight and the moon hung in the sky like one of the shiny ornaments on their tree. Felix leaned easily into the wall of snow and ice behind him, cigarette tucked neatly between the middle two fingers of his right hand. He looked up at the moon, inhaled deeply, then casually blew three perfectly formed smoke rings into the night air. "I agree," he said to Volkhov, "it's rather hopeless at this point."

They were talking about the battle that had been raging to try to recapture Mga. The Germans seemed especially determined not to be defeated there. They had already lost Tikhvin to the Red Army. If they lost Mga, their stranglehold over Leningrad would come to an end.

"I think we've lost the momentum," Felix added. "I don't see the lines around Leningrad changing until spring brings warmer weather."

Felix's partisans were not engaged in the battle for Mga. They were still near Tikhvin, awaiting orders of where specifically they were to go behind enemy lines.

Most of partisans were gathered around the campfire drinking. It was a cloudless, windless evening, and Misha was the life of the party. He had covered a pocket comb with cigarette paper, and, holding it to his mouth, was playing the national anthem. When he finished that, he led everyone in singing a round of "Dark Night," an appropriately melancholy song for the times:

> ... ♪ *You are waiting for me, standing by the crib,*
> *and wiping away the tears so no one sees.*
> *I am not afraid of death. I met him a few times in battle.*
> *And even now he is circling around me* ♪ ...

After that, they sang the ever popular "Katyusha," about Russia's top secret mobile multiple rocket launcher that was much feared by the Germans:

> ... ♪ *Fly toward the clear sun*
> *And to the warrior on a far away border*
> *Bring Katyusha's greeting* ♪ ...

Near the end of the song, Misha crouched down to the ground then leaped in the air, then bent low again and alternately kicked each leg as high as he could – performing the traditional Ukrainian Gopak dance clumsily but with enthusiasm. By the time he finished, there wasn't a single person who wasn't laughing.

When the stroke of midnight finally came, the night sky erupted with shouts and yells and gunfire. Volkhov was standing next to Felix and was the only sober one of the bunch. Misha came over and handed Felix the bottle of booze he was carrying around, then wished Volkhov "Happy New Year," slapping him on the back.

"This is ridiculous," Volkhov responded. "What's there to celebrate? You think 1942 will be any better? It'll probably be just as miserable – maybe even more so – than '41."

"Celebrate that you're alive, man!" Misha said. "You can't have fun when you're dead."

"He's got a point there," Felix said and took a drink from the bottle. It tasted like gasoline and he nearly gagged. The other bottles Felix had drank from were either diluted or mixed with something. Misha's wasn't.

"You can't tell jokes when you're dead, can't laugh," Misha continued, "can't read poetry, can't write love letters."

"So what?" Volkhov said.

Felix watched Misha lean back and look at the stars. "Look at that," he said to Volkhov and pointed into the sky.

"At what?" Volkhov said.

"The stars, man! You can't look at the stars when you're dead. Don't you get it?"

"No," Volkhov said, "and you don't either. We're fighting a war."

"But I *do* get it," Misha said, slurring his words. "If there's one thing I've learned from this war it's to never get distracted from what's beautiful in life."

"You're drunk," Volkhov said.

"Thank you," Misha answered, "I've been trying very hard tonight to reach that supreme state of bliss."

Natasha emerged from nearby shadows, her nose red, her green eyes glossy, a smile on her cute face. She walked up to Felix and stood in front of him. "How about a New Year's kiss?" she said.

Felix had drank his fair share that night and, without much thought, put his arms around her waist and leaned forward to give her a short kiss.

"You certainly can't kiss women when you're dead either," Felix heard Misha say to Volkhov.

After a couple seconds of kissing, Felix dropped his arms and pulled away. But Natasha didn't. She squeezed her arms around him and pressed her lips back to his. Felix resisted at first, but then gave in and they kissed long and hard. The softness of her lips and the feel of her tongue on his filled him with desire.

"What are you trying to do?" he asked with a grin when she finally let up.

"Give you something to live for," she answered, pressing her lips back to his.

He hadn't thought of intimacy in such a long time, and it washed over him now like a tidal wave. There was nowhere to hide from this animal instinct, this primordial appetite of his body. Even through her many layers of clothing, he could feel her breasts pressing against him. His breath became short and he could hardly believe how strong his urge was to have sex. Within a matter of seconds, everything had shifted. He could think of nothing other than his own physical desire.

"How about we go to my hut?" Natasha suggested. "We can be alone there."

Felix couldn't find his voice, but managed to nod his head. He wondered why he had paid so little attention to her obvious interest in him thus far. He fantasized now how amazing it was going to be to touch her bare skin, to press his lips to her nipples, to hold her naked body up tight against his.

Inside her hut, they resumed kissing. Felix worked his hands through layer after layer of clothing, until he came to her soft warm skin. It was so smooth, and she shuddered as he ran his fingertips up the side of her waist.

They were there kissing and caressing for ten minutes when someone from outside the hut shouted, "Felix! Are you in there?"

Felix recognized Yuri's voice and decided not to answer. Both he and Natasha were naked from the waist up, and Felix was blind with desire. He felt like a balloon that was going to burst if it didn't release some air.

"Are you sure he's in there?" Yuri asked somebody.

"Yes, I saw him go in there," Volkhov answered.

"Felix! We have a New Year's present for you," Yuri hollered.

"Give it to me later," Felix called out as he pulled Natasha's supple body up close to his.

"No," Yuri said, "this one can't wait."

Felix kissed Natasha again then reluctantly pulled away. "Wait here," he whispered. "I'll be right back."

Natasha kept her arms around Felix's neck. "Don't go," she said.

"I'll be quick," he answered. "I know Yuri, and he's not going to leave me alone until I do this." He dressed quickly and went outside.

Yuri was standing with his rifle pointed at a young German soldier. Volkhov stood to the left of Yuri, and their commissar looked like a dwarf next to the massive Siberian.

"Here's your present," Yuri said, grinning. He was wearing his white camouflage but had a dark fur hat on. An inch of fresh snow lay on top of his hat.

Felix sighed. He had hoped to just grab some sort of gift of food or tobacco from them and then go back to Natasha. He was disappointed to realize that wasn't going to happen. "Where did you get him?" he asked Yuri.

The German soldier's eyes darted from speaker to speaker.

"On the road just south of us. There were two of them. I think they were lost."

"So where's the second one?"

"He was a little *stubborn*," Yuri said. "He didn't want to cooperate."

Felix understood that meant Yuri had shot the man. "All right," Felix said, "let's see if this one can tell us something interesting. Take him to our hut.

Comrade Volkhov, could you go get Sergei." Sergei was the newly joined partisan who spoke German.

"Already did," Volkhov answered. "He's waiting in our hut." Volkhov did a sharp turn and led the way. He took long strides for his size, and his boots made small, precise indentations in the snow.

The hut Felix, Yuri, Misha, and Volkhov shared was the largest of them all. In addition to being the place where they slept, it also served as a gathering place. When Felix crawled inside it now, he found it full of drunk and boisterous partisans. They were passing a bottle around, eating chocolate, and trading black humor jokes about the war. Felix considered kicking them outside, but the wind had started gusting and dark clouds now blotted out the light of the moon. Besides, they were all having a good time, and Felix wanted them to enjoy themselves.

He cleared people out of a corner of the hut and Yuri pushed the German down to the ground there. The German sat on the ground with his legs crossed, Yuri towering over him, gripping his rifle tightly and keeping his finger on the trigger. Felix wanted to tell him to relax, but had learned that never did any good with Yuri.

Volkhov sat next to Felix. Their translator, Sergei, sat between them and the German prisoner.

"Put out that candle," Felix ordered Sergei.

"But why, comrade?" Volkhov asked Felix. "It's not very light in here as it is."

Felix hated being in such close proximity to cockroaches, and the light made it worse.

"There's plenty of light in here without that candle," Felix said.

Sergei blew the candle out.

Volkhov had a pencil and a small notebook in his lap. "Have you been a part of many interrogations?" he asked Felix.

Felix thought back to when he and Dima were prisoners of the Germans. "A few," he answered.

"I haven't done any," Volkhov said, "so I'll defer to you for now."

Sergei asked the German something, got a response, then addressed Felix and Volkhov, "His name is Friedrich von Manstein."

"I didn't ask for his name," Felix said irritably.

"I'm sorry, comrade," Sergei replied. "I just assumed . . . ."

Felix didn't like to be reminded that the cockroaches had names. "Ask him where he was going tonight," he said.

Sergei conversed back and forth with the German for a minute or two. "Well?" Felix asked impatiently.

"He won't say," Sergei said.

"What?" Volkhov shouted over the din in the hut. "Speak up. We can't hear you."

"I said, 'He won't tell us,'" Sergei said louder.

Volkhov looked to Felix. Felix took a deep breath, letting it out slowly. He didn't want to be doing this right now.

"Tell him we'll kill him if he doesn't answer us," Felix said.

Sergei told the man, then reported back, "He says we're going to kill him anyway, so what does it matter."

Natasha came into the hut and asked Felix how much longer the interrogation would take. Felix smelled she was wearing perfume now and felt an intense desire rise from his waist and spread throughout his entire body. He shivered slightly and tried to refocus on the situation at hand.

Volkhov wiped his glasses on his shirt and said to Natasha, "As long as it needs to take."

Felix arched his eyebrows and gave Volkhov a sidelong glance, at which point Volkhov said, "My apologies, Comrade Lieutenant. She was obviously talking to you." He put his glasses back on and looked away.

"Tell him we'll give him a drink of alcohol and a cigarette if he tells us how many men they have defending the big hills south of here," Felix said to Sergei.

Sergei translated, then said back, "He says to give him the booze and cigarette first. Then he'll tell you."

Felix yelled to the four men playing cards in the opposite corner to pass him the bottle they were sharing. Then he gave it to the German and motioned for him to take a drink.

The young prisoner was dressed poorly for the cold weather. Instead of a winter coat, he wore an autumn jacket with a rain coat over top. His gloves were thin, and his thick, full beard was more likely out of necessity than anything else. There was a fresh scar on his left temple that looked like a bullet had recently grazed him. Felix reveled in the thought that it was probably from the rifle of one of his partisans. They'd been harassing the Germans for the past couple weeks.

The man took a big gulp from the bottle, then his face turned red and he fell into a coughing fit. Everyone in the hut laughed. Even Volkhov grinned.

"What's the matter, German," someone yelled. "Can't handle fine Russian liqueur?"

"That's Siberian tea!" someone else said. "It keeps you warm at night!"

"He probably thought it was beer!" another man yelled.

Felix waited for the men to stop laughing and for the German to stop coughing, then he addressed Sergei. "Tell him he'll get the cigarette after he answers us."

The German said something to Sergei, who then reported to Felix that he'd requested a drink of water.

"Not until we get an answer," Felix said.

The German started speaking at length and Sergei translated. "He says there's ten men . . ."

Volkhov held his hand to his ear. "What?" he shouted.

"Quiet down!" Felix yelled to everyone in the hut.

Sergei started again, "He says there's ten men there – two groups of three near the road, and a group of four on the right flank. He claims the left flank is currently undefended."

"He's lying," Volkhov said to Felix. "We know for a fact they have at least fifteen men defending those hills. We've spotted that many. Who knows how many more we haven't seen?"

Felix knew that already. That was why he started with that question – to see if the man was going to tell the truth.

"Tell him he's lying and we know it," Felix said. He smelled Natasha's perfume again and felt his patience for his current activity decline even further. He closed his eyes for a second and imagined taking Natasha's numerous layers of clothing off one by one.

The noise level had already returned to its previous level, and Sergei shouted over it, "Tell him what?"

"Felix," Natasha said, pulling on his sleeve, "come on. You should do this tomorrow."

Felix agreed. There was too much chaos for an interrogation. Besides, he'd much rather be back in Natasha's hut. "I think he'll be more willing to tell the truth after a night without food or heat," Felix said to Volkhov, then got up from his chair. He shook his head at how loud everyone was talking.

Yuri's long bushy eyebrows pulled together and thick wrinkles layered his forehead as he watched Felix put his mittens on and turn toward the door. "Are we giving up? You want me to shoot him?" he asked.

"You're finished?" Natasha said and smiled widely. "You're going to do it tomorrow?"

Felix glanced at her and saw how pleased she was. "Yes, might as well," he answered. "We're not getting anywhere."

The crack of a gun suddenly rang out and everyone in the hut stopped talking and turned their head to the corner where the German was. The man slumped sideways to the ground, a pool of blood forming on the ground below him.

Yuri still held tightly to the rifle he'd just fired. "What the hell did you just do?!" Felix yelled at him.

"I asked if you wanted me to shoot him," Yuri said, "and you said, 'Yes, might as well. We're not getting anywhere.'"

"I wasn't talking to *you!*" Felix said. He went over to the man and felt the pulse in his neck. It was fading fast. Felix rolled him onto his back so he could inspect the wound. It didn't take him long to find the small hole in the middle of the man's chest. Bright red blood was gushing out of it.

There was nothing to be done, Felix knew. The young man would be dead in a matter of minutes. He saw the edge of something white on the inside of the man's jacket and pulled out a small photograph. Felix was completely dumbfounded when he saw it. He had to look twice, then three times, then four before he was sure.

It was a picture of a young woman with a long thin neck, sad dark eyes, and hair that fell to the sides, naturally framing her face. There was an expression on her lips that looked almost like a smile, but not quite. Felix was convinced at first that it was Katya. Only after staring at the photo for a long time did he find the subtle differences that told him the woman was German. Still, he couldn't pull himself away from it. He was mesmerized by the uncanny likeness.

Volkhov came up and took the photo from Felix's hand to look at it.

"Felix, what's wrong?" Natasha asked. She took him by the arm and tried to get him to face her, but Felix shook free and fled to the outside. He was overcome with emotion and could hardly think. He had to get away from everyone and everything.

He went deep into the woods where he could be alone with the evergreens and the falling snow. They had been trying to communicate with him for a long time, he now knew. Thinking back to when he thought he'd heard the forest whispering his name, he felt angry and ashamed for having ignored it. He had done his best not to hear it, because he hadn't wanted to face the darkness he knew it would speak of. But now he had to listen. He had to know what it was trying to tell him.

As he opened himself to what it had to say, he was surprised to find a sense of comfort and familiarity coming from it. It was the same feeling as when he was a kid lost in the playground and heard his mother's voice calling him to her outstretched arms.

The thing spoke to him for hours, and Felix watched with intense curiosity the emotions that came and went in his mind as he contemplated what was said about the universe, his life, and why he was in this uncomfortable situation of war and separation. He recalled the mystical experience he'd had as a boy with the being named Ariel, remembering how it said that he had chosen a challenging path for this life – how he would either succumb to bitterness and contempt, or undergo a great transformation under the most trying of circumstances. Felix could see now that the decision was his.

He closed his eyes to think, leaning his head back so that the snow fell onto his face. And all the while, Katya and the German woman in the photo looked down at him; waiting, it seemed, for him to emerge from a black thick-walled cocoon that he was just now beginning to see surrounded him.

The morning came quickly, and after tossing and turning for several hours trying to get to sleep Felix was glad the night was over. He lit a candle and placed it at the foot of his bed, then tried to pack his things quietly so as not to wake Yuri, Misha, and Volkhov.

When he came to Katya's letter, he held it to his nose and inhaled. She'd put a purple lilac flower in it, but he could no longer smell its fragrance. He ran his fingers along the paper. Then he unfolded it carefully and admired the thin, flowing style of her handwriting. In the top corner, she'd drawn a picture of a unicorn flying toward a crescent moon.

Yuri began to stir, and Felix quickly folded the letter, tucked it in his pocket, and finished packing. Just as he was getting ready to leave, Yuri awoke and turned his head toward Felix. He saw the pack and rifle around Felix's shoulders and asked, "Where are we going now?"

Felix had planned on slipping out unnoticed and just leaving a note behind, but now he decided to tell. "I'm going to Leningrad," he said.

"Very funny," Misha said, now awake. "Seriously, where are you going?" He sat up in bed, then groaned in agony. "Oh, that hurts," he said and held his hand to his forehead. "You know most everyone is probably a bit hung over. Can't we stay put at least one more day?"

"I don't recall us discussing any plans for moving out today," Volkhov, now also awake, said. "Did we finally get our orders?"

"No, the orders haven't come yet. You might as well stay put until they do," Felix said.

"Son-of-a-bitch," Misha muttered. "You're serious, aren't you? You're leaving."

"Comrade, what is this about?" Volkhov asked.

Misha took a quick drink of water from his canteen. "How the hell do you think you're going to get to Leningrad?" he said.

"Over the Ice Road," Felix answered.

"Over Lake Ladoga? That's crazy," Yuri said.

"You might make it to the lake," Volkhov said, "but I doubt you'll get across it. If the Germans don't stop you, then your own comrades in the Red Army will."

"He's right," Misha said. "They're not going to let you cross the lake and they're sure as hell not going to let you in the city. I'm speaking from experience here. I was nearly sent to the firing squad when I entered the city without permission back in August."

"I know this is difficult to understand, but it's something I need to do," Felix said.

"What on earth is this about," Volkhov asked again.

"This isn't about that girl you left behind, is it?" Misha said. "She's probably dead, and even if she's not, what can *you* do?"

"I don't know," Felix said. "But I'm going. I know that."

"Your country needs you *here*," Volkhov said, stressing the last word.

"*We* need you here," Yuri chimed in. He had his massive arms folded tightly in front of his chest. "Don't betray us like this."

"This has nothing to do with *you*," Felix said.

"The fight is here, comrade," Volkhov said. "It's not in Leningrad."

"Yes, listen to him," Yuri said. "He's right. We have to *fight* now. If we don't, we lose. That's why we're here – to fight for what's right."

Felix felt a strange sensation inside of him. With every word they said, it grew bigger. The harder they pushed, the larger this thing grew in return so it could push back. Felix couldn't put it into words, but he knew without a doubt they were wrong. This logic, this intellectual reasoning, this curse of the twentieth century, was a trap. It was a trick man played on one another so that no one thought outside the acceptable boundaries.

"Felix, you believe in equality, right?" Volkhov said. "In justice? In freedom? That's what the fight is about. This isn't just a battle to kick the Nazis off our land. This is a battle for what's *right*. We're fighting on behalf of the entire world against evil. You're not going to turn your back on the world, are you? Who's going to fight for those with no voice?"

He hit on Felix's weakness. That was how they always got to him and convinced him to keep playing the game. He felt himself slip a little, starting to fall prey to that insatiable beast.

"Comrade, you've been blinded by your personal desires," Volkhov continued. "Can't you see that? Love has no role in this world. Love, romance, compassion – they're all dead. They're tired cliches, useless concepts, that have no value anymore. You're stuck in that . . . in those fairy tales from the past. You've got to pull yourself out of it. The only emotion that's helpful these days is hate. It's fuel. It'll keep you alive. Hate is the only way we're going to win this war. That's what the Nazis came here with, and that's why they've been winning so far. We've got to 'out-hate' our enemies if we want to win."

Felix slipped another inch closer to the trap, but then the thing inside him suddenly swelled to twice its size and pushed the poison out of his head. Silently, Felix asked this thing, "What are you?" In response, he heard Katya's voice whispering that poem in his ear on that warm summer day last June: *Love is the beginning, and Love is the end, and here in the middle is where we must mend.* He had to go to her and he had to go now. He'd never been so sure of anything in his life.

"I'm going," Felix said with finality. "I hope none of you try to stop me." He was referring specifically to Volkhov and looked at him now.

Volkhov got up from his straw bed and put his glasses on. "In the short time I've known you," he said, "you've earned my respect. I won't try to stop you, but know, too, that I can't defend your decision if you're caught."

"I understand," Felix said. He handed Volkhov an envelope addressed to Katya. "Could you send this out in the next batch for me?"

Volkhov took it and nodded.

Felix had written several letters to Katya, though he had his doubts as to whether any of them made it to her. He began tightening his coat and scarf around him, getting ready for the bitter cold outside. Volkhov went to the other end of the hut with the letter, and Yuri began rummaging through his things looking for something. Felix pulled his hat down tight, took a deep breath and said to his three comrades, "I hope we all meet again one day after this madness is over. We'll drink a bottle or two and tell some jokes."

No one responded.

Felix saluted, said goodbye, then headed toward the door. Yuri grabbed Felix's right arm and stuck something in his hand. "You'll need this," Yuri said.

Felix looked down at his hand and saw some rubles. He had no money himself and felt very grateful. It was hard to come by these days and would come in handy if he needed to buy food when he got to Leningrad.

He looked up at Yuri's face, at that big forehead, bushy eyebrows, and dark eyes. "Thank you, my friend," Felix said.

"It's nothing," Yuri responded with a wave of his arm.

Felix knew better. He stepped forward and they embraced for a second, patting each other on the back.

Before Felix got to the door, Misha called out to him. "Wait," he said. "Let me go with you."

"No," Felix answered. "This is something I need to do on my own." He pulled the blanket hanging at the doorway aside and a gust of wind blew snow and cold air into the hut, extinguishing the candle at the foot of Felix's bed.

* * *

Misha finally caught up with Felix two hours later when Felix stopped at an infirmary. Misha had set out twenty minutes after him and followed his tracks from camp until they ended at the scattered tents erected on the frozen field. The infirmary was a dismal place that didn't have much to offer in the way of care. The first tent Misha went into had a sickening stench and was full of soldiers with chest wounds. Their sallow, expressionless faces reminded him of the dream he had where he was following the dead people. He felt nauseous and hastily left the tent. Except for a few scratches and bruises, he hadn't been wounded in the war and felt so very grateful for that now.

He found Felix in the third tent he checked. He was sitting next to one of the stoves warming his hands on a cup of tea. Misha walked up to him and said, "Wow, fancy meeting you here."

Felix looked up, but if he was surprised, he didn't show it. "Why are you here?" he asked.

"Just thought you could use some company, that's all," Misha said.

Felix pointed with his head to the other side of the tent. "There's some cups over there."

Misha went over and got a cup, filled it with hot water from the large homemade samovar, then sat down next to Felix. "What do you think? Are you impressed I found you?"

"No," Felix said. "I've learned that you're quite capable. If you set your mind to do something, you'll do it."

Misha squirmed in his seat. He'd been raised on criticism and felt uncomfortable with compliments or praise or anything even approaching it. He studied Felix's face, looking at the pink scar on his cheek just below his right eye where a bullet had grazed him in one of their first battles to retake Tikhvin. Misha was jealous of him. Felix had a way of being in the world that Misha didn't. Felix did all the same activities that Misha did – eating, drinking, sleeping, planning, fighting – but Felix did them all with a sense of purpose. Misha desperately wanted to figure out what this purpose was so he could live his life that way too. Even more than that though, Misha just wanted to be around Felix and help out any way he could.

He poured the hot water down his throat like it was a shot a vodka. "What are we waiting for?" he said and stood up. "Let's get going. Leningrad, here we come!"

Leningrad was two hundred miles east of Tikhvin. The first goal of their journey was to reach the town of Kabona on the edge of Lake Ladoga. Next was to gain access to the lake, then hitch a ride across it, then onto the road to Leningrad, and, lastly, into the city itself.

It took them seven days to get to Kabona – one to get arrested on the way there, three for Misha to talk and bribe them into letting he and Felix go, and three for the actual journey.

Kabona was a former sleepy village on the edge of Lake Ladoga that was quickly being transformed into a bustling port. Misha had actually driven through there before the war. Back then, it was a typical Russian village with a few hundred inhabitants working as fishermen in the summer and lumberjacks in the winter. It looked very different now. There were newly built warehouses and barracks, and lots of tents to house the road maintenance crews, drivers, and anti-aircraft garrisons. Everywhere Misha looked, he saw soldiers and civilians walking to and fro. There were hundreds of trucks and ambulances and staff cars, the majority of which were headed for the lake.

Felix and Misha walked past the village huts amid the sound of barking dogs. It wasn't long before the frozen expanse of Lake Ladoga came into view. It was the largest lake in Europe – 125 miles long and nearly 80 miles across at its widest point.

There were several roads leading to the lake, but they were all being filtered through one central gateway where Red Army soldiers stopped every truck and reviewed the papers of each of its occupants. Felix and Misha tried to hitch a ride with the trucks beforehand, but none of the drivers would take them through a checkpoint. They all said the same thing, "See me on the other side."

After having no success at three of the four checkpoints, Felix and Misha approached the last one feeling quite desperate. At the previous three, the soldiers wouldn't even talk to them as soon as they learned Felix and Misha didn't have the proper authorization to travel across the lake.

The traffic had thinned in the last fifteen minutes and the two soldiers Felix and Misha walked up to had no trucks waiting in their line.

"Let me do most of the talking," Misha said when they were less than ten yards away.

One of the soldiers was well over six feet tall and had a long drooping nose. The other man was short and had lots of acne scars on his cheeks. They both had the same fatigued, unhappy look on their faces as the others Felix and Misha had already spoken to. "Papers," the short one demanded and held out his hand.

Misha had tried to forge an official order but it hadn't fooled any of the others. He took it out now and handed it to the man, hoping for the best.

The man looked it over quickly and handed it back to Misha. "That's not getting you onto the lake," he said.

"What do you mean?" Misha asked. "Those are official orders from our commanding officer, Major Lestov."

"That may be," the man replied. "But they're not getting you past this checkpoint."

"What do we need to do to get past this checkpoint?" Misha asked.

"Get a valid pass," the man replied dryly.

"How do we go about that?"

The man shrugged his shoulders. "That's your problem," he said.

"Comrades, please! This is very important," Felix said. "I need to get to Leningrad as soon as possible. What's it to you if you let us pass?"

Misha cringed at Felix's words. He knew that wasn't going to work.

"We have strict orders from our commanding officer," the man said. "If it was up to me, I'd let you pass."

"Don't give me that!" Felix said angrily. "*You* are the one standing here who won't let us pass. No one else. Take some responsibility for your actions. Stop hiding behind the Red Army bureaucracy."

Felix's words had the opposite intended effect, as Misha knew they would. The men hardened their position and even threatened Misha and Felix with arrest.

For all Felix's leadership skills and bravery, he was clueless when it came to delicate situations like this. But Misha was pleased that he could help, pleased that he could do something better than Felix.

He convinced Felix to step back about fifty feet while he had a few words with the two men.

"You'll have to excuse the Lieutenant," Misha said. "His girl is in Leningrad, and we all know the situation there."

Both men nodded their heads and seemed to soften a little.

"They say 3,000 to 4,000 die every single day there," Misha continued. "So you can see why he's eager to get there."

"Without the appropriate orders, you aren't getting past this point," the short one said. "Now I suggest you turn back around and . . ."

"Whoa, let's slow down here," Misha said, pulling out a pack of cigarettes. "There's no reason why we can't discuss this a little and make sure we understand one another, right?" The two men eyed Misha's pack of cigarettes like it was a can of caviar. Misha had already made sure the pack contained five cigarettes. He took one for himself, then offered one each to the men. They looked around to make sure no one was looking, then each accepted the offer.

Misha lit his cigarette and offered the two men a light as well. They refused, choosing instead to tuck the cigarettes in their pockets.

"So what's the ration situation like around here?" Misha asked.

The tall one slowly shook his head. The short one said, "It's getting a little better."

"They give you plenty of bread?" Misha asked.

"Yes, we get enough bread," the short one replied. "Just hardly anything to go with it."

"That's not right," Misha said. "They probably save the good stuff for themselves."

The tall one nodded his head. "I saw the Major eating salted pork yesterday," he said to the short one.

"You guys have a harder job than just about anybody," Misha said. "If anyone deserves better rations, it's you guys. They should try your job for a week – standing on your feet all day long in this freezing cold day in and day out. Then they'd know how hard it is." Misha pulled out his flask and offered each of them a sip. "Go ahead," he said. "Nobody's looking."

They each took a sip and coughed afterwards. "It's strong stuff, huh?" Misha said, grinning. "That'll warm you up in no time." He took a small parcel from his pack and began to undo the paper it was wrapped in. "Perhaps the two of you might also enjoy this," he said. He finished opening it and gave them a peek at the cream-colored lump that was about the size of a tin of sardines. "It'll make that bread taste ten times better."

"Is that butter?" the short one asked.

"*Not* just butter," Misha said. "It's sweet cream butter. The best you've ever tasted."

The tall one reached for it. "Let me taste it," he said.

Misha pulled it away. "No, no," he said, "I don't work that way." He wrapped it back up. "You can taste the whole thing if you let me and the Lieutenant pass."

Neither man responded, instead looking to the other for the answer. Misha knew he had them. "Comrades," he said, "what's there to think about?"

Finally, the short one straightened up and tried to look resolute. "Throw in a pack of cigarettes and we'll look the other way for a minute," he said.

"Unfortunately, I'm down to my last pack," Misha said. He got it out of his pocket. "Just two measly cigarettes are all I have left."

The short one looked at him and pushed him bottom lip up. "Then give us each another cigarette," he said.

"You drive a hard bargain," Misha said.

The man smiled, revealing two missing upper teeth.

Misha actually had several more packs of cigarettes and anticipated having to give a few of them away in addition to the 'butter.'

"Here you go," Misha said, giving them each another cigarette. Then he handed them the butter. "I suggest you keep that well hidden," he added. "I'm sure you know the penalty for bribery." He imitated the sound of a gun firing.

The man stuck the butter in his pocket. "Just get going," he said gruffly, "before we change our minds."

Misha motioned with his arm to Felix and when he arrived the two soldiers pretended to be busy inspecting some spot on the ground.

"Come on," Misha said to Felix, "let's hurry."

"How did you get them to let us pass?" Felix asked.

"I bribed them with some butter," Misha said, quickening his pace.

"Butter? I didn't know you had any of that."

"I didn't," Misha said. "It's just soap. That's why we need to hurry."

Felix laughed and walked faster to keep up with Misha. They could see the ant-like lines of vehicles going in every direction across the lake in front of them.

"So tell me the truth," Felix said. "Why did you decide to join me?"

"I already told you," Misha answered. "I just thought you could use some help. You'd probably still be under arrest if it weren't for me. And you certainly never would have gotten past that checkpoint by yourself."

"There's no doubt you're a tremendous help," Felix said. "It took a little while. You were always drunk when I first met you, but I've learned I can count on you. You always come through. I've come to trust you and think of you as more than just a fellow soldier. I consider you my friend."

Misha felt a little choked up by what Felix had just said. It was a perfect example of why Misha had decided to join him. Felix was honest. He always spoke the truth, – sometimes to a fault. He wasn't afraid to express his gratitude or tell you how he truly felt about something. In short, Felix was able to do those things that Misha wished *he* could do.

"I'm still waiting for the real reason you came," Felix said.

"I guess I just like working with you," Misha said. "I don't have to pretend when I'm around you."

They walked on in silence for a minute, then Felix said, "I'm glad you're here."

Misha felt choked up again. Nobody had ever said that to him before. Amazing what a few kind words could do to somebody.

"We'll get to Leningrad," Misha said. "One way or another, we're gonna get there."

* * *

They were packed in tight in the cab of the truck and Felix struggled to get his arm out from behind Misha's so he could have a drink of water from his canteen. He had no idea how Misha had managed to get the truck driver to take them over Lake Ladoga, but he'd learned that Misha was quite good at that sort of thing. If a situation came up that involved bartering or bribery, Felix knew to let Misha handle it.

Their truck was only one of a twelve-truck convoy, and their convoy was only one of a never-ending stream of convoys going to Leningrad and back again. Twenty-four hours a day, seven days a week, the trucks rolled on.

The driver was jittery, didn't say much, and kept his left hand on the door as if he might jump out at any second and let the truck go on without him. He used his teeth to pull the mitten off his right hand, then took a cigarette out from his coat pocket. Both Felix and Misha noticed that his last two fingers had been severed below the knuckle.

"What happened?" Misha asked.

"The first truck I drove didn't have any heat," he said matter-of-factly.

Felix didn't understand at first, then it dawned on him. Frostbite. Sitting motionless in an unheated truck for hours on end with the nighttime temperature dipping to forty-five degrees below zero . . . he had to have two of his fingers amputated.

"Lucky they gave you this truck," Misha said. "It's got a good heater. What did they do with your old truck?"

The driver pointed below them.

"What do you mean?" Misha asked. "It's in the lake?"

"A few weeks after I started, there was a thaw," he said. "I jumped out just in time."

Felix understood now why the man kept his left hand on the door at all times.

"I take it you didn't fall in the water," Misha said.

The driver shook his head. "You fall in the water, you're dead in less than ten minutes."

After a short time, they came upon a small hand-painted sign that read, "Дорога Жизни" – Road of Life. Next to the sign was a snow-covered car sticking halfway out of a large bomb crater in the ice.

Every hundred feet along the road there was a small, colorful flag sticking out of the snow. The driver said they were markers to help them follow the road. If you saw a red flag, that was a warning to take a detour around a thin spot in the ice. In addition to the flags, there were traffic controllers every few hundred yards directing the convoys. The men wore white camouflage robes that stretched all the way to the snow, covering their dark boots. They had snub-nosed automatic guns slung around their necks and wore extra cartridge belts slung across their chest in a X formation.

Felix saw a board lying on the ice and a little flag fluttering in the wind above it. "What's that?" he asked the driver.

"That means there's open water there – a bomb crater. It'll be frozen over again in a day or two and they'll remove the board."

The driver had to hit the brakes suddenly to avoid hitting the truck in front of him. There wasn't much space between the trucks in the convoy and neither were the drivers to allow much.

"What are you hauling?" Misha asked.

"Food," came the response.

"Well, that's what they need, I've heard," Misha said. "How are things going in Leningrad?"

The driver turned his head to Misha and stared, expressionless. "You want to know how things are going in Leningrad?" he repeated. "Here comes your answer." He nodded his head toward a caravan of cars and trucks up ahead. They were stopped because the front truck was apparently experiencing some mechanical difficulties. One man stood leaning over the top of the engine, and another man was lying on the snow underneath the engine.

Felix and Misha leaned forward so they could get a better look. The vehicles in the caravan, like all vehicles on the lake, had been painted white for camouflage. The large army truck at the front was loaded with Leningraders fleeing the city. Felix saw them crammed into the back, peering out with ungodly big eyes and thin faces. He saw the red and white frost marks on their cheeks and knew they were already half-dead. They were little more than skeletons with skin, and Felix felt terrified. Was the entire city like this? Full of these subhuman creatures on the verge of dying at any moment? He shuddered to think that Katya might look like the people in the back of that truck.

Behind the truck was a bus that had obviously been outfitted with heat – puffs of smoke came out of a tin chimney in its roof. Behind the bus was a carload of people. The car could comfortably fit seven, maybe eight. Felix counted eleven people packed into it. Those seated in the back had a large tank of some sort on their laps. It was so crowded that Felix doubted they could move an arm or a leg more than an inch or two.

"What's that big tank on their laps?" Felix asked.

"Probably gasoline," the driver replied.

Felix imagined how miserable they must be – packed in there so tightly, gasoline fumes filling the air, stuck in an unmoving vehicle on a road of ice where the outside temperature was well below zero. And the Germans might attack with their long-range artillery or planes at any moment. He started to wonder how bad the situation in the city could be that people would submit themselves to that. Then he glanced back at the skeletons in the front truck and understood why they'd left.

In a truck behind the car, four men were dragging a body out and toward a round crater filled with blue water. The men had to stop and rest every few yards as they dragged the corpse over the ice. Felix could hardly comprehend it. He alone could pick up that thin corpse, toss it over his shoulder, and carry it to the crater in a matter of seconds. What had happened to these people? Were these just the extremely ill who were being evacuated? Felix could not – would not – believe that the whole city was filled with people like this. But certainly every person in the caravan before him was. All five trucks, two buses and three cars were packed full with half-dead men, women, and even children.

"I've heard dystrophy is rampant in the city," Felix said to the driver. "Are all these people sick with it?"

"Some, I imagine," he replied, shrugging his shoulders.

"Where are they going?" Misha asked.

"To their graves, most likely," the driver answered. "Most of them are too far gone to be saved."

"But I heard they increased the rations," Misha said.

"Too little, too late," the driver said.

Felid had to close his eyes. He couldn't take it all in. He had the thought that he was too late – that Katya was already dead. She was thin to begin with. She had no fat reserves to call upon.

When they passed the caravan, Felix looked in the mirror and watched the cars and trucks slowly disappear into the endless whiteness that surrounded them. He was impressed with how well the white camouflage worked but then looked out the window and saw the dark shadow the truck created. The sun never got very high in the sky this time of year, and there was no way German planes could miss the hundred-foot long shadow the truck made.

After another twenty minutes, the traffic slowed to a crawl again. There were abandoned and wrecked cars and trucks alongside the road, victims of either the cold weather, the perilous road, or the German Luftwaffe. After a few more minutes of slow going, their convoy came to a complete stop and Felix and Misha got out to stretch their legs and smoke a cigarette. A pair of nurses with sheepskin coats skied up close to them. They had red crosses on their left arms, submachine guns around their shoulders, and pulled small sleds packed full with medical supplies.

Misha nudged Felix with his arm. "Girls," he said, pointing at them.

The nurses heard and stopped when they reached him. "That's *Lieutenant*," the second one said, "and you'll salute before addressing me."

Misha came to attention and promptly saluted. "My apologies, Comrade Lieutenant," he said.

"Do you know what the hold up is about, Comrade Lieutenant?" Felix asked.

"There's only one lane open ahead," she said. "There's a large bomb crater in the road that hasn't frozen over yet."

"Those certainly look warm," Misha said, referring to their sheepskin coats.

"They are," the first one responded, "but they don't smell so good."

A long caravan of peasant sledges approached and began to pass by. The sledges were filled with straw and pulled by tired horses rhythmically nodding their head with each step. The horses had hoar-frost on their fur and their ribs stuck out.

The driver suddenly grabbed his automatic submachine gun and jumped out of the truck. "Down!" he yelled and started running away from the truck.

Felix couldn't understand why. Were the sledges part of a German trap?

The nurses started to ski away, then Felix saw the peasants halt their sledges and throw dirty white sheets over the horses. Two people emerged from the straw in the back of each sledge and started running away.

Then Felix heard it. Planes.

He and Misha ran about fifteen yards, then dove to the ground just as the bombs started whistling through the air. They exploded on the ice and sent geysers of water streaming into the sky.

An anti-aircraft battery that he hadn't seen before began pounding at the planes. The big guns were hidden behind walls of ice blocks and a heavy snow-laden net that sunk low over the top. Everything was camouflaged in white. Even the guns had been painted white.

The low-flying planes with the black crosses on their wings roared over Felix and Misha and then started to make a giant loop around for another pass. While they did that, a second wave of planes dropped their bombs on the column of trucks and sledges. Felix watched as one of the sledges, horse and all, suffered a direct hit and disappeared into the lake.

The deafening sounds of explosions and rushing water filled the air. When the second wave reached them, Felix rolled onto his back, aimed his rifle, and squeezed off several shots. The bullets clanged off the underbelly of the planes.

After the second wave came a third wave of planes. The bombs squealed as they dropped down to the ice. Felix could see several of the trucks burning, but so far the one he and Misha had been riding in had been spared.

The first wave of planes had circled around and was strafing the convoy with their machine guns now. The bullets hissed as they hit the ice. Felix heard one of the horses neigh wildly and watched its rear legs slump to the ice. The sledge's driver got up from the ice, shook his fist at the German planes, cursing them at the top of his voice. A second later, bullets cut him down and a pool of blood formed around his lifeless body.

It wasn't until the third wave of planes was flying over for the second time that the anti-aircraft guns finally hit one. The plane's left wing was split in two and the plane spun out of control, hitting the frozen lake with a tremendous thud that shook the ice and made long, lightening-like cracks in the ice that extended in all directions.

"Yeah!! Take that you bastards!" Felix heard someone shout.

Once the anti-aircraft guns stopped firing, Felix heard lots of shouting, but quickly realized they were not shouts of victory or vengeance, but of agony. Several people had been wounded in the attack.

Half of the dozen trucks in their convoy were on fire. The ice was dotted with craters where the dark blue water of the lake stood in stark contrast to the whiteness all around. The truck Felix and Misha had been riding in wasn't on fire, but it had been struck repeatedly by the planes' machine guns. Felix doubted it would be going anywhere for a while – if at all.

"Looks like you're going to have to dig into your bag of tricks and get us another ride over that lake," Felix said to Misha.

Misha didn't reply, and Felix turned around and saw he was still lying in the thick snow on top of the ice. "Misha," he shouted. "It's over. They're gone. You can get up now."

Still no response.

Felix felt his stomach tighten. "Misha!" he called out even louder and walked toward him.

As he got nearer, he saw the awful red snow under Misha's head. He knelt down and gently rolled Misha over. His right eye was drenched with blood and he was unconscious. One of the nurses skied over and kneeled down next to Felix. She worked without her mittens, placing her fingers in her mouth from time-to-time to keep them warm.

"He's still alive," she said after a minute, "but he needs to see a doctor. We have to get him to a medical station right away."

"We passed one not too long ago," Felix said.

"Yes, that's the closest one. It's about a mile and a half from here," she said.

Felix hesitated, looking to the other side of the lake where Leningrad was. If he went back with Misha, he'd be delayed for several hours – perhaps even a day. He started to mull over his options, but then stopped himself. He knew what he had to do.

He started looking for a means of transportation to take them to the medical station. The trucks were out, so that left the sledges. Carefully, Felix circled around the wide cracks in the ice that led to the numerous bomb craters. He saw four men gathered around the horse that had been wounded. They had cut open its belly and were emptying the still-warm carcass of its internal organs. They did it all with their bare hands, then dumped the inedible parts down one of the bomb craters. The horse's carcass was tied to one of the sledges to be dragged along behind. Its meat would not be wasted.

Felix came up to one of the sledge drivers as he shoveled fresh snow over the blood stains the horse had left on the ice. "Help me bury those two men," the man said to Felix, nodding with his head toward two bodies a little ways away from them.

Together they dragged the two bloody corpses to the nearest crater and dropped them in.

"Did you know them?" Felix asked.

"I was transporting them in my sledge," the man said.

"So you have some free space now?" Felix asked hopefully. "Can you take me and my comrade who's been wounded to the nearest medical station?"

The man shook his head. "My orders are to return immediately once I've finished. There's others waiting."

Felix tried to think of what Misha would do or say to convince the man. "We have some cigarettes we could give you," he said.

"I don't smoke," the man replied and started to walk away.

"Wait," Felix said, taking him by the arm. "My friend is badly injured. He needs to get to a medical station right away."

"There'll be a sledge along shortly to pick up the wounded," the man said.

"No, he can't wait."

"He'll have to. I'm not going that direction." The man tried to free his arm, but Felix wouldn't let go.

"I'll make you a deal," Felix said.

"What kind of deal?"

"You agree to take us to the medical station . . ."

"And?"

"And I promise I won't shoot you."

The man was taken aback. He opened his mouth but didn't say anything.

"Yes?" Felix said.

The man nodded his head slowly.

They loaded Misha into the back of the sledge, then Felix jumped in and covered them both with some straw to keep warm. The driver cracked his whip and the horse started forward.

It was a painfully slow trip. The horse moved just slightly faster than Felix could have walked. When they finally arrived at the medical station, it was dark and Misha was still unconscious. A pair of nurses came out of an ice hut and they helped roll Misha onto a stretcher and get him inside.

A young female doctor inspected his eye and promptly decided they needed to operate. They took him behind some curtains and told Felix to go to the hut next door and see if they had any room for him to sleep that night.

Felix didn't sleep well once again. He laid awake most of the night thinking either about Katya or Misha. He got up and left the hut just as the sun rose around ten in the morning.

Outside, he noticed one other ice hut in addition to the one he'd slept in and the one that served as a medical station. Two men came out of the hut, talking about how this was the harshest winter they could ever remember. Felix wanted some company and was pleased to see them walk in his direction. When they saw Felix and the lieutenant insignia on his coat, they saluted and walked on in silence.

Felix took his mittens off, then undid the insignia from his coat and put it in his pocket. He hated that a little piece of metal had such a profound effect on some people. It created a distance between them before they'd even met.

A truck with a humongous black pot in the back pulled up and the elderly woman driver honked the horn a few times before climbing out. Felix smelled something delicious – stew maybe – and realized this truck was the field kitchen.

"Good morning, young man," the woman said. "Are you hungry?"

"Always," Felix replied. He never got to eat three meals a day anymore. He ate *when* he could and *if* he could. It was usually the case that he got one meal a day, then snacked on some bread before he went to sleep.

The woman came closer and looked him over. "I can tell you're not from Leningrad," she said.

"No, but that's where I'm going," Felix replied.

"Well then you better get your fill now," she said. "Ain't no food in the city."

She got a large ladle out of the cab and then climbed up on the back of the truck. When she opened the lid on the black pot, a cloud of steam rose up. She stuck the ladle inside and began to stir.

"You got a bowl?" she asked.

"No."

"I've got one you can use then," she said. "But you have to give it back to me before I leave." She scooped a large helping of stew into a tin bowl and handed it to Felix. "There's some bread in there," she said, pointing to a bin next to the little fire under the pot. "Just pull that door up."

Felix opened it and saw a hundred thick slices of black bread. He could tell just by looking at it that it was good quality. He took a piece and settled onto a snow drift. Then he pulled his spoon out of his boot and started to eat.

The nurses, three in all, came out of the first hut and half a dozen soldiers out of the second and third huts. They all had their bowls in hand.

Felix asked one of the nurses how Misha was doing.

"He just woke up," she answered. "The doctor is checking him over now, but you can go see him in a few minutes if you like."

"Yes, I'll do that," Felix said. "Thank you."

When everyone had been served, the woman began packing things up to go to her next stop. Before she left, Felix went up to her and gave her the tin bowl back. She looked around and, seeing no one, slipped Felix a few extra pieces of bread. "Here," she said, "you're going to need this if you're going to Leningrad. Be safe."

Felix thanked her, then she got into the truck and pulled away in a cloud of exhaust.

Another truck pulled up just as the field kitchen departed and a woman opened the passenger-side door and hollered for Felix to help her carry a wounded man inside. The soldier was bleeding badly from his right leg and couldn't walk.

Felix helped get him inside, then went to check on Misha. He found his friend in the far corner. A pretty, young nurse with curly blonde hair was feeding him stew one spoonful at a time.

Felix held out his hand for the bowl. "I can do this," he said to her. "I'm sure you have plenty of other things you need to."

She handed him the stew. "Thank you, comrade," she said.

"What are you doing?" Misha said after the nurse was out of hearing range. "She completely adored me."

Felix laughed. He was glad Misha seemed to be himself already. There was a patch covering the eye that had been wounded, but other than that he looked fine.

"How are you feeling?" Felix asked.

"I've got one hell of a headache," Misha answered, "but the doctor tells me I'm lucky to be alive. She pulled one piece of shrapnel out. She thinks there might be another one, too, but said she couldn't find it."

"Is your eye going to be all right?"

Misha shook his head slightly. "What eye?" he said. "She took it out."

"I'm sorry," Felix said.

"Don't worry about it. This could be a good look for me," Misha joked. "Women love war heroes. And plus I've always wanted to be a pirate." He laughed at his joke then sat up in bed. A second later, he got a glazed look on his face and his head began going in circles.

A nurse rushed over and laid him back down. "Comrade, I told you not to try to get up. You've had a concussion and it's going to take a while for you to get your sense of balance back."

"Looks like I won't be going anywhere for a while," Misha said to Felix.

"How long will it take?" Felix asked the nurse.

"A few days minimum," she answered. "Possibly a week."

The truck driver who'd brought the wounded man, and the woman who'd hollered for Felix to help were in the hut. Felix overheard the truck driver saying his farewell to the woman.

"Off so soon?" the nurse standing next to Felix said.

"Yes," the driver answered. "Leningrad needs me."

"You're going to Leningrad now?" Felix asked.

The driver nodded. "You want a ride?"

Felix hesitated and looked at Misha.

"I know what you're thinking," Misha said. "You don't have to wait for me. I'll be all right."

357

"You sure?" Felix asked.

"Of course," Misha said. "Get out of here."

"Yes, I'll go with you," Felix said to the driver.

"All right. I'm leaving in five minutes," the driver said and left the hut.

Felix turned back to Misha, grabbed him by the arm and squeezed. "Listen," he said, "you've done a lot for me and I want to thank you for . . ."

"No, no. It was nothing," Misha interrupted.

"You don't even know what I was going to say thank you for," Felix said.

"Whatever it is, it was nothing," Misha said. "Let's just shake hands and say, 'Til next time.'"

Felix thought a moment. "No, I'm not going to do that. We might not ever see one another again and I don't want to regret not saying the things that need to be said. You've helped me and supported me every step of the way, and I wouldn't have made it this far without you."

Misha, clearly uncomfortable, started fidgeting with his hands.

"You've been a good friend, and . . ."

"Oh, come on, stop it," Misha said. "I'm just a drunk – a fool."

"No," Felix said emphatically. "You're not."

Misha was quiet, then slowly turned his head and met Felix's eyes. "Thanks," he said.

Felix got up to leave. "I won't forget you."

Misha smiled. His eye was watery. "You take care of yourself, Felix."

"You too," Felix said. "Goodbye, my friend."

"Do me a favor," Misha said as Felix started to walk away. "Before you leave, ask that nurse if she'll finish feeding me."

Felix laughed. "Okay," he said. "I'll do that."

* * *

It was morning and Petya was on his hands and knees on the sidewalk in front of their building. He was looking for clues as to his *mission* in the ice underneath the snow. It was a tedious process – scraping away inch after inch of compacted snow until the ice underneath could be seen. He thought for sure this was where God would leave the instructions for him.

For weeks, Petya had been using a magnifying glass to study the ice formations in the frost on their apartment windows because Katya told him that if he looked long and hard he'd find God's message there. She said God's message "was everywhere," but the ice crystals on the windows were a good place to start. Petya tried it for weeks, but couldn't find a single letter or number. He'd asked Katya to tell him what words she could see, but she only replied that God didn't communicate in Russian. When he asked what language he *did* communicate in, she'd only say that one had to figure that out for themselves.

Petya didn't believe her anymore, and as he carefully scraped away another patch of snow and recognized the Russian letter "К" in the ice, he was sure she'd been misleading him all this time. Of course the crack in the ice could have just been a random squiggle that by chance looked like a "К," but that's exactly what God would want the average person to think. His message was meant only for Petya, and Petya knew that squiggle that looked like a "К" was no mere coincidence.

It was a cloudless, windless day and the morning sun was shining brightly. It was bitterly cold out, and every time Petya exhaled, his breath obscured his vision. He used his hand to try to redirect the air from his mouth. After the "К," he found a "Д" and was especially pleased to have found two letters in one day. He'd add them to the ones he'd found on previous days: "А," "З," "Ц," "Х," and "Я." That afternoon, he'd see if he could arrange the letters into a word.

As he got up from the sidewalk, his left suspender came unhooked from his pants. He'd lost 83 pounds since the start of the blockade and suspenders were the only way he could keep any of his pants up. His weight – finally stable at 123 – was undeniably better than most. Many a man in the city considered himself fortunate if he weighed over 100.

He re-fastened the suspender and went to check the large bulletin board in the middle of their block. There were a number of pieces of paper on it, most of which Petya had already seen:

> *Missing: Five-year-old girl with black hair and brown eyes. Was last seen walking from here toward Nevsky Prospekt . . .*

> *For Sale: Phonograph and records, man's leather boots and fur coat, baby crib . . .*

> *Will remove corpses for food . . .*

The last one was his. He'd put them up all over the city. It was the only way he was making it through the blockade. All the able-bodied men were at the front, and most Leningraders – whether man or woman – simply didn't have the strength to take dead bodies down stairs and then pull them on sleds to the morgues or cemeteries.

Petya scanned through the notices quickly until he saw a new one. On January 8th – today – the Young Communists were having a winter coat and clothing collection for war orphans and soldiers at the front. As soon as Petya figured out what it was, he stopped reading and tried to quickly move on to another notice. But it was too late. That confounding voice in his head told him that he had to help, just as Petya feared it would. It was useless to try to fight it. If God told him to do something, he had no choice but to obey. He already had a lot to do that day but resigned himself to the fact that he now had even more to do.

When he got back to the apartment, Katya was in her usual place seated in a chair facing the front door. Petya squeezed by her, looking over her shoulder as he did so. He saw she was drawing another one of her endless pictures of Jesus. That was all she seemed to do every day now.

Each picture she drew was the same in one astonishing way – Jesus would be smiling and laughing. Petya still remembered the first time he saw one of those drawings and how stunned he'd been. Most every picture, painting, or drawing of Jesus he'd ever seen in his life was of the son of God in agony as he died of crucifixion. Or with a sad but peaceful look on his face as he looked upward in prayer. Or maybe Jesus with the crown of thorns on his head – blood streaming down his forehead, his face weary from the pain and humiliation. Never in his life had Petya seen pictures of Jesus like Katya's – with smiles and laughter, and happy expressions on all the disciples' faces.

The voice of God in Petya's head was strangely silent on the subject and Petya didn't know what to think. He'd asked her to explain the drawings to him once, and she'd simply said, "*My* Jesus was full of peace and joy. And that's what he tried to teach others."

Petya sat down across from Oksana, who was lying in bed moaning softly every now and then. She'd taken a turn for the worse in the past week and hadn't been able to make it into work. She complained incessantly that her stomach hurt, was convinced she had an ulcer, and that she was going to die. Petya thought she was probably right – half the food you ate these days was inedible. And ulcers were indeed fatal. He hoped she'd die soon; he had plans for her.

He wrote the letters "К" and "Д" in his journal. Then he grabbed a large brown bag for the coats and clothing he hoped his neighbors would donate, and left the apartment.

The first apartment he came to on the fourth floor was one he didn't particularly want to stop at. The woman that lived there didn't like Petya and usually didn't try to hide the fact.

"*You?*" she said, peeking through the crack in the door. She kept the chain on it locked. "I don't believe it. What are you up to?"

"I already told you," Petya said. "They're having a coat and clothing drive for soldiers at the front and war orphans. I just saw the notice on the bulletin board. The Young Communists are sponsoring it."

"I still don't believe you," the woman said. "You probably just want to sell whatever I give you on the market. Now go away." She slammed the door shut.

Petya trudged down the stairs and back to the bulletin board, took the notice down, then went back to the woman's apartment and knocked on her door again. She wouldn't open it to him, so he slid the notice under her door.

The End Of Sorrow

A minute later, she opened the door, keeping the chain locked, and squeezed a coat out the three-inch crack between the door and the doorframe. "Even if you are lying," she said, "ain't nobody gonna pay you a kopeck on the market for this old coat anyway."

"Thank you. You are a most kind and munificent woman," Petya said sarcastically and moved on.

At the next door, an old man covered with boils answered. After Petya's explanation, the man opened the door and let him in. The boils were another of the many results of malnutrition. Petya saw he even had boils on his fingers, several of them lanced and unhealed.

The windows were covered over with plywood and it was dark inside the apartment. The man's wife and aunt were busy packing things. He explained that they were being evacuated tomorrow. They were supposed to have left two days ago, but apparently the car that was to have taken them had broken down.

He was quite generous in donating children's clothes, and Petya learned why – both of their daughters had died the week before.

On the second floor, one of the doors opened as Petya walked up to it. The Lusinkii's lived there and Petya saw their eldest son, an officer in the navy, emerge. He looked comparatively healthy, as did most of his family. They certainly weren't flourishing, but neither had they lost anyone to starvation or disease either. Petya didn't know how they did it, but they were not alone. Death was busy knocking on nearly every door in Leningrad, but by no means all.

Petya asked them if they wanted to donate any clothing or coats. They said no, quickly closing the door.

No one responded to his knocks at the door across the hall, so he moved on to the next one where the Karpovskii's lived. The man's wife answered and Petya asked her if they had any coats they would like to donate. She invited him in and led him down a short hallway and through another door that opened into the kitchen. It was dark there and she lit a candle. The light glittered off the frost-covered walls.

She pointed to the floor by a boarded-up window. A corpse lay there. "You can have his coat," she said. "He doesn't need it anymore."

Petya didn't have to ask who it was. He knew it was Mr. Karpovsii. "When did he die?"

"Day before yesterday," she replied.

Dead bodies, even in apartments, did not stink or decompose because of the bitter cold.

"I can take care of the body for you, if you like," Petya said.

"How much?" the woman asked.

"A day's bread ration."

The woman contemplated for a few seconds. "No, I can't do it."

"You're just going to leave him here then?"

"Yes," she answered. "I can't give up an entire day's ration."

Petya saw the woman's teeth as she spoke. They were badly decayed. It was the same all over the city. There wasn't a single body part that didn't suffer from the effects of starvation.

"You're a neighbor," Petya said. "I'll do it for half the ration. How about that?"

She nodded, went into the other room, then returned a minute later with the bread. It didn't look like half the ration, but Petya wasn't going to argue with her.

He stuck the bread in his pocket, then went over to the body and took the coat off. "Here," he said, handing the coat to the woman. "Lay that out in the hallway for me. I'll come and get it later." Petya grabbed the body by the arms and pulled it off the table down to the floor. Then he dragged it out of the apartment to the hallway where he let it lay while he returned to the third floor to get one of their sleds and give Katya half of the bread he'd just received.

He was surprised when he didn't find her sitting in the chair in front of the door. Instead, he saw her in her bedroom walking from one side to the other. Her ankle had healed some, but she still walked with almost as big a limp as Petya did.

She seemed to be gathering things into a bag. Petya didn't bother asking her about it though. He knew she wouldn't answer him. He held out the bread to her, and she stopped doing whatever it was she was doing just long enough to take it.

Petya worried that no matter how much food she received now that it wouldn't help, that she was too far gone to be saved. There were tens of thousands of people like her – firmly in death's grasp, their bodies too depleted of nutrients to ever regain their health.

After Petya dragged the body of Mr. Karpovskii down the stairs to the outside, he loaded it onto the sled. But instead of taking it to the morgue or the cemetery, he made for a small shed in the courtyard across the street. All the apartment buildings there had been destroyed by the German's long-range artillery and the area was deserted now. The shed was the only structure still standing, and Petya unlocked the padlock he'd put on the door and started to drag the body inside.

There were disembodied arms and legs scattered about the floor, and Petya had to kick a head out of the way so he could get the new body in. The head rolled a foot or two under the workbench and came to a stop on its right ear. Petya quickly closed the door behind him and then tied a rope around the corpse.

This was his butcher shop, complete with a variety of knives and a small ceramic stove. Without this place, Petya figured he would have starved to death weeks ago. Labeling some of the meat 'Horse Sausage,' he'd recently started going to the Haymarket to try to sell it. The Haymarket, made famous by Dostoevsky's novel, *Crime and Punishment*, was the biggest marketplace in the city. Everything and anything was sold there: boots, coats, clothes, sleds, bread, and, of course, 'meat.' Most everyone knew what the meat was really made of but chose to feign ignorance, pretending it was actually whatever the seller said it was. Petya hadn't had much success at the Haymarket yet. There was stiff competition for those selling 'meat.'

He cleared away a pair of thin arms from his workbench, tossing them into the corner. The arms were sometimes too thin to do anything with, so he threw those away with the heads and other unuseable parts. Reaching under the workbench, he tried grabbing hold of the head he had kicked earlier. The old man – or maybe woman, Petya didn't remember and couldn't tell from looking at the head – didn't have much hair left. Starvation and lack of nutrition had seen to that while they were still alive. Petya grabbed what hair he could, lifting the head out from underneath the bench. But before he could toss it into the corner, the head dropped to the floor again, a handful of white hair clinging to Petya's still clenched fist. The head, with its sunken eyes and thin, nearly nonexistent lips, looked up at the ceiling. Its mouth was partially open, revealing several brown, severely decayed teeth and numerous gaps. Petya hated dealing with the heads, because they were the body parts most likely to speak to him. He bent over and closed his eyes as he grabbed the head with both hands. Then he carried it to the corner and set it down, leaning it against a severed foot so it would look toward the wall.

Using a set of pulleys he'd attached to the ceiling, Petya hoisted his new corpse up onto the workbench. Then he left the shed, making sure the padlock was secured, and returned to his apartment building.

He knocked on the doors on the first floor to see if anyone else had anything to donate, but no one answered. Next, he stuffed all the coats and clothing he'd collected into the big brown bag and tied it to the sled to take to the collection center. The Germans had started shelling with their long-range artillery again, so Petya listened to the explosions and the high-pitched whistling of the shells for a while to see where they were coming from. The Germans were systematic in their bombing and you could tell what area of the city they were targeting and whether your trip would be safe.

All along his journey, Petya saw the old-timers – thin and seemingly on the verge of death – at their posts waiting for an air raid alarm. There hadn't been any bombing runs by German planes since mid-December (rumor was it was so cold that it froze the fuel in the planes), but that didn't mean the guards didn't still have to sit in the freezing cold at their posts by gates, doorways, in halls, or stairwells.

Petya passed by the block with the abandoned building where he'd found Kolya. He didn't bother stopping. For a week after Kolya disappeared, Petya had checked the building every day for him. He never showed up, and Petya had given up on ever finding the boy.

The Germans stopped their shelling when Petya was about halfway to the collection center, and all was eerily quiet. He hated the silence. It wasn't only that that was when the voices usually spoke to him, but it also just wasn't right that such a large city *could be* that quiet.

At one point, he thought he heard the sound of dogs barking, but knew that couldn't be true. There were no dogs left in the city. There hadn't been for a long time. Besides the Leningraders themselves, there were hardly any animals at all left in the city. No cats. No birds. No squirrels. The only animal one rarely saw were rats. But most of them had either starved, been eaten, or departed for the trenches at the front where the food supply was better.

Just as Petya feared, a voice began speaking to him. It was the voice of God and it was telling Petya how pleased he was that so many of his children were being returned to him in heaven as a result of the war.

"But there is one who has not come home yet," the voice said. "One that I miss very deeply."

Petya knew who the voice was talking about. It wasn't the first time God had expressed his longing to be reunited with Katya.

"I am tired of waiting," the voice said now to Petya. "I want her returned to me."

Petya didn't have to ask "When?" out loud. All he had to do now was think the question and the voice would answer.

"Today," it said.

Petya wanted to argue. He wanted to fight, or at least plead, instead of just giving in. But what did it matter what he wanted? In the end, the voice would win. It always did.

* * *

The warmth of the inside of the truck's cab, along with the methodical rocking and steady hum of the engine, had lulled Felix to sleep. He had strange dreams of being entombed in a coffin so big that he could stand up and walk around – either that or the coffin was regular size and he was really small. He didn't know which, but the dream left him feeling uncomfortable to the point of sickness and he wished he could have made it into the city yesterday, instead of today, January 8th.

The trip across the lake to Leningrad had been slow going from the start. The traffic was heavy and they often spent more time at a dead halt than they did moving.

Felix was startled awake by a tremendous noise and thought for sure they were under attack. When he opened his eyes though, he immediately saw the source of the noise. Five huge snowplows were approaching from the opposite direction, creating another road.

"Good," the driver said in his thick Georgian accent. "We need another road. The Nazis have pretty much ruined this one."

"They certainly seem determined to put an end to this supply route into the city," Felix said.

"Yes, but we're more determined to keep it open," the driver said. "They can keep on destroying our roads, we'll just keep building more. They'll never win."

"How are you so confident?"

"Because we'll never give up. That's why," the driver said. "They're not going to win unless they kill every last one of us." He paused to swerve the truck around a piece of wreckage sticking out from the side of the road. "This is our home. It's where we're meant to be."

The man's comments didn't surprise Felix. He'd noticed a slow but steady shift in people's attitudes and actions since those first few months of the war. You rarely met anyone these days who was ambivalent about the war. Everyone had bonded together in a common cause – the defeat of the Nazis by any means. It was no longer a conflict of opposing ideologies, it had become a patriotic war.

Felix wanted to continue the conversation, but his body had other ideas. It was a rare thing to be seated in a warm place and have nothing to do, and he fell quickly back asleep.

When he next awoke, he saw trees outside his window. "We're off the lake?"

"Yeah," the driver said, "we finished with that a while ago."

"How much further?"

"Not much," the driver said and pointed ahead of them.

Felix looked where the driver was pointing and was surprised to see Leningrad's skyline coming into view. He knew he must have been sleeping quite a while because once you crossed the lake, it was still a long distance before you reached the city.

He reached into his pack for a cigarette, but then remembered he only had three left and decided not to have one right now. He'd had another full pack when he started the journey, but the driver made it clear to him that the ride wasn't for free. He'd wanted money, but Felix had already given what little money he had to Misha for an earlier bribe. Thankfully, the driver had accepted Felix's pack of cigarettes as payment.

They passed a small collection of ice huts where he saw two nurses with the customary red crosses on their arms. They were pulling a wounded man into one of the huts. A little ways after that, they passed a snow-covered truck tipped over on its side. A squirrel ran along the top of it.

The closer they got to the city, the more Felix could see how viciously Leningrad's once beautiful skyline had been ravaged by the German Luftwaffe and long-range artillery. He tried to prepare himself mentally for the devastation he knew he was about to experience.

They passed by two figures trudging away from the city, heading in the direction of the lake. One of them was wearing a man's fur coat that was much too big for them, and Felix wondered if the man had lost that much weight or if maybe the coat didn't belong to him. He was pulling a small brown sled with some bundles strapped to it. The fur wasn't as dark as most similar coats and it had an interesting pattern of stripes to it. It looked vaguely familiar to Felix and he thought for a second he might know the man, but he couldn't see his face because it was wrapped in a dark scarf.

The other person appeared to be an old woman. She was stooped, wore a wool shawl, and had rags wrapped around her boots. Felix had seen the rags or carpets wrapped around the feet before. It was an attempt to prevent frostbite.

"Where are they going?" Felix asked.

"To the lake," the driver said. "I see them all the time. They're evacuating on their own. They try to hitch a ride with us when we're headed back across."

"Do you pick them up?"

"Sure, if they can give me something – some cigarettes or bread, you know."

"And those who don't have anything to give?"

"Aww, come on. Everyone's got a least a little something. If they don't want to give us anything, then they can walk."

"Walk where? All the way across the lake?"

"That's their problem. We're not even supposed to pick them up in the first place."

Felix watched the two fade into the distance. It would be dark soon, and he wondered where they would sleep that night. He wondered too about the desperateness they must have experienced to take on such a journey – a journey where the odds of dying were far greater than the odds of living. He'd seen the lifeless bodies alongside the road multiply the closer they got to Leningrad. He'd assumed they were victims of bombings or shellings, but now he knew the truth.

When the outskirts of Leningrad spread out before them, the driver stopped the truck. "This is where you get off," he said. "They don't let us carry passengers into the city."

Felix buttoned up his coat and pulled his scarf tight around his neck. He thanked the driver for the ride and hopped out of the truck.

"One word of advice," the driver said. "Keep your wits about you if anyone approaches. Especially stay away from the river."

"What do you mean?" Felix said. "I already told you I don't have any money."

"It's not your money these people are after," he said.

"Then what?"

The driver bared his teeth and pretended to bite his own arm, then drove away. Felix wasn't sure what that meant and didn't spend any time trying to figure it out. He looked across the horizon at the faint sun and calculated there was about one hour of daylight left, which meant it was now about three p.m.. He got a piece of bread out, took a big bite of it, and set off for Katya's neighborhood. It was going to be a long walk, he knew. Several hours at least.

The section of the city he started out in wasn't familiar to him. Piles of rubble lay in the street and for some strange reason he kept smelling turpentine. Blackened, burnt-out buildings and dead trees jutted out from the ground. They balanced precariously, looking as though they might fall over after the next big gust of winter wind. Snow drifts reached to the windows of the second floor of some buildings. Streetcars and automobiles were frozen in place and partially, or in some cases completely, covered over with snow. Everything was quiet and he imagined that his own footsteps crunching the hard snow beneath him could be heard a mile away. It was like he was walking through the ruins of an ancient city.

He didn't encounter a single other person for the first forty minutes, and as he witnessed one frozen, lifeless block after another, he started to wonder who or what could possibly survive here. Then he saw them – dark figures trudging in the alleys and around the snow drifts. He came across three of them as he rounded the next corner. They wore black masks over their faces, with peepholes cut out for their eyes. Felix instinctively reached for his gun but realized they weren't out to rob him. They wore the masks to protect themselves against the cold of the arctic night.

An artillery shell exploded nearby, shaking the earth beneath him. Felix was about to dive to the ground when he noticed that nobody else seemed to even notice it. They just kept on walking as if nothing had happened. It was then that he realized how numb they were to the death and chaos around them.

He came across some soldiers on pass from the front to visit their families, and asked them for directions. Right after Felix left them, he saw a man and a woman wearing militia uniforms come up to them. "Your papers, please," the woman said.

Felix quickened his pace and hoped they wouldn't notice. He had no pass, no orders to be in the city. If he was caught, he could be sent to the firing squad for desertion.

He heard the woman yell in his direction, "Comrade, where are you bound?" Felix pretended that he didn't hear and kept walking. When he came to the next alley, he turned into it and, safely out of their sight, began running. He climbed over a couple snowdrifts and emerged on the other side, then resumed his walking. He wanted to blend in and knew he would attract a lot of attention if anyone saw him running. It was clear to him that anyone living here wasn't capable of doing that.

A five-ton truck rumbled down the road and Felix wondered if it might be carrying more people being evacuated. It slowed as it approached a corpse in the street, then slid to a halt a few yards beyond it. Three men got out of the truck and pulled the tarp from the back, revealing dozens of dead bodies stacked one on top of the other.

Felix watched them pick up the corpse in the street and throw it on top of the others, only to have it come tumbling back down to the ground. They tried again, pushing the arms and legs back behind the gate. Felix still didn't think it would stay, but the men were able to walk away without it falling. Before they got back in the truck, they poured something where the corpse had been lying. A second later, Felix smelled turpentine stronger than ever, and realized they were using it as a disinfectant. That was why the whole city smelled like it.

It was after five p.m. now and the sun had set. The city was usually quite busy at this time as all the workers headed home for the day. But there were no masses of people walking the sidewalks. There were no streetlights, no trolleys running, no cars going up and down the street. It was dark and quiet, and the moon shined its pale light on the plump, gray anti-aircraft balloons that hovered at varying altitudes.

Felix was still having trouble recognizing where he was. Not only were familiar buildings no longer there, but there were no street signs or block numbers. They'd all been painted over.

Nearly everywhere he looked in this part of the city, he saw corpses – on the sidewalks, the streets, in the doorways of buildings, even sitting up on curbs, frozen in place. At first, he kept count of them, but stopped after he passed fifty.

The thought came to him that Katya may have suffered the same fate. Perhaps she had already starved or froze to death. Or been a victim of the relentless German bombing. For a second, he felt foolish for thinking otherwise. What proof did he have that she was still alive? He hadn't received any letters from her, had heard nothing from anyone to suggest that she was still living and working in Leningrad. The rational conclusion was that she was dead.

But he knew somehow that wasn't true. He couldn't name it, but he was certain that she was still alive and that he had to go to her. This strange sense was very strong in him lately – this knowing of the truth of things that he couldn't otherwise prove.

He heard a squeaking sound that he recognized as coming from the runners of a sled, and it brought back fond memories from his childhood. He stopped for a second and looked around for the sled, expecting to see a young boy pulling it. Instead, he saw a gaunt, elderly man with the rope in his hand. There was a small blue body on the sled. It was wrapped in a blanket, but the young girl's long brown hair spilled out and trailed behind in the snow.

The man passed by Felix as though he wasn't even there, then stopped at a park bench. Felix thought he was going to sit down to rest, but he didn't.

From an alley in front of Felix, a man emerged wearing a blue militia coat.

He started walking right at Felix. "Halt!" the man yelled, taking his rifle from his shoulder.

Felix froze in place. There was nowhere to go. His heart and mind started racing as to what to do. Then, to his surprise, the militiaman walked right past him. He was heading toward the man who'd stopped at the park bench. Felix turned his head and saw what the man with the sled was doing. He was tearing planks from the bench, presumably for firewood.

"Halt!" the militiaman said again. "You are destroying government property."

Felix breathed a sigh of relief and resumed walking.

He noticed that all the apartment buildings he passed – even the ones still intact – looked deserted. Not a light. Not a sound. Where were the two and a half million inhabitants of this city?

He came upon a tremendous fire that lit the surrounding area like it was still daytime. There was a crowd of people gathered around the apartment building, but no one was trying to put the fire out. Instead, they had formed a chain and were handing possessions out of the building: a samovar, a kerosene stove, blankets . . . ..

Felix had heard about the scourge of fires that tormented Leningrad. It wasn't just the Germans and their incendiary bombs, hardly any of the makeshift stoves people had were installed properly. Every month, these stoves started hundreds of fires that burned down hundreds of buildings. There was no water to put the fires out.

Felix asked one of the persons at the fire which way the Kazansky Cathedral was. The person gave him a strange look, but then answered and pointed the way. It was only after hearing their voice that Felix could determine that the person was a female. He couldn't tell by sight alone whether these walking skeletons with their skin stretched tight over their faces were male or female.

As he headed off in the direction the woman had directed him, he noticed more people coming toward the fire. They were all carrying pails, except there was nothing in them. Felix looked over his shoulder as he continued on and saw that the fire was melting snow and ice and the people were gathering the precious water into their pails to take home with them.

After a few more blocks, his surroundings started to look more familiar. Part of that was because the bombed buildings had been covered over with plywood and painted to look as though they were still intact.

It took him nearly three hours from the outskirts of the city to finally reach the Kazansky Cathedral. Katya's apartment building wasn't far beyond that. Felix looked over his favorite cathedral and was pleased to see it undamaged. Its two giant wings remained resting on the ground, and Felix thought that if it hadn't flown away yet, it never would.

The moon was still shining and he expected to see its light glimmering off Kazansky's shiny cupola, but the top of the cathedral had been painted a dark color as camouflage. Felix couldn't remember if the cupola had been painted when he last saw the cathedral or not. Everything in the city looked so strange to him, like he was an unwitting character in a science fiction story. Everything that was once familiar to him looked mysterious and foreboding. It was both the city he knew so well and a strange place full of ruins and corpses and un-humanlike people.

As he approached Katya's neighborhood, a giant cloud moved in front of the moon and all became pitch-black. At first he had to feel his way along a nearby snowbank, but then his eyes adjusted and he could make out the edges of things. After he turned down Katya's block, he was devastated to find her apartment building lying in rubble.

He stood there staring at the dim outline of the ruined building, wondering how he could have been wrong. Wondering what to do next. Then the light of the moon returned and he saw that he was on the wrong block. Katya's apartment was one block farther still.

He hurried there and was relieved to find her building intact. It hadn't caught fire or been bombed. Giant icicles clung to the edge of the roof and there were dark streaks down the side of the building. The streaks weren't from smoke, Felix knew. People didn't have the energy to take their slop and garbage out. Instead, they threw it out the window into the street. It was going to be one hell of a mess come springtime.

Felix lit a match for light and walked up the stairs. The building, like the entire city, was eerily quiet. The only sound Felix heard was his own footsteps. He felt queasy and short of breath the closer he got to the third floor. He was so afraid to see how thin Katya must have become, but his biggest fear was not seeing her there at all.

The third floor hallway was pitch black. Felix's match was getting dangerously close to his fingers, so he blew it out and dropped it to the floor, walking the few last steps in darkness. Taking a deep breath, he prepared to knock on Katya's door, but saw that it hadn't been closed all the way. The door was open a crack and he could hear a man's voice inside. The person was speaking in a low whisper and Felix didn't recognize the voice.

"None of this is personal you know," the man said. "I don't even want to be doing this, but it's necessary for me to be able to continue."

Felix opened the door quietly and walked into the apartment. It sounded like the man was having a conversation with someone, but Felix never heard anyone answer.

"There is one thing I want to apologize to you about," the man whispered. "I'm not quite sure how to say it though."

The hallway of the apartment was dark and cold, but Felix could see candlelight coming from up ahead. He moved slowly and silently until he could see around the corner into the room that the hallway opened up into.

The room that Felix used to know so well was barely recognizable to him now. There was a stove in the middle and three beds circled around it.

The walls were stained black and had no wallpaper, and a stovepipe snaked through the room to one of the windows.

The man had his back to Felix and was leaning over someone lying in bed. Felix couldn't tell what the man was doing, but he saw that the bed was covered with blood.

"Who are you?" Felix demanded, stepping around the corner. "What are you doing?"

The man, wrapped in layers of blankets from head to toe, stopped talking and moving. He seemed frozen in place.

The light from the candle flickered and Felix repeated his questions.

"It's all right, Felix," the man answered and turned to face him. "It's God's will . . . all part of the mission."

That the man knew Felix's name frightened him because he had no idea who he was talking to. Felix moved closer so he could see the man's face better. The man lunged at him with a bloody knife. Felix caught his arm in the air and easily flung him down onto one of the beds. Then he grabbed the knife out of the man's hand and threw it across the room.

He turned to the thin, bloody corpse on the bed with the blanket covering its face. A large section of the person's right thigh was missing, and Felix didn't want to find out who was under that blanket.

The man continued lying where Felix had thrown him, making no attempt to get up or even roll over. "She waited for you, you know," he said.

"*Who* waited for me?" Felix said. Everything was swirling about him. Nothing made sense. Who was this man speaking to him? Who was this corpse under the blanket?

"She never gave up on you," the man continued. "Even when they told her you were dead. She sat in that chair staring at the door every day – just waiting for you to walk through."

Felix had to end the madness. He stepped over to the bloody body, pulled the blanket off, and stared at the face.

He didn't recognize the person. "Who is this?" he asked.

"You don't recognize her, either?" the man said.

Felix went back to the man, grabbed hold of the blankets wrapped around him, and lifted him into the air. "Enough of your games!" he yelled. "Who did you kill?"

"I didn't kill anyone," the man said. "That's Oksana. She was already dead when I got back."

"And who are you? Where is Katya?"

"It is I, Felix," the man answered. "Petya."

Felix looked closer and saw the man had a little black mole on his cheek just as he remembered Petya had. The man's vaguely familiar voice now became fully recognizable. "Petya?" Felix repeated. His hands started to tremble.

The man nodded. "Yes," he said. "I didn't think we'd ever meet again."

"Where is Katya?"

Petya didn't answer, and Felix lifted his limp body up higher into the air and looked him in the eyes. "I said, where's Katya?"

"Hopefully in a place far better than this," he said.

"Damn it, Petya! I'm not going to ask again," Felix said. "I'll throw you across the room if you don't answer me. Now where is she?"

"Gone," Petya said.

"Where?"

"To find you."

Felix let go of his grip and Petya fell back onto the bed. "She went to find *me*?" he said incredulously. He stumbled backwards a step, like the words were arrows that had pierced his chest.

"When I got back an hour ago, I found this," Petya said, holding up a piece of paper.

"Give it to me," Felix said, grabbing it out of Petya's hand.

Petya,

By the time you read this, I'll be gone. I've decided to go across the lake to find Felix. I know he's out there somewhere and that we'll be together again. I took the brown sled. Please say goodbye to Igor for me and give him the letter I wrote him.

– Katya

As soon as Felix finished reading the letter, he realized why that fur coat he'd seen on the person heading toward the lake had looked so familiar to him. It was Katya's father's old coat – the one he'd bought from the fur trader outside Archangel, the one he used to wear before he'd gotten a new one last year. Because of the fur coat, Felix thought it had been a man pulling the sled. Now he was sure it was Katya. He'd just missed her!

He turned and ran out of the apartment and down the stairs, crashing into the door to the outside. He could barely breathe, and ran into the night grasping at his chest, trying to get some air into his lungs before his heart burst.

He ran back the way he'd just come. Running and running until his legs were exhausted and forced him to slow to a walk. Dark, heavy clouds were converging on the city. The streets were empty.

* * *

Katya watched her companion fall to the snow-covered road for the second time in less than ten minutes. She stopped a few feet away from the woman, hoping her companion would be able to get back up again. Katya knew that she herself didn't have the strength to help her in any way. It was all she could do to put one foot in front of the other and not fall down herself.

Katya didn't know the woman. They just happened to both be heading to the lake and decided to accompany one another. The woman was hoping to make it to the south, Katya had learned, where she had a sister.

The sun had just set and the temperature was dropping, although Katya didn't notice any difference. Twenty degrees below zero and thirty degrees below zero felt the same to her.

After much effort, the woman made it back to her feet. "I'm so damn cold," she said.

"Why don't we trade coats?" Katya suggested. "I'm warm enough for now, and we can switch back once we reach a shelter and you're able to warm up a little."

"Are you sure?" the woman said.

Katya took off her fur coat and handed it to the woman to take. It made her feel good that she could help out in some way.

The woman took her ragged old coat off, gave it to Katya to wear, then pulled Katya's large fur coat tightly around her. "My goodness," she exclaimed. "It's so big."

"It was my father's coat," Katya said.

Once they had finished trading coats, they continued walking along the road. The trucks coming from the lake came at them in an endless stream. Trucks going the same direction they were heading were few and far between. Katya didn't bother waving for them to stop anymore. She'd learned that she didn't possess anything they wanted, and none of them would give her a ride for free.

It wasn't even another five minutes before Katya's companion fell again, this time into the thick snow on the side of the road. Katya pulled her sled up close and sat down next to her.

"I can't make it any further," the woman said.

Once off the road, the snow was very deep and Katya knew she couldn't possibly help the woman out. "I can't help you up," she said.

"I know, dear," the woman replied. "I don't expect you to. This is where I'm going to die."

Katya didn't argue with her. She'd thought of doing the same thing herself a few times already.

"Those truck drivers should have given us a ride," the woman said bitterly. "I worked as a schoolteacher for twenty-seven years and not once did I ever ask for a pack of cigarettes or a loaf of bread to teach a child."

Katya thought the woman shouldn't be dwelling on such things while on her deathbed, but it was *her* death she realized. Who was she to tell the woman how to spend her remaining time?

For the next ten minutes, she listened to the woman's persistent rant about how the truck drivers should have offered them a ride. Then the woman stopped talking altogether and closed her eyes. Katya took out a piece of bread and ate a few bites as the wind picked up and it started to snow.

The woman opened her eyes after a minute and looked at Katya. She seemed very calm, almost peaceful. "You may as well get going, my dear," she said. "You've got a long journey ahead of you."

Katya agreed with her. There was nothing she could do.

"Bless me before you go," the woman said.

Katya made the sign of the cross and said a short prayer out loud. The woman thanked her, then closed her eyes again. Her breathing was very shallow and Katya had an idea that she would be dead within a few minutes. Katya wanted to get her fur coat back, but realized it was too late now. The woman couldn't take it off, and Katya was much too weak to get if off of her. It was only with great effort that Katya had even been able to stand up again.

She grabbed the rope of her sled and started walking. She had no idea how much further it was to the lake but hoped she was at least past the halfway point.

The only way she'd made it this far was by focusing solely on the next segment of her journey. She thought only of reaching the next destination. To think of her final destination or the entire journey was too much – too daunting of a task. If she focused on the next one hundred steps, or just reaching the next intersection, then it was doable.

Katya saw corpse after corpse alongside the road. They had no effect on her. She never thought she could be so indifferent to death, but after you saw so much of it, you just stopped reacting. It became a normal part of one's daily life.

She had a strong desire sometimes to join them, to lay down in the thick, soft snow and close her eyes. Death didn't seem so bad at this point. She imagined it would be a lot like a deep, restful sleep.

She'd realized before she even left the apartment how much risk this trip would involve. She knew this could very well be the last journey she ever made, but it was worth gambling for. Something had been calling her for a long time. Something she had heard but been too afraid to answer. It was ironic to her that the final push she needed to answer the call was an even greater fear of staying. She knew if she stayed that she would die in that apartment. Either Petya would take that final plunge below the ice of sanity and murder her or she would simply give in one night to the cold and the hunger.

She caught herself reaching into her coat pocket for the bread Petya had given her earlier, and stopped herself. "Wait until you reach the lake," she said silently, "then we'll have a little bite of bread and a nice rest."

She noticed she had started referring to herself as 'we' and wondered what it meant.

The rope to the sled fell from her hand. It wasn't only that she had so little strength, it seemed that the signal from her brain to various parts of her body was either being ignored by the intended recipients or else getting lost along the way. Her joints hurt, even more than usual, and she found herself stumbling over her own feet and forgetting where she was and why she was out here.

This difficulty with thinking was nothing new. For the last month or so, she found her concentration lasted no more than a few seconds. It was similar to being really drunk – making a decision to do something and getting ready to do it, then forgetting what it was you wanted to do.

She decided to tie the rope around her waist. As she was preparing to do this, a truck barreled down the road in her direction. The road was narrow here and there wasn't enough room for both her and two lanes of trucks.

She moved to the side of the road and pulled her sled over so the truck wouldn't run over it. But as she did so, she lost her hold on the sled and it went racing down the four-foot slope on the side of the road. It came to a rest about thirty feet away.

She stared at the sled and sank down onto the snow. She knew she couldn't get the sled back. The snow was very deep, and though the top of the snow was hard, it wouldn't support her weight and she'd sink down to her waist.

The consequences of what had just happened were very clear to her. She had packed clothing and documents and half a loaf of bread on the sled, and they were all gone now. She had no energy to get upset about it though. She didn't view it as something that had gone terribly wrong. It had happened, and that was it.

She still had half of her lipstick that she could eat, and also the bread Petya had given her. She decided to eat some of the bread now and save the lipstick for later. When she finished, she willed herself up to her feet and started walking again, vowing not to stop until she reached either the lake or a shelter.

Dark clouds had moved in and blotted out the moon and stars. The wind had begun to gust from time to time and snowflakes the size of grains of sand swirled about. A blizzard was coming, Katya knew. The trucks had started to thin out and after a while stopped altogether.

She walked for thirty minutes that seemed more like three hundred, and then her legs stopped moving. She hadn't told them to. She felt dizzy, like she was floating on a magic carpet caught in a wind storm. Then her legs gave out from under her and she found herself lying in the thick, fluffy snow alongside the road. It was so very comfortable. She had no desire to get back up.

She closed her eyes and thought of her companion who lay in a similar position a few miles back. The words the woman had said to Katya still rang in her ears. Even on her deathbed, the woman had stubbornly clung to the belief that she was right, that the truck drivers *should* have given them a ride. Katya thought how everyone seemed to feel it necessary to prove their rightness, to prove they possessed the one-and-only truth. She didn't believe in any of that though. She didn't believe in aggression as the answer;

as self-righteous indignation as a necessity; in shame, anger, or hate as things effective or beneficial.

Her grandmother had taught her otherwise, but nobody else saw it that way. To them, animosity and rage were healthy – a natural and acceptable part of life. Where were the Peacemakers, Katya wanted to know. Where were the Righteous? The Merciful?

She was alone. Alone in so many ways. She felt like the only one in the world who still believed peace and understanding were the answer. The only one who thought that nobody *deserved* anything; the only one who thought that nothing was good or bad, right or wrong.

She wasn't mad about it, though, just sad. Sad that the world could be such a better place if only more people could see the beauty of Jesus' nonviolent teachings.

Katya noticed that her breathing was no longer automatic. If she didn't consciously tell her body to take a breath, it wouldn't. She took her mitten off and stuck her right hand inside her coat. When her fingers got to be too thin to hold the ring Felix had given her, she put it on a string and wore it around her neck. She held fast to the ring now and thought back to a dance where she realized for the first time she was in love with Felix. It was fascinating to her because no words were spoken. She didn't suddenly blurt out, "I love you," as if the sentiment was a complete surprise even to her. And neither did he prompt her feelings in any way by saying anything.

It happened when the band started to play a waltz. Felix came over to her, leaving his group of friends behind, and held out his hand for her to dance with him. She put her hand in his and they walked to the dance floor. When they came to a stop, he placed his left hand on her hip and held her right hand up to shoulder height, then looked her in the eyes, as if to say, "Ready?"

He had a confidence about him that she found mesmerizing, but her legs felt like rubber. He moved his left leg forward, but she didn't move backwards and he crushed her toes with his shoe. The pain was intense but she found herself laughing despite it. Felix apologized profusely. Then she admitted she didn't know how to waltz. "Close your eyes," he'd told her. "I'm going to lead and you only have to follow. Just relax and don't try to guess what you need to do. Just react. When you feel me moving toward you, move away. Keep your arms firm. Don't let my chest come any nearer to yours than it is now."

And then they began, ever so slowly to waltz. One-two-three. One-two-three. Katya kept her eyes closed the whole time and let herself be carried away by the music and Felix's sure grasp. They glided across the floor, spinning, swaying, Felix counting softly to her, one-two-three, one-two-three.

There was only that moment. Nothing else existed. Just her and Felix and the music moving as one. It was during that time that her heart seemed to grow as big as the entire dance hall and she knew beyond the inadequacy of words that she was madly in love with this man and that her life would never be the same.

Her right hand was starting to get numb from the cold but she refused to let go of the ring. She put her left hand over her right and closed her eyes even tighter, trying to return to that night when her heart was as big as the dance hall. Tears of sorrow welled in her eyes and the icy wind froze them to her eyelashes.

* * *

It had already been snowing for over an hour by the time Felix made it back to the place where he thought he'd seen Katya with the sled. His breath was short from the intense cold. The hairs on the inside of his nose felt like little frozen needles poking him on each inhalation. The wind gusted and belted him in the face, causing his cheeks and eyebrows to go numb. If he had ever been this cold before, he couldn't recall it.

There had been a long line of trucks coming from the lake, their headlights providing a constant source of light to see by. The trucks had started to thin out recently, and Felix had to use his flashlight quite often. There were very few trucks going the same direction he was, but he wouldn't ask them for a ride anyway. He needed to check the bodies lying along the side of the road – and there was at least one every hundred feet or so.

Only twenty minutes past where he thought he'd seen Katya, Felix thought he saw the fur coat with the familiar stripes. It was half buried under the sand-like snow, on a body that did not move.

"Katya!" he yelled and ran to her. Hurriedly brushing some of the snow off, he grabbed her by the arm and shook. There was no response. Her body was stiff and cold. He pulled the scarf away that covered her face and saw to his horror and relief that it wasn't Katya. It was an old woman.

Emotions swam frantically in every direction within him. Fear. If someone else had Katya's coat, did that mean Katya was dead? Regret. Why couldn't he have stood firm and made her leave on that train back in August? Guilt. Why had he taken so long to come back for her? Hopelessness. If she wasn't wearing that unique fur coat, how could he possibly find her?

He sat back on the snow, unsure what to do next. He could head back toward Leningrad to find some place to sleep for the night, or continue on in the hope that Katya might still be out there. This woman didn't have a sled after all, and he distinctly remembered seeing the person with the fur coat pulling a sled with some bundles strapped to it.

Something inside was telling him to keep going, to continue on toward Lake Ladoga (still many miles away), but Felix couldn't decide. A truck stopped near him and the driver hopped out to urinate on the side of the road. Felix asked him if he'd seen any people walking toward the lake.

"Sure, I see 'em all the time," he answered. "Poor souls. Hardly any of 'em ever make it."

"Tonight though," Felix said. "Did you see any tonight?"

"Tonight . . . hmm," he said. "I'm not sure. The days all kind of blend together."

Felix took a deep breath and closed his eyes. He was so cold and hungry and tired.

"You need a ride into the city?" the driver asked as he got back into his truck.

The wind was blowing harder, the snow falling heavier, and Felix found himself opening his mouth to say yes. But before he said it, he did his best to set his confusion aside for a second and just listen. Then there was no doubt. The message coming from within was loud and clear: *Don't give up. Not now. Not ever.*

He waved the driver off and marched on, checking every body alongside the road. He worried that Katya might have collapsed and that he would pass her by, so he was careful not to skip over any of them. He'd stop, brush off some of the snow, then study the person's face. He had to look closely because the corpses all looked the same to him. He could tell the old from the young, but that was about it. There wasn't enough light to tell any more.

After he'd walked nearly two miles from the spot where he'd thought he'd seen Katya, exhaustion – both physical and mental – started to take its toll on him. The weather was abysmal. The wind was blowing stronger than ever and the snow was traveling horizontally, blinding you if you tried to look into it. He'd checked dozens of bodies. They were all dead and frozen.

He passed by another corpse on the side of the road, but there was no sled nearby and he didn't want to stop to check the body. He was tired of disturbing the dead and wanted to let them rest in peace.

He sat down to rest on a snowbank a few yards past the corpse. His hands were cold and numb, and only with great difficulty was he able to get out the flask Misha had given him and open it. The liquor burned his throat, as usual, but his body welcomed the sensation – probably because the rest of it was frozen. His stomach growled, but there was nothing to be done about that. He'd eaten the last of his food several hours ago.

He prepared himself to go check the corpse. Taking the scarf off and studying the face was the hardest part, especially if they still had their eyes open. As he walked up to the body, he wondered if they might have some bread or something that they'd packed for the journey. They might have died before they had a chance to eat it, he thought.

There was a time when Felix would have found the idea of taking things from the dead revolting, but now he'd seen so much death that he had little reaction to it. Corpses were as familiar to him as flies in the summer. The dead had no need of their material possessions – especially food.

The body only had an inch of snow over top of it, so Felix guessed they hadn't died too long ago. He decided it would be easier to search for food before removing the person's thick scarf and seeing their face. As he brushed some of the snow off, he saw the person had both of their hands tucked inside their coat, just below their chin. The left hand covered the right, as if they were holding something precious. Felix pulled each arm out so he could see what it was they were holding. He was surprised at how easily the arms moved. The person couldn't have been dead long at all. Rigor mortis hadn't set in.

He used his flashlight to get a better look and saw the person was holding a ring hanging from a necklace. The ring had a small ruby in the middle and a petite diamond on each side. Felix recognized it of course. It was the ring he'd given Katya on that day long ago before he left for the front.

His jaw dropped. He hadn't expected this.

Unable to take in all the significance of the development, he simply stared at the ring. Then he placed his hand on the scarf that covered the person's face and braced himself. He removed it slowly, studying the face inch by inch. It was a second or two after he fully removed the scarf before he knew for sure. She was thin and pale and had those awful red and purple marks that indicated frost bite. Despite her taut skin and humongous eyes, Felix recognized her.

"Oh, Katya. My precious," he whispered as tears filled his eyes. He laid his head on her chest and held her. He was too late. She was gone. Grief filled his entire being like the thick, acrid smoke at the warehouse had, and he found it hard to breathe.

"My love," he cried softly, barely able to get the words out. He pressed his lips to her cheek. Her skin was cold, but he'd expected it to be colder. Cautiously, he removed the mitten from his right hand and felt for a pulse in her neck. He thought he felt something, but couldn't be sure. He stuck his fingers in his mouth to warm them up, then held his breath and tried again. And there it was – the faintest pulse he'd ever felt. She was alive!

Elation surged through his body like an electric current. *My God! She's alive!*

He took his flask out and carefully poured a little of the liquor in her mouth. Then he took out both of the blankets he carried in his pack and wrapped them tightly around her. He desperately hoped to see a truck and get a ride because it was critical that she warm up. But the trucks, which had been gradually thinning out, had now completely disappeared. Perhaps it was because of the weather, or an accident, or some other reason. Felix didn't know.

He remembered when he came into the city they passed by a collection of ice huts and that he'd seen two nurses pulling a wounded soldier into one of the them. He decided to take her there, hoping that hut served as a medical station. It was probably another two miles further, he guessed. He picked Katya up and was horrified at how light she was. She weighed no more than a child. He could tell there was no seductive curve from her waist to her hips anymore – her body had no curves at all now.

The road was slippery because the falling snow didn't pack, and underneath it were patches of ice. But it wasn't just the slippery conditions that made the trip difficult, Felix's legs were worn out. It was all he could do to keep from stumbling and falling to the ground.

He carried her in front of him with both arms, trying to keep her face close to his. After ten minutes, he stopped and poured a little more of the alcohol down her throat. She responded by coughing, and it was the most wonderful sound he'd ever heard.

"Katya," he called out over the roaring of the wind.

She moaned and moved her head slightly.

"Katya, open your eyes."

Her eyelids remained closed, but she did mumble something.

"What?" Felix said loudly in her ear. "I couldn't hear you." He pulled the scarf covering her face down to her chin.

"You're such a wonderful dancer," she said weakly.

Felix still wasn't sure he'd heard her correctly. A *dancer*?

"Katya, it's me. Felix."

"I know," she said, then finally opened her eyes. "Who else would it be?"

Felix wasn't sure she saw anything. Her eyes appeared unfocused and seemed to be looking past him. She started to speak again and he turned his ear toward her.

"Where did you learn to waltz like that?" she asked.

Felix didn't understand and thought she was delusional.

She squinted her eyes and looked him in the face. Then she wrinkled her forehead, looking confused. "You have a white beard," she said.

Felix was sure she had lost her senses, then realized that his beard probably was colored white from the cold and the snow.

"You look like Father Frost," she said.

A joke. *She told a joke*! Felix laughed loudly. It was the funniest, most beautiful wisecrack he'd ever heard her say. She was going to be all right. He just knew it. "Yes, that's right," he said, still laughing. "I'm Father Frost. Ho-ho-ho. And I brought a present for you, little girl."

Katya managed a narrow smile that lasted only the briefest of seconds. "Oh Felix, I knew I'd find you," she said. "I just knew it."

The wind blew snow as fine as table salt directly into Felix's face and he bent his head forward as he carried her. "Yes, you found me," he said. "Everything's going to be fine now. We're together again."

"I'm really tired," she said. "I'm going to sleep for a little while."

"No," Felix said emphatically. He knew what falling asleep meant for someone in her condition. It wasn't slumber she would be surrendering to, it was death. "You need to stay awake, Katya," he said. "Okay?" She had already closed her eyes and didn't open them.

"Katya," he shouted in her ear, "promise me you won't fall asleep."

She said something in response but it was so faint that Felix couldn't hear it. "I didn't hear you," he said and leaned his right ear as close as he could to her mouth. "Say it again."

"Aaa promiss," she said in a whisper.

"You don't have to speak," Felix said. "Just listen to me. Just stay awake and listen to me."

He knew he had to talk about something that would keep her attention if he was to have any hope of keeping her awake. "Do you remember that day we skipped school and went to the museums instead?" he began. "It was a spur-of-the-moment decision. We'd arrived at school at the same time and it was the first nice day of spring. Neither of us wanted to go to class. Just as we were about to walk through the front door, you said, 'Let's get out of here.' I thought you were joking, but you were serious, so I asked, 'Where?' And you said, 'Anywhere. Anywhere at all so long as we can be together today.' So we did it. And we had such a wonderful day. I still remember eating chocolate ice cream in the park, and that one painting we saw. It was . . ."

Felix tried to cover every detail of the story, both to keep it interesting and to stretch it out as long as possible. As soon as he finished telling it, he started on another story.

The wind had stopped gusting. It blew hard non-stop now. The snow came down heavier than ever and hard little snowflakes found their way past Felix's scarf and down his back. The storm had become a full-fledged blizzard, and the blinding snow and lack of light made it nearly impossible to see. If it weren't for the large snowbanks on each side of the road that Felix bumped into repeatedly, he probably would have lost his way.

The physical toll of the trip continued to mount. He'd been walking, running, trudging through deep snow, and stepping carefully on slippery surfaces for over seven hours straight. Miniature icicles hung from where his breath warmed his scarf. He stumbled a few times and wanted badly to rest for a couple of minutes but wouldn't allow it. He knew he didn't have a minute to spare in getting Katya medical attention.

After telling several stories in succession, he was starting to have difficulty thinking of new ones.

"Oh, I know," he said after a brief pause. "How could I forget this one? Remember that time you stole your father's bottle of brandy, and Dima picked the lock on the door to the roof of his apartment building? The three of us sat up there all night long talking and staring at the stars. We ended up falling asleep up there and you had an exam the next morning and you ran into class twenty minutes late. You told me later you still got an A on it. Do you remember that, Katya?" Felix put his ear close to her mouth to hear if she responded. He thought he heard something like a "yes" or a small laugh, so he continued on.

An hour later – just as Felix's endurance was breaking down and he was running out of stories – he saw the snow-covered truck tipped over on its side that told him the ice huts were only another ten to fifteen minutes further.

"We're almost there, my love," he said. "Just hang in there a few more minutes. Then everything will be all right." He didn't hear a response from her, but then he hadn't heard one for at least half an hour.

The ice huts came into view and Felix saw someone exiting one of them. "Is there a medical station here? A doctor? Or nurse?" he yelled to them.

"Yes," the man replied. "In that next hut there. Here, follow me."

The man led Felix to the medical station and helped him pull Katya through the waist-high entrance. Then they laid Katya down on one of the small, hard beds as two nurses came over and began tending to her.

Felix collapsed down onto the floor of the hut from sheer exhaustion. He watched one of the nurses put another blanket over Katya while the other checked her pulse and listened to her chest with a stethoscope.

"Should I go get the doctor?" the first nurse asked.

The other nurse pulled the stethoscope away from Katya's chest and shook her head. Then she pulled the blanket up so that it covered Katya's face.

Felix made it back to his feet. "What are you doing?" he asked.

"I'm sorry, comrade," the nurse with the stethoscope said.

"What do you mean, *you're sorry*? I brought her here so you could help her. Give her a transfusion or something."

"Comrade, she's dead. There's nothing we can do."

"No!" Felix shouted. "She can't be dead! You've got to do something." He went over and pulled the blanket down from Katya's face. He put his fingers on her neck to find a pulse. His own heart was racing, pounding, aching. When he couldn't find a pulse, he put his ear next to her nose to listen for her breathing. Nothing.

"Comrade, it's no use," the nurse said and tried to pull him away by the arm.

Felix shook his arm free and pushed her away. "There has to be *something* we can do," he said.

"There's nothing," the nurse said. "She's in God's hands now."

The finality of the words stopped him. *In God's hand now*. A tear slid down the side of his nose and caught in his beard. He wiped his watering eyes with the back of his hands and bent toward Katya's pale face. He pressed his lips to hers and for the first time ever, there was no response. Her lips were thin and cold. Her *entire face* felt so very cold, and he knew then that it was over. She was gone.

He took her mittens off, wrapped his hands around hers, and rested his head on top of her. Through his tears he sang that silly nursery rhyme she was so fond of: ♪ *Silly as a duck, what dumb luck, we're meant to be together, meant to be to-ge-ther* ♪ . . . .

When he finished, he felt crazed – mad with bitterness – and had to get away. He went outside and thought to scream. But who at? What would he say? He kept thinking it can't end like this. *It just can't!*

What good were the trees? The sky? The air he breathed? What good was any of it when life at its core was hollow?

He had to *do* something. He had to let it out, to throw back at life all the ugliness that had penetrated him, poisoned him. He opened his mouth to cry out, but no sound came. There was nothing he could do or say that was going to change anything. There was only that infuriating feeling that he was trapped. There was no escape from this pain. No escape from death. No escape from sorrow.

He spread his arms wide and fell straight back into the thick snow. Everything he held dear in his life had been taken from him: his hopes and dreams; his beloved city; his best friend, Dima; and now the love of his life, Katya. It was as if the universe – knowing he wouldn't take that pilgrimage into darkness willingly – had thrown him headfirst into the abyss. He was in freefall on that most frightening of human journeys, *the Descent*.

The snow continued to fall, slowly knitting a blanket of white over him. Felix felt the earth trying to reclaim him in some way, and he didn't resist. He welcomed it.

~

Глава Десятая — Chapter Ten

Those Who Would Not be Defeated

A Blue Jay chirps outside my window
    as I contemplate why the door to my room
    is always open.
I'm expecting no one.
I didn't even expect the Blue Jay.
I think I should shut the door.
No sense in leaving it open.
And then I hear it . . .
Laughter.
It bounces off the walls,
    up the stairs,
    and into my uncomprehending ears.
I ask it what it's doing here.
But laughter only laughs. It doesn't understand.
"Don't leave me," I say.
And it doesn't.
And we sit together for a while,
    remembering those endless summer nights,
    those endless summer dreams,
    with our youth, and our convictions,
    that our endless lives would always be just that.
I look away – only for a moment –
    and laughter slips away.
I am bitter,
    but leave the door open anyway.

The End Of Sorrow

The dentist put his flashlight and tool down in exasperation. "You're going to have to hold still for me to be able to do this," he said in his thick Lithuanian accent.

Felix took a deep breath and tried to relax all his facial muscles. He'd developed a blinding toothache that morning that blurred part of his vision. He was on leave from the front to have a dentist look at it. The tooth Dima knocked loose so long ago had never really healed. Nor had Felix wanted it to. He liked the pain. It served as a distraction and blocked other pain – emotional or other – out of his mind. It was also a constant reminder of the cruelty and confusion that defined the times in which he was living.

He'd been wandering aimlessly in the depths of sorrow for weeks on end but was hesitant, even now, to get rid of the tooth. It was like a comfortable old companion to him, someone he'd grown to trust. But a part of him knew it was time to move on. He was ready. Ready to feel again.

The dentist poked at his teeth and gums with a sharp metal object. "Ah yes, I see the problem," he said. He set the tool down and picked up a different one that looked like a pair of pliers. "Are you sure you don't want a little alcohol to numb the pain? This is going to hurt."

Besides some strong alcohol that you could swish around in your mouth and then swallow, the dentist had no anesthesia. Even if he did have anesthesia, Felix wouldn't have accepted it. He wanted to feel every ounce of the pain when the tooth was removed. That was important to him.

The dentist stuck the plier-like tool in Felix's mouth and clamped down on the tooth. "Ready?" he asked.

Felix heard the dentist, but didn't reply because he was busy creating a different world in his mind. A world in which there was no hate, no shame, no arrogance. A world where poetry and legends were more important than money and philosophy.

After the dentist yanked the tooth from his jaw, Felix thought he would die from the pain.

The dentist put a small piece of cloth in Felix's mouth when he was done. "Bite down on that," he said, "but not too hard. It'll help stop the bleeding."

Felix was glad it was over but also filled with a great sadness. It was goodbye. Goodbye to a way of life that he'd grown accustomed to.

"Well, my son," the dentist said, "you're just about all grown up now. A 'mature adult' as they say."

Felix wanted to spit some of the blood out of his mouth, but the dentist had already told him not to do that as it would slow the clotting process. "What do you mean?" he struggled to say while still biting down on the piece of cloth.

The dentist was washing his hands over a bucket of water. "Your wisdom teeth are coming in," he answered.

It was March and the great cleanup of the city had begun. Felix passed by thousands of Leningraders busily clearing away snow and slop and corpses from the thawing streets. The workers were weak and thin and nearly all women. They used crowbars and hammers to chop the ice, snow, and debris from the sidewalks, then carried it on flat sheets of plywood to the river. Felix didn't want to think about how filthy the river would be when its ice finally melted and all that stuff sunk to the bottom. That was a problem for another day.

The ration situation had finally stabilized. Bread was plentiful. One could even get sugar, butter, and meat. The devastating months of January and February were behind them now, and Leningraders were daring to hope again. Hoping they'd already endured the worst. Hoping the blockade would be broken soon.

Felix passed by a bulletin board where a woman was putting up the latest issue of Leningradskaya Pravda. In his former existence, he would have stopped and read every article. But he'd stopped reading newspapers altogether now. He'd been concerned that they distorted his view of the world, so he'd went a week without reading any. He liked it so much that he stopped listening to the news on the radio too. He found that his whole demeanor changed. He felt lighter and more understanding of what it was that he was supposed to do with his life. Never again would he read a story or article that would anger him. Instead, he would spend his time talking to the trees and the animals and the snowflakes. He didn't always understand what they were saying, but it was immensely gratifying trying to figure it out.

There was a long line of people standing at the front door of a school. They were waiting to get inoculations, Felix knew. With spring fast approaching, it was feared that epidemics would break out and kill the remaining Leningraders who had somehow made it through the winter. Vaccines for typhus, cholera, plague, smallpox, and others were flown in from Moscow. Every hospital and school served as an inoculation station. Those too weak to make it there would get their shots at their home by visiting nurses.

A gust of wind picked up and it started to snow – big, wet, milky-white snowflakes filling the sky. As one passed by his ear, he heard a whisper. He didn't look around for another person. He knew who it was.

Everywhere he looked now, he saw Katya. She was in the monuments, the bridges, the canals, the Neva river. Her voice floated on the wind. Her eyes looked back at him from everyone he met. She was everywhere – inseparable from the city and people she loved so dearly. Everything she believed in was still here, and Felix awoke each morning knowing she was in his heart, her spirit guiding him with every step he took.

He was approaching the Kazansky Cathedral now and saw a small group of people gathered there. A beautiful, haunting piece of symphonic music was coming from the outside loudspeakers, and he stopped to listen. He was enchanted by the unfettered confidence of the piece. It was clear the composer had mastered his craft. It was also clear that he'd been very inspired when he wrote it. New ideas washed ashore in the music like giant waves, the tone changing seamlessly from vibrant to fearsome to dread and back again. The brass and percussion thundered in, then faded away, only to return in a more sinister form later on.

Felix didn't try to find any meaning or symbolism in the music. He was tired of philosophy and contemplation, always wanting to know things *for certain*. He was tired of thinking each new epiphany would be the one that changed his life forever. He'd had dozens of insights in his life and each time believed he'd found 'the answer.' He now understood that there actually was no answer and he should stop expecting one.

The music moved him. He found himself thinking of the proud and courageous people of Leningrad. How they refused to give up. He recalled the time at the end of January when the power stations had run out of fuel – halting the city's last remaining water-pumping station. Without water, the bread bakeries couldn't operate. A call went out for help, and two thousand Young Communists answered it. They formed a chain, passing buckets of water from the frozen Neva to the nearest bakery. They kept up the strenuous work in the bitter cold for hours on end, saving countless thousands of lives.

Then Felix thought of the truck drivers who tirelessly brought food into the city, risking their lives every minute they were on the ice, driving until fingers and toes had to be amputated. He thought of the starving workers who continued to produce shells and bullets in the freezing-cold factories, of the soldiers on the front lines who fought against the Germans and the cold and hunger day after day. All in order to save Leningrad. There were so many who had sacrificed everything – even their lives – for the sake of their country. Felix was filled with gratitude and awe at their bravery and selflessness.

Bits and pieces of the music sounded familiar. Felix asked a fellow soldier standing next to him what it was. "Shostakovich's Seventh Symphony," the man replied. "It's being performed in Moscow."

It was then Felix knew Russia would ultimately prevail over the Germans. Shostakovich composed that symphony while living in Leningrad under siege. Now it was being performed for the whole world to hear. A testament to the fact that they'd absorbed the deadliest blow any army had ever inflicted on another, and they were still standing.

He walked on. The pain from his tooth was fading, gradually being replaced by a tingling sensation in his stomach. He'd felt it for most of his life, but always thought it signified a weakness. The night Katya died, he learned otherwise. Her death had triggered something in him. A part of him he hadn't known existed came to life. It was a fierceness, centered in his belly, that gave him profound strength to keep his heart open to the world no matter the circumstances. He could speak of his grief and his sorrow and his joy. He could listen to others express their feelings. It was all part of a greater conversation to him, one he had daily with things both living and non-living.

As he'd laid there on the earth that night, being covered over with falling snow, he'd had the awful sensation that this life he was living was not really his. Awful, because he knew for certain that things would never be the same and he'd have to let go of the way he used to exist in the world. His life did not belong to him. It belonged to something larger, something he didn't completely comprehend yet. He'd struggled to find the words, ultimately settling on Divine Mother Nature. *She* was the one who had given birth to him, and he was filled with awe at his unity with such largeness. The price of that precious birth was steep. The price was that everything and everyone he held dear belonged to Her, and She would reclaim them all – sometimes one by one, sometimes a thousand at a time.

He understood after that night he was always meant to be in complete servitude to Her. He'd known that as a small child, but had somehow forgot it as he got older. It took him nearly fifteen years to come full circle, to regain that knowledge of who he was and was always meant to be. That one night of unbearable angst and sorrow had accomplished what would have otherwise taken him decades to understand. Because of that great and awful secret that had been whispered to him when he reached the bottom of the pit of despair, he could no longer look at anything or anyone the same as before. His thoughts coagulated into slow, black sludge at one point on that night. Each thought the same – a tiny speck of black that combined to form an infinity of darkness. He struggled to comprehend it: the lack of colors, the void of emotion, the silence complete. He struggled and finally understood the futility of it. It was beyond his comprehension. It always had been.

He no longer cared about satisfying his petty desires. He no longer wanted to be understood. He was finished looking for answers. The only thing that mattered to him now was the mystery. The mystery of life.

It was going to take a lifetime of vigilance for it to sink into his being completely. All he knew right now was that he accepted the world exactly as it was and it gave him a sense of peace like he'd never known before. Peace so great, it burned through the darkness around him.

~

Epilogue

It was a warm sunny day in May and the five university students sat at a table next to an open window. Greenfinches sang from the treetops and pigeons strutted along the sidewalk looking for crumbs. Kyra, one of the students, had a big bag of puffed corn and threw a handful of it out the window for the pigeons to eat.

"So everyone knows their role for the presentation, right?" Igor asked.

The others either answered yes or nodded their head.

"Good," Kyra said, "we're done then. Now let's get out of here and enjoy this beautiful weather!"

Papers were hurriedly shoved in bags, books were shut with loud snaps, and the doors to the outside were flung open with abandon. Kyra began skipping and singing and raising her arms toward the bright blue sky. "Oh, how I love spring!" she exclaimed. She set her books and bag down and sprawled out in the grass. The others shared cigarettes and told jokes around a bench under a big oak tree.

Igor sat down on the grass next to Kyra, pensively looking at the passing cars and trolleys on the street. Kyra squeezed his ankle to get his attention. "Kiss me," she said.

Igor smiled, then leaned over and touched his lips to hers. She wrapped her arms around his neck and pulled him down so that he fell on top of her, and they both laughed for a long time.

"You're going with us for the picnic, right?" Kyra asked. "We're celebrating Sasha's eighteenth birthday. We'll go right after the parade."

"No, I can't," Igor answered. "I've got other plans today."

Kyra pretended to frown. "Oh, you're no fun," she said.

Igor felt hot in the sun and rolled his sleeves up beyond his elbows. He had hard muscular forearms. Kyra ran her fingers along them.

"You're at least coming to the party tonight, aren't you?" she asked.

He stood up. "Yes, I'll be at the party."

"You better be," she said as Igor started to walk away.

On his way past the others gathered around the bench, Igor plucked a half-finished cigarette from his best friend's lips, then smoked it himself as he continued on.

"I'll get you for that," his friend jested. "Just when you least suspect it too."

"Eight o'clock sharp, Igor!" Kyra called out after him. "You better not be late!"

A lone white cloud floated in the sky and Igor shielded his eyes from the sun to take a peek at it. Today was a special day – May 9th – Victory Day. The whole country took this specific day of every year off to celebrate their victory over the Nazis in WWII. May 9th meant even more than that to Igor though. It was the day he chose to give thanks to a person who had changed his life.

He passed under a tree full of blooming white flowers and thought of a story Katya had told him about a tree and how it was never really born and would never really die. The thought was comforting to him because it made him realize somehow that he wasn't alone in the world. There were others out there who believed as he did in the oneness and connectedness of everything. They may be hundreds of miles away or they may be next door; they may speak Japanese or Swedish or English or Swahili – or even German! But they *were* out there, and he knew it. He was not alone. Kyra was proof of that. Kyra, with her child-like laugh and spontaneity. She believed as Igor did, and that's what had drawn them to one another.

The ten-foot-tall iron gates of the cemetery were wide open and Igor walked in and turned to the right. There was a bush on top of a small hill that bloomed bright pink flowers whose fragrance would sometimes be carried his way by the breeze. He liked the smell. It was familiar to him, though he couldn't quite place it. He went up to the bush and broke off a small branch of the flowers.

As he walked among the graves and tombstones, he thought back to that horrible time when nearly half of the city's population perished due to starvation or cold or the enemy's bombs. The number still staggered him – over one million people dead in such a short amount of time.

The Great Patriotic War, as it was now called, had been a war like no other. Unprecedented in its savagery, and so too, in its bravery. Igor pulled out the medal he'd been given as a survivor of the blockade. Every Leningrader who had made it through that hell had been given one. He held it tight in his hand and thought of how many times the Red Army had tried to break the blockade. He thought of the Ice Road and how there were as many as sixty routes over it at one time. They'd even built an entire railroad over the frozen Lake Ladoga one winter. For 900 days they'd endured the siege, until the tide finally shifted irrevocably and the Soviet Army burst forth and didn't stop until it reached Berlin.

Igor saw a lone figure kneeling by the tomb he was headed for. He knew who it was. He saw him there on this day every year. It was Felix Varilensky. Everyone knew him – the decorated war hero wounded on nine separate occasions and returned to fight each time. Old ladies kissed him on the cheek. Children sang nursery rhymes about him. A poster of him receiving the Order of Lenin medal adorned the interior of nearly every Post Office building in the city.

All to his embarrassment, Igor knew. They talked once or twice a year and one thing Igor was always amazed at was Felix's humbleness. He didn't like all the praise and attention, and didn't think he deserved it. He wasn't proud of what he'd done in the war, but neither did he regret it. It was something that had happened and it was over. "Why can't we just leave it at that?" Igor had heard him say more than once.

Not wanting to intrude, Igor stopped and leaned against a tree to wait. Felix was sitting on the grass in between two graves. He was speaking in a soft voice and rubbing his eyes with the backs of his hands. He made the sign of the cross, then folded his hands together in front of him and stayed that way for a long time.

An attractive young woman with brown, shoulder-length hair, a light-blue dress, and a yellow sun hat approached in the distance. She held two small children – one boy and one girl – by the hand. She was walking slowly so they could keep up. Each child held a dandelion with their free hand. The sky was a soft blend of blue and white, and the lone cloud Igor had seen earlier was gone.

When the woman got close enough, the children let go of her hand and started running. "Daddy! Daddy!" they yelled.

Felix caught them in his arms, then picked them up and spun around in circles while they laughed and squealed. The woman came up and gave Felix a kiss on the lips, then the four of them started to walk away.

Igor started toward the grave. When he got there, Felix looked over his shoulder and saw him. Igor waved, and Felix shouted to him to stop by for dinner sometime next week.

The grave was covered with fresh-cut flowers: red roses, purple lilacs, white daffodils, and two yellow dandelions. Igor added to the mix the pink flowers he'd picked from the bush, then he sat down and pulled a small brown book from his bag.

He thought back once more to those days that so changed his life. The misery, the despair, the destruction. And yet through it all, he remembered mostly just the kindness of one person.

He held the book up in front of him. "You see," he said aloud. "I told you last year that I would get your poems published. It's been receiving great reviews since it came out last month. Anna Akhmatova herself even wrote a glowing review of it."

He opened the book and began reading from the beginning. He read for an hour and a half, not stopping until he reached the last part of the last poem, his favorite:

> *I follow the path and come across a great lake of joy,*
>   *and see it's fed by this abundant river of sorrow.*
> *This maddening dichotomy has evaded me for so long:*
>   *One cannot exist without the other.*

He left the cemetery and strolled leisurely along the Neva. Everywhere one looked now there was new life: birds singing as they flew from tree to tree, green buds sprouting from the dark soil, trees and bushes overflowing with young flowers. A light breeze picked up the scent of linden trees which were just coming into bloom. A pigeon on the sidewalk in front of him hooted softly and then flew away.

People were lined up along the bridges and riverbanks to watch the ice from Lake Ladoga pass through. It was an annual event that every Leningrader loved to watch. Igor found an empty spot along the railing and stopped for a minute. The gray water was full of ice floes of various sizes that shifted and squeezed and forced their way downriver.

Igor watched as a group of small children, no more than four years old, passed by him. They each held part of a rope being pulled by a short, thick-waisted woman. A group of ducks were gathered nearby, and a little girl with brown eyes and brown hair let go of the rope and ran after them.

"Katya!" the woman at the front of the rope yelled at her. "Come back here!"

The little girl stopped, looked back, started to frown. Then the frown turned into a mischievous grin and she turned and ran for the ducks again just as fast as her tiny legs could carry her.

Igor smiled as he watched the little girl run and giggle and the short woman chase after her. There was a large oak tree next to the river, its brown leaves still clinging to the branches, just as they had all winter long. A breeze picked up and one of the leaves finally let go. It sailed slowly toward the ground, gracefully coming to rest on a large ice floe making its way out to sea.

~ ~ ~

Resources

The following excellent books have been referenced in the writing of this novel:

Erickson, John & Ljubica, *The Eastern Front*, Carlton Books Limited, 2001.

Salisbury, Harrison E., *The 900 Days: The Siege of Leningrad*, Da Capo Press, 1985.

Shostakovich, Dmitry, *Testimony: The Memoirs of Dmitry Shostakovich*, Harper & Row, 1979.

Skrjabina, Elena, *Siege and Survival: The Odyssey of a Leningrader*, Southern Illinois University Press, 1971

Wayne, Kyra Petrovskaya, *Shurik: A Story of the Siege of Leningrad*, Lyons & Burford, 1970.

Lightning Source UK Ltd.
Milton Keynes UK
30 November 2009

146901UK00002B/27/A